# THE AMATEUR MARRIAGE

Anne Tyler was born in Minneapolis in 1941. She is the Pulitzer Prize-winning author of *Breathing Lessons* and other bestselling novels, including *The Accidental Tourist*, *Ladder of Years*, *A Patchwork Planet* and *Back When We Were Grownups*. In 1994 she was nominated by Roddy Doyle and Nick Hornby as 'the greatest novelist writing in English'. She lives in Baltimore, where her novels are set.

## ALSO BY ANNE TYLER

Anne Tyler

# THE AMATEUR MARRIAGE

VINTAGE

Published by Vintage 2004

This edition published 2005

Copyright © Anne Tyler, 2004

Anne Tyler has asserted her right under the Copyright,
Designs and Patents Act, 1988 to be identified as the author
of this work

First published in Great Britain in 2004 by
Chatto & Windus

First published in the United States of America in 2004 by
Alfred A. Knopf

Vintage
Random House, 20 Vauxhall Bridge Road,
London SW1V 2SA

Random House Australia (Pty) Limited
20 Alfred Street, Milsons Point, Sydney
New South Wales 2061, Australia

Random House New Zealand Limited
18 Poland Road, Glenfield,
Auckland 10, New Zealand

Random House (Pty) Limited
Endulini, 5A Jubilee Road, Parktown 2193,
South Africa

The Random House Group Limited Reg. No. 954009
www.randomhouse.co.uk/vintage

A CIP catalogue record for this book
is available from the British Library

ISBN 0 09 949987 8

Papers used by Random House are natural, recyclable
products made from wood grown in sustainable forests.
The manufacturing processes conform to the environ-
mental regulations of the country of origin

Printed and bound in Great Britain by
Bookmarque Ltd, Croydon, Surrey

# Contents

# The Amateur Marriage

# 1. Common Knowledge

Anyone in the neighborhood could tell you how Michael and Pauline first met.

It happened on a Monday afternoon early in December of 1941. St. Cassian was its usual poky self that day—a street of narrow East Baltimore row houses, carefully kept little homes intermingled with shops no bigger than small parlors. The Golka twins, identically kerchiefed, compared cake rouges through the window of Sweda's Drugs. Mrs. Pozniak stepped out of the hardware store with a tiny brown paper bag that jingled. Mr. Kostka's Model-B Ford puttered past, followed by a stranger's sleekly swishing Chrysler Airstream and then by Ernie Moskowicz on the butcher's battered delivery bike.

In Anton's Grocery—a dim, cram-packed cubbyhole with an L-shaped wooden counter and shelves that reached the low ceiling—Michael's mother wrapped two tins of peas for Mrs. Brunek. She tied them up tightly and handed them over without a smile, without a "Come back soon" or a "Nice to see you." (Mrs. Anton had had a hard life.) One of Mrs. Brunek's boys—Carl? Paul? Peter? they all looked so much alike—pressed his nose to the glass of the penny-candy display. A floorboard creaked near the cereals, but that was just the bones of the elderly building settling deeper into the ground.

Michael was shelving Woodbury's soap bars behind the longer,

3

left-hand section of the counter. He was twenty at the time, a tall young man in ill-fitting clothes, his hair very black and cut too short, his face a shade too thin, with that dark kind of whiskers that always showed no matter how often he shaved. He was stacking the soap in a pyramid, a base of five topped by four, topped by three . . . although his mother had announced, more than once, that she preferred a more compact, less creative arrangement.

Then, *tinkle, tinkle!* and *wham!* and what seemed at first glance a torrent of young women exploded through the door. They brought a gust of cold air with them and the smell of auto exhaust. "Help us!" Wanda Bryk shrilled. Her best friend, Katie Vilna, had her arm around an unfamiliar girl in a red coat, and another girl pressed a handkerchief to the red-coated girl's right temple. "She's been hurt! She needs first aid!" Wanda cried.

Michael stopped his shelving. Mrs. Brunek clapped a hand to her cheek, and Carl or Paul or Peter drew in a whistle of a breath. But Mrs. Anton did not so much as blink. "Why bring her here?" she asked. "Take her to the drugstore."

"The drugstore's closed," Katie told her.

"Closed?"

"It says so on the door. Mr. Sweda's joined the Coast Guard."

"He's done *what?*"

The girl in the red coat was very pretty, despite the trickle of blood running past one ear. She was taller than the two neighborhood girls but slender, more slightly built, with a leafy cap of dark-blond hair and an upper lip that rose in two little points so sharp they might have been drawn with a pen. Michael came out from behind the counter to take a closer look at her. "What happened?" he asked her—only her, gazing at her intently.

"Get her a Band-Aid! Get iodine!" Wanda Bryk commanded. She had gone through grade school with Michael. She seemed to feel she could boss him around.

The girl said, "I jumped off a streetcar."

Her voice was low and husky, a shock after Wanda's thin violin notes. Her eyes were the purple-blue color of pansies. Michael swallowed.

4

"A parade's begun on Dubrowski Street," Katie was telling the others. "All six of the Szapp boys are enlisting, haven't you heard? And a couple of their friends besides. They've got this banner— 'Watch out, Japs! Here come the Szapps!'—and everyone's seeing them off. They've gathered such a crowd that the traffic can't hardly get through. So Pauline here—she was heading home from work; places are closing early—what does she do? Jumps off a speeding streetcar to join in."

The streetcar couldn't have been speeding all that fast, if traffic was clogged, but nobody pointed that out. Mrs. Brunek gave a sympathetic murmur. Carl or Paul or Peter said, "Can *I* go, Mama? Can I? Can I go watch the parade?"

"I just thought we should try and support our boys," Pauline told Michael.

He swallowed again. He said, "Well, of course."

"You're not going to help our boys any knocking yourself silly," the girl with the handkerchief said. From her tolerant tone, you could see that she and Pauline were friends, although she was less attractive—a brown-haired girl with a calm expression and eyebrows so long and level that she seemed lacking in emotion.

"We think she hit her head against a lamppost," Wanda said, "but nobody could be sure in all the fuss. She landed in our laps, just about, with Anna here a ways behind her. I said, 'Jeepers! Are you okay?' Well, *somebody* had to do *something*; we couldn't just let her bleed to death. Don't you people have Band-Aids?"

"This place is not a pharmacy," Mrs. Anton said. And then, pursuing an obvious connection, "Whatever got into Nick Sweda? He must be thirty-five if he's a day!"

Michael, meanwhile, had turned away from Pauline to join his mother behind the counter—the shorter, end section of the counter where the cash register stood. He bent down, briefly disappeared, and emerged with a cigar box. "Bandages," he explained.

Not Band-Aids, but old-fashioned cotton batting rolled in dark-blue tissue the exact shade of Pauline's eyes, and a spool of white adhesive tape, and an oxblood-colored bottle of iodine. Wanda stepped forward to take them; but no, Michael unrolled the cotton himself

5

and tore a wad from one corner. He soaked the wad with iodine and came back to stand in front of Pauline. "Let me see," he said.

There was a reverent, alert silence, as if everyone understood that this moment was significant—even the girl with the handkerchief, the one Wanda had called Anna, although Anna could not have known that Michael Anton was ordinarily the most reserved boy in the parish. She removed the handkerchief from Pauline's temple. Michael pried away a petal of Pauline's hair and started dabbing with the cotton wad. Pauline held very still.

The wound, it seemed, was a two-inch red line, long but not deep, already closing. "Ah," Mrs. Brunek said. "No need for stitches."

"We can't be sure of that!" Wanda cried, unwilling to let go of the drama.

But Michael said, "She'll be fine," and he tore off a new wad of cotton. He plastered it to Pauline's temple with a crisscross of adhesive tape.

Now she looked like a fight victim in a comic strip. As if she knew that, she laughed. It turned out she had a dimple in each cheek. "Thanks very much," she told him. "Come and watch the parade with us."

He said, "All right."

Just that easily.

"Can I come too?" the Brunek boy asked. "Can I, Mama? Please?"

Mrs. Brunek said, "Ssh."

"But who will help with the store?" Mrs. Anton asked Michael.

As if he hadn't heard her, he turned to take his jacket from the coat tree in the corner. It was a schoolboy kind of jacket—a big, rough plaid in shades of gray and charcoal. He shrugged himself into it, leaving it unbuttoned. "Ready?" he asked the girls.

The others watched after him—his mother and Mrs. Brunek, and Carl or Paul or Peter, and little old Miss Pelowski, who chanced to be approaching just as Michael and the four girls came barreling out the door. "What . . . ?" Miss Pelowski asked. "What on earth . . . ? Where . . . ?"

Michael didn't even slow down. He was halfway up the block

now, with three girls trailing him and a fourth one at his side. She clung to the crook of his left arm and skimmed along next to him in her brilliant red coat.

Even then, Miss Pelowski said later, she had known that he was a goner.

"Parade" was too formal a word, really, for the commotion on Dubrowski Street. It was true that several dozen young men were walking down the center of the pavement, but they were still in civilian clothes and they made no attempt to keep in step. The older of John Piazy's sons wore John's sailor cap from the Great War. Another boy, name unknown, had flung a regulation Army blanket around his shoulders like a cape. It was a shabby, straggly, unkempt little regiment, their faces chapped, their noses running in the cold.

Even so, people were enthusiastic. They waved homemade signs and American flags and the front page of the *Baltimore Sun*. They cheered at speeches—any speeches, any rousing phrases shouted over their heads. "You'll be home by New Year's, boys!" a man in earmuffs called, and "New Year's Day! Hurray!" zigzagged through the crowd.

When Michael Anton showed up with four girls, everybody assumed he was enlisting too. "Go get 'em, Michael!" someone shouted. Though John Piazy's wife said, "Ah, no. It would be the death of his mother, poor soul, with all she's had to suffer."

One of the four girls, the one in red, asked, "*Will* you be going, Michael?" An outsider, she was, but very easy on the eyes. The red of her coat brought out the natural glow of her skin, and a bandage on her temple made her look madcap and rakish. No wonder Michael gave her a long, considering stare before he spoke.

"Well," he said finally, and then he kind of hitched up his shoulders. "Well, naturally I will be!" he said.

A ragged cheer rang out from everyone standing nearby, and another of the girls—Wanda Bryk, in fact—pushed him forward until he had merged with the young men in the street. Leo Kazmerow walked on his left; the four girls scurried along the sidewalk on his right. "We love you, Michael!" Wanda cried, and Katie Vilna called, "Come back soon!" as if he were embarking for the trenches that very instant.

Then Michael was forgotten. He was swept away, and other young men replaced him: Davey Witt, Joe Dobek, Joey Serge. "You go show those Japs what we're made of!" Davey's father was shouting. For after all, a man was saying, who could tell when they'd have another chance to get even over Poland? An old woman was crying. John Piazy was telling everybody that neither one of his sons knew the meaning of the word "fear." And several people were starting in on the where-were-you-when-you-heard discussion. One had not heard till that morning; he'd been burying his mother. One had heard first thing, the first announcement on the radio, but had dismissed it as another Orson Welles hoax. And one, a woman, had been soaking in the bath-tub when her husband knocked on the door. "You're never going to believe this," he'd called. "I just sat there," she said. "I just sat and sat. I sat until the water got cold."

Wanda Bryk returned with Katie Vilna and the brown-haired girl, but not the girl in red. The girl in red had vanished. It seemed she'd marched off to war with Michael Anton, somebody said.

They did all notice—those in the crowd who knew Michael. It was enough of a surprise so they noticed, and remarked to each other, and remembered for some time afterward.

Word got out, the next day, that Leo Kazmerow had been rejected because he was color-blind. Color-blind! people said. What did color have to do with fighting for your country? Unless maybe he couldn't recognize the color of someone's uniform. If he was aiming his gun in battle, say. But everyone agreed that there were ways to get around that. Put him on a ship! Sit him behind a cannon and show him where to shoot!

This conversation took place in Anton's Grocery. Mrs. Anton was answering the phone, but as soon as she hung up, someone asked, "And what's the news of Michael, Mrs. Anton?"

"News?" she said.

"Has he left yet?"

"Oh, Michael's not going anyplace," she said.

They slid their eyes toward each other—Mrs. Pozniak, Mrs. Kowalski, and one of Mrs. Kowalski's daughters. But nobody wanted to argue. Mrs. Anton had lost her husband in 1935, and then her firstborn son two years later—handsome, charming Danny Anton, dead of a progressive disease that took him away inch by inch and muscle by muscle. Mrs. Anton had been a changed woman ever since, and who could blame her?

Mrs. Pozniak asked for Cream of Wheat, Fels Naphtha, and a tin of Heinz baked beans. Mrs. Anton set each item flatly on the counter. She was a straight-faced woman, gray all over. Not just her hair was gray but her dull, slack skin and her lusterless eyes and her stretched-out, pilled, man's sweater worn over a gingham dress. She had a way of looking past her customers' shoulders while she dealt with them, as if she hoped someone else would show up, someone less disappointing.

Then the bell on the door tinkled and in burst a girl in a red coat, carrying a tissue-wrapped parcel. "Mrs. Anton?" she said. "Do you remember me?"

Mrs. Pozniak hadn't completed her order. She turned, one finger poised on her grocery list, and opened her mouth to protest.

"Pauline Barclay," the girl explained. "I cut my forehead and your son gave me a bandage. I've knitted him a scarf. I hope I'm not too late."

"Too late for what?" Mrs. Anton asked.

"Has Michael left for the front yet?"

"The front?"

Mrs. Anton pronounced the word with a little halt, a little different sound to the *o*. It seemed possible that she was picturing the front of a room or a piece of furniture.

Before Pauline could elaborate, the door tinkled open again and here came Michael in his shaggy plaid jacket. He must have caught sight of Pauline from the street; you could tell by his artificial start of surprise. "Oh! Pauline! It's you!" he said. (He'd never have made an actor.)

9

"I knitted you a warm scarf," she told him. She held up her parcel in both gloved hands; she tilted her fine-boned, delicate face. The little store was so crowded by now that they were standing almost nose to nose.

Michael said, "For me?"

"To wear to the front."

He sent a quick glance toward his mother. Then he took hold of Pauline's elbow. "Let's go get a Coke," he said.

"Oh, why, that would be—"

"Michael? We have another telephone order," Mrs. Anton said.

But he said, "I'll be back soon," and he guided Pauline out the door.

They left behind a larger space than they had occupied, somehow. Mrs. Pozniak paused for a moment longer, just in case Mrs. Anton had something interesting to say. She didn't, though. She was staring grimly after her son, one hand tracing the Cream of Wheat box as if to square off its corners.

Mrs. Pozniak cleared her throat and asked for a bottle of molasses.


The parlor windows on St. Cassian Street developed a military theme, the Blessed Virgins and china poodles and silk flowers replaced overnight by American flags, swoops of red, white, and blue bunting, and grade-school geography books laid open to maps of Europe. Although in some cases, the religious items stayed put. Mrs. Szapp's bleached-out Palm Sunday palm fronds, for instance, remained in place even after a banner bearing six satin stars was tacked to the wooden sash. And why not? You need all the intervention you can get, when every last one of your sons is off risking his life for his country.

Mr. Kostka asked Michael what branch of the service he'd joined. This was in Sweda's Drugs, which had reopened under the management of Mr. Sweda's brother-in-law. Michael and Pauline were sitting at one of the marble-topped tables; they'd been observed together often over the past few days. Michael said, "The Army," and Mr. Kostka said, "Is that a fact! I'd have thought the Navy."

"Yes, but I get seasick," Michael told him.

Mr. Kostka said, "Well, young fellow, the Army's not going to ship you over by motorcar, you know."

Michael got a sort of startled look.

"And when do you leave for boot camp?" Mr. Kostka inquired.

Michael paused. Then, "Monday," he said.

"Monday!" By now it was Saturday. "Has your mother lined up any help at the store?"

Oh, sneaky; very sneaky. Everybody knew that Mrs. Anton had no idea Michael had enlisted. But who was going to tell her? Even Mrs. Zack, famous for interfering, claimed she hadn't the heart. They were all waiting for Michael to do it; but here he sat, sipping Coke with Pauline, and the only thing he would say was "I'm sure she'll find someone or other."

Pauline was wearing red again. Red seemed to be her color. A red sweater over a crisp white shirt with a rounded collar. It was known by now that she came from a neighborhood north of Eastern Avenue; that she wasn't even Catholic; that she worked as a receptionist in her father's realty office. *How* this was known was through Wanda Bryk, who had somehow become Pauline's new best friend. It was Wanda who reported that Pauline was just the nicest person imaginable, and so much fun! So vivacious! Just always up to some mischief. But others had their reservations. Those seated at the soda fountain, now. You think they weren't cocking their ears to hear what foolish talk she might be filling Michael's head with? Not to mention they could see her in the long mirror behind the counter. They saw how she tucked her face down, all dimpling and demure, fingers toying coquettishly with the straw in her Coca-Cola. They heard her murmuring that she wouldn't be able to sleep a wink nights, fearing for his safety. What right did she have to fear for his safety? She barely even knew him! Michael was one of their own, one of the neighborhood favorites, although not till now considered the romantic type. (Over the past few days a number of girls, Katie Vilna and several others, had started wondering if he might possess some unsuspected qualities.)

Old Miss Jakubek, drinking seltzer at the counter with Miss Pelowski, reported that the evening before, she had gone up to Pauline at the movies and told her she looked like Deanna Durbin. "Well, she does, in a way," she defended herself. "I know she's a blonde, but she does have that, oh, that dentable soft skin. But what did she say? 'Deanna Durbin!' she said. 'That's just not true! I look like me! I don't look *like* anyone!' "

"Tsk, tsk," Miss Pelowski sympathized. "You were only trying to be nice."

"I myself would love it if someone told me I looked like Deanna Durbin."

Miss Pelowski drew back on her stool and studied Miss Jakubek. "Well, you do, around the chin, a little," she said.

"His poor, poor mother, is all I can think. And the girl is nothing; no nationality. Not even Ukrainian; not even Italian! Italian I might be able to handle. But 'Barclay'! She and Michael don't have the least little thing in common."

"It's like *Romeo and Juliet*," Miss Pelowski said.

Both women thought for a moment. Then they glanced toward the mirror again. They saw that Pauline was crying; that Michael was leaning across the table to cup her chrysanthemum head in both hands.

"They do seem very much in love," Miss Jakubek said.

That night there was a huge going-away party for Jerry Kowalski. Depend on the Kowalskis to make more of a fuss than other people. Other people had been seeing their boys off all week with no more than a nice family dinner, but the Kowalskis rented the Sons of Warsaw Fellowship Hall and hired Lenny Zee and his Dulcetones to play. Mrs. Kowalski and her mother cooked for days; giant kegs of beer were rolled in. The whole of St. Cassian's Church was invited, as well as a few from St. Stan.

And of course, everyone came. Even babies and small children; even Mr. Zynda in his cane-seated wooden wheelchair. Mrs. Anton arrived in a ruffly blouse and ribbon-trimmed dirndl skirt that made her look grayer than ever, and Michael wore a pinchy suit that might have been his father's. His raw, bare wrist bones poked forth from the sleeves. A white flake of toilet paper clung to a nick on his chin.

But where was Pauline?

Most certainly she had been invited, at least by implication. "Feel free to bring a date," Mrs. Kowalski had told Michael—in his mother's presence, no less. (Oh, Mrs. Kowalski was widely known to be a bit of an imp.) But the only girls here were neighborhood girls, and when the first polka started sawing away, it was Katie Vilna who came over to Michael and pulled him onto the dance floor. She was the forward one of the group. She kept tight hold of his hand even when he resisted. Eventually, he gave in and began awkwardly hippity-hopping, every now and then glancing toward the door as if he were expecting somebody.

The Fellowship Hall was a warehouse-like building with splintery floors and metal rafters and naked overhead lightbulbs. Card tables draped with hand-stitched heirloom linens lined the far wall, and it was here that the older women gathered, scrutinizing Mrs. Kowalski's pierogi and finickily readjusting the sprigs of parsley garnish after one or another of the men had passed through loading his plate. When they stood back to watch the dancing, they tended to clasp their hands on their stomachs as if folding them beneath aprons, even though not a one of them actually wore an apron. They commented on Grandfather Kowalski's sprightly step, on the evident chill between the Wysockis (newlyweds), and—of course—on Katie Vilna's unbelievable nerve. "I swear, she has no shame," Mrs. Golka said. "I'd die if one of *my* girls was to chase a boy that way."

"Fine chance she has, anyhow, with that Pauline person in the picture."

"Where *is* Pauline, though? Wouldn't you think she would be here?"

"She's not coming," Wanda announced.

Wanda had approached unnoticed, her footsteps drowned out by the music. (Otherwise, the women never would have said what they did about Katie.) She forked a kielbasa onto her plate. She said, "Pauline's miffed that Michael wouldn't call for her."

"Call for her?"

"At her folks' house."

"But why—?"

"He wanted to spare his mother's feelings. You know how his mother can be. He told Pauline to meet him here; they'd act like it was just happenstance when they ran into each other. And first she said okay, but then I guess she reconsidered because when I phoned her this evening, she told me she wasn't coming. She said she was the kind of girl a fellow should be proud to be seen with, not all ashamed and hidey-corner."

Wanda moved off toward the dessert table, leaving a silence behind her. "Well, she's right," Mrs. Golka said finally. "A girl has to set some standards."

"He was only thinking of his mother, though."

"And what good will that do him, might I ask, when Dolly Anton's dead and gone and Michael's a seedy old bachelor?"

"For mercy's sake," Mrs. Pozniak said, "the boy is twenty years old! He's got a long way to go before he's a seedy old bachelor."

Mrs. Golka didn't seem convinced. She was gazing after Wanda. "But does he know," she said, "or not?"

"Know what?"

"Does he know that Pauline's miffed? Did Wanda tell him?"

Now several of the women began to show some sense of urgency. "Wanda!" one called. "Wanda Bryk!"

She turned, her plate in midair.

"Did you tell Michael that Pauline's not coming?"

"No, she wants him to worry," Wanda said, and she turned back and plucked a pastry from a tray.

There was another silence. Then, "Ah," the women said in unison.

The Dulcetones stopped playing and Mr. Kowalski tapped the microphone, sending a series of furry-sounding thwacks through the hall. "On behalf of myself and Barbara . . ." he said. His lips were too close to the mike and each *b* was an explosion. Several people covered their ears. Meanwhile, the children were getting up a game of Duck, Duck, Goose, and the babies were fussing themselves to sleep in nests of their mothers' coats, and several young men near the beer kegs were growing loud-voiced and boastful.

So nobody noticed when Michael slipped away. Or maybe he

didn't slip away; maybe he walked out openly. Even his mother was absorbed by then in the goings-on, the speeches wishing Jerry well and the prayer from Father Pasko and the cheers and the rounds of applause.

But they noticed when he returned, all right, later in the evening. Here he came, brave as you please, leading Pauline by the hand through the big plank doors. And when he helped her take her coat off—which no one had even realized Michael knew to do—it emerged that she was wearing a slim black dress that set her apart from the other girls in their lace-up waistcoats and drawstring blouses and flouncy embroidered skirts. But it was her eyes that caused the most comment. They were wet. Each of those long lashes was a separate, damp spike. And the smile she gave Wanda Bryk was the rueful, wan, chastened smile of someone who had just come through a crying spell.

Oh, plainly she and Michael had been having words of some kind.

She turned from Wanda and looked at Michael expectantly, and he gathered himself together and squared his shoulders and took hold of her hand again. He led her further into the hall, past the microphone where Jerry himself now stood, foolishly grinning, past the accordionist who was flirting with Katie, over to the women on their cluster of folding chairs. "Mama," he said to his mother, "I know you remember Pauline."

His mother held a plate in both hands on the very tip end of her lap—a single beet swimming in horseradish sauce. She gazed up at him bleakly.

"Pauline is sort of . . . my girl," he told her.

Even this late, the noise was deafening (all those overtired children on the loose), but where Mrs. Anton sat, the silence spread around her like ripples around a stone.

Pauline stepped forward, and this time her smile was heartfelt, her dimples deep as finger pokes. "Oh, Mrs. Anton," she said, "we're going to be such good friends! We're going to keep each other company while Michael is away."

Mrs. Anton said, "Away?"

Pauline went on smiling at her. Even with her damp lashes, she had a natural kind of joyousness. Her skin seemed to radiate light.

"I've joined the Army, Mama," Michael said.

Mrs. Anton froze. Then she stood up, but so unsteadily that the woman next to her stood up too and took away her plate. Mrs. Anton relinquished it without a glance. It appeared that she would just as soon have dropped it on the floor. "You can't," she told Michael. "You're all I've got left. They would never make you join."

"I've enlisted. I report for training Monday."

Mrs. Anton fainted.

She fell in an oddly vertical manner, not keeling over backwards but slowly sinking, erect, into the folds of her skirt. (Like the Wicked Witch melting in *The Wizard of Oz,* a child reported later.) It should have been possible to catch her, but nobody moved fast enough. Even Michael just watched, dumbstruck, until she reached the floor. Then he said, "Mama?" and he dropped sharply to his knees and started patting both her cheeks. "Mama! Talk to me! Wake up!"

"Stand back and give her air," the women told him. They were rising and moving their chairs away and shooing off the men. "Lay her flat. Keep her head down." Mrs. Pozniak took Pauline by the elbows and planted her to one side. Mrs. Golka sent one of her twins off for water.

"Call a doctor! Call an ambulance!" Michael shouted, but the women told him, "She'll be all right," and one of them—Mrs. Serge, a widow—heaved a sigh and said, "Let her have her rest, poor soul."

Mrs. Anton opened her eyes. She looked at Michael and closed them again.

Two women helped her to a sitting position, and a moment later they lifted her onto her chair, all the time saying, "You'll be just fine. Don't rush yourself. Take it easy." Once she was seated, Mrs. Anton bent double and buried her face in her hands. Mrs. Pozniak patted her shoulder and made soft clucking sounds.

Michael stood at a distance, now, with his palms clamped in his armpits. Various men kept slapping him reassuringly on the back, but it didn't seem to do any good. And Pauline had simply vanished. Not even Wanda Bryk had seen her go.

The Dulcetones were drifting helplessly among their instruments; some of the children were quarreling; Jerry Kowalski was standing slack-jawed at the microphone. Cigarette smoke hung in veils beneath the high rafters. The air smelled of pickled cabbage and sweat. The tables had a ravaged look—platters almost empty and puddled with brownish juices, serving spoons staining the linens, parsley sprigs limp and bedraggled.

Everybody said later that the party had been a mistake. You don't throw a celebration, they said, when your sons are leaving home to fight and die.

The windows above Anton's Grocery stayed dark all the next day, not even a glimmer showing behind the lace curtains. The store, of course, was closed, since it was a Sunday. Neither Michael nor his mother came to church, but that was not unusual. After Danny got sick, the Antons appeared to have fallen away somewhat from their faith. Still, people said, in view of the situation, wouldn't you think Michael's mother would want to offer up a prayer?

This was not a neighborhood of drop-in visits—or any visits, really, other than from blood relatives. Houses were too small and too close together, too exposed, without so much as a shrub to shield them from prying eyes. Best to avoid becoming overfamiliar. But toward evening, Mrs. Nowak from across the street called Mrs. Anton on the phone. She planned to inquire after Mrs. Anton's health and maybe bring by a casserole if she received any encouragement. Nobody answered, though. She told Mrs. Kostka later that she had a definite sense that the ringing was being *listened* to, in silence. You know how you get that feeling sometimes. Eight rings, nine . . . with a kind of watchfulness in between. But that could have been her imagination. Maybe the Antons were out. Mrs. Anton did have a brother-in-law, an unsocial sort who ran a dry-goods store over near Patterson Park. It seemed unlikely, however. Surely somebody would have noticed them walking.

Several times during the evening, Mrs. Nowak glanced across the street again. But all she could see were those secretive curtains and the display window below them, ANTON'S GROCERY in curly gold letters in front of fifteen Campbell's soup cans neatly arranged in the pyramid style that Michael was so fond of.

The Army hired a special bus to take recruits to Virginia. It was a school bus, from the looks of it, repainted a matte olive drab, and at eight o'clock Monday morning it stood waiting on the designated corner within eyeshot of the seafood market. By fours and by sixes, families approached in a lagging, hanging-back manner, always with at least one young man in the lead. The young men carried suitcases made of cardboard or leather. Their relatives carried lunch boxes and cake tins and thermoses. It was a raw, windy day, but no one seemed in any hurry to pack the young men onto the bus. They stood in small groups clutching their burdens, stamping their feet for warmth. A few of the families knew each other, but a lot more didn't; the bus served a fairly wide area. Still, people made a point of exchanging greetings even if they were strangers. They sent quick, searching smiles toward the young men and from then on averted their eyes, giving the families their privacy.

The Kowalskis came with Jerry and Jerry's girlfriend and Mrs. Sweda, who was Mrs. Kowalski's sister. The Witts came. Mrs. Serge and Joey came.

Mrs. Anton and Michael came.

Mrs. Anton looked even drearier than usual, and she barely responded when her neighbors said hello. She wore a gray tweed overcoat and thin, short socks half swallowed by her brown oxfords. Her hands were thrust deep in her pockets; it was Michael who carried his lunch, in addition to a mildewed black gladstone bag. Around his neck he had wound Pauline's scarf—broad bands of navy blue and white, a pattern any neighborhood girl would have considered too simple.

Just as they arrived, a beefy man in uniform lumbered down the steps of the bus with a clipboard under one arm. No one had even known he was there; all they had seen was the driver, who sat staring ahead expressionlessly with the motor loudly idling.

"All right, men," the man in uniform called. "Line up here to my left."

People began milling in his direction, the relatives as well as the recruits. Michael, however, stayed where he was. He gazed northward, straight up Broadway to where it crossed Eastern Avenue.

"Move along, men. Say your goodbyes."

Mr. Kowalski raised his Kodak and snapped a picture of Jerry grinning stiffly and unnaturally. Jerry's little sister blew on a painted tin horn. His girlfriend threw her arms around him and buried her face in his neck.

"Let's get going, men, double-time."

But it was from the east, from St. Cassian Street, that Pauline came running. She had her red coat on, which was how they could all spot her from such a distance. They said, "Michael! Look!" and Michael turned at once in the right direction, although Pauline herself had not called out. When she came nearer they could see why. She had no breath left, poor thing. She was gasping and tousle-haired and flushed—really not at her prettiest, but who in the world cared? She was holding out her arms, and Michael dropped his belongings and started running too, and when they collided he swooped her up so her feet completely left the ground. Everybody said "Ah" in one long, satisfied sigh—everybody except his mother, but even she watched with something close to sympathy. How could she not? They were hugging as if they would never let go, and Pauline was speaking in broken gasps: ". . . thought you were leaving by train, but . . . went to your house . . . went to Wanda's . . . finally asked a man on the street and . . . Michael, I'm so sorry, I'm so sorry, I'm so sorry."

"All aboard!" the man in uniform bellowed.

Michael and Pauline tore apart. He turned and went back for his belongings. He ducked his head to let his mother kiss him. He sent one last look toward Pauline and then he climbed onto the bus.

When it pulled out, Pauline and Mrs. Anton were standing side by side, both waving with all their hearts.

\*   \*   \*

Now carved wooden creches and plaster Santas and ten-inch-tall, cone-shaped green straw Christmas trees blobbed with soap-flake snow stood among the flags in the parlor windows. Mrs. Szapp's famous angels—a dozen of them, handblown glass—fought for space beneath the palm fronds. Mrs. Brunek marched eight china reindeer straight across her map of Czechoslovakia.

Almost none of the boys who'd enlisted returned for the holidays. They had left too recently; they were confined to their various posts. In theory, this was something that their families had been prepared for, but still it came as a shock. The streets all at once seemed so quiet. Their sons' bedrooms seemed so empty. The dinner tables were too sedate and orderly—no long-armed, greedy boys pouncing on the last chicken wing or gulping down milk by the quart.

Instead, there were mere letters, all of which might have been written by the same person. "Got a 'grand' bunch of guys in my unit" and "You wouldn't believe the tons of gear we have to lug" and "Sure do miss those Sunday evenings with you folks around the radio." These identical lines, with only minor differences, were read aloud in the grocery store by Mrs. Witt, Mrs. Serge, Mrs. Kowalski, Mrs. Dobek . . . and yet their sons were not alike in any way, or at least had not seemed so till now. "Could take my weapon apart blindfolded and put it together again," Michael Anton wrote—Michael! so peaceful, so unmechanical!—as did Joey Serge and Davey Witt. It wasn't just their similar experiences (the KP duty, tetanus shots, blistered feet) but the way they worded things—the slangy, loping language, with too many sets of quotation marks and not enough commas. "Took a 20 mi. hike yesterday and I can tell you my 'dogs' are the worse for it . . . Wish you could see how neat I make my bed mom now that I've got a 'sarge' standing over me watching."

Maybe the letters they wrote their girlfriends were more distinctive. Or maybe not; who knew? There were only so many ways to say "I love you" and "I miss you." But their girlfriends kept their letters to themselves, disclosing only a sentence or two and then just to the other girls. So the older women had to speculate about that.

Michael wrote Pauline every day, Katie and Wanda reported. Sometimes he wrote twice a day. But none of the lines they quoted revealed anything interesting. He didn't like the food. The guy in the bunk next to him had a constant, honking cough. Life in camp alternated between working your head off one moment and sitting around, sitting around, sitting around the next, just waiting for the war to be over. By now it was a whole new year, 1942, and you would have thought they could have wrapped things up weeks ago.

Every so often, in the late afternoon, the three girls would stop by Anton's Grocery—Katie and Wanda and Pauline, sometimes with Pauline's friend Anna tagging along. "How are you bearing up, Mrs. Anton?" Pauline would say. "Michael asked me to check on you. He's worried how you're doing. Have you heard from him lately?"

Mrs. Anton was her usual gray self ("If he's as worried as all that, he never should have gone and enlisted," she said once), but those who knew her well could detect the gratified pleats at the corners of her mouth. And she always said, "*You've* heard, I guess," which was her devious way of asking without asking.

"Yes, a letter came this morning. He's managing okay, he says."

After the girls had left, the women would tell Mrs. Anton how sweet it was of Pauline to stop by. "She's trying to be nice," they told her. "You have to hand her that much."

Mrs. Anton just said, "Hmpf. For somebody holding down a job, she certainly has a lot of spare time, is all *I* can say."

Mrs. Anton had hired a colored man to help out in Michael's stead. Eustace, his name was. He was small and dry and toasty brown, of an indeterminate age, and he always wore a suitcoat over his bib overalls. Any time Mrs. Anton assigned him a chore, he said, "Yes-sum," and touched the brim of his hat in a dignified and respectful manner, but she told the other women she couldn't wait to be rid of him. "This is a family business," she said. "I can't afford to hire some stranger off the streets! I just want Michael home again. I don't understand what's keeping him."

In February he did come home, but only briefly. By this time people were growing accustomed to the sight of uniforms in their neighborhood, their sons returning for visits in glaringly short haircuts and government-issue woolens. But Michael seemed more changed than the other boys. His face was positively gaunt, with hollows below the cheekbones and shadows the color of bruises underneath his eyes. He was less attentive to his mother, almost not in evidence around the store, and absentminded when friends addressed him on the street. Every fiber of his being, it seemed, was focused on Pauline.

Well, that was something else people were growing accustomed to: these intense wartime romances. Three of the Szapp boys had married within a single week! But since Pauline was from away, this meant Michael all but disappeared from view. He spent most of his time at her family's house. Her family loved him, Wanda reported. They were very doting and welcoming—a household of daughters, four of them, only one as yet married. They cooked for him and made a big fuss whenever he showed up. And Pauline, of course, was in heaven. It was a perfect, blissful five days, by all accounts, and then he shipped out for special training in California. (Was it his gift for reassembling rifles? Some fund of superior intelligence up till now kept hidden?) Mrs. Anton was left looking more bereft than ever. She no longer discussed her plans to fire Eustace.

Mrs. Szapp asked Mrs. Anton if Michael and Pauline were thinking of marriage. This was not very tactful of her. The other customers tensed. But Mrs. Anton surprised them. Yes, she said mildly, he'd said something about it. He said the subject had come up between them. And it was a fact that a Baltimore girl would be preferable to somebody French or English.

Oh, well, of course. Sure couldn't argue with *that,* people said, tumbling over each other's words in their haste to reassure her.

But you never knew, Mrs. Anton went on. There was many a slip betwixt cup and lip. She wasn't holding her breath.

She brightened as she said this—unbecomingly, some agreed later, discussing it among themselves.


Katie Vilna left the cannery and took a job making airplane parts. The Golka twins journeyed daily to the steel mill out at Sparrows Point. And Wanda Bryk might join the Women's Army Auxiliary Corps, as soon as they began accepting applications. Should she?

Shouldn't she? she asked, twirling on her stool at the soda fountain. Yes! the other girls told her. Do it! *They* would join in a flash, if only their parents would let them.

Pauline didn't come around St. Cassian Street much anymore. She was busy with her volunteer work. The neighborhood girls had their own volunteer work (they must have rolled a million bandages by now, all the while wearing white headdresses that made them look like sphinxes), but Pauline's sounded more interesting. She was helping out at a Red Cross canteen, Katie said, serving coffee and doughnuts to lonesome soldiers passing through the port. Sometimes Katie helped too. Katie couldn't count all the fellows she'd met! She said her biggest expense these days was stationery.

A number of the girls asked if they could come with her next time.

In Anton's Grocery, Mrs. Szapp said, "Where has Pauline got to? Nobody seems to have seen her."

"Oh, she's around," Mrs. Anton said.

"I thought she might have gone off somewhere."

"She's around, I tell you! She was in here just . . . when was it. Just last week, or the week before. Talking on and on about Michael. You know how she talks."

Mrs. Szapp was quiet a moment, and then she asked how many ration points a pound of sausage would cost her.

The younger of the Piazy boys went down with his ship in the Coral Sea. It was the parish's first casualty. Mr. Piazy completely stopped speaking. The neighbors walked around for days with pale, tight faces, silently shaking their heads, murmuring phrases of disbelief when they met on the street. So this was for real! they seemed to be saying to each other. Wait a minute! No one had told them things would get so serious!

The Dobeks received a telegram saying Joe was missing in action.

23

Davey Witt was sent home with some kind of nervous trouble that the Witts preferred not to discuss. Jerry Kowalski caught malaria. And Michael Anton was shot in the back and sidelined to the infirmary.

Mrs. Anton said she was glad. She said, "Every day he spends lying in that hospital bed is a day he's not overseas getting killed." Nobody could blame her.

Pauline got more letters than ever, now, and already she had three shoeboxes full. She kept referring to Michael's having been "wounded." And of course, he had been wounded, but only by mistake. Some stupid, careless mistake on the part of a fellow trainee. To hear Pauline talk, though, you would think he'd been in hand-to-hand combat.

The elderly Japanese man who cleaned fish in the Broadway Market had quietly disappeared. Where had he gone? He'd been perfectly nice! Oh, things were dragging on too long, here. This war was lasting forever; everything was taking more time than anyone had expected. Already it was summer. Pearl Harbor seemed to have happened about a hundred years ago.

The oddest items were in short supply. Hairpins, for instance. Who would have thought *hairpins?* Gasoline, all right, but . . . And the littlest of the Brunek boys couldn't have the tricycle he'd requested for his birthday. Rubber tires were the reason. But try explaining that to Petey Brunek!

Then the War Office sent the Szapps two telegrams in the space of three days, and everybody felt guilty for complaining about trivia.

Although still, it would have been nice if Petey could have had his tricycle.

When Michael Anton came home to stay, he wrote ahead to his mother and said he would like for Pauline to meet his train alone. Mrs. Anton didn't appear to take offense. She supposed he planned to pop the question, she told the other women, and she spoke calmly, with a light shrug. As well she could afford to, now that she had her son back.

The reason for his discharge was a pronounced and permanent

limp. All his mother had dared hope was that he'd be transferred to a desk job, but mysteriously, unexplainably, he was sent home instead. He would never, ever in his life have to partake in combat. Mrs. Anton said soldiers called that a "million-dollar wound." Then she stammered and glanced toward Mrs. Szapp, but Mrs. Szapp said, kindly, "*Ten* million dollars, I would term it. God's been good to you, Dolly."

At around the time Michael and Pauline were expected to alight from the streetcar—toward noon on a Wednesday at the very tail end of August—women started showing up at the grocery store to make single, random purchases. One box of Jell-O. A flyswatter. They lingered a long while, chitchatting, casting sidelong glances at Mrs. Anton who wore a nicer-than-usual dress and a dab of lipstick. Eventually, having no further excuse to stay, they moved out onto the sidewalk and stood around in front of Mrs. Serge's parlor window next door. Mrs. Serge had a row of china nuns lined up beneath her service banner—little cute nuns, singing O-mouthed over hymn books or kneeling in prayer with tiny gold dots of rosaries painted across their fronts. It was hot as blazes, the sun glistening on the women's faces and spreading darkened half-moons beneath their arms, but still they went on studying Mrs. Serge's nuns.

Might have known the train would be late, they murmured to each other. Trains nowadays were always late, always crowded with soldiers and subject to unexplained stops.

Twice Mrs. Anton joined them, on the pretext of seeing a customer to the door—not something she would ordinarily do. She looked toward Dubrowski Street and then ducked back inside. She was wearing actual stockings, the women realized.

The third time she came out, she called, "Eustace? Is Eustace with you all?" although she had no possible grounds for imagining that he would be. And then she looked up the street and cried, "There he is!"

Not Eustace, of course, but Michael, with Pauline beside him. From a distance, they were as small and tidily matched as a couple on a wedding cake—Pauline in something pastel, Michael in summer khakis. Oh, couldn't a uniform stab your heart, and fill you with love and grief and longing! It was true that Michael carried a cane. He leaned on it fairly heavily, tilting as he swung his right leg, and Pauline was lugging his gladstone bag in front of her with both hands. But still they made good time. The women let him come to them. They stood waiting, absorbing the sight of him.

Then he was close enough so they could make out his broad grin, which stretched his face to a diamond shape and reminded them of the rambunctious kid he had been back in grade school. And his mother gave a sound that seemed wrenched from her chest, and set off at a hobbling run to meet him.

Long, long afterward, reminiscing together about how oddly exhilarating those hard, sad war years had been, more than one of the women privately summoned the picture of Michael Anton and his mother hugging on the sidewalk while Pauline watched, smiling, tipping slightly backward against the weight of his bag.


He said he was in no pain at all, except for when it rained. Then he might get a twinge in his hip joint. For he had been shot in the hip, not the back. In the rear end, to put it plainly. ("Back" had been a politeness.) Out in the woods on maneuvers, clambering over a log, he had felt a kind of slamming sensation and a deep, flaring ache, and next thing he knew he was lying facedown on a pile of moldering leaves. Lucky he'd been mounting that log or he *would* have been shot in the back, possibly straight through the heart. And yes, he could say who had done it: that fellow with the constant cough who'd bunked next to him in Virginia. Wouldn't you just know that of all the men he'd trained with, that was the one they would ship west with him? The guy's rifle had gone off when he stumbled—an accident, but one that never should have happened in view of the safety measures drilled into them from the start. Still, look at it this way: that fellow was a whole lot worse off now than Michael. *He* was still in the Army.

It was Thursday afternoon, and Michael, wearing gray work trousers and a blue plaid cotton shirt washed nearly translucent, was shelving pinto beans as he spoke. Mrs. Brunek, Miss Jakubek, and Mrs.

Serge stood at the counter, each ostentatiously displaying a grocery list, but they weren't fooling a soul. People had been coming in all day on the flimsiest of excuses, just wanting to wish Michael well and hear what he had to say for himself.

He said it would take him a while to catch on to this ration-point business. So complicated! So many forms! And there were other things to get used to. The skylight in Penn Station, he said, had been painted over completely, that pretty compass-rose sort of glass made opaque in case of air raids. Did they know that? No, they did not. They didn't have much reason to ride the train these days.

And it was such a surprise, he went on, to see the blackout shades in everybody's windows. Why, things were no different here than out west! Evidently he had expected that home would be exempt somehow—that the war was only elsewhere.

Well, just look at Davey Witt. Davey refused to sleep in a room alone now. Lord only knew what those poor boys had been through, so far away from Baltimore.

Mrs. Anton punched the keys of the sculptured brass cash register and the drawer slid open with its musical chin-*chink!* She was wearing her normal clothes again, but her manner was livelier than the three women had seen in ages, and when she told them "Come back soon!" she was very nearly singing.

Halfway out the door, the women caught sight of Pauline. She was flying toward them in a drift of pink-flowered white muslin, holding onto her straw hat so it wouldn't blow away in the breeze she'd set up. Interesting how she'd changed her colors just at the very time when she was changing in people's opinions. From dangerous and dramatic red to gentle, soft pastels, she'd gone. Probably that was due to the season, but still, they did like her so much! She was just what Michael needed, someone to warm up his life. Notice how she greeted all the women by name. "Hello, Mrs. Brunek! Hi, Miss Jakubek! Hi, Mrs. Serge!" And how at home she seemed, darting past them into the grocery store, trilling her fingers at Michael's mother and tossing Michael a dimpled smile that turned him sweetly self-conscious. For of course the women followed her back inside. It would be a shame to miss this!

She said, "Guess what, Michael."

"What," he said, beaming. He reached for the cane that he'd hooked on the edge of the counter.

"Guess!"

"Well, I don't know, Polly."

"Reverend Dane said we can be married in his church."

"He did? Really? That's great!" Michael said.

Pegging the length of the counter so that he could come out and join her, he flicked a glance toward his mother in passing. The neighbor women checked too. How would she take the news? Her son getting married in a Protestant church: not what most mothers would hope for.

Mrs. Anton was stalwart. She raised her chin and said, "Isn't that nice!"

"Naturally you're all invited," Pauline told the women.

They looked at each other and murmured their thanks. (Father Pasko would throw a fit.)

"Also, guess what, Michael," Pauline said.

He was standing in front of her now, leaning stiff-armed on his cane and smiling down at her. He said, "What."

"Guess!"

Michael was so slow and stodgy; the women had never realized how stodgy. "*What,* Polly," he said.

"My father's going to find an apartment for us."

Michael blinked. He said, "Why would we need an apartment?"

"To live in, silly!"

"But we have a place to live in. Here above the store."

"Yes, but Dad says he can find us something of our own. Lots of times he hears first when people are getting evicted, he says, when they come to him looking for someplace cheap in a hurry. All he has to ask them is, 'Where was it you've been living till now?' and if their landlord hasn't—"

"But we can't afford our own place, hon. I already told you. Mama's going to move out of her bedroom and you can decorate it yourself, any way you like."

Mrs. Anton was giving up her bedroom? So she'd have to sleep in that sliver of a room that used to be Michael and Danny's. (It wasn't very hard to figure this out, with houses all more or less the same floor plan.) What a sacrifice! The women sent Mrs. Anton a look, but she didn't respond. She was watching Michael and Pauline.

Pauline said, "Oh."

Michael said, "You understand."

"Well," she said.

She took a step backward. She was wearing flimsy sandals in an impossibly narrow size, something none of the hefty neighborhood girls could have dreamed of fitting into, and even on this creaky floor her step was so light and dainty that she didn't make a sound. She spun around, and just like that she was gone. The screen door swung shut. The rusty spring on top vibrated twangily.

Michael turned to the women with such a perplexed expression that Mrs. Brunek, for one, seemed to feel the need to explain. She gave a tinkle of a laugh and said, "Oh, you know: bridal jitters!"

He said, "Maybe I should go talk to her."

He left, his rubber-tipped cane chirping in an anxious-sounding way.

Miss Jakubek was so distracted that she started shopping all over again, even though she was already carrying a little parcel of canned goods.

Sometimes it seemed that the war was blurring St. Cassian's edges. The factory girls were dating fellows from South Carolina and West Virginia; the boys overseas were writing home about girls with English accents. A number of the neighborhood women—respectable women, married, with children—had taken jobs at Glenn L. Martin. They set off for work each morning in coarse blue denim coveralls while their mothers, wearing scarves knotted under their chins and dresses shaped like potato sacks tied in the middle, watched after them and shook their heads. Who knew where it would end?

You didn't hear just polkas anymore; you heard "Chattanooga Choo Choo" and "The White Cliffs of Dover" and "I've Got a Gal in Kalamazoo." You heard "Blues in the Night" and "Take Me" and "I

Don't Want to Walk Without You." Young people danced cheek to cheek, so slowly they might be sleepwalking. Katie Vilna got pregnant. Jerry Kowalski's girlfriend ran off with a sailor from Memphis. Everyone in the neighborhood learned how to identify airplanes.

Joe Dobek's body was found and shipped home, and they held a funeral for him on the first cool day in September. Even before the war began, St. Cassian's cemetery had been running out of room, but they squeezed him between two strangers' graves from long, long ago when the neighborhood was Irish. The mossy headstones of O'Malley and O'Leary flanked Joe's pearly white one, and Mrs. Dobek fell into the habit of laying flowers on all three graves when she came to visit Joe. John O'Malley had lived ninety-two years and died at rest in the Lord. O'Leary (no first name) had come into this world and left again in the space of a single day. Mrs. Dobek told her friends that sometimes, when she should have been praying for Joe, she thought instead about the O'Leary baby's mother—how terribly, achingly sad she must have been to lose her infant, but how much more she *could* have lost: all the years of his growing up and becoming a separate person with quirks and foibles and special ways of doing things, like half breaking her neck when he hugged her, and turning the dog's ears inside out, and pretending to mistake his little sister for Betty Grable.

She also said that when she first heard they'd found Joe's body, she had felt a bolt of something she would almost have to call anger. They made it sound as if he'd just been thoughtlessly mislaid, she said. Like somebody's cast-off toy. When she herself had been so careful, all these years, to keep him safe and healthy.

Nowadays so many couples were marrying in a hurry that people had grown accustomed to abbreviated, slapdash weddings. In the past there would have been months of sewing, weeks of cooking, a giant party afterwards where the guests tossed envelopes of money into the bride's scooped apron, but lately it seemed that getting married required no more forethought than going to the movies.

So when Mrs. Anton told her customers, on a Friday in late September, that Michael's wedding would take place the following afternoon, they weren't completely scandalized. And when she said they were welcome to come if they wanted, eight or nine women accepted. No men, as it happened. The men claimed they couldn't see themselves entering a Protestant church, but that was just an excuse. You know how men are about wearing ties on a Saturday.

Even though people talked as if Pauline hailed from the moon, her neighborhood was barely a twenty-minute walk from St. Cassian Street—a very pleasant walk, if the weather was good. And the weather on Michael's wedding day was beautiful. The air was crisp and fall-like, and as the women left their own neighborhood behind they began to see little fenced trees that were turning lipstick red or egg-yolk yellow. They strolled at a leisurely pace, commenting on the houses they passed, which were row houses still but wider and somehow messier—the fronts not perfectly uniform, the curtains all different colors, the stoops surrounded by disorganized bits of green. The church, when it came into view, was clapboard, and the windows were not stained glass but a monotone pink, pebbled like the windows in bathrooms. About this the women said nothing. They were determined to behave impeccably. They all wore their most American clothes, dark and severe, with dark hats and spotless white gloves, and they carried wrapped and ribboned gifts because where Pauline lived, brides were given items from Hutzler's. Everybody knew that much.

Leading the way was Wanda Bryk—the youngest by twenty years or more, but clearly the one in charge. She instructed them as they climbed the church steps. "Pauline's parents will be here, of course, and her three sisters, and her oldest sister's husband who's got asthma so don't say anything, I mean don't ask why he hasn't enlisted because he feels just awful about it . . . No, no bridesmaids, no best man . . . not even a real procession! We'll just all sit near the front and the minister's going to—oh, there she is! There's Pauline now!"

Pauline? Herself? Yes, that was who it was, all right. She was standing in the foyer, big as life, wearing a disappointingly plain ivory-colored street dress and talking to an old man. When she saw the women she said, "Oh! How nice of you all to come! Michael, look who's here!"

Good Lord, yes, there was Michael, too, leaning on his cane not a yard away from his bride. Apparently they saw no harm in meeting before the wedding. Michael wore his pinchy suit and a white shirt and a red tie. He looked so handsome! The women were proud of him. They kissed him, patted his arm, pretended his collar needed straightening. "Mama's on her way," he told them. "She's coming with Uncle Bron." Then he introduced them to Pauline's mother. "Mom Barclay," he called her; goodness, that was fast! Mrs. Barclay was trim and attractive, with Pauline's dark-blond hair, and she made such a to-do over the St. Cassian's women, complimenting their dresses and their hats and their wrapping paper, exclaiming at how far they must have walked, that they began to feel uncertain. Then a young sailor arrived, and Mrs. Barclay turned her gracious smile on him, and the women were free to go on inside.

The church had baby-blue walls and blond wood pews, which made it seem lacking in mystery. Up front, Pauline's friend Anna—the girl with the handkerchief that first day in Anton's Grocery—was playing the piano, her back to the congregation but her smooth brown pageboy and her faultless posture easily identifiable. Already several guests were sitting here and there. None of them was familiar, but shortly after the women had arranged themselves along the length of one pew, Michael's mother came down the aisle on the arm of her brother-in-law. She wore a navy polka-dot dress they'd never seen before, and a white cloth rose was pinned to the V of her neckline. When Mrs. Serge said "Psst!" Mrs. Anton gave the women a squinty, superficial smile and then instantly sobered, as if she had to keep her full attention on the business at hand. Elsewhere, though, people were talking in normal tones and even getting up to join in other conversations. None of them seemed to have presents. Were presents *wrong* in some way? The seating appeared to be random, but Mrs. Anton settled in a first-row pew, which the St. Cassian's women agreed was only proper.

A door opened behind the altar and a pale young man in a black suit emerged. He walked over to the pulpit, set down a Bible, and smiled at the congregation. For a while this had no effect, but gradually the guests who'd risen to converse went into a little flurry of returning to their seats. Then Mrs. Barclay came down the aisle with a worn-looking gray-haired man—no doubt Mr. Barclay—and they settled in the other front pew. Anna stopped playing the piano. The minister cleared his throat. A hush fell. Everyone looked toward the door at the rear.

Nothing happened.

People exchanged glances. Maybe the couple would enter from elsewhere; was that the plan? They faced forward again. The minister started leafing through his Bible, but not as if he meant to read from it.

Whispers started circulating up and down the pews. A child asked a question that was laughingly silenced, after which the atmosphere relaxed. Casual conversations resumed in several spots. Mrs. Anton's back stayed rigid and she went on looking straight ahead, but Mrs. Barclay kept twisting in her seat to check behind her. Obviously she had no more information than her guests.

"What's going on?" Mrs. Nowak asked Wanda.

Instead of answering, Wanda rose and stepped out of the pew. She started back up the side aisle, her heels clopping briskly, while the women looked at each other.

A glass of water stood at the right-hand edge of the pulpit, and now the minister picked it up and took a token, unconvincing sip. He set the glass back down. He coughed. He really was astonishingly young. "I hope they're not experiencing any last-minute doubts, haha," he said.

A few people tittered dutifully.

Behind the St. Cassian's women, two men were discussing the Orioles. One of them said he'd given up hope. The other said just to wait. Everything would be different, he said, in 1943.

Wanda came back and sat down, out of breath, rustling and bustling importantly.

What was it? the women asked, leaning forward.

Pauline had changed her mind.

Had *what?*

The answer came in patches, altering slightly from woman to woman as it was relayed down the row, whispered even in this hubbub so that no one in any other pew could hear.

Says she doesn't know what she was thinking . . . says all they do is fight . . . says he never wants to go anyplace and . . . always so unsocial and . . . such a different style of person from her, so set in his ways, won't budge . . .

"Always does *what?* Never wants to go *where?*" Mrs. Serge asked from the far end. "Wait, I didn't catch that."

Mrs. Zack said every bride felt that way. That was what weddings were all about! Wanda said Michael had said the same thing. He'd said, "Now, Poll, you're just overwrought," and Pauline had said, "Don't tell *me* I'm—"

"Ssh!" Mrs. Serge said.

Seated closest to the aisle, she was the first to notice the stir at the rear of the church. The women turned. The other guests turned. The piano came to with a start and started playing "Here Comes the Bride" as Michael and Pauline walked toward the altar hand in hand. Not arm in arm, the way people did at snootier, more stilted weddings, but tightly holding hands and wearing radiant smiles.

They were such a perfect couple. They were taking their very first steps on the amazing journey of marriage, and wonderful adventures were about to unfold in front of them.

# 2. Dandelion Clock

Pauline said, "Once upon a time, there was a woman who had a birthday."

Michael stopped pouring his cereal and looked across the table at her.

"It was January fifth," Pauline said. "The woman was twenty-three."

"Why, that's *your* birthday, too!" Michael's mother told her. "That's how old *you* turned, only yesterday!"

"And because this woman happened to be at a low point in her life," Pauline went on, "she was feeling very sensitive about her age."

Michael said, cautiously, "A low point in her life?"

Pauline rose to reposition the baby in her high chair. The baby had reached the stage where she could sit up, but just barely. Left on her own, she tended to slide gradually downwards until her chin was resting on her chest.

"Yes, she wasn't awfully attractive just then," Pauline said, taking her seat again. "She was two months pregnant and sick as a dog, and she still hadn't got her figure back from the *last* time she was pregnant. Also, her husband was a quarter-year younger than she was. For three months after every birthday, she was an Older Woman. Can you imagine how that felt? She was old and fat and ugly, and her bosom was starting to sag."

Pauline herself was prettier than ever, in Michael's opinion. This early in the morning, unrouged and unlipsticked, wearing a flowered chintz housecoat, she looked as fresh as a child. The second pregnancy had not begun to show yet, whatever she might imagine, and the only apparent effect of the first was the thrilling new roundness and weightiness of her breasts. Michael could almost feel them filling his hands as she spoke. He smiled; he tried to catch her eye. But Pauline was saying, "More coffee, Mother Anton?"

"No, thank you, dear. You know what it does to my stomach," Michael's mother said.

"Luckily for this woman," Pauline continued, "her husband was very understanding. He hated for her to feel bad! He decided he would devote himself to making her birthday perfect."

Michael stirred uneasily. He had certainly not *forgotten* her birthday—nothing so unforgivable as that—but neither could he say he had devoted himself to making it perfect. (It had fallen on a weekday this year. He did have a business to run.)

"He got up in the morning," Pauline said, "he tiptoed out to the kitchen, he fixed her French toast and orange juice. He came back with a tray and said, 'Happy birthday, darling!' Then he brought her the flowers that he'd stowed earlier on the fire escape. A dozen long-stemmed roses; never mind the expense. 'You're worth every bit of it, darling,' he said. 'I just wish they could be rubies.' "

Pauline was bright-eyed and her voice had a cheery ring to it, so that Michael's mother was fooled completely. She gave a sigh of satisfaction. "Wasn't that romantic!" she told Michael. (Since those two dizzy spells last summer, she had seemed less quick-witted.) But Michael watched Pauline in silence, his fingers tight on his napkin.

"And her present," Pauline said, "was . . ."

For the first time, she faltered. She turned to untie the baby's bib.

". . . was something personal," she said finally. "A bottle of cologne, or a see-through nightie. He would never give her anything useful! And he'd never just tell her to buy it herself! He'd never say, 'Happy birthday, hon, and why don't you stop by Zack's Housewares and pick up one of those family-size canning kettles you've been telling me you needed.' "

Michael felt his mother send him an uncertain glance. She said, "Oh. Well . . ."

"But what am I boring *you* with this for?" Pauline caroled. "It's not as if we live that way ourselves, now, is it?"

And she sprang lightly to her feet and lifted Lindy from the high chair and carried her out of the kitchen.

Downstairs in the grocery store, Michael slit open a cardboard carton and unpacked tins of peaches. He stacked them on a shelf above a tab that read 17¢—18 POINTS. In his head he was defending himself. "Was I supposed to read your mind, or what?" he silently asked Pauline. "How would I know what you want for your birthday? I'm twenty-two years old! The only woman I've ever bought a gift for is my mother! And Mama's always loved getting presents that were useful!"

He recalled the moment when the inspiration of the canning kettle had hit him—the flood of relief as he remembered Pauline's complaints about his mother's little dinky one. He had been so proud of himself! Now a wounded feeling swept through him.

And notice how she had said nothing about her birthday cake. Chocolate cake, with chocolate icing spread not just across the top ("flat top" style, as the Ration Board called it) but down the sides as well. Who did she imagine had asked his mother to make that cake? Left to her own devices, his mother probably wouldn't have remembered what day it was, even.

Eustace emerged from the stockroom, toting a crate of eggs. He set it down by the refrigerator case and straightened, groaning, to massage the small of his back. "Must be going to snow," he said, "achy as my bones has been."

"Yup, my hip says the same," Michael told him.

"You got them items ready for Miz Pozniak?"

"They're over by the register."

Eustace went to check. The groceries were in a canvas sack of the sort that newsboys carried, with a strap that crossed the chest bandolier-fashion. (Eustace was too old, he claimed, to learn to ride the delivery bike with its oversized wire basket that Michael had used as a boy.) He heaved the sack onto his shoulder and approached the door just as Mrs. Serge walked in. "Morning, Eustace! Morning, Michael!" she said, stepping to one side so Eustace could pass.

"Good morning, Mrs. Serge," Michael said. He rose from the carton of peaches and reached for his cane. "Cold enough for you?"

"Oh, yes. My, yes," she said, and she clutched her coat collar more tightly around her throat. In fact, coming from just next door she must have barely had time to feel the cold. But people seemed to expect this kind of small talk, Michael had found. "How's your mama?" she asked him. "How's Pauline? How's that darlin' Lindy?"

"They're all fine. What do you hear from Joey?"

"He's coming home on leave tomorrow afternoon."

"That's wonderful!"

"Yes, so I'll need some tinned milk, because I want to fix him some ice cream."

"Tinned milk," Michael said, and he turned back to the shelves. "One can, or two?"

"Better make it two. You must think I'm crazy, doing this in January."

"No, ma'am," Michael said. "I know how Joey loves ice cream." He set the cans on the counter. "Anything else?"

"Well, let's see. A box of gelatin, and I might as well get some vanilla extract just to play it safe . . . Did Pauline try that ginger tea I was telling her about?"

"I'm not sure," Michael said.

"A quarter-teaspoon of powdered ginger in half a cup of hot water, I told her. Sip it real slow before breakfast. I did that every morning back when I was expecting Joey and it worked just like a charm."

"I'll make her some tomorrow," Michael said.

"Poor thing. Skinny as *she* is, she can't afford to stop eating."

"No, it's been hard on her," Michael agreed.

Although later, when Mrs. Serge had left, he added to himself, "And she's not the only one it's been hard on."

Well, he knew he shouldn't complain. How would *he* behave, if he couldn't keep a morsel of food down? Plus pregnancy in general, all those female troubles.

He wasn't certain, though, how much of Pauline's moodiness was due to pregnancy and how much just, well, things going wrong between the two of them. Oh, women were so mystifying! And he was so inexperienced! "What did I say? What did I do? What *was* it?" he always seemed to be asking. Did other men have this problem? Was there anyone he could discuss this with? If he somehow had the right words—the right touch, the proper instincts—would his wife be a happier person?

She'd been a constitutionally happy person when they met, he believed. Pauline with her soft dimples and her liquid, chuckly laugh! She had slipped her hand into his so trustfully the first time they went on a date—her slim fingers, impossibly smooth, nestling into the cup of his palm when he had assumed it would be weeks before he could hope they would get so familiar. He had felt himself expanding with the sense of responsibility. He had wished for something dangerous—a bully, a runaway car—so that he could protect her.

But then he'd made some mistakes. He was willing to admit that. The time he asked her to meet him at the Kowalskis' party, for instance, instead of calling for her and escorting her, just to spare his mother's feelings. That was wrong, wrong, wrong, and Pauline had been perfectly right not to show up. He'd realized that almost at once—had had a sudden, disturbing view of himself as a mama's boy, a coward, and run all the way to her house and rung her doorbell and begged Mr. Barclay to fetch her so that he could apologize and persuade her to come back with him. But then later that same evening, when his mother had crumpled up in a faint—well, what was he to do? He couldn't just ignore her! So Pauline had disappeared, vanished into the night, and he'd had to go to her house all over again and bother Mr. Barclay again (now in bathrobe and pajamas) only to be turned away. "Sorry, son, afraid she's not accepting visitors at the moment." Not at that moment and not the next day, when Mrs. Barclay had stepped in to offer one excuse after the other. Pauline was still asleep; then she was indisposed; then, "I guess it's best to stop calling, dear," or something of the sort, some statement to that effect.

With all the many times since that he'd stood on the Barclays' front porch, these scenes tended to blur together in his mind.

But he knew that on his deathbed, the last, best memory he would cling to would be the sight of Pauline in her red coat, flying down Aliceanna Street to see him off to war. Wasn't that worth all the rest? Every other edgy, imperfect, exasperating moment of their marriage?

Mrs. Piazy came in wanting Spam and a box of elbow macaroni. "I'm serving this new recipe for supper," she told Michael. "I cut it out of a magazine. How's Pauline feeling today?"

"Still not so good," he said.

"Has she tried saltine crackers? That's what I used to do. She should eat six or eight as soon as she wakes up, and more any time she feels queasy."

"I'll tell her, Mrs. Piazy. Thanks."

"And stop that worrying, Michael. You can't fool me! I see that long face! I know how you fret about her! But take my word, she'll be fine. Just fine."

"Well, thank you, Mrs. Piazy."

"You two are so precious together," she said.

And she gave a fond, indulgent smile as she dug in her bag for her change purse.


At noon he went looking for Eustace, who had finished all his deliveries and was hidden away in the dimness of the stockroom. "Eustace?" he called. "You there?"

"I'm here."

"Guess I'll be going to lunch now."

"Okay, then," Eustace said, and he struggled up from behind a pickle barrel, a half-eaten sandwich of homemade bread clutched in one gnarled hand.

Michael said, "Oh. You want me to wait till you finish that?"

"No, sir. You just go on now."

What Michael had meant to say was that he preferred for Eustace not to eat in front of customers—something he himself wouldn't do.

But he wasn't sure how to put it. The fact was, he felt uncomfortable bossing around an employee. Before the war they'd never had an employee. But first with his enlisting, and then his mother's health, and Pauline so tied up with the baby . . .

He continued through the stockroom and climbed the stairs at the rear, relying on the handrail instead of his cane for support. Not that he needed much support anymore. His limp had become just a hitch in his step, a side-to-side motion as he swung the one leg forward, and he was sheepishly aware that he used the cane primarily to fend off strangers' questions about why he wasn't in uniform.

Pauline said that was silly of him. "What do you care what people think?" she would ask. "You and I know the truth of the matter."

In many ways, Pauline was a much stronger person than he was.

His mother was already seated at the kitchen table while Pauline stood at the stove, the baby astride her waist, and stirred a saucepan of soup. "Hi, there," Michael said, and his mother said, "Hello, dear," but Pauline was silent. He pretended not to notice. He said, "Lindy-Lou!" and reached for the baby, and Pauline let go of her so carelessly and abruptly that Michael almost dropped her. He sank into a chair with her, holding her compact little body close against his rib cage. "Daddy's here," he told her. "Say, 'Daddy! Welcome home! I've been pining for you all morning!' "

Lindy studied his lips intently. She was a solemn, focused sort of baby, with Michael's black hair and straight features. Her eyes were a shade of slate that would probably turn brown like his as she grew older, and already she had his thin hands and long, thin fingers. Was it only her resemblance to him that made him feel so connected to her? He had always just assumed that he would have children, the way he'd assumed he would have a wife and maybe someday an automobile, but he had never imagined that a child could tug on his heart so.

His mother was relating a recent run-in with Leo Kazmerow. "He takes his duties too seriously," she said. "An air raid warden's not God. Leave one little light on during a drill and 'Mrs. Anton,' he says, 'how would you feel if Baltimore got bombed clear off the map and you were the household responsible?' "

4 1

"It's all because he's 4-F," Pauline told her. "He thinks he has to make up for it."

Her tone was relaxed and pleasant. She and Michael's mother were cozy friends, and Michael was the outsider pressing his nose to the window glass. He sighed and offered Lindy a spoon. "Don't you plan to dine with us?" he asked when she didn't take it. As if he had convinced her, she reached out and grasped the spoon and pulled it from his hand with surprising strength. He lowered his face to the top of her head and breathed in the scent of her hair. Underneath the talcum he caught a hint of fresh sweat, which he found endearing and faintly comical.

Pauline ladled out the soup—cream of tomato. She sat down and unfolded her napkin. Michael wrested his spoon from Lindy's fist and started eating, and his mother picked up her own spoon, but Pauline just sat there, staring into her bowl.

"Hon?" Michael said finally. "Can't you manage even a little?"

"Not unless I want it all to come back up again," she said.

"Mrs. Piazy says to try saltine crackers."

There was a box of saltines on the table, but she didn't reach for it. Instead she said, "Will you all please excuse me?" and she laid her napkin next to her bowl and stood up and left the kitchen.

Michael and his mother looked at each other. The bedroom door closed quietly.

"She's going to waste away to nothing," his mother said after a moment.

Perversely, Michael felt a pang of almost brotherly jealousy. Didn't he deserve a little sympathy too? This wasn't much fun for him!

When they had finished eating (the clinks of their spoons too loud, guiltily healthy-sounding, and their remarks to the baby too chirpy), Michael told his mother that he thought he'd go check on Pauline. "Yes, why don't you do that," she said. "I'll see to the dishes." He hoisted Lindy out of her high chair and took her with him.

Playing it extra safe, he knocked on the bedroom door first. Nobody said, "Come in," but after a brief pause, he went in anyway.

Pauline was not lying in bed, as he had expected, but standing near the window at the foot of Lindy's crib. She had lifted one lace panel to gaze out, and she didn't look around when Michael entered. "Pauline," he said.

"What."

"I wish you'd try and eat a little something."

She went on staring out the window, although the view was just the flat faces of the houses across the side street.

This room, which had once belonged to Michael's parents, had developed a kind of dual personality since his marriage. His parents' white iron bed and glass-knobbed mahogany nightstand kept company now with Pauline's autograph quilt from her girlhood, and her senior-prom corsage all faded and hardened on the bureau, and snapshots of her high-school friends tucked in the frame of the mirror. Her decorating style was so personal. Even the few pieces of furniture that she'd introduced—a child's rocker, a hope chest—had their intimate associations, their long-winded, confidential histories.

He went over to stand next to her. "See Mommy?" he asked Lindy. "*Poor* Mommy. She's not feeling well."

Sadly, Pauline said, "You don't even know what's wrong, do you."

"Actually, I believe I do know," Michael said. He kept his voice very even, so as not to upset her further. "Or I know what you *think* is wrong. You think I should have made more of a fuss about your birthday."

Pauline started to say something, but he held up the flat of his free hand. "Now, I'm sorry that you feel that way," he said. "I certainly never meant to disappoint you. But what I suspect is that you're under a little strain these days. You're pregnant, you're morning sick, and you're none too pleased anyhow—neither one of us is—about having a second baby so soon. That's what's really bothering you."

"How do *you* know what's bothering me?" Pauline asked, wheeling around.

Lindy whimpered, and Michael patted the small of her back. He said, "Now, Pauline. Now, hon. Calm yourself, hon."

"Don't you 'hon' me! Don't you tell me to calm myself! So all-knowing and superior. I'm the only one who can say what bothers me and what doesn't!"

Anyone could have heard her—his mother, for sure, and maybe even Eustace and whatever customers might be down in the store. Her voice had risen at least an octave and turned thin and wiry, nothing like her usual appealing croak. And she was so physical in her fury, putting her whole body into emphasizing each word, that her curls stood out from her head in an electric, exaggerated way. (Like a dandelion clock, Michael suddenly fancied.) When things reached this state, he felt helpless. He had no means of controlling her. However he tried to quiet her only made her louder. "Sweetheart," he tried, and "Poll, hon," and "Be reasonable, Pauline." But she advanced, both fists clenched tight. She grabbed the baby, who was crying now, and she hugged her to her breast and shouted, "Go away! Just go! Just take your stuffy pompous boring self-righteous self away and leave us in peace!"

He turned without another word. Now was when he most hated limping, because instead of striding out he had to leave the room in a halting and victimlike manner. Still, he did his best. In the kitchen he passed his mother, who stared at him from the sink with a dish towel gripped in both hands.

"Guess I'll get back to work," he told her, and he smiled at her, or tried to smile, and lurched past her and out the door.


Was it possible to dislike your own wife?

Well, no, of course not. This was just one of those ups-and-downs that every couple experienced. He'd seen the topic referred to on the covers of those magazines that Pauline was always buying: "How to Stop Marital Fights Before They Start" and "Inside: 'Why Do We Argue So Often?' "

But surely most other wives were not so baffling as Pauline. So changeable, so illogical.

He transferred three onions from the scale to a brown paper bag and set them on the counter for Mrs. Golka. She was considering a pound of sugar but she hated to use all her points up. The twins had a terrible sweet tooth, she said. Michael said, "Sweet tooth, yes . . ."

and then fell to studying the scoop of the scale, which bore a dent from when Pauline had slung it down too hard during a quarrel.

Oh, there had been any number of quarrels. Quarrels about money: she spent money on what seemed to him unnecessary, household knick-knacks and baby things and decorative objects of no earthly practical use, while Michael was more prudent. (Stingy, she called it.) Quarrels about the apartment: she swore that she was going mad, stuck in those airless, dark rooms cheek to jowl with his mother, and she wanted them to move to the county as soon as the war was over—someplace with yards and trees and *side* yards, too, not one of those row-house developments that were starting to sprout here and there. When Michael pointed out that they couldn't afford the county, she said her father would help; he'd already offered. (Already offered! Michael had felt his face grow hot with shame.) When he said they would be too far from the store, she'd told him to move the store as well. "And what will St. Cassian people do for groceries, then?" he'd asked her, but she'd said, "St. Cassian people! Who cares? I'm tired to my bones of St. Cassian people! Everyone knowing everyone's business from three generations back. It's time we broadened our horizons!"

Even their sex life was grounds for dispute. Did he have to start out the same, exact way every single time? The same rote moves, the same one position? Michael had been dumbfounded. "Well, but, I mean, how else . . . ?" he had stammered, and she had said, "Oh, never mind. If I have to say it, forget it." And then he *had* forgotten it, to all intents and purposes, for nowadays they didn't have much of a sex life at all, though he supposed that was understandable in view of her condition.

But the worst quarrels, he reflected (fetching the sugar for Mrs. Golka, who had decided to go on and buy it) were the ones where he couldn't pinpoint the cause. The ones that simply materialized, developing less from something they said than from who they were, by nature. By nature, Pauline tumbled through life helter-skelter while Michael proceeded deliberately. By nature, Pauline felt entitled to spill anything that came into her head while Michael measured out every word. She was brimming with energy—a floor pacer, a foot jiggler, a

45

finger drummer—while he was slow and plodding and secretly some-what lazy. Everything to her was all or nothing—every new friend her best friend, every minor disagreement an end to the friendship for-ever after—while to him the world was calibrated more incremen-tally and more fuzzily.

Pauline believed that marriage was an interweaving of souls, while Michael viewed it as two people traveling side by side but sep-arately. "What are you thinking about?" she liked to say, and "Tell me what you honestly feel." She customarily opened his mail. She never failed to ask whom he'd been talking to on the phone. Even her eter-nal guess-whats ("Guess what, Michael . . . No, seriously, guess . . . Come on. Just take a guess . . . Wrong. Guess again . . . Come on!") seemed to him a form of intrusion.

How could two people so unlike ever hope to interweave? Which only proved, Michael felt, that his view of marriage was the right one.

"Well, that's Michael for you," he imagined her saying. "Never been wrong in his life, if you ask *Michael*."

He set the sugar carefully upright on the counter. "Anything else?" Mrs. Golka asked him.

He said, "Pardon?"

" 'Anything else I can get for you, Mrs. Golka?' "

"Oh," he said. "Sorry."

She smiled, shaking her head, and handed him her ration book.


A grocery store's business comes in waves: the early rush for staples depleted overnight; the late-morning rush for the children's lunches before they walked home from school; the afternoon rush for supper supplies. By five o'clock, things had slowed to a trickle and only Wanda Bryk stood at the counter. Wanda Lipska, she was now. She had finished all her shopping but she lingered to gossip with Michael. Had he heard that Ernie Moskowicz had been drafted? "Ernie Mos-kowicz!" Michael said. "He's just a kid!" And Nick the Greek's café had caught fire, and Anna Grant had married a colonel and moved to Arizona. "You remember Anna, the girl who played the piano at your wedding," Wanda said. Michael said, "Sure," for of course he remembered Anna—her archless, level eyebrows and smooth brown turned-under hair. He was surprised by a twinge of wistfulness. Why couldn't he have fallen for a woman like Anna Grant? he wondered. His life would have been so simple and serene!

Or Wanda, even. He used to find Wanda irritating, but here she stood, six months pregnant and rosily, bloomingly healthy, hugging her sack of groceries. Her tan cloth coat, which was slightly too short and didn't quite meet across her stomach, had the well-worn, comfortable look of the clothes that his mother and her friends wore, and her broad Polish face shone with contentment.

"Tell Pauline I asked about her," she said as she turned to leave. "Tell her I hope she's feeling—oh, there you are! Hi!"

It was Pauline herself, toting Lindy, entering through the street door with a string shopping bag on one shoulder. She wore her red coat and the hat Michael called her Robin Hood hat—a matching red felt that she normally saved for Sundays, with a narrow, asymmetrical brim and a dashing black feather. He used to look for that shade of red on the street when they were first courting. A flash of it glimpsed in a crowd could make his heart race.

"Hello, Wanda! Hello, Michael!" she said. "I thought I'd come in this way and see if you're closing up yet."

"Is she a little sweetheart," Wanda told Lindy. "Is she a little angel child," and she made a series of kissing sounds. Lindy was all decked out as well, in a pink wool coat and bonnet. She studied Wanda soberly and then looked toward Michael as if to ask "What's happening here?" He gazed back at her, not smiling.

"We went to the butcher's," Pauline was saying. "I thought I'd buy pork chops for Michael's supper. Isn't pork expensive these days! And seven points a pound. But Michael works so hard, I want to be sure he gets enough protein."

"You don't know the half of it," Wanda told her, "married to a grocer. I'd love to be in your shoes, with all the coffee and sugar I needed waiting just downstairs."

Pauline gave her chuckly laugh. "Oh," she said, "I'm lucky, all right!" and she cocked her head at Michael, waiting for him to laugh too.

He didn't, though. He just stared at her stonily, till Wanda cleared her throat and announced she'd be running along.


Pauline must think words were like dust, or scuff marks, or spilled milk, easily wiped away and leaving no trace. She must think a mere apology—or not even that; just a change in her mood—could erase from a person's mind the fact that she'd called him stuffy and pompous and boring and self-righteous. Watch how lightheartedly she moved around the kitchen table, humming "People Will Say We're in Love" as she forked a pork chop onto each plate. She'd prepared the pork chops the way Michael liked them, a coating of nothing but flour, salt, and pepper and a quick, hard fry in bacon fat. (Ordinarily she had a weakness for experiment, mucking up good food with spices and runny sauces.) And the vegetable was his favorite, canned asparagus spears, and the potatoes were served plain with a pat of real butter. "Isn't this nice?" his mother said happily, smoothing her napkin across her lap. Lindy crowed in her high chair and squeezed an asparagus spear until it oozed out either side of her fist. Michael said "Hmm" and reached for the salt.

During the course of the meal, Pauline reported all the news she had gathered while she was out shopping. Mr. Zynda's daughter was visiting from Richmond. Henry Piazy had married an English girl, or maybe just gotten engaged to one. Little Tessie Dobek had been taken to the hospital last night with a burst appendix. "Oh, my land," Michael's mother said. "Poor Tom and Grace! First losing their only boy, and now this. They must be worried out of their minds." Michael just went on eating. To hear Pauline talk, you would think she cared. You would think she actually felt some attachment to the neighborhood, instead of scorning it and maligning it and itching to leave it behind.

His mother said, "How old would Tessie be now, I'm wondering. Twelve? Thirteen? Michael, *you* must know"—trying to rope him into the conversation.

48

But Michael just said "Nope" and helped himself to another slice of bread.

"His hip has been acting up," Pauline explained to his mother. "I'll bet it's going to snow. Did you notice how he's been walking today? And he couldn't finish his exercises this morning." As if he weren't in the room; as if his mother didn't know the real cause of his behavior.

And his mother went along with it. "Oh," she said, "I can *feel* the snow! Every joint in my body is giving me fits."

"Did you take your pills?" Pauline asked her.

"I forgot! Thanks for reminding me."

"I'll fetch them. You sit still."

"No, no! Stay where you are!"

Like partners in some elaborate dance, both women half-stood and appeared to curtsy to each other. Then Pauline sat back down and Michael's mother rose all the way and shuffled out of the kitchen.

"I should have thought to remind her earlier," Pauline told Michael. "It's a whole lot easier to stave off pain than to cure it once it's set in."

Michael said nothing. He tore a bite-size piece from his slice of bread and set it on Lindy's high-chair tray.

"But of course, you'd know that better than I would," Pauline said. "Accustomed as you are to living with your hip."

He was silent.

"Michael?"

"Try some bread, Lindy. It's delicious," Michael said.

"Michael, aren't you going to talk to me?"

"Yum, bread. Can you say, 'Bread'?"

Lindy grinned at him, showing two tiny bottom teeth coated green with mashed asparagus.

"Please don't be this way, Michael. Can't we make up?"

"Bread," he told Lindy distinctly.

"I didn't mean what I said, honest! It's just I was feeling so under the weather. Michael, I can't bear it when you're mad at me!"

"I'm not mad at you," he said. He was still facing the high chair; he seemed to be addressing the baby.

49

Pauline said, "You're not?"

"I'm just fed up with you. I'm disgusted. I'm sick to death of you and your nasty disposition. I never should have married you."

This time the silence was sharper—a sort of hole in the air of the kitchen.

Then his mother's footsteps came fumbling out of her bedroom. "Found them!" she called in a loud, carrying voice.

She entered the kitchen holding aloft a blue cardboard pillbox from Sweda's. Michael said, "Well, good," and Pauline sat up straighter and asked, "You want something to take those with, Mother Anton?"

"No, thank you, dear, I still have my water," Michael's mother said, and she lowered herself into her chair.

Michael picked up his fork and resumed eating, but Pauline went on sitting motionless with her hands at either side of her plate.

When the meal was finished, Michael's mother said she would do the dishes. "You two just clear out of here and go relax together," she told them. But Lindy was fussing by then, which meant she was nearing her bedtime; so Michael said, "I'll make up her bottle."

"Oh, I can do that, dear. You two run along."

As if she hadn't spoken, he went over to the rack of sterilized bottles on the counter. His mother offered no further argument.

Pauline carried Lindy off to the bedroom to change her while Michael filled a bottle with milk and set it to heat in a pan of water on the stove. He stood with his arms folded and his feet planted wide apart and watched the water start to simmer. Behind him, his mother scraped plates and collected glasses. "Don't let that get too hot," she told him after a while, and he said, "Hmm? Oh," and hastily plucked the bottle from the pan, burning his fingers. "Damn," he said. For once, his mother didn't comment on his language. He held the bottle under the sink tap while she stood back, and then he went off to the bedroom, shaking the bottle vigorously.

Nobody was there.

Lindy's crib was empty. Her blanket hung crumpled over the railing. The rubber sheet that Pauline always spread on their bed before changing her was still folded on the bureau.

He crossed the hall to the bathroom. Nobody there either. He even poked his head into his mother's little room, but of course they wouldn't be there.

They must have used the outdoor stairs. Not the safe, sheltered indoor stairs at the rear but the rickety metal fire escape that ran down the Porter Street side of the building. Pauline must have climbed through the bedroom window onto the landing, which was an open grid, and carried a wet, hungry, sleepy six-month-old baby down the slick steps and into the cold winter night with a north wind blowing up and a promise of snow before morning.

He went back into the kitchen and set the bottle on the drain board. His mother, swishing a handful of cutlery through the rinse water, sent him a questioning look.

"I guess they're taking a walk," he said.

She stopped swishing the cutlery.

"Having a little stroll around the neighborhood before bedtime," he said.

She said, "Ah."

She placed the cutlery in the dish rack. Michael picked up a towel and began to dry the spoons, thoroughly polishing the bowl of each one before putting it away. When he got to the forks, he started humming under his breath in a jaunty, carefree manner. Then he noticed what the tune was: "People Will Say We're in Love." But it was too late to change it.

Oh, and her inconsistency; had he included that fault on his list? Her fickle, irresponsible unpredictability. How would Lindy learn what a proper bedtime was, if she was carted off into the night whenever Pauline took the notion? By now it was almost nine o'clock; they'd been gone for more than two hours. Children needed schedules. They needed routines.

Wandering back to the crib on one of his restless journeys, he took Lindy's blanket from the railing and shook it straight and folded it. They needed neatness, too. You couldn't raise a child in chaos and then expect her to view the world as a stable, secure place. They needed the edges matched and the corners squared. They needed to feel certain that things were where they belonged.

He heard his mother emerge from the bathroom, hesitate in the hall, and then proceed to her own room—her slow, vague footsteps in heavy shoes. He should go back out to wish her good night, but it required too much effort. He heard her door latch shut in a way that seemed to him reproachful and resigned.

Lindy's blanket was one Pauline had sewn when she was pregnant, binding a length of pale-yellow wool with yellow satin on all four sides because, she said, babies loved to run their fingers across something smooth and slippery when they were trying to go to sleep. She somehow knew things like that. She knew that very young babies worried they'd fall apart; they liked to be wrapped into cylinders like stuffed cabbage leaves. She knew the level of voice they preferred—higher-pitched but not shrill—and she knew that while a swaying motion could be soothing, an up-and-down motion would cause a baby to stiffen every muscle.

Michael had no idea where she had learned all this. He suspected that she hadn't learned it—that it came from a natural, inborn fund of empathy.

He laid the folded blanket at the foot of the crib. He adjusted the green cloth frog that sat at the head. It was Pauline's frog, from her childhood. It had a faded, floppy, rubbed-bald look; you could tell it had been well loved. A gap at one corner of the stitched-on mouth turned its smile into a lopsided grin. The right arm had been reattached with brighter-green thread.

She was a rememberer and a saver and a compulsive souvenir keeper. She still had the red tin cricket from the box of Cracker Jack that he'd bought her on their first date. She had a cone-shaped paper cup, flattened now into a pie wedge, from the train they'd ridden on their honeymoon trip to Washington, D.C.

He circled the room, gathering further evidence of what kind of person she was. The laughing, affectionate faces of her friends in the snapshots tucked in the mirror. The fountain of maidenhair fern burgeoning on the windowsill. (She could grow anything, anywhere.

Her victory garden in the backyard—a yard the size of a scatter rug! packed as hard as a pavement!—had produced so many vegetables last summer that they had had extras to sell in the store. Although half the time, she had spontaneously given them to the neighbors before Michael could collect them.)

In the evenings, often, she and his mother put their heads together over one of her magazines and they would get the giggles. Anything might set them off—an extreme fashion photo or a ludicrous household hint. " 'Saving your silk stockings to donate for the war effort?' " Pauline would quote. " 'Crochet this lovely drawstring sack embroidered in a botanical theme to store them attractively out of sight!' " His mother would double over and make little snuffling sounds, shyly covering her mouth with one hand, her eyes two merry slits. Michael couldn't remember seeing his mother giggle before, not even when his father and his brother were alive. Only Pauline called up that sense of mirth in her.

He heard the tin alarm clock ticking away on the nightstand—every hollow, slow tick. Other than that, the room was silent. It was a silence that seemed directed toward him personally. "See there?" it asked. "See how little you would have, if you didn't have Pauline?"

He took his jacket from the closet, and he opened the bedroom door and walked out.

Yes, it was surely going to snow. He could tell by the color of the sky—a pinkish tinge underlying the gray, like the pink in a hand-tinted photograph. There was a flinty smell to the air. The few pedestrians hurried past in a bunched and huddled manner. Each time Michael pegged the sidewalk with his cane a metallic sound rang out, as if the cane's rubber tip might have frozen solid.

He experienced Pauline's absence as a torn feeling deep inside him. It would not have been a great shock to discover he was bleeding.

When he was away in boot camp, he used to keep the scarf she'd knitted him folded beneath his pillow. He would pull it forth at night and press it to his face and inhale. At first, it had smelled of Pauline, or he had imagined it had—her almond lotion, her spearmint

53

breath, and even the applesauce scent of her mother's kitchen. But by the time he shipped out to California, those smells had faded, and the only one left was the yeasty smell of wool. He began to associate the smell of wool with Pauline. It got so *any* wool—Army blankets, a bunkmate's watch cap, the mittens some misguided ladies' club sent to his unit in June—called up in him an ache of almost pleasurable melancholy. He wrote her "I'm making myself sick over you" and "I really don't think I could live without you"—lines that sounded extreme, he knew, but every word was painfully, absolutely true.

And Pauline wrote back "Miss you!" and "Love you!" and "Wish you could have been here last night when all of us went bowling!" Then her letters grew farther apart and even those few personal remarks, unsatisfying as they were, dwindled to almost nothing. She talked more and more about the canteen where she served coffee and doughnuts to soldiers. She spoke of these soldiers as buddies, "nicest guy from Nebraska" and "the redheaded fellow named Dave, I think I told you about him"; but even so, he couldn't help worrying when she not only went bowling with them but roller-skating and dancing. "Have to do my patriotic duty!" she said about the dancing. "If jit-terbugging's what it takes, then jitterbug I will!" He read her letters with a narrow squint, struggling to see behind her words. He wrote, "You're not starting to forget me, I hope," and she wrote, "I would never forget you! But I can't just sit at home nights, I'm 21 years old, what do you expect?" In fact, he thought that sitting at home sounded like a fine idea, but he kept that observation to himself.

It didn't help that he hated the Army. The outdoor life made him miserable, and the lack of privacy drove him to distraction, and nearly all of the time he was afraid. He feared not only combat but the exercises meant to prepare him for it: crawling through scratchy underbrush, twanging between strands of barbed wire, lunging with his bayonet while too close on either side his fellow trainees, grunt-ing hideously, lunged also. In boot camp his secret prayer had been assignment to someplace stateside and safe—to a service battalion, say, in charge of foodstuffs. Wouldn't that make sense for a grocer's boy? But he could tell from what they taught him in California (all having to do with explosives) that the Army had other ideas. Special training was just more of the same; in fact he still, ironically, had to bunk beside Private Connor from Virginia with his everlasting cough.

Pauline, meanwhile, was dancing with soldiers and whispering secrets to her girlfriends and fluffing up her hair in front of mirrors. The image of her snug, lacy world filled Michael with longing, though at times it crossed his mind that it was her fault he had enlisted. Well, not her *fault,* maybe, but her influence—the influence of her admiring and expectant gaze. No, cancel that. A man had to take responsibility for his own decisions.

That was what he'd told himself, and yet daily his resentment against Army life had grown until he lived in a permanent state of barely suppressed rage. He raged against the itch of flying insects on the exercise field, and the increasing weight of his weapon as he stood rigid throughout some officer's interminable speech, and the infuriating hawk and gargle of Connor's cough. One night, after Pauline had allowed eight days to go by and then sent only a breezy note describing a visiting captain's "cultured" Boston accent, Michael leapt from his bed shouting "Stop it! Stop it! Stop it!" and clamped a pillow on Connor's face and held it down with all his might. It took three men to pull him off. Connor sat up, blinking in a dazed and disbelieving way, and Michael sank back on his cot and buried his head in his hands.

After that, the other men shunned him. He hadn't made any friends in this new camp anyhow, and now the few who'd been minimally polite began to leave a wide space around him. His superiors observed him too closely, and Connor (a loutish sort) made a point of harassing him every chance he got—"accidentally" upsetting Michael's coffee mug or jostling him out of formation. Then they took a hike through scrub and Connor's rifle went off and shattered Michael's left hip. Nobody even pretended it might have been a mistake. The only mistake, Michael knew, was that he'd been wounded rather than killed. But he was not so naive as to press charges.

And besides, the joke was on Connor, in the end. Michael got to go home.

He crossed Purslane Street and turned left. Now he was in front of the Barclay house, its ground-floor windows outlined by threads of

55

light around the edges of the shades and the wooden porch pillars a luminous white. Michael was not accustomed to porches. He thought of them as luxuries, although the Barclays' porch had a ramshackle air with its litter of tossed-off galoshes and the rusted snow shovel and stubby straw broom propped expectantly next to the door.

He rang the doorbell. Wiped his feet (unnecessarily) on the coco mat. Started to ring again but changed his mind and raked his fingers through his hair instead.

"Ah," Mr. Barclay said, finally appearing in a widening shaft of lamplight. "Michael."

"Hi there, Mr. Barclay."

"Hi."

Mr. Barclay stood aside. He wasn't yet in his bathrobe, at least. He wore a V-necked cardigan and baggy-kneed trousers. A section of the *News-Post* dangled from one hand, and his rimless reading glasses were sliding down his nose.

"I think it might be going to snow," Michael said as he stepped inside.

"Yes, that's what they're saying, all right." Mr. Barclay flapped his newspaper in the direction of the stairs. "She's up there with the baby," he said. Then he headed back to his armchair.

From her rocker, Pauline's mother gave Michael a friendly wave. "How're you doing, Michael?" she asked.

"Oh, I'm okay, Mom Barclay."

She was knitting something blue that flowed across her lap. A fire burned low in the fireplace, and music tinkled faintly from the radio with its fancy tilted dial that people didn't have to squat to adjust. When Mr. Barclay resettled himself, he gave a groaning sigh of contentment and opened out his paper.

Michael took in the scene for a moment before he turned away and started up the stairs.

In the larger of the rear bedrooms, the one that had once been Pauline's, Pauline stood jiggling the Barclays' old crib in the rhythm that always put Lindy back to sleep when she was fretful. The room was dark, but enough light spilled in from the hall so that Michael could see Pauline's expression when she raised her face to greet him.

Her eyes were damp and her mouth had a vulnerable look, the two little points of her upper lip touchingly hopeful.

"Sweetheart. Pauline," he said, and he let his cane fall to the floor and crossed the distance between them and wrapped his arms around her. He felt her tears dampening the skin just inside his collar. He was astonished all over again by how dear she was, and how fragile and slight. "I thought you'd never come for me, I thought you'd given up on me, I thought you didn't love me," she was whispering, and he said, "I could never give up. Of course I love you. I couldn't *not* love you. I wouldn't know how to not love you."

Hugging her close, gazing over her head and out the tall, dark window, he saw that the snow had finally begun. Soft white flakes drifted past, so weightless they were almost not even falling. He had the feeling that if he held his breath, the two of them could stay suspended forever in this moment of stopped time.

# 3. The Anxiety Committee

When the telephone rang, Pauline cried, "Sit still, everybody! I'll get that! Don't anybody move!"

Although none of the children was stirring, in fact. Lindy and George stared at her placidly over their morning toast. Karen, who was still too little to answer the phone, continued forcing sodden Wheaties into her doll's O-shaped mouth.

Mother Anton was shuffling down the carpeted corridor from her bedroom. When she saw Pauline approaching, she flattened herself against the wall and allowed her to race past. For Pauline wasn't picking up the telephone in the kitchen. She was running for the one in the rec room, all the way downstairs.

"Hello?" she said, out of breath, hopping on one foot because she'd stubbed a toe in her hurry.

"Hi, hon," her mother said.

"Oh. It's you."

"Well, *that's* a fine welcome!"

"I was just . . . How are you, Mom?"

"Very well, thanks, but I can't say the same for your sister. Seems last night she went into labor, or what she thought was labor, and so at two a.m. she telephoned, I got up, I got dressed, your dad drove me over to babysit, she and Doug went off with her little packed suitcase, and what happened? They told her it was a false alarm. 'False alarm!' she said. 'It can't be false! I'm an old hand at this! Don't you think I'd know it if—' "

One of the children had left a comic book on the bar and now an imprint remained—smatterings of backwards type in white balloons and an image of Minnie Mouse with her big red hairbow. It was silly to have a bar, really. Neither Pauline nor Michael drank much. But Pauline planned to start throwing neighborhood parties as soon as their lives got a little less hectic, and already she was thinking ahead to sock hops once the children hit their teens, with root beer floats and such just like at a soda fountain. Besides, the bar came with the house. You could choose Plan A, B, or C, and while Plans B and C were beyond their means (or beyond her father's means, for it was he who'd made the down payment), even Plan A, the California Ranchette, had some very impressive features, including not only the bar but a chimney-looking brick column catty-corner from it, except where the fireplace opening would have been there was a recessed cube for a TV set as soon as they could afford one.

Poor Donna had come home in tears, her mother was saying. "You know how wearisome it gets. Can't sleep nights, can't find the right position for your back . . ."

Pauline put her finger in the _1_ on the dial and rotated it the least little bit—not quite enough to cut her mother's voice off. Then she went a smidgen too far and her mother stopped short after "water retention." When she released the dial her mother was saying, ". . . ankles dented like bread dough . . ." Pauline hadn't missed a thing.

"Well, maybe I'll call her later," she said. "Try and boost her spirits."

"Oh, why don't you do that, hon. She's just so blue and discouraged."

"Gotta go now!" Pauline said.

And hung up, just like that.

But then stood there a moment longer staring at the phone. It didn't ring again, however.

Upstairs, Mother Anton was emptying the cupboard next to the stove—hauling forth salt, pepper, cornstarch, sugar, tapioca. Her hair was wrapped in a kerchief that was knotted over her forehead, and her legs stuck out all white and skinny and veiny beneath her housecoat.

"Are you looking for something?" Pauline asked her.

"Prunes."

"Sit down and I'll get them for you. George, stop playing with your toast. Either finish it or ask to be excused. And Lindy . . . Lindy, what is that you're *wearing*?"

Lindy was wearing denim shorts and a lace-trimmed, puff-sleeved pink blouse—the top half of a mother-daughter outfit she had so far refused to be seen in. Every Sunday morning as they were dressing for church, Pauline would ask, "Well? Should the two of us put on our outfits?" and Lindy always said no. She wanted to wear her sailor suit; she wanted to wear her blue plaid. Anything, it seemed, but an outfit that matched her mother's. She was such a contrary little person! Pauline had just about given up, resigned herself to waiting till the outfit could be handed down to Karen. Who was more the type for it anyway: soft and blond and blue-eyed, while Lindy had Michael's dark coloring and—even at age seven—his angular, sharp-edged frame. Someday Lindy was going to be a beauty, Pauline believed (though she admitted she might be biased). She'd be what people called striking, arresting—someone who could carry off those clothes you saw in *Vogue* magazine. But meanwhile, here she stood, a crazy mix of lace and denim on a Saturday morning when Pauline herself was in pedal pushers. "Lindy," Pauline said, "would you go put on a T-shirt, please? And hang that top on a hanger before it gets all wrinkled."

"I'm not in the mood for a T-shirt," Lindy told her. Chin raised defiantly, eyes squinched into splinters. Her hair hung straight as licorice sticks on either side of her face.

"Well, nobody's going to the pool with me dressed that way," Pauline told her. Then she turned her back and started hunting for the prunes, because you got a lot further with Lindy if you didn't force a confrontation. For a moment nothing happened, but eventually she heard Lindy slide out of her chair and stalk away.

"*I* can go to the pool," George announced. "*I'm* wearing a T-shirt."

"Yes, Georgie. Mother Anton, I can't find any prunes. I'm afraid you'll have to have something else for breakfast."

"But Dr. Stanek said prunes. He said lots of prunes and roughage."

"How about applesauce?" Pauline asked.

"Applesauce! Are you trying to kill me? You know applesauce is binding!"

"Fruit cocktail, then. I know I saw a can of fruit cocktail, somewhere or other . . ."

"I simply cannot figure," Mother Anton said, "how my son could be in the grocery business and still we never seem to have any food in the house."

Pauline made a face at a box of Grape-Nuts.

"And where is Michael, anyhow? It's Saturday! Didn't he promise he would start staying home on Saturdays?"

"Oh, you know how he is," Pauline said. "He refuses to believe that anyone could take his place. He got a call from Eustace about some problem with the fridge, and nothing else would do but that he go straight down and see to it."

"And rightly so," Mother Anton said, suddenly reversing herself. "Whoever heard of leaving your business in the total care of a darky?"

"Here," Pauline said. "All-Bran. Can't ask for any more roughage than that!"

Mother Anton poked her lips out in a discontented way, but she sat back in her chair and let Pauline pour her a bowl.

"Go get your towel and swim trunks," Pauline told George. "Karen, honey, finish your Wheaties. It's almost time for the pool to—"

The telephone rang again.

"I'll get it!" she cried.

She flew out of the kitchen and back down the corridor, down the stairs to the rec room. Each time she heard another ring she thanked her lucky stars, because you never knew when Mother Anton (seemingly deaf to phones and doorbells, as a rule) might take it into her head to pick up the receiver.

"Hello?" she said.

"Pauline?"

61

She said, "Oh! Alex! Hi!"

Very offhand and surprised, as if he'd been the farthest thing from her mind.

"I hope you're not up to your elbows in something."

"No, no."

"I know Saturday's a family day."

"Actually, Michael's gone into town," she said. "It's no different from any other day, for me."

"Well, I had this little research question I was hoping you could help me with."

"Shoot!" she told him.

She seemed to have become a different person all at once—somebody slangy and athletic, the type of woman you might find in a flippy little skirt on a golf course.

"It appears that my basement freezer has got these various meats in it," he said, "and they've been there quite a while. Ever since before . . . you know, the famous departure. So I was wondering, do you suppose it would kill me to eat them?"

"Oh. We-e-ell . . ." she said. She was drawing out her answer so as to make the conversation last longer.

"I'm not ready to leave this earth yet," he told her, "heartbroken though I may supposedly be."

"I should say not!" she agreed. "But your freezer hasn't been off at all, has it? Hasn't had any malfunctions or power interruptions."

"Not so far as I know."

"And Adelaide's been gone since . . ."

As often as they'd talked lately, this was the first time she had referred so directly to his wife's leaving. She felt very daring to be speaking the name out loud.

"Since May," Alex was saying. "But she was one of those far-sighted types. She could have bought that meat any number of weeks before then."

"Still," Pauline told him, "I imagine it would be safe."

"You think?"

"Maybe a slight loss of flavor, but—"

"I'm going to risk it, then," Alex said.

"Well, don't take my word for it!"

"Why not?" he asked her. "Who would know better? Gosh, you're Madame Betty Crocker! I haven't forgotten that dip you brought to the Fourth of July picnic."

"My Hawaiian Luau Dip," she said. She couldn't help feeling pleased.

"That was pretty amazing," he told her.

"Michael said it tasted too foreign."

"But that was what was good about it!"

"He asked me, he said, 'Why on earth for *Independence* Day would you serve a dish with soy sauce in it?' "

Lindy said, "Mom."

Pauline spun around so sharply that she knocked her elbow against the edge of the bar. "Well, hi!" she said.

Lindy was standing at the bottom of the stairs, one hand on the newel post. She had changed into a halter top that tightly banded her flat little chest. Pauline said, "What is it, honey?" but Lindy just went on looking at her, her eyes so dark that Pauline couldn't read them.

On the other end of the line, Alex was still speaking. ". . . got to admire a woman with cosmopolitan tastes," he was saying. Pauline interrupted him. "Oops!" she said gaily. "Here's my daughter!"

"Oh. Okay," Alex said.

"Bye-bye for now!"

"Goodbye, Pauline."

She hung up. Lindy said, "Who was that?"

"A friend."

"What friend?"

"Just a friend, Lindy, asking, you know, a freezer question."

"Freezer question?"

"A cooking question. *You* know."

Lindy went on studying her. "Let's get going," Pauline told her, and she walked briskly toward the stairs, rubbing the point of her elbow where she'd hit it against the bar.

\* \* \*

63

Someday they would have two cars, the way the people on the corner did, but right now they couldn't afford it. Pauline had to take the children everywhere on foot, or else drive Michael downtown and pick him up after work. Still, to her, Elmview Acres was worth it. It was so green and safe and peaceful, so structured, so beautifully organized!

Michael had been against moving here, at first. He had said it was too expensive, and too far from everybody they knew. But how long could they have gone on living in that little bitty apartment where the children had to sleep three to a room? Where Pauline and Michael didn't have a room, even—just a pull-out couch in the parlor? And anyone who visited had to enter through the kitchen?

Plus George and Lindy playing in the streets. That was the clincher. The two of them coming home grimy and gray, their knees dented with cinders. While out in Baltimore County every house had a lawn and every new development a swimming pool of its own.

The pool in Elmview Acres was a graceful blue guitar shape with folding chairs and recliners grouped around the shallow end for the women with young children. Today only two women sat there, though—just Mimi Drew and Joan Derby—because it was a Saturday morning, when most of the wives were running errands with their husbands. Pauline gave Mimi and Joan a wave and then wheeled the stroller toward the changing rooms. After her usual argument with George—"No, you cannot come to the ladies' side; you're old enough to go to the men's side on your own now"—he trudged off with his rolled-up towel beneath his arm. She parked the stroller at the entrance to the ladies' side and took her beach bag from the rear basket. Then she led Lindy and Karen into a chilly twilight that smelled of damp cement. A wooden bench ran the length of the room, and rough wooden booths lined the far wall. In one of the booths, she dressed Karen in a red-and-white swimsuit with rhumba ruffles across the seat to hide the bulkiness of her diaper. Lindy, meanwhile, clambered into a pair of boy's trunks and a sleeveless knit undershirt—the only bathing costume she would agree to. Pauline had given up on that particular battle.

She sent the girls out of the booth—"But don't leave the changing room, hear? You two sit right there on the bench and wait for me"—and got into her own suit, a blue gingham with wide, cuffed legs that were meant to be slimming. Lately it seemed she'd developed these bulges at the tops of her thighs.

If Alex Barrow should ever see those!

It often struck her as unfair, what a short time she'd been young and halfway decent to look at. Although Michael, bless his heart, contradicted her whenever she said so. "You're still young! You're not even thirty! You're still the prettiest girl in town." Which just went to show how little he noticed. Her face seemed to be growing heavier at the jowls, almost square, and only the unruly thickness of her hair could hide the fact that it was turning . . . not gray, quite yet, but duller, and crumblier in texture.

She hooked the straw handles of her beach bag over her shoulder and stepped out of the booth. Karen was sitting on the bench as she'd been told, sucking her thumb, but Lindy teetered on the ledge that marked the entranceway, half in and half out, her thin shoulders bright with sunshine while her pipe-cleaner legs stayed in the dark. "Lindy Anton!" Pauline said. "Did I or did I not tell you to sit on the bench?"

Without answering, Lindy shot out onto the deck. Pauline and Karen followed, joined by George as they passed the entrance to the men's side. Like Karen, George was a minder. He'd been waiting where he was supposed to, pudgy and fair-skinned and docile in his big seersucker trunks. He handed Pauline his towel and asked, "Can I go in now, Mama?" His best friend, Buddy Derby, was waging a water fight against the Drew boys on the other side of the pool.

Pauline said, "Go ahead," and he took off. "But no running!" she called, too late. Lindy was already in, having cannonballed with a huge splash the instant she reached the deck.

Pauline took Karen's hand—a silky little cream puff of a hand—and they walked over to the two women. "No husbands today?" she asked as she set down her beach bag.

"Brad's got one of his migraines," Mimi said on a long sigh, and Joan said, "Phil had to go in to work."

"Oh, so did Michael," Pauline told them.

Mimi Drew was a plump, peach-faced, ordinary woman, but Joan Derby could have been a model—tall and willowy, expressionless behind her cat's-eye dark glasses, her strapless black maillot sleekly following the lines of her elegant figure. Pauline always felt shy around Joan. She sat on the very end of the recliner to Mimi's left and gathered Karen between her knees, drawing confidence from Karen's sturdy little torso. "He promised he'd start staying home on Saturdays," she said, "but there always seems to be something that requires his going in."

"Oh, yes," Joan agreed. She had a voice that matched her looks—a drawling, amused, smoker's voice. She tipped her face to the sun and said, "Tell Phil the lawn needs mowing and it's, 'What a shame, my secretary's scheduled a very important meeting.'"

"Or cleaning the gutters!" Mimi chimed in. "Any time I bring up the gutters, you can be sure Brad's head'll start hurting."

Michael didn't know how to clean gutters. When they moved in, last fall, Bob Dean next door had pointed out that the neighborhood's one full-size tree had managed to litter every gutter on Winding Way and he would be more than happy to lend the Antons his ladder. Till the mention of the ladder, Michael said later, he had assumed Bob was talking about the gutters alongside the street. "Couldn't we just let the leaves be?" Michael had asked Pauline. "Isn't that what roof gutters are for—to catch the leaves?"

Pauline had spread her hands helplessly. She was a city girl herself, after all.

"It's bad enough I'll have to mow the lawn every week!" Michael had said.

And on Sunday afternoons, when whole families came to the pool, Michael was the husband who didn't know how to swim. The one whose trunks seemed floppier, whose chest seemed whiter and somehow more exposed-looking than the other men's.

Karen wriggled away from Pauline and set off toward the poolside. She wouldn't so much as dip a toe in, Pauline knew, and anyhow the teenaged lifeguard was watching from his chair; so Pauline slid back in her recliner and closed her eyes. The sun was still gentle, not yet a blast of heat the way it would be later in the day. A breeze was softly brushing her skin, and the smell of warm chlorine made her feel limp and languid, as if she were actually floating in the water.

Mimi was debating what to cook for dinner. ". . . already had tuna fish once this week," she was saying, "already had hamburgers, hot dogs . . ."

"I don't mind the *work* of meals; I mind thinking up what to fix," Joan said. "Sometimes I wish somebody would just hand me a week's menus. 'Here,' they'd say. 'It's Monday; cook this.' "

"I really should use that roast that's been sitting in the freezer," Mimi went on. "I'm not even sure it's any good anymore."

"Like Alex," Pauline said. She opened her eyes.

Mimi said, "Alex?"

Pauline felt her heart speeding up, as if she were about to do something dangerous. "Alex Barrow," she said. "That man is never going to get his freezer emptied."

"Alex Barrow talked to you about his freezer?"

"Why, yes," Pauline said. Her voice seemed to have a flutter, a breathy faintness. She shaded her eyes and looked toward Karen to give herself some time. "He's just so bewildered by kitchen things; you know how men are. Karen, honey, don't get too close to the edge!"

Karen, who was standing a good foot back from the edge, turned and gazed at Pauline over the thumb she was sucking.

"How did he happen to mention this?" Joan asked.

"It just came up once when we were on the phone."

"You were on the phone with Alex Barrow?"

"Well, sure!"

"Did you call him, or did he call you?"

"He called me, of course," Pauline said.

But already she was sorry she had mentioned it. She sat up higher in her recliner and called, "Karen? Want your snack now?"

"What else do you talk about?" Joan asked.

"Oh, this and that. Nothing much."

"I had no idea you two were so close!"

Pauline kept her eyes fixed on Karen.

"Has he told you why his wife left?" Mimi asked.

"Goodness, no!" Pauline said. She bent to rummage through her beach bag. "We never even touch on it. Poor man, it's the last thing in the world he wants to talk about."

She raised her head from the beach bag to find both women studying her. Mimi's mouth was a small, pursed O. Joan had removed her dark glasses and was thoughtfully chewing an earpiece, her naked-looking eyes narrowed and assessing.

"I just think it's so mysterious," Mimi said finally. "They were such an attractive couple! Alex all dark and handsome and witty, Adelaide that silver-blond ice-goddess type. I never once saw them fighting. Did you?"

"They didn't have any children, though," Joan told her. "Maybe that was the problem."

Pauline said, "Well, but—" Then she stopped herself. They'd be aghast if she told them she wasn't so very sure that children really did improve a marriage.

"And then one night," Mimi continued in a bemused, storytelling tone, "he comes home from work and she's gone. He's forced to ask the neighbors whether anyone has seen her. Oh! He must have felt so humiliated! That it was Laura Brown—a stranger, near about—who had to tell him his wife had decided to leave him."

"And even Laura didn't know why," Joan put in. "She said Adelaide had just rung her doorbell and handed over her house keys, told her she was moving back to her parents' place in Ohio."

"So *mysterious!*" Mimi said.

They looked expectantly at Pauline. But Pauline just called, "Here you go, sweetie!" and held up a box of animal crackers.


By the time they left the pool the sun was directly overhead, beating down on their faces like a sheet of blazing metal, and the children were pink-skinned and sweaty and cross. Karen threw a stiff-legged, buckle-backed tantrum in her stroller. George didn't see why he had to go home when Buddy Derby got to stay. "Well, maybe Buddy Derby doesn't have a grandma at home waiting for her lunch," Pauline snapped. Her bra straps were hurting her shoulders where they'd gotten sunburned. Her shoes—white ballerina flats, bought on sale the previous weekend—were scraping blisters on her heels. The thought of fixing lunch in a kitchen still littered with breakfast things, with dirty dishes and food-stained bibs and picture books and parts of toys, filled her with pure despair.

Abruptly, she took a left off Beverly onto Candlestick Lane.

Lindy said, "This is not the way to go home!"

Pauline didn't answer. (She was constantly surprised by Lindy's disconcerting *awareness*. Neither of the other two gave her that sense she was under a microscope.)

"Why are we taking this street, Mama?"

"I thought you might like a change of scenery," Pauline told her.

"I don't care about the scenery! I want to go home. I want my lunch."

"Well, *I* care. I'm tired of seeing the same old things day after day," Pauline said. And then she started humming, pushing the stroller more slowly and gazing ostentatiously left and right to admire the view. Which was not, as a matter of fact, any different from Winding Way's. Same low-slung ranch houses, lawns that ran into each other like one big golf green, slender saplings tied to stakes with strips of black rubber. George bobbed ahead at an uneven gait, avoiding all cracks in the sidewalk. Lindy lagged behind. Pauline could hear her scuffing the toes of her shoes as she'd been told a million times not to.

Toward the end of the second block, at the house before Alex Barrow's house, Pauline came to a stop. She smiled at a woman who was weeding a bed of petunias. "Pretty flowers!" she called.

"Well, thanks."

"Lovely day to be doing this!"

"Yes, it *is* nice."

The woman pulled another weed but then paused and sat back on her heels, perhaps wondering if some further exchange was expected of her. "All in all, it's been nice weather this whole summer," she offered.

"Oh, it has, hasn't it?"

Reluctantly, Pauline resumed walking. She wheeled the stroller inch by inch past Alex's house—his brick-and-flagstone Plan C, the Maison Deluxe. "This place has a built-in grill on the patio out back," she told Lindy. "Solid brick, with a cast-iron grate."

Lindy peered at the house. "How do you know that?" she asked.

"We went there once for cocktails."

"Can you roast marshmallows on a built-in grill?"

"Well, sure."

"That's what I would do, if I lived there."

"A man named Alex Barrow lives there," Pauline said.

Just to hear the words spoken aloud—the classy-sounding "Alex" and the easy, rolling "Barrow."

She stopped again, for a moment. But the house remained closed and blank-faced. Nobody came outside. Finally, she moved on.


Her mother-in-law was watching for them from the living-room window. Pauline saw the fishnet curtain twitch as they approached. By the time they walked in the back door, though, she was sitting in the kitchen with both hands grasping the table edge. "Where have you all been?" she cried. "I was out of my mind with worry!"

"We went to the pool, remember?"

"You weren't coming from the pool. You were coming from the other direction."

"We took a different way home," Pauline said. She set her beach bag in the one clear spot on the counter, and then she started stacking the breakfast dishes under Mother Anton's radar eyes. The woman wouldn't venture out the door since they'd moved here for fear of getting hopelessly lost, but she knew exactly what street Pauline should be on at any given moment, it seemed.

"First I thought, Oh, well, I guess they must be enjoying themselves too much to recall it's my lunchtime. Then I thought, What if one of them's drowned? What if something dreadful has happened?"

"We had a nice long visit at the pool with the Derbys and the Drews," Pauline said. "Then we came home by Candlestick Lane so as to get a little exercise."

"Swimming wasn't exercise enough?"

Pauline set the stack of dishes in the sink. She dampened a sponge and returned to the table, stepping around Karen, who was crooning to her doll in the middle of the floor. "What kind of soup would you like?" she asked her mother-in-law.

"I don't know that I can eat anymore. I've reached the stage where I got so hungry that I've gone *beyond* hunger. My stomach has that hollow, sickish feeling."

Pauline finished wiping the table and then chose a tin of chicken noodle from the cupboard. She had cranked the can opener completely around the rim before Mother Anton said, "Maybe vegetable beef."

"How about chicken noodle?"

"No, I think vegetable beef."

Pauline briefly closed her eyes. Then she set the chicken noodle aside and went back to the cupboard.

Karen was singing "Rockabye Baby." George and Lindy were quarreling over a box of alphabet magnets. "Lindy," Pauline said, "would you get your crayons off of my stove? They're going to melt into a puddle."

"I bet you stopped at Joan Derby's afterwards for a Coke," Mother Anton said. "That is the world's idlest woman, I swear. Nothing better to do than loll around the pool all morning and then go back to her house and gossip with her girlfriends."

"No," Pauline said, "Joan was still there when we left. The children and I came straight home."

"Well, not *straight* home. You just admitted as much not half a minute ago."

Sometimes, Pauline got a feeling like a terrible itch, like a kind of all-over vibration, and she thought that at any moment she might jump clear out of her skin.

"I used to like a boy from my church who had the nicest mother," she told Michael.

Michael had returned so late that the lunch things were cleared away, and Karen and Mother Anton were napping, and the older children were playing on the swing set in the backyard. Pauline had to fix a whole separate meal, tuna salad hurriedly assembled and coleslaw left over from yesterday, and although she had eaten with the others she couldn't stop herself from picking at the tuna as she sat keeping Michael company.

"Mrs. Dimity, her name was," she said. "Whenever I came by their house, she would serve me tea in her best china cups. She gave me perfume for my birthday, a bottle of Amour Amour that my parents wouldn't let me wear."

"*Who* was this?" Michael asked. He had been reaching for the coleslaw, but he stopped now to look at her.

"I told you. Mrs. Dimity."

"But whose mother, I meant."

"This boy from my church named Rodney."

"You never mentioned any boy from your church."

"Didn't I? His mother had seven sons and no daughters. She always said she wished I were her daughter."

"You never breathed a word about a boy from your church! You claim you've told me about everybody you were ever involved with, but I never heard about a boy from your church until this instant."

"Oh, well, involved," Pauline said. "We were thirteen years old. You couldn't really say we were involved."

"Then why bring him up?" Michael asked.

"I didn't bring *him* up; I brought up his mother. His mother was the one I loved. I just wish now I'd kept in touch with her."

Michael looked at Pauline a moment longer, and then he shook his head and reached again for the coleslaw.


Rodney Dimity! He'd had freckles and a button nose, and he used to blush like a girl any time she spoke to him. She supposed that had been his charm: he was safe. Not too manly or bold. They had never even so much as held hands; just exchanged a few secretive smiles that turned Rodney's face rosy red. Then she had outgrown him and moved on to other boys. Richard Brand, the first boy she kissed. Darryl Mace, who gave her his gigantic class ring to wear on a key chain beneath her blouse so that her parents wouldn't notice. Her parents had thought Darryl was too old for her. (He was eighteen to her fifteen.) Pauline had not been allowed to go alone with a boy to the movies yet, even, but already that warm, heavy ring was nestled between her breasts. Oh, she'd long ago left Rodney Dimity behind!

In high school it seemed that each boy she fell for had been more challenging, more daunting than the one before. She would start out assuming that surely this new boy would never give her a glance, but then he did and they would date for a time until gradually she would grow restless, and somebody else would catch her eye, someone supposedly unattainable, but even so . . . Now when she reviewed her past it was like gazing down a long flight of stairs. Sweet, nebulous Rodney stood at the bottom, and Roy Cannon—senior class president, football captain, most-sought-after boy in her school—stood at the top, his neck so big and muscular that it was almost indistinguishable from his mighty shoulders. Roy had gone into his uncle's used-car business after graduation, but by then Pauline's enthusiasm was fading. She began to notice how loud his voice was; in a suit instead of a football uniform, his neck seemed grotesquely misshapen. When she broke up with him, though, she had no one new on the horizon—a first. (She was out of school herself by that time, and working in her father's office, where meeting boys was more difficult.) She had no one to say goodbye to when the war began, and although some might say that was fortunate, she didn't *feel* fortunate. In that first, feverish rush after Pearl Harbor she saw couples embracing everywhere she looked, boys standing outside recruitment offices with girls clinging proudly, bravely to their arms, but Pauline was all by herself.

Except for Michael.

Was that the whole explanation? That she had just wanted a boy of her own to send off to war?

But also he'd been so kind and so handsome, and she had seen something so fine in his face. Well, he *was* fine! He was a decent, sober, hardworking man, and she could have done a lot worse, as she often reminded herself.

Still, during their courtship she had begun to notice certain flaws in him. She noticed and yet did not notice; she put them out of her mind. When he didn't get her jokes, when he sacrificed her feelings to his mother's feelings, when he showed a lack of imagination, when he criticized one of her friends, she gave a kind of mental blink and persevered in her original vision of him: he was the romance she had been waiting for all her life. And didn't everyone agree? They were such a perfect couple! So young, so attractive, so star-crossed, so tragic! He was leaving to fight for his country! She was staying home to wait for him! The radio was playing "I'll Never Smile Again" and the war was raging in Europe and the world was trying to tear them apart, but in the end they would prevail!

And so she had steadily, stubbornly, pigheadedly continued pursuing the wrong course. Oh, she could see that clearly enough in hindsight. She had dug herself in deeper and deeper, promising to write daily when she detested writing, when there was nothing new to tell a person if you had to write him every single blessed neverending day of the week and when his own letters were infinitesimally detailed accounts of mock battles in which so-and-so was behind such-and-such a tree, so-and-so on the right flank, so-and-so on the left, on and on and on . . . And promising not to see other men when she was bored half out of her mind, alone and without entertainment, and the city was teeming with good-looking soldiers and she was too *young* for this! This was such a waste!

Till finally she had thought, I'll end it. I'll write him and end it; what do I care? What does it matter what people will say?

While she was still choosing just the right words, though, Michael had his accident. You can't jilt a man in a hospital bed. She would wait a bit. Hold off writing her letter till he was on his feet again. But instead he was shipped home. He alighted from the train with deep new lines pulling down the corners of his mouth although he was barely twenty-one, and his khakis were so crisp and authoritative, and his limp so stirring; and Pauline was the soldier's young sweetheart running toward him in her summer dress. When he let his cane fall where it might and caught her up in his arms and asked if she would marry him, was it any wonder she had said yes?

Even then it had not been too late to back out. She could still call it off! And almost had, half a dozen times, including the very last possible minute before the wedding. But here she was, somehow, all these years later.

She chafed daily at his failings: his rigidity, his caution, his literalmindedness, his ponderous style of speech, his reluctance to spend money, his suspicion of anything unfamiliar, his tendency to pass judgment, his limited understanding of his own children, his uncharitable attitude toward people down on their luck, his dislike of all social occasions, his stodginess in bed, his magical ability to make her seem hysterical, his infuriatingly patient "Now, Poll," whenever she was upset, his fondness for reminding her during quarrels of weaknesses she had too gullibly confessed at happier moments. And yet underneath, she knew that none of these was the real problem. The real problem was that they were mismatched. They simply never should have married each other.

Although whenever he voiced this thought himself, it cut her to the heart. He would be willing to give her up? He could picture a life without her? Then she would see that perhaps it was not that he was too slow but that she was too quick and impatient, not that he was too deliberate but that she was too reckless, and so forth. And she would dissolve into tears and wish she could do it all over again— meet him, fall in love, marry him—but this time, properly valuing him.

The master bedroom was her pride and joy, the showpiece of the house. In the living room she'd had to make concessions to Mother Anton (Old Country lace doilies and hand-embroidered runners, a crucifix above one door), but step into the master bedroom and you knew you had entered the modern age. The carpet was a beige wall-to-wall, the furniture ash-blond wood with cream Formica tops and asymmetrical slashes of chrome for the drawer pulls. The bed had a white "crackle ice" vinyl headboard and a spread in a vibrant abstract print of red and yellow and royal blue. Over the bed was a framed Picasso that Michael always referred to as *Three Musicians After a Train Wreck*, and over the vanity a mirror shaped something like a boomerang.

The idea was that every horizontal surface should be bare, with perhaps a single tasteful object here and there for decoration, but that was easier said than done when you had small children. At the moment the bureau top was hidden beneath a mound of laundry waiting to be sorted, and a drift of Lindy's paper dolls, and the swim goggles that George had been hunting for this morning. Also, Pauline had a habit of strewing clothes around when she was dressing. Right now she was dressing for an afternoon canasta party, and first one thing didn't look right on her and then another; so there were skirts and tops and slacks piled on the bed and shoes pointing every which way across the carpet. She had just about decided on a pink V-necked blouse, but she couldn't think what to wear with it, and she was stepping out of a too-tight skirt when the phone rang. Half staggering, her feet entangled in pleats, she made a lunge for the extension on the nightstand. "Hello?" she said.

"Pauline?"

It was Alex.

"Oh!" she said. She looked toward the door, which was almost shut but not quite. "What do you want?" she asked.

She hadn't meant to sound so blunt. She pressed her fingers to her lips. He didn't take offense, though. He said, "Here I had thought I was thawing a steak, but just now when I unwrapped it I found out it was ground beef."

"Ground beef," she said, and then, audaciously, "Didn't Adelaide label her freezer packs?"

"Not this particular one," he said. "I had to guess from the shape alone, and obviously I flunked. So what do I do now? Help! I find myself in the throes of a culinary emergency!"

She laughed. Suddenly the world looked less serious, less important. Ground beef and Elmview Acres and domestic life in general were just . . . comical, in fact. She said, "Well, of course you could always have hamburgers."

"The last time I made hamburgers, they kept falling through the grate," he said. "Adelaide was ready to kill me. We had company and there I was, serving up these little charred bits of meat that I'd risked third-degree burns for plucking them from the fire. 'Here, folks, have some Beef Crumbs Flambé.' "

" 'Some Burgers Carbonisé,' " Pauline suggested, gargling her *r* the way she'd been taught in French I. Alex laughed, which gave her a flush of gratification. She said, "How about meat loaf, then?"

"Well, I *thought* about meat loaf . . ."

"I know that sounds kind of humdrum, but I have the best recipe! Meat Loaf Orientale, it's called. You just take any normal meat-loaf recipe from one of Adelaide's cookbooks, *Better Homes & Gardens* or some such, and you stir in a can of chop suey vegetables and half a can of chow mein noodles. It's delicious."

"Wait a minute; I'm writing this down. Chop suey vegetables . . ."

"But drain them first," she said. It was fun to feel like an expert at something.

"Chow mein noodles . . ."

"And what I do myself, I lay a sheet of foil across the pan when the meat starts to brown. I hate a meat loaf that's too brown and crusty on top."

"Sheet of foil . . ." Alex repeated. "Gee, thanks, Pauline. I knew you'd come to my rescue."

"Any time," she told him. "Hope it works out!"

Then they said goodbye and she hung up.

After that, it took no more than an instant to settle on what to wear. She slipped on a full white skirt and zipped the zipper, stepped into a pair of medium-heeled pumps, and grabbed her purse from the amoeba-shaped plastic chair in the corner. "I'm off," she told Michael as she passed through the kitchen. He was playing Go Fish at the kitchen table with George and Lindy. Karen, who had just awakened from her nap, sat on his lap, sucking her thumb and dreamily twining a curl around one chubby index finger. Pauline said, "There are cookies for the kids in the cookie jar, and chocolate milk in the fridge if they want it."

"Who was that on the phone?" Michael asked.

"Phone?"

"The telephone."

"Oh. Well. That was Wanda."

"Wanda! You're just about to see her in person!"

"So?"

"You were talking to her for ages!"

"You know how women are," Pauline said, and she gave him a breezy wave and walked out.


Their car was a 1940 Dodge Special—a dull-black, turtle-shaped model inherited from her father when he moved up to a pale-pink Deluxe after the war. Michael hadn't even known how to drive when they got it. Pauline had had to teach him. He'd been almost too good a student. Now any time she drove him to work he found fault with her gear shifting or wondered aloud why she revved the engine so hard. After she had shot backwards into the street and braked a little too sharply, not having noticed an approaching station wagon until it honked, she winced and glanced toward the house. But Michael must not have heard, because he didn't appear at the window.

She meandered through the curving streets of Elmview Acres and out the gate, took a wrong turn, corrected herself, and eventually ended up on Loch Raven, where she could settle behind a bus and relax into a daydream. Alex Barrow's broad face, with the roughened skin that gave him an air of experience. His powerful, packed, wrestler's body. The thick black fur at the base of his throat. It was wrong to call him handsome, although all the women did. Really he was almost ugly, but in a stirring, thrilling way that made her shift in her seat as she thought about him.

Last Christmastime, she and Michael had attended a dinner party so large that their hostess had had to rent an extra table for the dining room. Married couples were separated, the wife at one table and the husband at the other, and it so happened that Alex had been seated next to Pauline. Partway through the dinner, he leaned toward her and asked if she'd noticed that theirs was the frivolous table. "Frivolous?" she repeated, and he said, "Yes, our table's telling jokes, but the other one's talking politics. They're the sober half of these marriages and we're the jolly half."

It was true, she saw. Jack Casper, on her left, was in the midst of a very funny story about his three-year-old's visit to Santa, while his wife at the other table was attacking the Israeli Parliament's relocation to Jerusalem. When their own table erupted in laughter at the punch line of Jack's story, Alex told Pauline, "See?" and of course everybody wanted to know, "See what?"

He said, "We're the fun-loving ones. The other table's the responsible ones, the ones who balance the household accounts and tell us we can't afford that vacation trip we wanted."

Then the other table got wind of the discussion and joined in— Jack's wife protesting that they were fun-loving too; just because they'd been speaking seriously didn't mean they weren't. "But after all," she pointed out, "certain things are more important than fun, you have to admit."

Alex said, "They are?"

"I mean, you've got to accept reality."

"Reality!" Alex echoed in horror, and Jack Casper leapt to his feet, shouting, "Never! Never!" and pumped both fists in the air above his head. The rest of their table cheered and clapped, while the other table watched blankly.

Was that when Alex Barrow began to occupy Pauline's thoughts?

Oops. Somehow, she had arrived downtown. She should have taken a left back there. And the next street she came to had a sign reading No Left Turn; so she took a right instead. Then a left after that. But now where was she? She seemed to have gotten confused.

After another left, though, the scenery grew more familiar. She entered a hodgepodge of stores and houses, the stores' signs often Greek or Polish or Czech, the houses' stoops scrubbed white as soap bars and their parlor windows displaying artificial flowers, dolls dressed in native costumes, plaster Madonnas with their arms out-stretched in blessing. Black-garbed, kerchiefed old women plodded down the sidewalks laden with knobby shopping bags. Little girls played hopscotch or jacks; older girls in spaghetti-strapped sun-dresses sashayed past groups of teenaged boys and pretended not to hear their whistles.

Pauline had been right to urge Michael to leave this place. Life here was so jumbled, so gnarled and knotted and entangled.

The canasta party was at Katie Vilna's. It always was, because Katie was a divorcee—the only one of them free to have her girl-friends over any time she liked without a husband's barging in. She and her son lived in the apartment where she had grown up, above Golka's Barber Shop. As Pauline was maneuvering her car into a very obstinate parking space out front, she saw Wanda and her sister-in-law, Marilyn Bryk, walking toward her. She tapped her horn and they stopped to wait for her—Wanda square-hipped and dowdy in a flowered dress with cap sleeves, Marilyn (a New Jersey girl) more fashionable in a bouffant-skirted shirtwaist. "Okay, you're almost in," Wanda called. "Just swing her to the left a bit . . . back, back . . . whoa!"

Pauline cut the engine and stepped out of the car, leaving all her windows open because it was so much hotter here. "Hi, there!" she said. "Don't you look cute in that hairdo, Marilyn!" (She was speak-ing from a protective impulse, because actually Marilyn's hairdo—a tightly curled, skull-hugging poodle cut—made her face seem too big.) Each woman set an arm around Pauline in a brief embrace, and then the three of them entered the door to the right of the barber's.

The stairs inside were narrow and steep, with corrugated rubber treads, and the walls had not been painted for so long that the white had turned custard-yellow. When Katie flung open the door to her apartment, though, it was a whole other story. She had replaced her parents' dark furniture with the very latest style, all in an automotive motif. Bands of chrome trimmed every edge, the cushions were cov-ered in tangerine vinyl, and the rounded corners gave each piece an aerodynamic sleekness. "Come in! Come in!" she said. "You're late! I was starting to think you'd forgotten!"

Katie had aged the best of any of them, in Pauline's opinion. She still had her figure, and the hardships she had been through—the hasty marriage, "premature" baby, and contentious divorce—had given her face an intriguingly embittered look. Of the four women, she was the only one in slacks (capri pants in a chartreuse tropical print). The others seemed overdressed by comparison.

"Donald's at my aunt's," she told them. "She's keeping him for the night because I've got a date this evening and I figured I might as well take him there early and be done with it."

A date! Imagine. The old ladies in the neighborhood shook their heads over Katie, thankful that her parents weren't around to see how she'd turned out, but Pauline thought her life was fascinating. The ex-husband was heir to a brewing fortune in Milwaukee, and his alimony payments were how Katie could afford her new furniture and her clothes. She could even buy a better house, if she wanted, and Pauline couldn't see why she didn't. Pauline was always urging Katie to move out to Elmview Acres.

To be honest, the canasta game was only an excuse. It was true that they settled immediately around the folding table, and Marilyn shuffled the cards, and Wanda cut the deck . . . but meanwhile, they were talking a mile a minute. Katie's upcoming date was an unknown, the brother of a friend; not much material there, at least for now. But she did have news of Janet Witt. Janet was living out in Hollywood, California, of all places. She had married a set designer twenty years her senior. And then Wanda reported receiving a letter from Anna Grant, Pauline's old school friend, whom Pauline herself had just about lost touch with except for Christmas cards. "Does everybody know that Anna's pregnant?" Wanda asked. "Finally! You remember she wanted to get her music degree first, but now at long last she's expecting—in early September, she says." Which reminded the others to ask Pauline about her sister. "She's three weeks overdue, going on a month," Pauline said. "Bigger than a house, and about to lose her mind."

"Which is this, her third?" Katie asked.

"Her fourth. I don't know what she was thinking."

"I told Lukas," Marilyn said, "I told him, 'God gave me two hands, only two, to walk my children across the street with. There's a message there,' I said."

"Well, sure, if you can follow it," Wanda told her. (She herself had five daughters.) "Things don't always go the way you plan them."

"Isn't *that* the truth," Pauline said, and everybody smiled at her, because they'd been the ones who had to console her when she found she was pregnant with Karen. As a girl she had wanted lots of children, but she had changed her mind after those hard early years with the first two so close together.

"I'll never forget," Wanda said, "the summer I was expecting Claire and nobody knew it yet, and my mother-in-law kept bringing me vegetables to put up and I would say, 'Oh, I'm sorry, I'm not able to at this time of the month,' because I hated, hated, hated canning and Mother Lipska held to that old-time belief that women shouldn't preserve food on those certain days. She would say, 'Still?' and go away tut-tutting. Once she asked if I thought I should see a doctor. And then when she found out later that I'd been pregnant all along . . . !"

They laughed, even though they had heard that story before. There was something comforting about going over and over each other's memories until they seemed like their own.

Marilyn was dealing. "One, one, one, one," she said. "Two, two, two, two"—laying out each card meticulously, pausing now and then to take a puff of the cigarette that rested in the ashtray standing between her and Katie. Pauline checked her cards as she got them, but the others left them lying facedown while they went on with their conversation.

What they didn't know, she thought (moving a three of spades next to a four of spades), was that Karen had not actually been an out-and-out mistake. She was the result of a reconciliation—Pauline and Michael flinging themselves together wildly, almost crazily, after one of their terrible fights, letting what happened happen, in fact wanting it to happen, at least at that particular instant. Was that why Karen was the sweetest-natured of the three children? A love child, Pauline called her in her mind. Even though she knew that a love child was something else entirely.

"Eleven," Marilyn announced at last, and the rest of them picked up their cards.

Nor did Pauline mention Alex Barrow at any point. First off, they wouldn't have known who he was. But also, she regretted dropping his name at the pool. So she kept quiet, much quieter than usual, and listened more than she talked. She listened to what Wanda's husband had said about the new carpet; then to what Marilyn's husband had said about her golabki—both remarks insulting, so that the other women gave scandalized little gasps of laughter. (Never mind that Marilyn's husband was Wanda's brother. In this room, he was The Opposite Side.) Did *all* wives believe they had chosen the wrong course?

When they had finished their game, drunk their coffee, eaten the last of the little sugared pastries from Kostka Brothers and wiped their fingers on Katie's jazzy Miro-print napkins, it was Pauline who made the first move to leave. "Oh, not yet!" the others cried, but she said, "I've got a drive ahead, remember. And no doubt the Anxiety Committee will be wringing his hands at the window." So they let her go, with hugs and pats and promises to phone.

She descended the wooden stairs feeling the faint sense of bereavement that always overtook her when she parted from her girlfriends.

As usual, the trip home seemed to take less time than traveling in the other direction. And certainly she had less trouble finding her way. Before she knew it she was back on Loch Raven, speeding northward, rolling her window almost shut to stop her hair from blowing. She had a tune repeating in her brain, something her children liked to sing that she hummed in disjointed snatches. *I'm sorry, playmates, I cannot play with you . . .*

The entrance to Elmview Acres was a double wrought-iron gate

83

that always stood open, rising in two graceful curves from two square brick pillars. On the right-hand pillar, a black-and-brass sign read ELMVIEW ACRES, EST. 1947.

*My dolly has the flu, boo-hoo, boo-hoo, boo-hoo . . .*

She turned right on Santa Rosa, passing the pool, which was unpopulated now except for the lifeguard silhouetted against the sunset on his high white chair; passing the clubhouse with its glass-encased bulletin board out front (bridge classes, child study classes, Garden Club workshops). She turned right on Beverly Drive and then, for the second time that day, she took an unpremeditated left onto Candlestick Lane.

If he happened to be in his yard, she would stop and roll down her window and call out some friendly question about the progress of his meat loaf. If he was not in his yard, she would drive on.

He was not in his yard. But she didn't drive on.

She slowed and came to a halt and studied the front of his house. It was a very unrevealing house. The front door was solid, without even the smallest glass panes. The giant picture window was shielded by white fabric so textureless and opaque that it might have been some sort of liner, like the waterproof inner curtain on a shower stall.

She turned off the ignition and got out of the car. She marched up the front walk in a businesslike manner, her purse clamped under her arm—a woman just doing her duty.

Before she could press the buzzer, though, he opened the door. "Pauline?" he said. She had neglected to remember how thick and kinky his hair was, and how closely it bracketed his dramatically dense black eyebrows. He was wearing a white shirt with the sleeves rolled up so high that she could see the bulge of his biceps.

"I was just driving back from the city," she said. ("The city" sounded more sophisticated than "my girlfriend's place.") "I thought I should stop and ask how your meat loaf is doing."

"Well, aren't you thoughtful! Come in," he said, stepping back and gesturing toward the foyer. He was barely taller than she was; that was sort of a shock. Although he gave the impression of mass and muscle, so that when she moved past him to enter the house she felt petite by comparison.

"The meat loaf has been compiled, so to speak," he told her, "but it hasn't gone into the oven yet. You can see if it passes inspection."

He led the way toward the kitchen, through a layout eerily similar to that of her own house but airier and more open. The place was very tidy. He hadn't let things slide the way a lot of men would. And the kitchen was immaculate. If not for the loaf pan on the counter beside the stove, you would never have known he'd been cooking.

The meat loaf was an unappetizing brown rather than a nice fresh red. Pauline bent close and sniffed it. It did smell all right, she thought. "Well, good for you!" she told him. "This looks delicious!" She straightened and surveyed her surroundings. The window curtains were printed with fruits in a repeating white-lattice framework, a pattern her mother would have liked. Pauline herself would never have chosen anything so old-fashioned. A wall calendar hung next to the phone with nothing written in.

"Forget delicious," Alex was saying. "I'll settle for just edible. You're looking at a man in crisis. Last night I made military beans and they were a disaster."

"Military beans?"

"Or . . . no, army beans."

Pauline wrinkled her forehead. Then it came to her. "Navy beans!" She laughed.

"Yes, that's it, navy beans."

"Well, navy beans are tricky. You have to cook them forever. Why on earth would you choose navy beans?"

"I assumed they'd be a cinch," he told her. "My mom used to make them; she cooked them with a can of tomatoes. I thought, What could be simpler than that? But at ten o'clock at night they were still these little hard pebbles. I ended up throwing them out."

Pauline studied him a moment. Then she said, "It's difficult, isn't it. Being on your own."

Once again she was amazed at her daring, but Alex seemed to take it in stride. "Yes," he said, "in some ways it is. In practical ways, like figuring out how to work the washing machine and such. Gosh, houses have so many parts to them! But in other ways, it's kind of a relief."

Pauline cocked her head and waited. She hadn't seen him so serious before. He was leaning back against the counter with his arms tightly folded across his chest, his biceps all the more noticeable.

"I couldn't do anything right, towards the end," he said. "Nothing I did would satisfy her. She had this way of going silent and then glancing off to one side and raising her eyebrows. I got the feeling someone was standing there agreeing I was hopeless."

"Oh, I *know!*" Pauline said. It just burst out of her, somehow.

He was about to continue speaking, but he paused and looked at her.

"I know exactly what you mean," she said in a lower voice.

"You do?"

"And there's that compressed thing they do with their mouths, like they could think of lots to say except they're too self-controlled to say it."

"Exactly," Alex said. "But I can't believe anyone would do that with *you*."

"Try telling that to my husband," she said.

"I always thought your husband looked like a pretty nice guy."

"Nice!" she said. "Well, yes. But, oh, you know how it is when someone's constantly disappointed in you. Disapproving of you. Judging you and finding you lacking."

"Frowning in this unamused way," Alex said, "when you say something you'd fancied was funny."

"He doesn't even like music," Pauline said. "He prefers dead quiet. If I have the radio on when he comes home—just something lively, you know, to brighten up the atmosphere—he right away clicks it off. Sometimes that's my first inkling that Michael's in the house: this sudden silence."

"Well, how about if you're *making* the music?" Alex asked her. "Me, now, I play the trumpet."

"You do?"

"I was in the marching band in high school."

"Oh, I love the trumpet! It's so energetic."

"But when I tried to play it after we married, Adelaide worried it would bother the neighbors. She wanted me to use a mute. It's not the same instrument with a mute."

"Well, of course not," Pauline said.

"There are so many shoulds in their lives," Alex said.

"They haven't got any talent for enjoyment," Pauline said.

They were quiet a moment. Pauline felt suddenly bashful. She looked downward and hugged her purse. Then Alex reached for the purse and gently lifted it from her grasp, and she looked up and found him gazing into her eyes. Not so much as glancing away from her, he set the purse on the counter next to the meat loaf and leaned closer to kiss her on the lips. His mouth was very warm. He smelled like thyme or marjoram—something green and on the verge of bitter.

When they separated, she felt no less bashful than before. To cover her embarrassment beneath his grave, steady scrutiny, she stepped forward and tipped her face to him again and they went back to kissing. His hands slid up under the tail of her blouse, heating her skin through her slip. Oh, Lord, what bra was she wearing? Was it the one with the safety pin? Now he was working around toward her breasts, and she pulled away and smoothed her blouse down and gave him a shaky smile.

"Goodness!" she said.

He was out of breath, she saw. And not smiling.

"Well, I'd better be—goodness! Look at the time!"

In fact there wasn't a clock in sight, as far as she could tell, although certainly the kitchen had grown dimmer.

"Pauline," he said.

She retrieved her purse from the counter and faced him, wearing what she hoped was a bright and interested expression.

"I'm sorry," he told her. "I shouldn't have done that."

"Oh, that's okay!" she said.

She hoped he didn't mean he regretted it.

He said, "Can't we . . . ? Do you really have to go just now? I'd like for you to stay."

"I'm already very late," she told her. "They'll be wondering where their supper is."

"Couldn't I see you afterward? This evening? How about if I sort of, say, walked past your house after dark? Couldn't you come outside and just talk with me? Only talk?"

"I'm not sure," she said.

"You could say you want a breath of fresh air; you're going to take a stroll."

She had never in her life said she wanted a breath of fresh air. She and Michael were not the types to take a stroll with no purpose. But she found herself saying, "Michael goes to bed before I do, often. Usually about nine or so."

"Nine, then," Alex said.

"This would be just to talk, though."

"Yes, of course," Alex told her. "Honest. I promise."

To emphasize the promise he reached out and took hold of her wrist, encircling it completely with his strong, thick fingers. She needed all of her resolve to draw away from him and leave.


It seemed that she'd been in his house no more than two minutes, but outside the sky was white and flat, edging on toward twilight. She started the car too abruptly and took off too fast, speeding down Candlestick Lane to Pasadena and then swerving right onto Winding Way, approaching her house from the wrong direction so that what mattered to her most was getting into the driveway before anybody noticed. She parked haphazardly the instant she'd turned in, well before reaching the carport, and flung herself out of the car and hurried up the front walk. But then at the door, she paused. She touched her fingers to her lips and reached up to pat her hair and checked to make sure her blouse was tucked firmly back into her skirt. Really what she needed was a kind of margin, here—a no-man's-land between the two houses where she could regain her composure. But already the door was opening and "Mom!" Lindy cried. "Tell George he's not allowed to play with my Silly Putty! He's messed it all up with different colors from his stupid comic books!" Karen, who had something black smudged around her mouth, was holding out her arms and saying, "Up, Mama, up," and Mother Anton was hovering behind in that shadowy, dithery way she had, so irritating, so helpless. "Did I misunderstand?" she asked Pauline. "I had thought you'd be home long before this. Was there something I should have done about supper?"

"No, no . . . Karen, what is that on your face? Don't hang on me, Lindy; let me catch my breath. Where's your father?"

"He's in the kitchen trying to make soup," Lindy said.

"Soup! What's he want soup for? I've got supper all ready to go into the oven!"

She forged a path through the dining room, hindered by children clinging to her skirt or her ankles or wherever they could reach—it felt like a dozen children, not three—and followed by Mother Anton with her put-upon expression. Michael was struggling to open a can with the little pocket-size can opener that Pauline used only on picnics. He turned when she came in and said, "Thank goodness you're here! The children were crying with hunger!"

"Oh, for mercy's sake," she told him. "It's not as if they're in danger of starvation." She set her purse on the counter and took the can opener from him. "I'll throw dinner in the oven and it'll be ready in an hour."

"An hour!" Michael said.

She pretended not to hear him. (In fact, it would be more than an hour, since the oven needed preheating. But maybe she could jack up the temperature a bit and hurry things along.) She set the thermostat to 400° and took a Pyrex casserole out of the fridge along with a head of iceberg lettuce. The clipping sound of her heels made her seem brisk and efficient, she hoped; but no, Michael was still watching her with those reproachful eyes of his. "Where *were* you all this time?" he asked.

"It's not so late!" she told him. "My stars! If you people didn't insist on eating before the sun goes down—"

"I phoned Katie and she said you'd left ages ago."

"Yes, well, I just . . . stopped by my folks' house," Pauline told him. She was fitting the casserole into the oven now, so she didn't have to look him in the face. He said, "Your folks?" but then Karen began clamoring for him to pick her up—a providential distraction.

"How's poor Megan?" Mother Anton asked. "Has she had that baby yet?"

"You mean Donna," Pauline told her. The woman could not seem to get Pauline's sisters' names right, which usually was an annoyance, but tonight Pauline welcomed the change of subject. "It's Donna who's having the baby," she said. "No, it still hasn't come, after they went to all that trouble last night getting her to the hospital, calling Mom over to babysit . . . and then it was false labor."

"Gracious, you'd think she'd recognize false labor by now," Mother Anton said. "Isn't this her third?"

"Her fourth."

"Oh, I thought she had two."

"It's Megan who has two."

"Isn't Megan who we're talking about?"

Pauline stopped unwrapping the head of lettuce and sent Michael a despairing glance, but he stared back at her without expression. Karen was scrambling all over him, working her way from his arms to his shoulders while he stood there like an inanimate object. "What's that around Karen's mouth?" Pauline asked him. (Might as well take the offensive.) "I leave her in your charge and come home to find her turned into a tar baby!"

"It's chewing gum," George piped up. He was sitting on the floor with a comic book. "She got chewing gum in her hair, even, and Daddy had to cut it off with scissors."

Pauline gave Karen a closer look. Sure enough, a spot above her left ear had been sheared right down to the scalp. She said, "Oh, for— you know she's too young to have chewing gum!"

Michael didn't answer. He continued to watch her, no doubt winning points in heaven for his forbearance, and it was George who said, "*Daddy* didn't give it to her. She got hold of it off your dresser top."

"Well, Lord knows how we'll ever clean her up," Pauline said. "She may just have to grow old that way."

And she began cutting the lettuce into wedges, stubbornly not meeting Michael's gaze.

In the end, cleaning Karen up required nail-polish remover. Soap and water weren't enough. Pauline had to wrestle her to the ground and practically sit on her to keep her from twisting free, and the whole time Karen behaved as if she were being murdered, her shrieks reverberating off the bathroom tiles. "Stop that," Pauline told her. "You're hurting my ears." Lindy watched from the doorway, looking pleasantly entertained, while George—soaking in bubble bath—peered wide-eyed over the rim of the tub. Then, of course, Karen had to be returned to the tub herself, hiccuping and sniffing, because now she smelled like a manicure parlor.

At least it occupied the time till dinner was ready. The children seemed to have forgotten they were hungry. Even when they were settled around the dining-room table, finally, damp and pale and subdued in their fresh pajamas, they made no move toward the plates Pauline had filled for them. "Eat," she told them, and she picked up her fork with a broader gesture than necessary, setting an example. She was slightly damp herself by now, her blouse and skirt splashed with bathwater, her face filmed with sweat. And she had no more appetite than they did, but she cut into her chicken breast with ostentatious enthusiasm. "I got this recipe from Mimi Drew," she told Michael. "I think you're going to like it."

It would be a miracle if he liked it (there were water chestnuts in it), but for once he didn't make one of his disparaging remarks. Instead, he rose and went to the kitchen for . . . what? For butter. She took it as a reproof; he could have asked her to fetch it. She would have been glad to fetch it. But no, he had to limp all the way across the dining room, all the way into the kitchen and back, swinging his bad leg extra widely from the hip as he tended to do when he was tired. He placed the butter dish in front of his mother and inched back down onto his chair with a grunt. That the butter was for his mother added insult to injury; it implied that Pauline was not properly alert to his mother's needs. His mother sliced into the butter at once and spread it directly on her bread, as if she'd been too desperate to allow it that ceremonial rest stop on her dinner plate. Michael took a mouthful of chicken and chewed steadily and doggedly. A little vein or muscle flickered in his left temple every time his jaws closed. He made eating seem like hard work.

"Well!" Pauline said brightly. "It was a real experience being back in the old neighborhood. I know you're used to it, Michael, going to the store every day, but for me it's always such a surprise! I think, Did we really live in this place? All the houses are so narrow and skinny!"

"You can buy a spool of thread there, though, and not have to get into a car to do it," Mother Anton pointed out.

"Well, yes . . ."

"It's a compromise," Michael said.

George said, "Mama, me and Buddy—" but Pauline told him, "Hush, George, Daddy was speaking."

Michael had to finish chewing his mouthful of chicken first. Then he had to swallow. Then he had to take a drink of water. The silence grew so heavy that it was almost visible.

George tried again. "Me and Buddy—"

"There are pluses and there are minuses," Michael finally said. "We were aware of that when we decided to move out here. Yes, we do have more space now. So in terms of the children, in terms of their . . . oh, shall we say, recreational activities, I admit one could very well argue that . . ."

If he chose the wrong word just once, what difference would it make? If he failed to find the perfect, exactly right terminology, would life as they knew it come to an end?

". . . and yet sometimes I can't help feeling that the space is, why, almost a . . . drawback," he went on. "I mean a, what do I mean, a . . . detriment. I feel that as a family, that is, as a cohesive family unit, if you follow my drift . . ."

Pauline cut into her wedge of lettuce, and her fork went *chink!* and the lettuce skittered off her plate. George and Lindy giggled. Michael stopped speaking and looked at her.

"Sorry," Pauline told him.

*  *  *

There was a polka program on the radio that Mother Anton liked to listen to every Saturday night at 8:30. She sat on the living-room sofa with some mending in her lap—a pair of Karen's footed pajamas, one of the soles coming loose—and nodded as Frankie Yankovic seesawed away on "Don't Flirt with My Girl." She didn't nod in rhythm; it was a slow, stiff, stately nodding, as if she were merely agreeing with the announcer's taste in music.

On the opposite end of the sofa, Michael sat reading the paper. It was the Saturday paper, slimmer than on other days, with small-print headlines that Pauline couldn't read from where she sat. She was leafing through a *Ladies' Home Journal* in the armchair across the room. All she could see of Michael were his fingers at either edge of the paper and his long, thin, gray-clad legs and heavy brown shoes.

"Maybe I should use a bigger needle for this work," Mother Anton told Pauline. "These soles are double-layered. I'm having trouble poking through."

"Shall I bring you one?" Pauline asked. Anyhow, her magazine was failing to hold her attention.

"No, wait a bit; let's see how it goes."

Behind his paper, Michael yawned aloud. Pauline could tell that the yawn was manufactured. He folded his paper, set it aside, and stretched extravagantly. "Aaah," he said, yawning once again. "Hoo, I'm bushed. Guess it's time for bed."

Pauline turned a page. A woman in a frilled apron was holding up a pot roast on a platter.

"Pauline? You coming too?"

"Pretty soon," she said.

She turned another page.

Michael stood up. He hesitated. She could sense his eyes on her. Saturday night was lovemaking night; that was how predictable he was. He liked his set ways of doing things. She pursed her lips and frowned intently at a recipe for Potatoes au Gratin.

"Well, then," Michael said finally. "So, um, sleep well, Mama."

"You too, son," his mother said.

But he went on standing there. Finally Pauline looked up, making a show of marking her place on the page with an index finger.

"Guess I'll see you in a minute, huh?" he said.

"Okay."

She lowered her eyes to her magazine. He turned and limped out of the room.

The radio was playing the "Good Night Polka" now, signaling the end of the program. It must be nine o'clock. Mother Anton bit off the tail of her thread and jabbed her needle into the sofa arm. "All finished?" Pauline asked her.

"Good as new," Mother Anton said.

She laid Karen's pajamas on the coffee table and gathered herself to rise, but Pauline suddenly felt an urgent need to keep her there. She grew breathless and trembly; she seemed to have all the symptoms of fear. (Why, though? She was only planning to take an innocent evening stroll.) "Well!" she said. "Thank you for doing that!" Her voice came out oddly thin, but Mother Anton didn't appear to notice.

"You're very welcome," she said.

She stood up, first hitching forward on the sofa and then struggling to her feet, pushing off with both palms, but Pauline chattered on. "Let's just hope Karen gets to wear them again, as fast as she's been growing lately. By the time the weather's cool enough, maybe they'll be too small! Do you suppose?"

"Yes, she's shooting up, all right," Mother Anton said absently, moving toward the corridor.

"And that would be a shame, all your hard work going to waste."

"Well, no matter."

"Because it's not as if we'd be having any more children to hand them down to!"

Finally, Mother Anton's attention was snagged. She paused and turned, greedily curious. "Oh?" she said. "Oh, now, you never can be certain of that."

"Three is such a handful, though," Pauline told her. "Don't you agree? We women are the ones who have to cope with it all; we're the ones everything falls on. Men don't have the slightest idea. Wouldn't you agree?"

Mother Anton cocked her head to consider the question. "You know," she said, "I don't believe my John ever had any inkling what-all I went through. I remember once when Danny and Michael both had the scarlet fever. I was so beat I thought I would die! I fell asleep with my clothes on one time, and next thing I knew it was morning and John was standing over me. 'Hon?' he was saying. 'Hon? I don't see any breakfast on!' "

Pauline laughed. "You know what I mean, then," she said.

"Yes, and you have the three! All's I had was the two."

But then, oh-oh, she seemed to recollect herself. "Well, this is not getting me into bed," she said, and she turned away again with a flap of one arm and resumed her trip toward the corridor. "Night, dear," she called back.

"Good night, Mother Anton."

Pauline closed her magazine and set it aside. She reached over to switch the radio off. She listened to her mother-in-law's shoes shuffling down the corridor. The trembly feeling came back to her.

The water spots on her clothes had long since dried, and with a little smoothing and straightening she would look acceptable. But she did want to fix her face a bit. Dust her nose with powder, put on lipstick.

Instead, she went on sitting.

The house was so quiet that she could hear the attic fan humming overhead, bringing a drift of lukewarm air through the nearest window. She heard a car whispering past, and the music box in the Dean baby's bedroom next door tinkling out "Waltzing Matilda."

The telephone rang.

Her first thought was that it would be Alex. She sprang up and raced toward the kitchen, frantic to cut off the ringing before Michael answered instead. But then she realized that Alex would have known enough not to call at this hour. Fumbling in the dark, she felt for the receiver and lifted it and said, "Hello?"

"Pauline?" her mother said.

"Mom?"

"You didn't phone!"

"What?"

"You didn't phone me back, you didn't phone your sister—"

"I don't know what you're talking about!"

"I left a message," her mother said. "Didn't Michael tell you? Donna had her baby."

"She did?"

"A little girl. Jean Marie. Seven pounds, four ounces."

"He never said a word!"

"Mother and daughter both doing fine. He promised he'd let you know."

"Wait. When was this?" Pauline asked.

"One o'clock this afternoon. Two and a half hours of labor; a lot less time than she took with—"

"When did you call, though? Where was I?"

"He said you were playing canasta."

Pauline was silent. A slow, deep wash of blood seemed to be flooding through her whole body.

"Pauline?"

What had she said to Michael, exactly? Had she said in so many words that she was at her mother's?

Yes, she was almost certain she had.

And he had said . . . The expression on his face had been . . .

"Pauline, are you going to phone Donna? She may be asleep already, but—"

"I'll call her first thing in the morning," she said. "Thanks, Mom. Bye."

She replaced the receiver with the quietest possible click.

The Dean baby's music box wasn't tinkling anymore, or at least it wasn't audible from this end of the house, but she could still hear the attic fan. She looked toward the luminous face of the clock among the stove dials: 9:22. She turned and looked toward the window over the breakfast table. Outdoors it was brighter than indoors. There must be a full moon tonight. She could see the Swensons' hydrangea bush on the other side of the street—a pale, pearly cloud billowing next to their mailbox—and the gleam along the rooftop of their car. She could see when a man walked by very slowly, paused in front of her house, and walked on. She saw him reappear from the opposite direction a couple of minutes later. He paused again, and walked on again. But Pauline stayed where she was.


The bedroom was pitch black, shielded from the moonlight by the heavy curtains. She had to grope her way around the foot of the bed and step blindly toward her closet. Once she'd found it she stripped her clothes off, letting them fall to the carpet, and took her night-gown from its hook and slipped it over her head. It smelled like fresh ironing, a homey smell. She went back to the bed, which was dimly visible now, and stretched out next to Michael.

He was facing away from her, lying on his side and breathing very evenly. She couldn't tell whether he was really asleep. She moved closer. She wrapped herself around him and pressed her cheek to his back. But he went on lying motionless, and his breath went on rising and falling, and his heart went on beating steadfastly beneath his smooth, unreadable skin.

# 4. Whispering Hope

Separately, Karen and George both checked to see if Lindy had come home last night. Karen checked first. A worrier by nature, she couldn't burrow back into her late-Sunday-morning sleep until she had stumbled out of bed and down the hall to Lindy's room. And then—because she found the bed not slept in and the room silent and empty—she was still awake to hear George check later, returning from a noisy pee in the bathroom. He was more nonchalant about it, slapping his knuckles just once on the door before he twisted the knob, and she knew he would poke just his head in, barely bothering to look, instead of tiptoeing into the room as she herself had done and peering around wide-eyed, wondering where Lindy had got to.

For a long time now, they had been expecting to find her not there someday. She was almost not there as it was—seventeen years old and a senior in high school (when she deigned to attend), riding about with strange kids all in black whole hours past her curfew, coming home with beer on her breath and a weird burnt smell in her clothes and quarreling with her parents, sneering at their "suburban" routine, dreaming aloud of the day when she could begin her real life on the road like her favorite author, Jack Kerook. When Karen thought of Lindy, she pictured her poised on the doorstep, leaning outward, long black hair streaming straight behind her, like a figure-head on a ship. She pictured her cocking her thumb in the wind, or loping down the highway beneath a knapsack bigger than she was. Never just staying at home behaving. That, Lindy left to the other two.

And as if there were set amounts for such things—as if only so much rebelliousness were allotted to each household—the other two did behave. They studied hard, obeyed all the rules, and sat unnaturally straight and quiet at the dinner table, willing Lindy to follow their example, praying that no shouting matches would erupt before dessert, silently pleading with their parents to notice them, the good ones, and not Lindy slouching opposite, chewing on a strand of hair and rolling her crayon-rimmed eyes when anybody said anything.

Karen was assistant secretary of her seventh-grade class. George was a member of the Honor Society. Although he was sixteen, he so far did not have his driver's license, probably because he hadn't found a girlfriend yet and therefore could live without one. (Lindy had no license either, but that hadn't stopped her from taking their mother's car one night without permission and denting the right front fender against the Deans' mailbox post.)

There was some kind of progression here; that was why Karen and George had grown so vigilant. Last month, a few weeks after school began, Lindy had failed to come home one afternoon. At first no one had thought a thing about it, but then as it grew later their mother started telephoning all of Lindy's old girlfriends whom Lindy didn't even see anymore, asking where she might be. (It wasn't as if anyone knew the names of those kids in black.) She'd telephoned the store and their father had cut his workday short; no supper had been served; no one had asked Karen whether she'd finished her homework before she started watching TV. The police had been phoned but had stalled, suggesting another call if Lindy wasn't back by morning. Then along about ten o'clock or so, while their mother was still telling the police what she thought of their attitude, in waltzed Lindy, looking bored, not even taking the trouble to make up a good excuse. She'd been hanging out with some friends, she said. Which friends? Where? She just shrugged.

What the other two suddenly realized was, their parents didn't have anywhere near the power they'd always claimed to have.

And then the previous Saturday she'd gone somewhere with another girl—a girl with the same raccoon-style eye makeup as Lindy's, was all they had managed to gather when her car pulled into the driveway—and at seven the next morning she still was not in her bed. Nor at seven-thirty. But Karen must have dozed off after that, because at a little past eight she heard George's fierce whisper in the hall—"Where've you *been*, you numbskull?"—and Lindy's curt, unintelligible murmur. And when their mother knocked on Lindy's door at ten-fifteen and caroled, "Lindy? You coming to church?" Lindy was there to give her an answer, although it wasn't a very polite one. (She always referred to Heavenly Comforter Church as "Heavenly Quilt," which George and Karen found hilarious but clearly their mother did not.)

So: that could happen again. The clock radio on Karen's nightstand read 8:25 now, but Lindy could still show up.

On the other hand, maybe this was the day they'd all been more or less braced for. The day she turned out to be gone for good.

At breakfast they didn't lie, but neither did they tell the whole truth. "Is Lindy getting up?" their mother asked. "Has anyone heard her stirring?" George beetled his brows and grunted in a way that could have meant anything. Karen fixed her eyes on her pancakes and imperceptibly shook her head.

"But she did come home last night," their mother said. She shot a quick glance toward their father.

George said nothing. Karen, after a pause, felt forced to offer, "Oh, yes! I peeked into her room."

If not for the "yes," she would have been blameless. As usual, she had said too much. She bent lower over her plate. She felt a jab of anger, not just at George (the coward), who was smugly tucking butter pats between his pancakes, but also at her parents. Why hadn't they checked for themselves, for Lord's sake? And why hadn't they stayed up waiting last night? Other parents did, with much less reason for concern.

But here they sat, in their bathrobes, ignorant as babies. Their father was reading a newspaper section folded into quarters. Their mother was dreamily watching a sparrow at the windowsill feeder. The two of them were in one of those lulls that generally followed their fights—a huge fight, this time, about a check to the Orphans' Fund that their mother had written without their father's permission. He had accused her of wastefulness and willfulness and cottoning up to the woman in charge of collecting. "It wasn't even a cause you cared about!" he had said. "The Holy Shepherd Orphans' Fund, when we don't belong to Holy Shepherd! You just gave that money because you wanted Sissy Moss to like you."

"That is absolutely not true!" she'd cried. "I care deeply about orphans! It doesn't matter to me in the least which church is helping them!"

"And all for what?" he had asked her. "Does Sissy Moss have the slightest bit of interest in you? Has she ever invited you to her house? Ever called you on the phone?"

"Well, yes, she has, as a matter of fact."

"Oh? When was that?"

"Well, on Friday when I called her, she told me wasn't that funny, she'd just been thinking of calling me."

"Pauline," their father had said, in a heavy, sighing tone, and after that had come the usual ruffled feathers and sharp words and tears and shouting and slamming and painful, obvious silences followed by (even worse) the icky-poo reconciliation scene a couple of days later, all lovey-dovey and cooing, the bedroom door shut and furtively locked and their shy, foolish faces afterward. Now there would be peace—for weeks, if all went well. Karen prayed that it would. Her father, refolding the paper, hummed beneath his breath. When her mother rose for the coffee, she trailed her fingers across his back in passing.

If Lindy had been here, even the air would have felt different—spiky and unreliable. Lindy had an entire long side of the table to herself, opposite George and Karen, and whenever she made one of her pronouncements she tended to stretch out her arms and grip both corners as she spoke, taking over not just the table but the whole kitchen. This was a skinny, bony girl (deliberately skinny, calorie-obsessed—a girl who weighed all her clothes before deciding what to wear to the doctor's office), but somehow she managed to loom; she managed to seem bigger than the four others put together. She spat out words like "middle class" and "domestic" as if they were curses. She quoted a line from a poem called "Howl" that got her banished to her room. She urged books upon her parents—her beloved Jack Kerook and someone named Albert Caymus—but when her father asked if they had Language (as he called it), she said, "Oh, what's the use? Nothing's going to change you. I don't know why I bother."

With all these literary interests you would think she would make straight A's, but in fact she'd had to repeat a semester of English last summer, and her first-term report card this fall had had no grade higher than a C; and that too was a subject for endless altercation— her father saying, "Caymus-Shaymus, if you can't even pass a test on *Silas Marner*," and Lindy saying, "If that is not typical! You're so stuck in your narrow-minded little money-grubbing rut, nothing matters if it isn't for credit, if it can't fit into a high-school transcript, if it doesn't look good on a resumé," and their mother saying, "Now, Michael, it's nice she's doing some independent reading," and their father saying, "If you wouldn't always take her side, Pauline, she might learn a little self-discipline," and their mother saying, "Oh, fine! I suppose it's all *my* fault your daughter's flunking out . . ."

Their mother returned with the coffee pot and leaned into their father's shoulder as she filled his cup. "Thanks, sweetheart," he said, and he reached up to pat her hand before he took his first sip.


When they found out Lindy was missing, Karen would be held accountable for her "yes." Oh, yes, she had said, Lindy had come home all right; Karen had peeked into her room. Dressing after breakfast, she felt a dull, dank weight growing in the pit of her stomach. She stripped off her pajama top, tugged on a sleeveless undershirt, and then sat numbly on the edge of her bed, staring down at her rabbit slippers. Her parents would point out that because she had told a lie, the authorities' search for her sister had been tragically delayed. If Lindy was in trouble somewhere—say, buried in an underground vault with a twelve-hour supply of oxygen—it would be Karen's fault she died.

Goose bumps were prickling her arms and she was starting to shiver with cold; so she stood up and finished dressing. She put on the underpants embroidered with SUNDAY, her rosebud-printed blouse, her pink corduroy jumper and pink knee socks. But no shoes. Instead she padded out the door, making as little noise as possible, and went down the hall to Lindy's room.

You might expect someone as wild as Lindy to be messy and disorganized, but the odd thing was that she kept her room very neat. Her clothes (mostly black, except for those that their mother had bought without consulting her) hung in a row in the closet. The bulletin board intended for party invitations and team pennants and snapshots of her classmates displayed a single poster: James Dean smoking a cigarette. The books in the bookcase were lined up according to height, and the bureau top was bare except for three family photos in dimestore gilt frames. It almost seemed nobody lived here. Was that the whole point? The phrase "clean getaway" popped into Karen's mind.

Neatest of all was the bed: the pillow plumped, the top sheet folded over, the coverlet stretched taut. It was unthinkable that anyone glancing into this room could imagine that bed was inhabited.

Karen went to the closet for Lindy's bathrobe—an old man's ratty thrift-shop overcoat that always made their mother shudder. She crossed to the bed, drew back the covers, and laid the robe in a long, bulky shape down the center. When she pulled the covers up again it looked as if someone without a head were sleeping there, but she solved that problem by rearranging the pillow, bunching it in such a way that a head might be buried beneath.

If you just peeked in, only peeked, you could be excused for supposing that the bed was occupied.

On her way out, Karen stopped by the bureau to study the photos. One was on her own bureau too, as well as on George's—though pretty well hidden, in both cases, by piles of clutter. It was their parents' fifteenth-anniversary picture, a full-color studio portrait that their mother had framed for each of them. Their father was in his dark suit and their mother in a gray dress, so that the most noticeable color was the blue satin fake-sky backdrop. Both of them looked self-conscious and stiff and surprisingly young, although it wasn't that long ago.

The second photo was last year's Christmas card. FROM OUR HOUSE TO YOUR HOUSE, HOLIDAY GREETINGS 1959, the caption read, beneath a picture of George and Karen smiling and Lindy scowling. They all three wore red-and-white reindeer sweaters, which might explain Lindy's expression. An accident of composition—the vertical line of a curtain edge separating her from the other two—accentuated Lindy's difference, her darkness and thinness and sharpness next to George and Karen's soft blondness. Their mother had found the photo disappointing, although it was the best of the bunch. Signing the cards at the desk in the TV room, she had repeatedly grimaced. Wouldn't you know that Lindy would snitch one and go off and buy a frame for it, as if to make a statement!

The third photo was Grandma Anton, who had died when Karen was in kindergarten. Karen barely remembered that seamed and pocketed face, that no-color, no-style hair, but Lindy still missed her because their grandma had loved Lindy best, or so Lindy claimed. She claimed Grandma Anton was watching over her from heaven; that nothing could go wrong in her life because she was under Grandma Anton's constant care, which she knew for a fact because at difficult moments her grandma's favorite song, "Whispering Hope," would come wafting into her head for no reason. Karen thought Lindy was probably right. It was such a namby-pamby song, so old-ladyish (nothing like the hammering rock-and-roll music Lindy ordinarily listened to), how else to explain its presence?

Their grandma had died of a stroke, and their mother had taken it terribly. This was their father's mother, not their mother's, but their father had acted just quietly sad while their mother had cried for weeks. She said she should have been more sensitive to Grandma Anton's feelings, more considerate, more responsive to her complaints. She worried that God would punish her; that she would get old herself one day and find out how it felt to live far away from her friends, the only grandma in the neighborhood, nothing to do and no place to go unless her daughter-in-law condescended to drive her, which she oftentimes might not. Their father told her she was making too much of it. "Making too much!" their mother cried. "How can you say that!" and their father told her, "Now, calm yourself, Poll." The C word, Lindy called it. "Calm yourself; calm down"—always guaranteed to get their mother going. Plus she hated the name Poll. Everybody knew that, most certainly including their father.

Lindy herself hated the name Lindy. She said it sounded like a girl in pink gingham. At the beginning of this school year she'd started making all her teachers address her by her full name, Linnet. (She'd been named for an English bird that a soldier had mentioned to their mother during the war.) At first Karen had tried to call her that too, but it had felt so unnatural that she'd gradually given it up. Still, she sympathized, and once when a teacher phoned and asked for "Lin-NET Anton's mother or father"—stressing the wrong syllable, as everyone tended to do—Karen had felt a kind of bruise deepening in her chest. She had had a glimpse then of what it must feel like to be misunderstood and peculiar and not well thought of by grownups.

She set an ear against the door, listening for her parents, before she stepped out of Lindy's room and padded back to her own.

In the car, their mother said you couldn't very well force children to go to church if their own father wouldn't go. Then she slammed on the brakes and said, "Oh! I'm so embarrassed! I thought part of this road was for me." She was speaking to the driver of an oncoming station wagon, although of course he couldn't hear her. "I beg your humble pardon," she told him. Then she took a sudden right without a signal, her right rear tire bumping over the curb. It was Karen's turn to sit up front and she pointedly grabbed the dashboard, but her mother wasn't paying attention. "Mimi Drew makes her children go to church and Sunday school both," she was saying, "and afterwards at the dinner table they each have to talk about one thing they learned there. But then, her husband is a deacon. Whatever a deacon is."

She was silent for a moment, perhaps considering the question of deacons. When she wasn't talking she drove better. She had on the blue angora knit that she worried made her look fat; it did cling slightly to the gentle swell of her stomach but it also showed up the blue of her eyes, which Karen always thought of as *true* blue—a deep and sincere blue. A nearly invisible blond fuzz gilded the skin above her pointy-lipped, bright mouth. Karen's friends were constantly telling her she had the prettiest mother. Karen always said, "Oh! Do you think so?" as if it were a brand-new idea. Secretly, though, she agreed.

They took a left on Turtle Dove Lane, where Karen's best friend Maureen lived; but Maureen went to church in the city somewhere and they hardly ever got to see each other on Sundays. Karen stared longingly at Maureen's house as they passed it—the screened side porch where they'd spent the summer weaving lanyards, and the little staked tree in the yard with its leaves turning such a vivid yellow that they made her eyes squinch up.

"If your father went to church I'd be more in my rights to tell Lindy she had to go too," their mother said. "I know you can't cram religion down people's throats, but church would give her sort of an outlet, don't you think? She could join the Sunday-night youth group and meet a more wholesome brand of young person. What did she say, George?" she asked, looking at him in the mirror. "Did she say she wasn't coming to church because she was opposed to church, or just because she wanted to sleep?"

George must have shrugged. "Ah, well," their mother said. Karen twisted in her seat to see George's expression, but he was gazing serenely out the side window, his hands relaxed on his knees. Butter wouldn't melt in his mouth! "Go ask Lindy if she's coming with us," their mother had told him before they set off, and he had returned a moment later and said, "Nah. She's going to stay home." If it occurred to him that he was as guilty now as Karen—that Lindy might be running out of oxygen at any second—he didn't seem concerned.

"I don't believe he's antireligious so much as he's antisocial," their mother said. Evidently she was back on the subject of their father. "I mean, the man has no friends, have you noticed? Not counting his customers in the grocery store, or the neighbors whose parties I drag him to, he doesn't know a soul! Whereas I, on the other hand . . . Why, I can't think what I'd do without friends! I just need to share my feelings with people. Sometimes I don't even *know* what I'm feeling till I've said it out loud to Mimi or Dot. Oh, excusez-moi, monsieur, I didn't realize we were supposed to exceed the speed limit here."

In fact she had slowed to a crawl—something she often did while talking—but now she accelerated just as the car that had honked behind her was veering left to overtake her. The other car dropped back again. She said, "You know what I mean, Karen. When you and Maureen get together, gabbing to each other . . . And George, you're pretty social too, considering you're a boy. But Lindy is more like your father. A person can't guess what might be on her mind! She's got me totally baffled."

Karen had a sudden idea. Maybe George really had talked to Lindy. If Lindy had crept to her room unnoticed—which of course she would try to do, wanting to avoid a scene—and slipped between the covers, because naturally she'd be sleepy . . . Then George had stuck his head in and said, "Lin? You coming to church?"

"Go away," she'd have told him, muffled. "No. Leave me alone."

And he had said "Okay" and closed her door.

Karen should have considered that possibility before. She sat back in her seat, feeling much better. They passed a fish pond carpeted over with red and yellow leaves. This was such a beautiful fall day.

But when she checked Lindy's room again after they got home from church, the old man's overcoat still lay in the bed like a log. (Now she wondered how she could have imagined it would fool anyone.) The pillow was still bunched where Lindy's head should be. Karen closed the door again and returned to the kitchen. She was feeling faintly sick. The smell of Sunday dinner—something "gourmet" involving curry powder—itched the inside of her nose.

"Whose turn is it to set the table?" her mother asked. "Is it Lindy's? Go wake her up! There's a limit to how long a person should sleep."

Karen could probably have evaded a while longer, but all at once a kind of tiredness swept over her. "She's not there," she told her mother.

"Not there?"

Karen kept her face expressionless.

"What do you mean, she's not there?"

"She isn't in her bed. I just looked."

"But where is she, then?"

"I don't know."

Her mother turned to George, who was filching bits of icing off a devil's-food cake on the counter. "Have *you* seen her?" she asked.

He said, "Nope." His voice was as flat as Karen's had been. He may have felt equally tired.

"Well, she didn't just vanish into thin air! Both of you saw her earlier; how far could she have gone?"

George and Karen said nothing.

"This kind of thing's got to stop," their mother said. "Where's your father? Michael!" And she slammed her spatula into the skillet and went out into the hall. "Michael!" she called. They heard her opening Lindy's door, stepping into the room for a moment before she continued toward the stairs. Presumably she was going down to the TV room, where their father spent his Sunday mornings working on the household accounts. But whatever they said to each other couldn't be heard from the kitchen.

At dinner, all their mother wanted to talk about was Lindy's disappearance. "She made her bed up so it looks as if she's in it," she said. "This was premeditated! Something's going on."

Their father, on the other hand, was more interested in reviewing the budget. "Every month," he said, "I assume a certain amount will be spent on a certain category. I've told you this before, Pauline."

"How can you think of money when your daughter's missing?" she asked.

It did seem hardhearted of him, till Karen remembered that as far as their parents knew, Lindy had been missing no more than an hour or so. Then their mother looked ridiculous, with her eyebrows knitted so anxiously and her fists clenched on either side of her plate. When she was upset, she used fancier words. "Unconscionable," she said, and "fathom." "I cannot fathom why a girl in Lindy's circumstances, from a loving and caring home—"

"We'll have to have a talk with her," their father said. "Now, charitable donations, for instance. Charitable donations are no different from any other expense. It's true they benefit someone else, but still we need to budget for them. We can't just give to all and sundry any time the whim overtakes us."

Oh, great, he was back on the Orphans' Fund. Their mother sat up straighter and asked, "Haven't we *had* this discussion?"

"Yes, but now I see you also wrote a check to the—"

"Michael! Your oldest daughter's in some undisclosed location with a bunch of shiftless deadbeats in black turtlenecks, and all you can think of is—"

"Well, for God's sake, Pauline, you're the girl's mother! Why don't you put your foot down?"

They faced each other from opposite ends of the table, their eyes hard and narrowly focused. At such moments, Karen always felt that the children in this family might as well not exist. Her parents were such a *couple!* So self-centered! She fixed her mind on her plate; she tried to fork up her rice without including any of the yellow stuff on top. George, however, was eating everything item by item, plowing through his string beans first and then his rice-and-yellow-stuff and then his Waldorf salad. He had one elbow on the table and his free hand was supporting his head, but nobody bothered correcting him.

Across from Karen, Lindy's glass of milk stood untouched, growing warmer by the minute. There was nothing more disgusting than room-temperature milk. Just thinking about it made Karen's stomach turn over.

* * *

Their father went into the city to check on the store and their mother didn't object, although ordinarily she would have. (The store wasn't even open on Sundays. Sometimes it seemed he just got the fidgets any time he was home too long.) Instead she seized her chance to telephone each of her sisters and consult with them about Lindy. "I mean, *you* never had this happen, did you?" she asked one of them. (Sherry? Megan?) "The child is completely beyond our control! I don't know who we think we're kidding, here."

George was working on his history project—a diorama of the First Continental Congress—and he shooed Karen out of his room when she tried to talk to him. She decided she might as well assemble her costume for Halloween. She was planning to go as Castro; already she had a cigar borrowed from Maureen's father. The beard would be a problem, though. She wanted actual texture, not something drawn on with eyebrow pencil. In the end, she found a ball of black yarn in her mother's sewing cabinet and took it back to her room to experiment with.

"I just can't read her. I can't understand her," their mother said into the phone. "And yet I know that in some ways, she does still care about us. Or have some need of us, at least. She reminds me of this cat I once had—this very unfriendly black tom who flinched if you tried to pat him. But go to another part of the house and sooner or later you'd find him there too, strolling in like by accident to the very room you had just settled in."

She couldn't be talking to her sisters anymore, if she had to explain which cat she meant. She must have moved on to one of her girlfriends, Joan or Dot or Mimi, or Wanda from the old neighborhood.

Karen cut the yarn into inch-long pieces, collecting them in a pile on top of her dresser. She was trying to add up the hours that Lindy had been gone. What time had they eaten supper last night? Six, or maybe six-thirty. And Lindy hadn't stayed through dessert. "Sit!" their mother had said. "You haven't been excused yet, miss. The rest of us aren't finished." For a while after that, Lindy had more or less percolated in place—you could practically hear the springs coiled inside her, like in a jack-in-the-box—and then, "Mom!" she had said. "I promised! I'm late!" And their mother had said "Well-l-l," on a sigh, and Lindy had exploded from her seat and left the room. That must have been at seven or so. Seven last night till seven this morning was twelve hours, and five more hours till noon made seventeen, and now it was past three p.m. and Lindy had been missing almost one full day.

If Karen told their mother now, with their father not around to keep things on an even keel, their mother was sure to panic. (She was always so ready to leap ahead to the direst possibility—the corpse by the side of the road, the gauze-wrapped mummy in the hospital bed.) But if she waited until their father came home, he would ask some uncomfortable questions. Why had she said yes, Lindy was in her room this morning? Why had George claimed that Lindy had told him she wasn't going to church? Their father was so upright. So honest. As their mother had said, more than once, "We're talking about a man who insists on putting money in the parking meter even when he finds that someone else has left enough minutes on it." It was better to tell their mother alone. You could rely on her to understand if you did something a little bit wrong now and then. She was more willing to see the other person's side.

Karen squirted a drop of Elmer's glue onto her index finger and then dabbed it on her chin. She had her mother's chin, small and definite. In the mirror it shone white with glue; she may have used too much. She wiped her finger on a tissue and then picked up a cluster of yarn bits and pressed them against the glued place. They stuck out every which way; some clung to her finger even though she'd wiped it, and some fell off when she lowered her hand. Now the person in the mirror had three or four wild black hairs sprouting from a single spot, and her eyes were dark with worry, almost not blue anymore, tensed in a way that made them seem rectangular.

George pushed open her door, which was nearly all the way shut. He could have knocked. He said, "What's that on your *face?*"

"I'm supposed to be Castro," she told him.

"Why don't you go as a witch with a wart on her chin?"

"Everyone goes as a witch."

"Everyone goes as Castro," he said.

"They do not."

"Do so."

She gave up and wiped the yarn off her chin with another tissue. "Listen," she said. "I think we ought to tell Mom."

He didn't ask what she was talking about. He stepped further into her room and closed the door behind him. "Yeah, well, I don't know," he said. "Maybe by and by, if Lindy's not back soon."

"She's been gone for over twenty hours! She's never been this late!"

"Aw, she's just off with those friends of hers. And remember, she's got Grandma watching over her."

"I don't think Grandma's enough," Karen said.

He shrugged. He was fiddling with the yarn bits now, gathering them up and aligning them into a tidy sheaf between his fingers.

"I don't think Grandma knows about all the bad things that can happen nowadays," Karen told him. "I don't think even Mom and Dad know, maybe."

"Oh, those kids are okay," George said. He must mean the kids in black. "They're just a little freaky, is all."

"It's not them, so much; it's the . . . what they get into," Karen said.

Although she wasn't sure, herself, what exactly they got into. It just seemed to her that Lindy was different after she'd been with them. She looked different, smelled different, spoke in a different, lofty tone of voice. Instead of raging at her parents she acted coolly amused by them, which somehow seemed much worse. She baited their father with questions about Eustace—he was pretty hardworking for a colored man, wasn't he? almost like a member of the family, wouldn't you say?—and their father was too dense to catch it. She complimented their mother on her inventive use of canned pineapple rings—"The Dole people ought to put your picture in a magazine ad!"—and her world-famous Pu Pu Sauce (enunciating the name too distinctly, while George and Karen tried not to laugh), and their mother, who was smarter than their father, took on a faintly uncertain expression before she said, "Why . . . thank you." At such moments

Karen felt that her parents were so innocent it was scary. How could they be relied on, even? How could they be trusted to raise three children to adulthood?

"Here's the thing," she told George. "We'll go to Mom and say we both all at once remembered we didn't actually hear Lindy speak when we peeked into her room. We just *assumed* she spoke. So we realize she might have been gone since yesterday evening."

"Why don't we wait for Dad," George said.

"Yes, but Dad will think we weren't being truthful or something."

"But you know how Mom can get sometimes."

"I say we tell her," Karen said.

"*You* do it, then, if you don't mind all that screeching."

They faced each other, both with their jaws set. On the phone their mother was saying, "Oh, yes! Men. Nothing they do would surprise me." To Karen, this was reassuring. Somebody—someone or other—must be spinning out some long-winded grievance of her own. Their mother wasn't so unusual after all; she had lots of company in her . . . well, not craziness, maybe, but . . .

If they told her about Lindy, it could be she'd act perfectly reasonable.

But George was still wearing his set-jawed expression, and Karen saw that he wasn't about to change his mind.

Then all at once their mother said, "Wait!"

She was off the phone, finally, and busy with her house plants—watering and misting and rotating her multitudes of thriving greenery, pinching off dead leaves, clucking over a fern that had dared to wilt despite her loving care. "Hold on a sec!" she said. She turned to Karen with a startled look. "How come Lindy's bed was made up the way it was?"

For a moment, Karen feared she'd been found out. She was on the verge of confessing—"You're right; it was all my doing; I'm the one who put that overcoat there"—but then her mother said, "She had to have done that last night."

"Last night?" Karen asked.

"Because why would she rig her bed in the morning? It doesn't make good sense, if she slept there last night and then got up and left while we were at church. But you say you did see her there when you peeked in before breakfast."

"Well," Karen said, "I *thought* I saw her."

"What exactly did you see?"

"Oh, um . . . a lump in the bed?"

Her mother looked at her for a moment. Then she set down her watering can. "George?" she called. "George!" And off she went to his room, with Karen trailing behind.

George was still working on his diorama. Cardboard men in white pigtails lay in a row across his desk—all of them cut from a single pattern, which struck Karen as unconvincing—and he was coloring their faces bright pink in assembly-line fashion. He didn't even glance around when their mother burst through his door. "George, think," she said. "When you asked Lindy was she coming to church, did she answer? Or just go on sleeping."

"She went on sleeping," he said, reaching for the next cardboard man.

"Did she move? Did you see her stir?"

"Nope. She was just lying there."

"But earlier you said . . . Didn't you say she told you she wanted to sleep late?"

"I said she *was* sleeping late," he said.

He sounded so sure of himself, and he seemed so genuinely absorbed in his work (bending closer to color in the touchy spot next to a hairline), that Karen half believed that really was what he had said. Had he? Now she didn't know anymore.

Their mother said, "Oh, God."

"Mom," George said, finally glancing up, "Lindy will be fine. What's your problem?"

"I'd just like to hear what you sound like when it's *your* child," their mother told him. Then she was off again, out of his room and down the hall. Karen, following, expected her to head back to the phone and start calling more of her friends; but no, she went into the living room. She lifted an edge of the fishnet curtain and stared out the picture window toward the road. "Oh," she wailed, "where is your *father?* The man might as well move into that store; I swear he's as good as married to it. Where is he? What can he possibly find to do there all this time?"

"Maybe you could phone him," Karen suggested. It made her anxious to have to handle her mother without any help.

"Sometimes I think he goes there to spite me," her mother said. "I was the one who wanted us to move someplace nice and now he's making me pay for it. That store could run itself, near about! Tell those six or eight old-lady customers he's got left just to plunk their money on the counter and take whatever they want; either that or close it down altogether and open something new out here in Baltimore County."

"A supermarket would be good," Karen said. She no longer liked her father's store, which smelled of stale bread and old cheddar. When she was little she had enjoyed taking her friends in for free candy, but over the years she'd grown slightly ashamed of the place.

"I think Lindy's gone to Mexico," her mother said, turning from the window.

"Mexico!"

"You know how she's always reading those books about people traveling across the country, hitchhiking or stealing cars or riding the rails to Mexico where life is simple and peasanty."

She was clutching a fistful of curtain convulsively as she said this, but Karen found the thought a relief. Oh, only Mexico! She'd been fearing much worse than that: kidnappers or rapists. She'd been remembering one night when Lindy was waiting for a ride to the movies, watching at this very window, and as soon as she'd spotted a pair of headlights pulling up alongside the curb she had run out and opened the car door and jumped in and only at that moment realized that the driver was someone unknown to her. Telling Karen and George about it later—about the middle-aged man looking first taken aback and then (according to Lindy) delighted, reaching over to pat her knee and assuring her he would drive her wherever on earth she liked—

Lindy had been breathless with laughter, but Karen had been horrified. Anything might have happened! This country was riddled with danger! A peasanty life in Mexico sounded so safe by comparison.

"Karen, does Lindy have a boyfriend?" her mother asked. "Somebody special among those people she runs around with? You can tell *me*."

"She hasn't mentioned one," Karen said.

"I'm worried she's eloped."

Karen's mouth dropped open.

"Would you tell me if she had?"

"Lindy would never get married!" Karen said. "She doesn't believe in marriage."

Her mother gave a low moan.

Then their father's Chevy pulled into the driveway—a dear and comforting sight. "Here's Dad," Karen said.

"Wonders never cease," her mother said, turning back to the window.

Her father had a way of sort of unskeining himself from his car—hauling his long legs out from among the pedals, gripping the top of the door as he straightened. He limped heavily as he started up the walk.

Once he had said to their mother, "You know what I'd like, Pauline? Not to be hit first thing with bad news. When I come home from work in the evening, maybe you could let me put the car keys down and take my jacket off and catch my breath and *then* you could tell me the toilet's blocked." But this afternoon he hadn't even reached the front steps before their mother had the door open, crying, "Lindy's run off to Mexico!"

"What?"

"Or someplace. I knew this would happen!"

"Start over, Poll. *What's* she done?"

"She isn't here and now I see she wasn't ever here, I mean not since yesterday evening. We just *assumed* she'd come home. She's disappeared!"

He looked at Karen.

"I guess maybe me and George thought she was in her bed this morning when all it was was a rolled-up bathrobe," Karen said.

" 'George and I,' " her father corrected her.

"We have to call the police," her mother told him. "You do it, Michael. They'll pay more attention to a man."

"Oh, well, the police," he said. He walked past them into the living room and sank onto the couch, still wearing his jacket. "You know what the police will tell us. Call back when it's been twenty-four hours."

"But it already has been! Or just about. She left in the middle of supper. Now it's past four the next day!"

"Pauline. Why don't you begin at the beginning. Lindy wasn't here this morning?"

"She just made up her bed so it looked like she was."

"But George said . . . and Karen said . . ."

"They were fooled too! She went out yesterday evening and nobody's seen her since!"

For once, he didn't tell their mother to calm down. He sat very still on the couch, with his hands gripping his knees.

"Michael, please call," their mother said.

At some point George had arrived in the hall doorway, and now their father looked over at him without changing expression. "Let's see," he said after a moment. "Say six or seven o'clock last night; really more like seven. Till four o'clock today . . . That's only twenty-one hours."

Their mother let out an exasperated pouf of a breath.

"Tell them she left at four," George suggested.

"What, lie to them?" their father asked. "That would certainly help our case! No, we'll wait till seven. Then I'll phone."

"Michael, for heaven's sake!" their mother wailed.

"Meanwhile, let's take stock here. Have you contacted the other parents?"

"What other parents? We don't even know them! We don't know who she goes around with, what their names are, where they live . . ."

"How can that be?" their father asked. He seemed honestly surprised, although Karen had heard their mother tell him this any number of times. "Karen? George? You must know these kids."

"Well," Karen said, "there's Smoke."

"Smoke?"

"He's the one who lends her those books she's always talking about."

"Well, does—Smoke? What kind of a name is 'Smoke'?—does Smoke have a *last* name, by any chance?"

"I don't know," Karen said. "I don't even know his first name, because I think it's something different."

Her mother said, "Could this be a boyfriend?"

"I don't know," Karen said. "I don't think so."

"Oh, why is she so *mysterious?* What is she trying to hide?"

"Pauline, pull yourself together," their father said. "It's no use going into hysterics."

"For pity's sake, Michael! Our oldest daughter has vanished off the face of the earth!"

"She's late getting home, is all we can say for a fact. She could very well be . . . oh, maybe at a slumber party. You know how a slumber party can run so late the next day."

"Slumber party!" their mother said, and then she seemed to give up. She dropped into a chair and squeezed her forehead between both hands.

"At seven o'clock precisely," their father said, "I'll telephone the police."

He glanced at the pendulum clock on the bookcase. Four-seventeen, it read. He looked around at his family. They all looked back at him. The clock ticked as loudly as footsteps.


Two policemen answered the call—one oldish and one young. They parked their car at the curb for all the neighbors to see and then they clomped up the front walk, but before they could ring the bell Karen's mother opened the door. "Come in, officers! Thank you for arriving so promptly. You have no idea how . . ."

Karen thought her mother sounded silly. ("Officer" was such a fake word; it was like referring to a stranger as a "gentleman" just because he was listening.) All of a sudden this whole situation seemed silly: her mother rushing around the living room frantically slapping cushions and her father so serious and important and manly. The policemen chose the two most uncomfortable chairs in the room— matching ladder-back chairs that used to be Grandma Anton's. They settled themselves with creaking sounds, perhaps from their stiff black leather holsters that seemed never to have been touched, much less opened; or from their uniforms that seemed made of something more rigid than mere fabric. The older man was small and wiry but the younger one was almost fat, with a babyish, whiskerless face. He was the one who asked the first questions. He asked for Lindy's full name, her age, and her description, including what clothes she'd been wearing. (Black, was all anyone could say.) He wrote their answers in a spiral-topped stenographic pad you could buy at any Woolworth's. His pen was a Paper-Mate, ballpoint, retractable.

"We see a lot of this," the older one told her parents. "They take up with a boyfriend, start ignoring their curfews . . . Oftentimes where we find them is Elkton, Maryland. Running off to get married where the waiting period is shorter."

"Oh, but I don't believe there's a boyfriend in the picture," Karen's mother said.

"Pardon me for saying this, ma'am, but the parents are generally the last to know."

"See, Lindy's more the type to go about with a crowd. A group of kids all together, not just one single boy."

The younger man didn't write this down, although Karen had expected him to. He glanced across at the older man, who said "I see" in a deeper voice than he'd been using up till now. "I see," he said again, and then, "How many would she run around with at one time, would you estimate?"

"Oh, maybe . . . how many, Michael? Five? Six?"

"And she stays out all night with these boys?"

"Oh, goodness, no! She does have a certain hour to be home. And it isn't just boys. Is it, Karen? No, there are other girls, too, of course. This is a group, officer; an ordinary group of boys and girls together. It isn't only boys."

"Do you know if she drinks, Mrs. Anton?"

"Drinks . . . alcohol? Well, of course not! She's seventeen years old! And up till sophomore year, she was always on the honor roll!"

"Till sophomore year," the older man said. He and the younger man exchanged another glance. Then he said, "Tell me this: does she have any favorite hangouts? Any bars or night spots where the customers might remember her?"

"Bars!" Karen's mother said, at the same time that her father said, "Sir, I think you may have gotten the wrong idea, here."

Both men looked over at him, the younger one clicking his pen shut to show he was paying attention.

"Our daughter may be a little bit rebellious," her father said, "a little late getting home some nights, maybe; a little critical of the older generation. But she is not out carousing in bars with a bunch of lowlifes. She isn't some sort of gang moll. She isn't . . . trash, understand?"

"Yes, sir," the older one said. But the two men's faces didn't change. They stayed coolly, blankly polite.

Now it was the Antons' turn to trade glances. All around the room they looked at each other—the parents on the couch, George in the armchair, and Karen perched on the ottoman in front of it. They didn't say anything, they didn't even move; but Karen had the feeling they had somehow drawn closer together.


Ordinarily on Sundays they ate an extra-early supper, but no one had had any appetite while they were waiting for the police to be called. After the two men had left, though, Karen's mother said, "I'm starving!" and her father said, "Me too. Why don't I fix grilled cheese sandwiches?"—his one and only specialty, served just a few times a year.

So they all went out to the kitchen, where he brought forth the big square griddle pan and the giant brick of Velveeta, and in minutes the room took on a delicious browned-butter smell that made Karen start feeling festive. Oh, that weight still dragged at her stomach, and part of her still listened alertly for any sound at the door. ("My prediction is, your daughter will be home tonight with her tail between her legs," the older policeman had said.) But even so, she was filled with an odd sense of celebration. Maybe it was relief at having the house to themselves again—those two thickheaded men finally gone, the occasional startling, painful crackle of the older one's radio finally silenced. And the rest of the family appeared to feel the same way. Her father clowned around at the stove, brandishing his spatula and putting on a French-chef accent. Her mother grew loose and chuckly. Her brother lounged in a kitchen chair, uncharacteristically social.

"Zees ees zee ra-r-r-re one," her father said, removing a pale-beige sandwich from the pan, "for zee young man who dislikes zee browned toast," and he set it on a plate and presented the plate to Karen, who was nearest. Karen curtsied and accepted the plate on the flat of both hands as if she were a waitress.

" 'Tail between her legs,' " her mother said. "I hate that expression, don't you?"

"Ah, what do they know?" her father said. "And how that one guy ever made it onto the force! Don't they have any weight limit? Whatever happened to physical fitness?"

Turning to give George his sandwich, Karen saw that he was the only one not smiling. He wore a grim, disapproving expression, and for an instant she wondered what could possibly be troubling him. Then she remembered. Oh, she thought. Lindy. It came to her with a thud.

She pictured Lindy pulling on her long black skinny tights, Lindy slamming her bedroom door so violently that the frame came loose, Lindy doubling over with glee as she described jumping into that stranger's car. Every image was full of movement; always Lindy was shaking her fists or shouting or sobbing or laughing. She was the household's spark and color, the spunky one, the adventurer.

Karen felt her heart was breaking, but she set George's plate in front of him and said, "Your sand-weech, monsieur."

For a moment, he seemed to be deciding something. Then his face relaxed and he said, "Merci beaucoup, mademoiselle," and he smiled.

It was true that Lindy was still missing, but Karen all at once felt filled with hope, almost lightheaded. It seemed to her that maybe now, at long last, their family could be happy.

# 5. Heidi's Grandfather

Michael had one childhood memory that wouldn't go away.

He was walking down Boston Street with his mother and his brother. He was probably about eight years old, which meant that Danny would have been twelve. They were shopping for something, but he couldn't remember now what—some household necessity or other. It was an errand that made him feel tired and cross even before they reached whatever store they were heading for, and he lagged farther and farther behind, squinting under the blaze of the sun, wrinkling his nose against the disgusting smell of hot tomatoes from the cannery. "Pick up your feet," his mother told him, and all at once, Danny crumpled to the sidewalk. Michael started laughing. He assumed that Danny—the family comic—was teasing their humorless mother by picking up *both* feet and therefore toppling over. "Hee-hee!" he said, covering his mouth with one hand, but then he saw Danny's face and he took a sharp step backward.

"Danny?" their mother cried. "Danny!"

"I don't know what's happened," Danny said.

Just then, still backing away, hand still covering his mouth, Michael caught sight of Johnny Dymski and Johnny Ganek half a block ahead—the two best baseball players in St. Cassian Elementary. And his immediate thought was Please, God, don't let them see this.

After that day, Danny could sometimes walk just fine but sometimes not. He could sometimes raise a glass of milk to his lips but sometimes he'd let it drop. You just never could be sure anymore.

Of course they consulted a doctor—several doctors, in fact—and Michael's parents must have discussed the problem with the neighbors. But during those first few months, when the symptoms were on-again-off-again, Michael thought of Danny's illness as something to be concealed. In public situations he stayed rigid with anxiety, every one of his muscles tensed, willing Danny's muscles not to fail. It would be so humiliating if outsiders guessed the family's secret!

His memories of the later, harder stages were dimmer. He retained only sketchy impressions of Danny in a wheelchair, Danny flat in bed, Danny sipping through a straw while their mother held the glass. And mercifully, Michael had been sound asleep when Danny died one winter night shortly before Danny's nineteenth birthday. Michael woke up in the morning and Danny was gone. In time, the sound of his voice was gone too, and the wry little twist he used to give to his mouth just before he said something funny. But the memory of that day on Boston Street stayed on.

The boring, comforting ordinariness suddenly yanked away. The horrified realization. The sideways glance to find out whether anyone else had noticed that something was wrong with the Antons.

Now he thought that his whole life was a version of that walk down Boston Street. He would always have something to hide. Surely other people's marriages were not so ragged and uneven! Other people's daughters were not so difficult! He studied his neighbors, hoping for flaws. He never saw anything serious. If Mimi Drew snapped at her husband, why, the very next moment she looped an arm affectionately through his. If the Brians' daughter came home late from a date, she was grounded and she accepted it, matter-of-factly if not graciously.

And she *had* come home, after all.

After Lindy's first disappearance, it seemed she got into the habit. It seemed she couldn't be contained; she popped out of her parents' hands any time they tightened their grip. The police grew wearier and less interested with every call. The school principal asked insulting questions about the Antons' home life.

The fall of her senior year, she was suspended twice. (Cutting class, the first time, and smoking, the second—one day's suspension for each.) Over Christmas vacation she disappeared, was gone three days and returned with no explanation. They took her to a psychologist recommended by the school counselor. She slouched in his office with her chin on her chest and refused to say a word.

Spring semester, she was kicked out of school a full week for bringing a six-pack of beer to phys ed. The principal suggested a facility for troubled girls in West Virginia, but neither Michael nor Pauline could bear the thought of shipping her off like that. They didn't know what to do. They felt they were in way over their heads. Lindy spent her week of suspension watching TV in the rec room—a jagged dark knife of a person sending out billows of discontent from her father's La-Z-Boy. Pauline told Michael that when she vacuumed, Lindy kept a stubborn silence and stared straight through her at Dave Garroway, although she'd always derided television as "pablum for the masses."

One afternoon she had visitors. Three boys and a girl, all in all-black, trooped purposefully down to the basement single file. Things had come to such a pass that Pauline actually welcomed these people. She brought them a tray of Cokes and a Tupperware bowl full of pretzels. They stopped talking when she entered, but at least they mumbled their thanks and shuffled their feet a bit. "It's such a pretty day," she told them. "Why not sit out on the patio?"

"Mom," Lindy said, "do you mind?"

Pauline said, "Well. I only thought."

When she reported this later to Michael, she said that one of the boys—the skinniest and tallest, the unhealthy-looking one with a scribble of beard on his chin—had seemed to be the leader. At any rate, it was his voice she'd heard steadily murmuring when she listened from upstairs. He'd been sitting on an arm of the La-Z-Boy, she said, more or less draped around Lindy. Michael was shocked by his gratification at hearing that his daughter was the one the leader favored.

That was on a Friday. Monday Lindy went back to school, docile and unprotesting, lugging her three-ring notebook and her striped beige canvas gym bag. Pauline told Michael later (telephoning him at the store once the other two had left) that she honestly thought this latest suspension might have done the trick. "I mean, a week's an awfully long time to loll around on your backside," she said. "For once I didn't have to nag her to get ready this morning. She seemed almost glad to go. I believe she's learned her lesson."

Michael went through the day feeling blessedly free. Apparently he'd been laboring under a sense of dread for months, although he hadn't been fully aware of it till it was lifted.

Karen returned from school at three, bringing her friend Maureen in for milk and cookies. George got home about four-thirty. Lindy didn't appear.

At six o'clock, when Michael arrived, Pauline was beside herself. "What are we going to do?" she asked, pouncing on him first thing at the door the way he wished she wouldn't. "We can't telephone the school! They'll think something must be wrong."

"Maybe she's catching up on her work," Michael suggested. "Meeting with her teachers about missed assignments and such. She did lose a full week of classes, remember."

"Teachers don't meet students at six!"

"Or maybe . . ."

"And she's not *allowed* to make up missed assignments. That's the whole point of suspension."

"Pauline. Let's take stock here. It's early yet. Seniors in high school often stay on for . . . whatnot. For extracurricular activities and such."

"Oh, for God's sake, Michael, do you imagine she's rehearsing the lead role in the senior play?"

He hated it when she adopted that tone—so biting and sarcastic.

They put off supper till seven-thirty and then ate without conversation, the younger two hunching over their plates and keeping their thoughts to themselves. Michael had trouble swallowing. The sense of dread had returned.

Had he realized, even then, that this time Lindy was gone for good? Later he seemed to remember he had, but that could have been mere hindsight. He could summon up so distinctly the picture of Lindy leaving for school that morning, as described for him by Pauline, and it seemed to him that he himself would have suspected something, that the visible weight of her gym bag or the absence of any textbooks or—most telling of all—a certain defensiveness in her shoulders would have warned him. Shouldn't Pauline have guessed, somehow? She was supposed to be the intuitive one! Inwardly, he held her responsible. During the days and days of interviews with policemen, school authorities, neighbors, classmates, other parents, he said almost nothing and watched with critical eyes while Pauline fluttered and babbled and buried her head in her hands and wept and carried on. It occurred to him for the first time that she wasn't very bright. Always it had been assumed that he was slower-witted than she, but look at her! Just look!

"I want you to understand that my daughter is a decent girl," she told a police detective. "This is not some juvenile delinquent you're hunting down. She doesn't come from a broken home. She's never committed a crime. She's just . . . young! She's just . . . Oh, I don't *know* what she is! I'm so surprised by this! I never saw it coming! Growing up, I swear, she was no different from any other child. Perfectly average behavior, nothing you would think twice about. Of course, she's always been strong-willed. Definitely a handful. But I never would have foretold that she'd do something so extreme. It's like she took a . . . leap of some kind! A leap past any logical progression! Well, *you* must have children. You know how they can be. So contrary and perverse, sometimes. But that doesn't mean they'll vanish, does it? So why has Lindy vanished? Why? Till now I blamed the class of people she hung out with, but yesterday, when Leila Brand came to see me . . . Have you spoken with Mrs. Brand? Howard Brand's mother; they call him Smoke; he's one of the other two that are missing? Why, Leila turned out to be the most regular, most normal, most nicely brought-up person. She was wearing the same identical jumper I bought last month at Penney's—we had a good laugh about that—and this soft, short, pretty hairdo. With a son so scraggy-bearded and strange, who would ever have guessed it? And I bet she looked at me the same way. I was the mother of that wicked Lindy Anton who led her innocent boy astray, she must have thought. She must have thought I was terrible!"

Then she couldn't go on because she started crying again, but Michael made no move to comfort her. He continued sitting erect, hands clamping his knees, eyes fixed unwaveringly upon the detective. It occurred to him that not once had Pauline said "we," or referred to Lindy as "ours." Everything had been "I" and "my," as if this drama were hers alone. He felt himself hardening toward her. He hoped the detective understood that the two of them were not the least bit alike.

At first he supposed that Lindy would show up at any moment, today or tomorrow or day after tomorrow. Weeks passed where every time the telephone rang at work, it might be Pauline calling to say that Lindy had just walked in. Or she might slip into the house overnight; she might be found the following morning peacefully asleep in her bed. Every day when he woke up, Michael would check her room. He supposed that Pauline did the same. The door of the room stayed wide open now—significant, and sad, when you considered how ferociously Lindy had once guarded her privacy.

Then, as the weeks stretched into months, they both lost hope. They no longer badgered the police or lay in bed at night discussing the what-ifs. ("Do you remember that friend of hers who moved away to Maine in sixth grade? What if *that's* who she's gone to? Do you remember her name?") Amazingly, Michael began to have mornings when Lindy's absence was not his first thought upon waking. Instead he would travel toward the realization in a kind of two-step process, floating contentedly upward into the warmth of the summer sunlight, the chug-chug of a neighbor's car starting, the musical murmur of voices elsewhere in the house, until all at once—*Something's wrong.* And his eyes would fly open and he would know: Lindy's missing.

How could he have forgotten that, even for a split second?

He knew that Pauline never forgot. He saw how she carried the knowledge constantly at the front of her mind; he saw how it aged her and wore her away. Two horizontal seams were deepening in her forehead, and her perkily swaybacked stance had sagged into a middle-aged stoop. Even when she was smiling at one of George's corny jokes or listening to Karen's schoolgirl gossip, she had the look of someone just barely managing to rise above her grief.

Yet it didn't bring them closer together. You certainly couldn't say that. Sometimes Michael thought it might very well be the end of them. Lindy's defection, he imagined, was a pronouncement upon their marriage: *You two are putting on an act. You're not really a couple at all. And this is not really a family.* Maybe that was why he hated talking about it with outsiders—with new neighbors who by some miracle had not already heard. (And wasn't it incredible that by now there were several neighbors Lindy had never laid eyes on?) Pauline would volunteer every last detail at the drop of a hat—it appeared to be a compulsion—but when people asked Michael how many children he had, he would tell them, "Two. A boy sixteen, a girl twelve." Pauline had a fit when he did that. "How can you deny your own daughter?" she would ask later, and he would say, "They only wanted to know if we have any kids at home the right age for *their* kids. I was only being practical."

"Practical! I call it disloyal. You're ashamed, is what it is."

"Some might say ashamed; some might say discreet. I've never seen the point in spilling our business to all and sundry."

"This is not *business,* Michael! It's a central fact of our lives! A terrible, unthinkable, unendurable fact of our lives!"

"There's no need for melodrama," he told her.

"Well, at least I'm not a block of wood, like some others I could name!"

And so on, and so on, and so on.


Now that he no longer thought "Maybe today" or "Maybe next week," he began to look for Lindy at family milestones instead. Labor Day, for instance when they traditionally threw a backyard barbecue. Surely she wouldn't skip that; she used to love it! But she stayed stubbornly, cruelly absent. Christmas Eve of 1961 he left the tree lights lit through the night, fire hazard or no, and Christmas morning he got up at the crack of dawn like some overexcited toddler and crept out to the living room, but all he found was Pauline sound asleep in an armchair.

He knew Pauline had hopes for her birthday—at least for a card or a phone call. When he asked if she would like to go out to dinner, she said she'd just as soon eat in. He suspected she spent the day watching for the mailman, dashing for the telephone every time it rang. But all for nothing. Michael offered her the only kindness he could think of: he pretended not to notice. Not that she did the same for him, on his own birthday three months later. As they were going to bed at the end of the day she said, "Honey, don't take it to heart. I'm sure she just forgot."

"*Who* forgot?" he demanded, and she kissed his cheek and turned out the light.

If George and Karen nourished their own expectations, they never let on to their parents. They had changed since Lindy's leaving—become more muted and withdrawn. The house grew uncomfortably quiet. Now the tumult that had surrounded Lindy—the dinner-table arguments, power struggles, scenes of open defiance—seemed the natural accompaniment to a vital, free-thinking spirit; and Michael was guiltily aware that he found the younger two dull by comparison. George's plodding conformity and Karen's good-girl blandness filled him with irritation. He wanted to shake them up; he wanted to say, "Show some life, there!"

Although he knew that he himself was equally lackluster.

Sometimes the police detective phoned. Michael imagined he had a reminder note jotted on his calendar. "Just touching base; nothing much to report. Young lady caught stealing a car in Oklahoma looked for a minute like she answered your daughter's description, but no; false alarm . . ." Michael was barely polite to the man. He had come to believe that the police were worse than useless. If they had acted fast enough, the trail would still have been warm and they could easily have found her. But they'd been so sure she would come back on her own at the very first little hardship—first rainstorm or spell of cold weather—that they hadn't taken things seriously. And then after the one kid, Smoke, sent a postcard to his cousin (the Grand Canyon in full color, and on the reverse, "Check it out, man! We camped last night where the X is"), the police grew all the more casual; for this proved to them that there'd been no foul play. Kids would be kids, was their attitude.

But she was only eighteen! She was out there alone in the universe!

Smoke's parents moved to Florida and stopped keeping in touch. In 1963 the second boy, Clement Ames, was found living in Chicago with a Puerto Rican girl. He told his parents he'd parted ways with the other two less than a week after leaving home—some argument about money. He had no idea what had become of Lindy.

The thought of her clouded every day. It meant that Michael never again had a moment of pure joy. In the midst of a family gathering, or celebrating a special event, or just savoring a good meal, he would wonder, What is Lindy doing now?

Is she all right? Is she hungry? Sick?

Is she alive?

It flabbergasted him, when he thought about it, that he could still watch a basketball game. Make love to Pauline. Whistle to a tune on the radio.

The milestones at which he looked for Lindy grew farther apart and more improbable: Pauline's mother's funeral, the grand opening of his new store in the suburbs, George and Sally's wedding. How likely was it that she would have heard about those? But even so, his eyes swept the crowd. And each time she failed to appear, it was as if she had left them all over again. Her absence seemed pointed; it seemed mean, a slap in the face. He always felt the wind whoosh out of his lungs as he acknowledged yet again that she wouldn't be coming.

Lately it had occurred to him that even if she did come, he might not recognize her. What would she look like now? She was almost twenty-five years old. She'd been gone for more than a quarter of her life. And Michael didn't have the slightest idea what those years had done to her.


On a warm, breezy afternoon in May of 1968, Pauline telephoned Michael at work and started talking a mile a minute as soon as he answered. "Your cousin Adam just phoned and Lindy's in San Francisco and they've put her in a hospital and her son's been left with the landlady and we have to go and get them."

Michael sat down on a carton of payroll forms.

The only chair in his office was occupied at the moment by the woman who did his accounts. She went on placidly punching the buttons of her adding machine, although Michael would have thought that she could hear his heart racketing in his chest.

"We have to go, you have to come home, how will we get there?" Pauline was asking, but all Michael seemed able to think of was "Cousin Adam? I don't understand."

"We have to buy airplane tickets, how do people do that?"

"Cousin Adam as in Uncle Bron's Adam? I barely even know Cousin Adam! I've seen him maybe twice in my life!"

"Michael, please. Concentrate."

He paused. He made himself take a deep breath. "What's wrong with her?" he asked finally.

"It's something mental, I don't know; some kind of mental thing."

"Oh, God."

"Will you come home, please?"

"I'm coming," he said. He hung up.

Mrs. Bird's fingers had slowed now, and her back gave off an air of alertness, but he left the office without explaining. He walked past the meat counter, past the dairy cooler, past the three registers up front. This wasn't a very large store. It was bigger and brighter than the old one but still small enough so that he knew each employee intimately. All he said to his manager, though, was "You'll have to close tonight, Bart." Then he pushed through the glass door and went out to the parking lot.

While he was driving home he tried to picture Lindy in a hospital. For the first time in seven years he knew her whereabouts, but the old uncertainty seemed preferable to this new image of Lindy huddled white-faced and shivering in a room with a barred window.

Well, she would be all right. She'd be fine. They would bring her home and take care of her and she would recover in no time.

But a son.

A son would take a little while to get his mind around. He would deal with that one later.


Pauline said that the landlady must have been proceeding in alphabetical order, and that was why she'd phoned Adam first. "I guess she told the operator to begin with the A's and work down," she said. She was packing as she talked, moving between the bureau and a suitcase laid flat on the bed while Michael watched from the doorway. She wore nothing but a white lace slip and nylons, as if she planned to dress right now for the trip even though they'd found out they couldn't get a flight until tomorrow. Two scratched-looking patches of pink stained her cheeks. Her hands shook slightly as she smoothed one of Michael's T-shirts. She said, "The landlady asked Adam if he had a daughter named Linnet, and Adam said no, he didn't, but he thought he could tell her who did."

"I'm surprised he was able to," Michael said. "It's not as if Adam's ever had much to do with the Anton side of the family."

"Well, maybe from that newspaper item back when Lindy first left."

Michael winced. It mortified him all over again to recall how their private troubles had been bandied about in public.

"Then she asked if he would get in touch with us because she was on the long distance, and he said yes, and he looked us up in the book and called and announced it like a weather report. 'Mrs. Anton,' he said—'Mrs. Anton!' Can you imagine?—'I believe your daughter Linnet's in San Francisco and you should phone this number.'"

When Pauline quoted other people she captured their tone so exactly that Michael always felt he was hearing them in person. His cousin Adam had been a thick, pale, bulgy-eyed boy, a carbon copy of

Uncle Bron's ex-wife, and now he trudged into Michael's mind six feet tall but still that young boy, his hands hanging limp at his sides and his mouth perpetually open.

"So I called and I guess the landlady was waiting by the phone because she answered right away. I said, 'This is Pauline Anton, Lindy Anton's mother. I just had word from my husband's cousin that—' "

"But what did *she* say?" Michael broke in. He had reached the point where he didn't think he could stand another minute of this.

Pauline gave him a hurt look, her mouth pooched out like a wrinkled red raspberry. "Well, I was preparing to tell you, Michael, if you'd give me half a chance. She said Lindy and her little boy had been renting one of her rooms for the past few weeks and she didn't know where they'd lived before or who the little boy's father was or . . . and then two days ago Lindy 'freaked out,' was how she put it; I don't know, just 'freaked out,' and now she's in a, maybe she didn't say hospital but some sort of clinic or facility . . . and someone has to come take care of the little boy because the landlady's not used to children and besides which he seems upset."

"How old is he?" Michael asked.

"She said she didn't know."

"Well, she must know more or less."

"He's not in school yet, evidently, because she kept complaining about him being there at the house every minute of the day."

"Does he talk?"

"She said he's stopped talking."

"Jesus," Michael said.

It occurred to him, all at once, that he was a grandfather. Pauline was a grandmother. A child directly related to them was so upset that he'd stopped talking.

"I wish they'd had a flight that left today," he said.

"We have to pick up our tickets when we get to the airport," Pauline told him. She was padding out to the hall now in her stocking feet, no doubt heading for Karen's bedroom closet, which she had taken over the instant Karen left home. (Was it from superstition that of the three children's rooms, only Lindy's remained unchanged—

no clothing packed away, no sewing machine or income-tax records moved in?) "I don't even want to tell you how much this is going to cost," she said. She returned, carrying over her arm a daisy-splashed minidress on a hanger.

Michael said, "You think I care how much it costs?"

"Destiny gave me the number of a not-too-expensive tourist home and I called and reserved a room."

He thought this over a minute. He said, "Destiny gave you . . ."

"Destiny, the landlady."

"Well, that was quick," he said, meaning the intimacy of first names. Pauline appeared not to understand; she sent him an innocent, round-eyed look before she turned away to hang the dress on her closet door. "How long did you take the room for?" he asked her. "When's our return flight? Do you think they'll let us bring Lindy home right away?"

"Well, of course," Pauline said. "We're her family! I've got the room booked for just the one night. And I reserved us four seats on the plane coming back the next morning."

He tried to imagine that: the four of them seated two by two, he and Pauline and then Lindy (in a hospital gown, he pictured) and a faceless little boy.

He couldn't figure out how his life had come to be so strange.


Neither one of them had ever been on a plane before, but Sally—George's wife—was an experienced flier, and she kept reassuring them as she drove them to the airport. "Don't worry about crashing," she said. "Look at the statistics! Air travel is a whole lot safer than automobiles."

It wasn't crashing that worried Michael; it was the question of proper behavior. What would he do with their suitcase? Where should he pay for their tickets? Did the tickets get punched, as they did on trains? He was relieved when Sally insisted on parking and coming in with them. Sometimes he found his daughter-in-law a little wearing—she was a sunny, bouncy blond gal with a take-charge attitude—but today he gratefully followed the confident sashay of her tennis skirt through Friendship Airport.

Pauline was the one who feared crashing. She wrung several tissues into shreds while they were waiting to board, and as she was kissing Sally goodbye she said, "If anything should happen to us, I've left a note in my jewelry box about what should go to whom."

"Listen to you!" Sally cried. "Nothing's going to happen!"

"I know it's only costume stuff, but there are several pieces that different people have admired in the past."

Sally hugged her. "You-all have a good trip," she said. "Give Lindy my love, hear?"—although of course she and Lindy had never met. She shooed the two of them toward the door, and they turned to follow the others onto the tarmac.

The flight itself struck Michael as something of a disappointment. He had expected more of a sense of being airborne, but once the plane had taken off (laboriously, like some out-of-practice water bird), it was steady as a locomotive, and the rows of other passengers on either side of the aisle made him feel that he was just in an extra-narrow waiting room. He almost couldn't tell they were moving. "Look!" Pauline told him, pointing out her window. (She was her usual dauntless self again.) He leaned past her and saw a river far below, long and winding and yet apparently motionless, reflecting a striated, silvery gray like the trail left by the broad side of a pencil lead. No highways or buildings showed anywhere; nothing but clustered tree-tops as green as broccoli florets. Hawks would have seen this sight, and bald eagles, when the country was unexplored wilderness. Then the plane climbed into a bank of clouds and the window turned white, and Michael sat back in his seat.

"I'm wondering if I should have brought Lindy's medical records," Pauline said.

"What medical records?" he asked.

"They must still have them on file at her pediatrician's office."

"Oh, hon . . ." he said. But he didn't add that their daughter was long past the age for a pediatrician.

Pauline was quiet after that. While he watched, her eyelids began to flutter shut, and several times she blinked and sat straighter before she let her head nod against the window. Michael couldn't sleep himself, although they'd had to wake up very early for their flight. He studied the emergency instructions he found in the seat-back pocket; he leafed through a *Newsweek* handed to him by the stewardess. Pauline gave a little snorting sound and her mouth fell open. She would have been embarrassed if she'd known. In honor of the trip she had put on a darker-red lipstick, which always made her look older, and powder that was caking in her dimples. He saw that her dimples were more like tiny dry incisions now—something he hadn't noticed till this moment. And her eyelids had a crumpled look, and her stockinged thighs bulged like sausages below her miniskirt.

Back in 1957, for their fifteenth anniversary, Pauline had proposed that they dress up and have a formal photograph taken. She said that already she'd had to pluck four gray hairs from her head and that was just the beginning; she was starting to grow old and she would never, ever look this good again. Michael had been amused. Okay with him, he'd said, if that was what she wanted. So they'd gone to Aronson's Portrait Studio—Michael in his suit, Pauline in her gray silk—and the photographer had arranged them in front of a velvet curtain that puddled in artful folds around their feet. "A little closer together," he'd said. "Mrs., lift your chin a bit . . . Mr., put your arm around Mrs. . . . ." Michael had obeyed, encircling Pauline's waist and clasping her elbow just inside the hem of her sleeve; and something or other—the new sponginess of her bare skin, perhaps, or the unfamiliar scent of the silk—had made him feel for just an instant that he was standing next to a stranger. Who *was* this woman? What did she have to do with him? How could they be expected to share a house, rear children together, combine their separate lives for all time? The knob of her shoulder pressing into his armpit had felt like an inanimate object.

Yet the finished photo on Pauline's bureau showed an ordinary couple: Mr. and Mrs. Perfectly Fine, standing side by side and smiling the same stiff smile. A gilt-framed commercial. An advertisement for marriage.

\* \* \*

From the air, San Francisco looked beautiful. It appeared to be mostly water, so much so that for a moment, Michael thought their plane was going to miss dry land altogether; and Pauline pointed out a distant bridge that could be the Golden Gate, although it was actually red. Then during the cab ride from the airport, they saw more water and dramatic mountains with picturesque little settlements tumbling down their sides. Poor, plain, humble Baltimore wasn't even in the running.

The cabdriver was an elderly man in a brown felt hat that rested squarely on his ears. He was not the talkative sort, although Pauline tried to get a conversation going once she'd given him the address. "Have you lived here all your life?" she asked him.

He said, "Yup."

"Well, it sure is a *pretty* place."

He said, "Mmhmm."

"We just got in from Baltimore, Maryland. This is the first time I personally have been west of the Mississippi."

No response.

The silence made Michael feel self-conscious, so that he spoke in a soft, furry mumble when he picked up the tail of an argument they'd been having before they landed. "The trouble with going to the hospital first—" he confided to Pauline.

"What, Michael? I can't hear you," she said in a bugle voice.

He closed his eyes and then opened them and started over, more distinctly but just as quietly. "If we go to the hospital first, we'll have to carry our luggage."

"So? It's one little suitcase."

"Yes, but then if they let us take Lindy and she has luggage, too—"

"Michael, I refuse to waste time unpacking my nightgown when I've got a sick daughter waiting."

"No one's asking you to unpack your nightgown. All I'm saying is—"

"Our daughter's in the hospital," Pauline told the driver, raising her voice even further. "We learned about it just yesterday."

"Retreat," the driver said.

"Pardon?"

"They call the place a retreat, not a hospital."

Michael had thought, for a second, that the driver had been telling *them* to retreat. Even in these circumstances, he found the misunderstanding comical.

Pauline said, "How do you know that?"

"Everybody knows Nineteen Fleet Street."

"It's a . . . retreat?"

"It's run by the brothers," the driver said.

"Oh, Catholic brothers?"

"More like . . . yogis or something."

Pauline sent Michael a look he couldn't read.

"Hold on, there," she said to the driver. "Are you telling me our daughter's joined a cult?"

"Naw, it's not the kind of thing you'd *join*," the driver said. "They go out and pick you up. That's their what-do-you-say, mission. They scrape people off the street and haul them in to tend them."

"Scrape people off the—"

"Your drugged-out types. Your druggy, hippie, beatnik types on the LSD and the mushrooms and such."

Michael decided he disliked the man intensely. He turned toward Pauline and said, in a low, urgent voice, "We could go to the tourist home beforehand and leave the suitcase there. You said yourself the landlady said it's an easy walk to—"

"Actually, our daughter's had a nervous breakdown," Pauline told the driver. "We've come to take her back east with us. We've always been a very close, very loving family and we know that she'll be fine once she's in familiar surroundings."

The driver merely flicked his turn signal on.

They were traveling through the city now. At first, Michael found the houses impressive. They were strikingly handsome antiques with lacy trim, turrets and balconies and widow's walks, stained-glass windows, steep roofs. But gradually they grew seedier. As if the cab were swooping forward in time, the paint started peeling and the shutters started sagging and the gingerbread chipped and crumbled. The window curtains changed to Indian bedspreads or faded American flags. Then some windows were boarded over. A boy with long hair, in layers of rags, leaned against a lamppost with his eyes closed. The cabdriver punched down his door lock; so Michael and Pauline punched down theirs.

Nineteen Fleet Street was just another worn-out house. Not even a sign identified it. Pauline asked the driver, "Are you sure this is the place?"

He said, "Yup."

She was the one sitting on the curb side of the cab and so she yanked her door handle, apparently forgetting that she had punched the lock down. "Oops," she said. Her mistake seemed to undo her. She slid lower in her seat and let out a whimper of a breath. Before Michael could come to her rescue, the driver reached back and pulled up the button. "There you go," he told her.

She yanked the handle again and stumbled out onto the sidewalk, her miniskirt rucked up and her purse strap catching briefly on the window crank.

"Hope it turns out all right," the driver told Michael.

But Michael still disliked him. He gave him a measly dollar tip, even though the fare was astronomical.

The man who answered their ring didn't appear the slightest bit religious. He was tall and gray-haired and clean-shaven, good-looking in a weathered sort of way, and he wore a plaid flannel shirt and jeans and sharp-toed cowboy boots. "Yes?" he said, filling the door frame.

"I'm Michael Anton," Michael told him. He set down their suitcase. "This is my wife, Pauline. I believe you have our daughter here."

There was a pause. The man tilted his head.

"Our daughter Lindy. Linnet," Michael said.

"In this house, all are free of labels," the man told him.

"Excuse me?"

"Family names, given names . . . The trappings of our old lives are cast off as we move forward."

So the man was religious after all. That earnest, jargony way of talking made it only too clear. Michael assumed an expression of courteous attention. "Isn't that interesting!" he said. "Well, she was brought in about three days ago. I believe she, um, freaked out. She's about yay high and she's got more or less my coloring: brown eyes, black hair, though I can't say for certain what *style* of hair—"

"Serenity," someone said.

Michael broke off. He stared at the boy who had materialized next to the man—a scarily thin teenager in a white gauze tunic and flowered bell-bottoms.

"Right," the man agreed. "That would be Serenity. She came to share our lives on Monday."

Pauline said, "Can we see her?"—jumping in too fast.

"Ah, no," the man said sadly. "I'm afraid that won't be possible. In this house, all are free of the bonds of home and family."

"Now, just a minute," Pauline said.

Michael said, "Hon. Do you mind?" He turned to the man, who fixed him with a dispassionate gaze. "I guess you don't understand," he said. "We haven't heard from our daughter in over seven years. Till yesterday, we didn't even know for sure if she was alive. We only want to pay her a visit, see how she's getting along."

"And then take her home and make her well," Pauline added at his elbow.

Michael said, "Please. Pauline. Let me handle this." He told the man, "We'll just find out how she feels. If she wants to come home with us, well and good. Otherwise we'll leave without her."

"I am so sorry, my friends," the man said gently. "Serenity's not available."

Pauline said, "What is this, some kind of prison? Are you holding our daughter captive?"

"Pauline—"

"We wouldn't do her any harm! We aren't one of those . . . damaging families! Just ask Lindy! Just let her come out for one second and speak to us! You have no right to shut her away from us!"

The man took a step backward to reveal the room behind him— an entry hall furnished with a small, round, doily-topped table and nothing else. "Do you see any bars or locks?" he asked Pauline in the mildest tone. He gestured toward the boy. "Tarragon here can leave us any time he likes. Tarragon, would you like to leave?"

The boy shrank back and shook his head.

Michael said, "Naturally, we're not accusing you of anything." He felt Pauline's glare of protest, but he kept his eyes on the man. "If you could just tell our daughter we're here, though," he said. "Tell her and see what *she* says. Offer her a choice."

"She's made her choice," the man said, still mildly. "She made it when she was brought to us."

Pauline gave an odd, strangled sound.

Michael said, "Ah. Well." He stood straighter. "So, what's the procedure, exactly?" he asked. "You release people when they're . . . themselves again? Is there a certain length of time involved?"

"We 'release' them, as you say, when they decide they are ready for birth," the man said. "When they open this front door and are born again into the world."

"Oh, God in *heaven!*" Pauline exploded.

The man surveyed her benignly. Then he turned to Michael. "Perhaps you'd like to phone now and then," he said. "Ask how Serenity is growing. We have no secrets here. We're in the book: Fleet Street Retreat. My name is Becoming."

For the second time that day, Michael had to stifle an inappropriate guffaw.


The landlady had recommended the tourist home for its location. It was three blocks from Nineteen Fleet Street and two from her own house, on Haight. Unfortunately, that meant it shared the same depressed surroundings. Michael vividly remembered the TV footage of Haight-Ashbury in its glory days—the bevies of "love children" thronging the streets—but now the place had an atmosphere of morning-after-the-party desolation. A few forlorn stragglers dotted the sidewalks, and wastepaper clogged the gutters. A starved-looking boy asked them for a quarter. (Not even Pauline responded.) An old man wearing a biblical robe sat on his heels in a doorway. Dusty store windows displayed muddles of merchandise: Mexican blouses, Chinese slippers, wind chimes, sticks of incense, and various tiny pipes and cigarette holders and Middle Eastern hookahs.

Michael took it all in, intrigued in spite of himself, but Pauline trotted ahead with her shoulders hunched and her arms tightly folded. Twice she said she was cold; then finally she asked him to stop and let her unpack the sweater she'd brought. It was true that the air had a chill to it, as if San Francisco's seasons, as well as its clocks, were lagging behind the East Coast's. "Now you see I was right to want to keep our suitcase with us," she told him as she wriggled her arms into her sleeves.

Michael sighed, and she said, "What."

"The reason we kept the suitcase, Pauline, is that you were set on going first to Fleet Street."

"Well? So? Can you blame me?"

"I'm not blaming you; I'm just saying—"

Although now he wondered what difference it made.

"I wanted to see my daughter!" Pauline cried. "I waited seven years, I flew clear across the continent, and then you asked me to wait some more just so you could dump your suitcase in some stupid rented room!"

"Poll—"

"And once we get there, what do you do? Stand there like a . . . Milquetoast. 'Oh, excuse me very much, sir,' you say. 'You won't let her out of your clutches? You refuse to let us see her? Fine, sir. Whatever you wish, sir.' "

"She's over twenty-one, Pauline. She signed herself in of her own accord, so far as we know, and their policy is—"

"Oh, policy! Rules! What do I care about rules? I'm her mother and this is tearing me apart! It's killing me! It's eating me up! I can't stand this anymore!"

Tears were streaming down her cheeks. She spun around and took off again, her purse bouncing on her hip and her back stiff and indignant. Michael picked up the suitcase and followed, but he didn't try to reason with her.

What could he have said, anyhow?

On the corner a couple much like themselves—late forties, the man in a sport coat, the woman in a short skirt—stood admiring a psychedelic poster that was peeling off the side of a building. The man raised the camera that was slung around his neck, and Michael suddenly felt the way he had when they visited Karen during Parents' Weekend last fall: he was just one more in a pack of stuffy oldsters doing their best to keep up with the young folk. And Pauline in her minidress looked clunky and ridiculous, her feathered blond hairdo laughably ornate compared to the flowing tresses of the two young girls crossing the street ahead of them.

When Michael had first heard about hippies—about the love-ins and the sit-ins and the antiwar protests, and tuning in and turning on and dropping out and such—he had secretly felt pleased. So Lindy had just been ahead of her time! And he and Pauline weren't alone anymore!

He wondered now if the couple with the camera had come in search of a missing son or daughter themselves. But no, they had the look of people on vacation. They wouldn't be taking photographs if they felt the way he and Pauline felt.

He caught up with her on the far curb and set his free hand on the small of her back. "That should be the tourist home, on the left," he told her.

It was another rundown Victorian, with gray wooden steps that buckled beneath their feet and a handwritten sign above the doorbell, DOESN'T WORK, and the woman who answered their knock seemed run-down herself, still in her thirties but slack-faced and sullen, wearing a housecoat of a type Michael hadn't seen since he moved out of the old neighborhood. "We're the Antons," he told her. She turned without a word and led them toward the rear of the house. The door of the last room stood open, exposing two narrow beds pushed together and a low, ugly vanity bearing a very old TV. "Bathroom's across the hall," the woman said. "Payment's in advance, no checks. Nine dollars even." She held forth the flat of her palm, and Michael counted the money into it. "Take that key on top of the TV if you go out," she said. Then she left.

Go out? All Michael wanted to do was drop onto the nearer of the beds; never mind that it was barely past noon. He was so tired that even this bleak, stark room seemed like a haven. But Pauline said, "You want to use the bathroom before we leave?"

"Leave for where?"

"Michael! We have to go find our grandson!"

"Right now?" he asked.

"He's waiting for us! Don't you want to meet him?"

No, he didn't, really. This child had been sprung on them too suddenly. Most grandparents were given nine months to prepare themselves. Shoot, they were given years, as a rule, while their daughters courted, got engaged, had formal weddings . . . But Pauline was so eager, with her tears wiped away now and her face lit up and animated. So he said, "All right, hon," and went off to use the bathroom.

When they started out again, they disagreed about which direction to take. Michael knew for a fact that Haight Street lay to their right. Already the neighborhood's general design was becoming clear to him. But Pauline said no, the landlady had told her it was a left. So they stood there on the steps while she dug through her purse for her notes. Out came her billfold, her cosmetic kit, her eyeglass case . . . and a tiny red metal fire engine still in its cellophane-windowed box. Michael pretended not to notice, but when she said, "Yes, turn right. Didn't I say turn right?" he told her, "Sure, hon," and reached out to cup her elbow as they descended the steps.

The air smelled like chili con carne. It reminded him how long it had been since breakfast—if you could call that limp, stale pastry and canned orange juice on the plane a breakfast. "Hey, Poll?" he said. "Maybe we could take the little boy out for a hot dog."

"That's a good idea."

"The landlady would probably be glad to get rid of him for a couple of hours."

"Couple of hours?" Pauline asked. She stopped walking and looked at him. "What are you talking about? He's not the landlady's responsibility; he's yours and mine."

"Well, but—"

"We're taking him for good, Michael. We're packing him up and taking him with us, because we are all he's got."

Michael had known this, of course, and yet somehow he hadn't absorbed the full implications. He said, "Right this minute we're taking him?"

"Where has your *mind* been?"

"Well, it's just that . . . I guess I was thinking, you know, we'd wait till we had Lindy too."

"When might that be, though?" Pauline asked him. "We can't leave a child unattended in some rooming house! We have to collect him immediately. But what to do after that . . . I don't know. I don't know." They started walking again. "That person at the retreat didn't give us the faintest idea how long Lindy might be staying there."

"I'm going to phone the guy this evening," Michael said. He had already decided that. Pauline was right; he had given in too easily. "Who knows, she may already be coming out of whatever it was. Lots of times, people have these flash-in-the-pan bad spells. But if she isn't, I'll say, 'Look. We feel she would do better on home ground.' Why, Baltimore's got the best medical experts in the country! And if he still tries to keep us from seeing her—"

"Here's the place," Pauline said, coming to a stop.

She was looking at a house even more ramshackle than its neighbors, although it must once have been the height of elegance. The double front door had two oval windows, one with an etched, beveled-glass pane and the other covered over with cardboard. Lindy had climbed these very steps, skirting the one that was rotten. She had turned this very doorknob, which hung loose above a missing lock that was now just a shredded hole in the wood.

"It's the number she told me, all right," Pauline said, clearly wishing it weren't.

They climbed the steps themselves, and Michael pressed the cracked rubber button to the left of the door.

"How do I look?" Pauline asked him.

"You look fine, hon."

It seemed odd to him that she would care, when they were meeting a mere child.

A young girl with pale, stringy hair opened the door and cocked her head at them. She wore a blue gingham dress, long-sleeved and ankle-length like something from pioneer days. Another boarder, Michael assumed—maybe even another missing daughter. But Pauline said, "Destiny?"

"Yes?"

"Well, hi! I'm Pauline. This is my husband, Michael."

"Oh, good," the girl said. "You got here."

Pauline stepped into the entrance hall, but Michael felt he needed a moment to adjust. (The word "landlady" had conjured up an entirely different image.)

"I didn't want to call the welfare people if there was any way around it," Destiny was telling Pauline in a low, confiding voice.

"Welfare!"

"I don't trust those people as far as I can throw them. But I knew I'd have to do something. He just stays shut away in their room; he won't leave it no matter what. Sometimes I hear him tiptoe off to the bathroom, but then when I start up the stairs he scoots back and slams the door."

She was leading them up the stairs as she spoke, past brittle, yellowed wallpaper curling off the walls. The house smelled of mice. The banister looked sticky, and Michael avoided touching it.

"I've been taking him his meals but I don't see as he's eaten," Destiny was saying. "Of course, I haven't a clue what a kid that age would like. I say, 'Here! You care for some lentils?' but he just stares at me so I set down the bowl and leave. Well, I do want to give him his space, right?"

She turned, having reached the top of the stairs, and raised her transparent eyebrows. Two complicated brass earrings hung nearly to her shoulders.

"What's his name?" Pauline asked her.

"Pagan."

*"Pagan?"* Michael and Pauline said together.

She shrugged. The earrings tinkled. "What can I tell you," she said. "His mom always struck me as kind of wifty, if you don't mind me saying so."

She turned again and started down the dark hall, passing two closed doors before she stopped at the third. "Knock-knock!" she called. "Anyone home?"

No answer.

"Coming in, then!" She turned the knob.

The room was scarcely bigger than a closet, with a single, clouded window and water-stained ivory walls. On the bare floor lay a mattress heaped with tangled blankets and clothing. While Michael watched, one piece of clothing stirred. A small boy sat up and blinked at them. Then he scooted backwards to the far edge of the mattress.

"Hello, Pagan," Pauline said softly.

He stared at her without answering. His eyes were a liquid brown and his hair was black and shaggy. It was *foreign* hair, Michael thought—a deeper, shinier black than any Anton's hair. There were bluish shadows beneath his eyes, which gave him a world-weary look although he couldn't have been much older than three.

"I'm your grandma!" Pauline was saying. "Your mommy's mother. This is your grandpa! We've come all the way from Baltimore, Maryland, to see you!"

Silence.

"I'll just get his things together," Destiny said. "He doesn't have all that many."

So she really was expecting them to take him with them. Michael knew he should be used to the notion by now, but he felt a thump of shock even so. He watched Destiny drift about, collecting a T-shirt here and a sweater there and folding them over one arm. When she approached the mattress, Pagan scrambled to his feet, hugging a small blanket. His clothes were unexpectedly conventional (a striped red jersey, jeans, red sneakers) but very dirty, and his fingernails were rimmed with black. Because the mattress occupied the entire length of the far wall, he had no choice but to step into the center of the room, and the sight of such a small, frightened child standing so undefended wrenched Michael's heart. Instinctively he drew backward, almost into the hall, to show that he meant no harm. Pauline, on the other hand, rushed forward. "Sweetheart," she said, and she dropped to her knees in front of the child and folded her arms around him. "Oh, honey pie, sweetheart, oh, my poor, sweet little one!"

Michael was horrified. So was Destiny, evidently, for she straightened, holding a jacket, and gaped at the two of them.

For a moment, Pagan stood frozen within the circle of Pauline's arms. Then he dropped his head to her shoulder. One grimy little hand reached around to pat her back.

Michael felt his eyes fill. He had to look away.

"I guess I'll just donate a pillowcase for you to carry his stuff in," Destiny said finally. She started cramming what she had gathered into a pillowcase more gray than white. "His mom has their only bag. I packed it up for her after she left, and my husband took it to Fleet Street."

Destiny had a husband? Somehow, Michael hadn't pictured that. He watched her shake out a sheet and stoop to retrieve a red sock. "Say," he said, suddenly hopeful. "Do you happen to know if Lindy, if our daughter, might be married?"

"Not that *I* ever heard," Destiny said cheerfully.

"I was just wondering about, ah, Pagan's dad."

"Oh, you know how those things can be."

He didn't know. He waited, in case she cared to explain. On the floor, Pauline was crooning, "It's all, all, all right, sweetheart. Everything's going to be fine now."

Michael said, "Well, could you tell us a little more about what happened here?"

"Happened?" Destiny said.

"How Lindy, um, freaked out?"

Destiny flicked a glance toward Pagan. "I don't guess now would be a good moment," she said.

"Oh. Okay."

"For sure, she's in a great place, though! The retreat is *great*. She's one lucky lady."

Michael said, "The thing of it is, we had planned to take her home with us. Then when we got there we found we weren't even allowed to talk to her. I worry she's being kept against her will."

"Nah, it's cool. You don't want to interrupt her in mid-birth."

Michael had been about to say more, but he closed his mouth abruptly. He felt he'd landed in one of those science fiction movies where the hero all at once understands that everybody else's mind has been taken over by aliens.

"So anyhow," Destiny said, handing Michael the pillowcase, "here's all his gear. I *think* it's all. I'm not refunding the rest of her rent on account of the long-distance phone call, and also the window."

"Window?" Michael asked.

"So this is goodbye, kid," Destiny told Pagan. "It's been nice knowing you. Have a cool life."

Pauline rose and took Pagan by the hand. He was still holding on to the blanket—a scrap of a thing, washed-out blue flannel—and she asked Destiny, "Is the blanket yours?"

"No, it's his," Destiny said—unnecessarily, since Pagan had already torn free of Pauline to clutch it even more tightly.

"It's okay, sugar," Pauline told him. She guided him out of the room and toward the stairs, followed by Destiny and Michael. "We're going to take you where Grandma and Grandpa are staying! Going to give you a bath, change you into clean clothes . . ."

All the way down the stairs the only voice was Pauline's, murmuring and soothing. Even when she told Destiny goodbye at the door, she used that lullaby tone. "Thanks for getting in touch with us, hear? Thanks for everything."

When Michael saw how she went first down the steps but then turned back to wait for Pagan once she'd reached the bottom, diplomatically protective, he felt a flood of love for her.


Walking a small child was like herding water, Michael used to think when his own children were small. Heaven only knew what they'd take it into their heads to do next—dart in front of a speeding car or throw a tantrum in mid-traffic or stop to pick a soaked cigar butt out of the gutter. So how to explain *this* child? He trudged between them in silence, incurious and resigned, hugging the bunched-up blanket with both arms. At the first intersection, he untangled one hand from the blanket and reached for Pauline's hand in an automatic way, not looking at her and apparently not thinking about it—a gesture that Michael found reassuring. Someone had once cared for the boy, you would have to surmise. He hadn't always been expected to manage on his own.

Other clues followed, now that Michael was watching for them—signposts that suggested the shape of Pagan's past life. For instance, he seemed very much accustomed to eating out. At the Good Feelings Deli & Pizza, half a block before the tourist home, he draped his blanket efficiently over the back of a chair and then clambered up and settled himself and waited for his food. But it appeared that he had never encountered a hot dog before, because when it arrived—ordered for him by Michael—he first surveyed it dubiously and then, once he'd figured out how to grasp it, ate it like an ear of corn, nibbling small, shallow rows from left to right. Nor did he seem familiar with soft drinks. His first sip of Pepsi made him wrinkle his nose, although he adjusted soon enough and downed the rest in no time. Michael supposed that this meant he'd been reared on hippie food, sugar-free and meatless and all that. He did seem to have some experience with potato chips, however. He ate all of his and then most of Pauline's, licking his gray-creased fingers after each one. "Good?" Pauline asked him. He nodded.

Maybe he *couldn't* speak. Maybe Destiny had only assumed that he used to speak before. Michael couldn't remember now at what age children started talking. "How old are you?" he asked, not expecting an answer.

To his surprise, Pagan looked at him directly. He had eyebrows no thicker than threads, much lighter than his hair color, and now they drew up the skin at the center of his forehead like stitches gathering up cloth. Finally, he arrived at a conclusion. "Four," he said. His voice was incongruously deep—not a small child's voice at all.

Pauline gave a little cry and blotted her mouth with her napkin. "Four years old! What a *clever* boy!" she said. "He's four," she told Michael.

"So I gathered," he said drily.

That Pagan had spoken his age instead of holding up four fingers might be another clue. He'd been blessed with the kind of mother who conversed with him intelligently. Or was Michael just grasping at straws now?

151

He so much wanted to believe the best about Lindy.

"So I guess you must go to school," Pauline was saying. "Preschool, play group, nursery school . . . ," offering every possible term for it. But Pagan seemed to consider the discussion finished. Either that, or the very notion of attending school was new to him, because he just reached for another potato chip.

"How are we doing here?" the waitress asked. "Anyone want dessert?"

"I guess not, thanks," Michael told her.

She was the cheerful, plump, motherly style of waitress he was used to seeing in Baltimore. He wished he could let her know somehow that it wasn't their fault their grandchild was so dirty.

And what to make of the fact that Pagan had no idea what to do with the fire engine? Pauline fished it from her purse and set it on the foot of one bed as soon as they reached their room. "Ooh!" she said. "What have we *here?*" But he treated it with suspicion, viewing it from a distance for several long minutes before daring to set one tentative finger atop the cellophane window. By the time Michael returned from inquiring about an extra cot (there wasn't one; they would have to make do), the situation had progressed only slightly: Pagan had wrapped the boxed fire engine tidily in his blanket, its front end poking forth like a baby's face from the flannel.

And he didn't seem to know about television, either. He watched it sitting next to Pauline, propped against the pillow at the head of her bed, open-mouthed and disbelieving at the sight of an ordinary Benson & Hedges ad. Game shows followed soap operas and were followed in turn by the evening news, every flickering black-and-white scene earning his undivided attention. "Say," Michael said at one point. "Isn't there someplace you'd like to go? A park? A playground?" But Pagan's silver-edged profile remained pointed toward the screen, and Michael himself was too done in to persist.

It could be the boy was shell-shocked. Perhaps he wasn't watching television at all, because when a clown took a comic pratfall in a used-car commercial, Pagan kept the same stony expression.

At one point during the news (Vietnam and more Vietnam), Michael fell asleep sitting up, letting his head tip back against the metal headrail of his bed. He awoke dry-mouthed and befuddled, although he could tell he must have slept only minutes because the screen showed a bunch of soldiers tramping through a jungle with fancy arrangements of leaves on their helmets. The room was almost dark now, lit bluish by the TV. He looked at his watch and said, "What do you say I go get a pizza for supper?"

Pagan perked up and nodded emphatically. (Another clue.) Although he wouldn't commit himself as to toppings. "Plain? Mushroom? Pepperoni?" Michael asked. No answer.

"Toad-frog?" Pauline suggested, and was rewarded with a pinched, reluctant smile that made her laugh and turn triumphantly to Michael. "Bring us a toad-frog pizza, please, Grandpa."

"Sure thing," Michael said too heartily, struggling up from his bed.

He had always imagined that his grandchildren would call him "Dziadziu"—the name he had used for his own grandfather. Well, but, okay. "Grandpa" was all right too.


While he was waiting at the Good Feelings for his pizza (plain, with extra cheese, which seemed safest), he used the pay phone in one corner of the café. He got the number from Information, dropped in his coins and dialed, and then had to wait for ten or twelve rings before a woman answered. "Fleet Street Retreat?" she said, sounding doubtful.

Michael said, "Yes, may I speak to . . . Becoming, please."

The phone at the other end clattered and went silent. Behind the counter, the chef spread watery pink tomato sauce across a pizza shell.

"This is Becoming," a voice said in Michael's ear. "How may I offer help?"

"It's Michael Anton. The father of, you know, Serenity."

"Ah."

"Look. We've reserved my daughter a seat tomorrow on the morning flight to Baltimore. Her mother and I will be traveling with

153

her and also her little boy. Surely you agree that she and her little boy should be together."

"I wasn't aware that she had a child," Becoming said.

Could she not even have mentioned the fact? How disturbed *was* she? Michael's thoughts were deflected, for a moment, but he pulled himself together and said, "So now you understand—"

"This makes it very sad, yes, very difficult. So sad when a child is involved."

"Now you understand why we should take her back with us."

"Dear friend," Becoming said in an alarmingly solicitous tone, "I don't think you fully comprehend what it is we're dealing with."

"All right," Michael said. "Tell me what we're dealing with."

"This is a young woman so zonked, so zapped and fried and hopped up and wigged out and blown away by drugs—"

"By drugs!"

"—she would never make it onto the airplane, friend. She wouldn't make it down the front steps."

"Do you mean drugs like . . . narcotics?"

"Every pill, every tab, every pop, every powder and capsule and button you can name. Every upper, every downer, every over-the-counter, under-the-counter . . ."

Michael sagged against the wall.

"And even if she were able to walk out of here, which she's not, how would you two handle her? How would you protect her little boy from the sight of her?"

Michael couldn't answer. It seemed his throat had closed over.

"Brother? Are you with me?"

He replaced the receiver.

The Good Feelings Deli was not equipped for takeout, and Michael had to carry the pizza wrapped in aluminum foil that let the heat burn through to the palms of his hands. But that was all right; he felt chilled to the bone. His teeth were chattering and his feet seemed too heavy, his limp more pronounced than usual.

"Zonked," he heard in his mind, and "zapped" and "hopped up" and "wigged out"—terms that were brand-new to him. And Destiny's word, "wifty," also unfamiliar. Destiny's face rose up before him, a faint green mark on one side of her jaw where her earring had rubbed as it swung. He hadn't noticed the mark at the time, but now it seemed indented in his memory like a scar.

When he got back to the room, he didn't tell Pauline what he had learned. Of course he would tell her eventually, but right now he couldn't bear to speak the words. All he said was "I talked again with Becoming on the phone, and it does appear it will be some time before Lindy's ready to travel."

He braced himself for questions, protests, cross-examination, but Pauline just said, "Oh," and sat silent for a moment. Maybe she'd somehow guessed. "So," she said finally. "I guess we'd better just go ahead and fly back tomorrow without her, right?"

"It looks that way," Michael said.

Pauline straightened her shoulders—squared her edges, so to speak—and rose to switch the light on.

The pizza was soggy and tasteless, but Michael suspected none of them would have enjoyed it in any case. Since he hadn't thought to buy drinks, Pauline fetched three tiny paper cups of lukewarm water from the bathroom across the hall. "Cheers!" she said as she distributed them. But she seemed to have her mind elsewhere. Several times she trailed off in mid-sentence. "Oh, *good* boy, Pagan; let's just wipe your . . . Isn't this cozy and . . . Who's for more? Anybody want . . . ?"

Pagan took dainty, unenthusiastic bites from just the tip of his pizza slice, leaving a broad swath of crust, never removing his eyes from the television screen. "How is it?" Michael asked him. Pagan didn't answer. In the harsh glare of the overhead bulb his eyes were squinty, and he looked hunched and furtive.

Face it, this child was just a substitute. He was not their *real* child, the one they'd flown across the continent to find.

He didn't own a toothbrush. He didn't own a comb or a hairbrush, unless Destiny had forgotten to pack them. He wasn't used to baths. (Could that be possible?) He had to be coaxed inch by inch into the claw-footed tub after first backing into a corner, bony-ribbed and shivering in his frayed gray underpants. But he did own a pair of pajamas, which he put on without assistance—footed pajamas patterned with spaceships, not entirely clean. (Every piece of clothing in that pillowcase had a close, sweet smell something like caramel, as did Pagan himself.)

He raised no objection when the light was switched off or when the window shade was pulled down to block the light from the street. He climbed obediently into Pauline's bed and settled himself in a curled position with his blanket tucked in the crook of his neck, the fire engine still swaddled within in its crackling box. He fell asleep almost at once and breathed evenly but too quickly, it seemed to Michael—shallow, whispery, kitten breaths. He was not a thumb sucker or a fidgeter or a snorer. During the night, though, he wet the bed. Michael woke to the smell of warm urine and the bump and tumble of Pauline climbing over him to slip under the covers on his other side. He didn't consider the bed-wetting to be a clue, however. He knew that even the best-trained child could regress in trying situations.

He lay wide-eyed on his back with Pauline's arm flung across his chest and her hair tickling his shoulder. It was a long time since they had slept snuggled so close together.

All these years, more years even than Lindy had been gone, Michael had spent wondering where they had made their mistake. Had they been too permissive? Too harsh? Neither one of them believed in physical punishment, but he could summon several shameful memories of gripping Lindy's arm too tightly when she was small or setting her aside too firmly. And Pauline, with her fondness for saying whatever came into her head—oh, she could be a real tongue-lasher when a child made her angry. It was hard not to blame her too for those character flaws he saw in Lindy that seemed Pauline's direct hand-me-downs: the explosiveness, the extreme emotions, the unpredictability. (Though hadn't Pauline, more than once, pointed out that Lindy's dark, glowering expression mirrored Michael's exactly?) Or maybe their attention had been spread too thin among the three children. Or they'd showered Lindy with too *much* attention—focused on her too closely, expected more of her than they ought to. What was it? What? What? What?

Drugs, though. Drugs were so . . . chemical, so physical. They were really not an interesting explanation. The mystery of Lindy Anton should arise from something more complex than a mere handful of pharmaceuticals.

He fell back into sleep as if sleep were a defeat, as if he were flinging out his hands and saying, "Forget it. I give up."

WELCOME HOME LINDY, Sally's placard read. And George was holding a cone of flowers such as street peddlers sold, and Karen—who should have been in class—was standing so close to the gate that the other arriving passengers had to swerve to avoid her. "Here we are! Over here!" she cried, jumping up and down. She wore a pink-and-orange psychedelic-print minidress, although her usual style was jeans and T-shirts, and her hair seemed to have mushroomed into a giant blond pouf that made her resemble those magazine ads where big photographs of heads were set on tiny pen-and-ink bodies. She must have been working on her appearance since crack of dawn. Michael felt an inner lurch of pity as he watched her search the approaching faces, while George craned his neck to gaze at the passengers beyond. Sally, having no inkling yet, continued to beam vivaciously, but the smiles of the other two were fading. "Where is she?" George asked his parents.

Instead of answering, Pauline pushed Pagan forward. "Look who *we've* got!" she told them. "This is Pagan, Lindy's little boy. Pagan, here's your aunt Karen, your aunt Sally, your uncle George . . ."

"Where's Lindy?" Karen demanded.

"Oh, she'll be along! But right now she's staying on a little while in San Francisco."

"Why? Is she all right? Did you get to see her?"

"Well, not in person, exactly, but—"

"Guess what I have, Pagan!" Sally said. "Ta-da!" and she pulled out a small brown felt kangaroo with a baby kangaroo in its pocket. "For you," she told him.

Pagan reached for it, his eyes raised somberly to Sally's.

"What do you say?" Pauline prompted.

"Thank you," he said distinctly, in his surprising bass growl.

The women fell upon him with little cries, as if he'd performed a miracle.

On the ride home—the men in front, the women in back, with Pagan perched on Pauline's knees—Pauline began constructing the story she would tell from now on about Lindy. Michael watched it taking shape—a fascinating process. "San Francisco was gorgeous," she began. "You-all will have to go there. And Lindy is in such a fine place! We spoke with the director. Of course we wish we could have brought her home right then and there but they have their procedures, you know, their proven methods for helping people sort out their stresses and tensions. They're so far ahead of Baltimore in that way! So she's going to join us later. But meanwhile, we have Pagan! Isn't that lovely? Our boy Pagan! Don't you think he resembles Lindy around the eyes?"

Another time, Michael might have felt annoyed by this rouged and lipsticked version of the truth. Such concern for the looks of things, even within the family! But today, he was touched. It occurred to him that his wife had amazing reserves of strength, that women like Pauline were the ones who kept the planet spinning. Or at least, they made it appear to keep spinning, however it might in fact be wobbling on its axis.


His respect for Pauline persisted over the next few weeks. He was awestruck by her devotion to Pagan and her unflagging energy, not just physical but emotional—her zest and warmth and optimism. Certainly Michael contributed; he read to Pagan every evening after supper or played a baby form of softball in the backyard. Pauline, however, had the minute-by-minute tasks, and the sad truth was that they weren't very rewarding. No fault of Pagan's, of course. He had to have been shaken and confused by all these changes. But he was so unresponsive—so boneless, somehow, and lacking in joy. He had a habit of staring at people with an expression that seemed censorious, his eyes unblinking and peculiarly opaque. He spoke as little as possible and he almost never answered questions. Friendly overtures of any kind appeared to put him on guard; conspicuous shows of enthusiasm turned him as wary as some small animal. "Pagan-boy!" Pauline would cry, swooping in on him in the morning. (He slept in Lindy's old room. Like an overly timid houseguest, he remained in bed until he was summoned, however long that might take.) "Pay-Pay! Pagan the Perfect! Come see what a yummy breakfast I fixed you!" Pagan merely stared. He was like blotting paper, Michael thought—just that dense and matte-surfaced, absorbing all that came his way and giving nothing back. But Pauline refused to be discouraged. "Egg-in-a-hole, Pay-Pay! And orange juice, freshly squeezed!"

She was a good person, really. Well, and so was Michael himself, he believed. It was only that the two of them together weren't good. Or weren't . . . what was he trying to say, weren't *nice*. They weren't always very nice to each other; he couldn't explain just why.

Every evening at seven or so—four p.m. West Coast time—Michael phoned the retreat. He figured that was late enough so a patient's progress for the day would have been evaluated. "May I speak to Becoming, please," he would say in a forthright manner. The name had stopped sounding odd to him. Even Lindy's new name rolled off his tongue without a hitch. "I'm inquiring about Serenity. This is her father."

The name "Serenity" had no significance for Pagan, Michael assumed. But something must have alerted him, because midway through Michael's third phone call he found Pagan at his elbow, mutely attentive, not moving and almost not breathing. "She's coming along, coming along," Becoming was reporting. "She knows now you have her little boy; we told her."

"And what did she say about that?" Michael asked.

"Oh, well, 'say'; she's not so very talkative yet. But we continue to have faith!"

When Michael hung up, he told Pagan, "Doing okay, it seems. Be a little while yet." His wording was deliberately ambiguous, in case Pagan had been standing there only by chance, but he could tell from the sudden droop in the child's shoulders that he did know—that he'd been listening with all his heart, concentrating fiercely on the news from the other end of the line. What else did he know? How much was he aware of?

The children's old pediatrician, Dr. Amble, was still in practice, and after Pagan had been with them several weeks they took him in for a physical. The first thing they learned was that he might not ever have visited a doctor before, because at the start he was unsuspecting—mildly, distantly interested in the waiting room with its toys and puzzles and nursery-rhyme decor—and then outraged and incredulous during the exam. He fought silently to keep his clothes on, scrambled off the scales in horror, and flung away the stethoscope the instant it touched his chest. "Hmm," Dr. Amble said thoughtfully. Then he told them that Pagan was most likely three years old. "He told us four," Michael said. "Couldn't he just be small for his age?" But Dr. Amble said no, he would pretty much stake his professional reputation on three. This gave Michael a new perspective. Replaying Pagan's "Four" in his mind, he now saw the child's long pause and knitted brow as preparation for a leap into an inflated and more impressive age. He grinned. It was the first time he felt some hope for his grandson's . . . oh, sense of self, he supposed.

At the end of the exam, Dr. Amble had Michael come into his office while Pauline helped Pagan dress. "Well," Dr. Amble said as he settled into his chair, "there's lots we can only guess at, of course. I'd say it's very possible he's never been immunized. I'll have my nurse see to that." He picked up a ballpoint pen and then, looking down at his papers, said, "No birth date, no birthplace, no middle name . . . and we can't be sure of his last name either, according to your wife."

"I'm fairly certain it's Anton," Michael said.

He fought off the urge to remind Dr. Amble that none of this was *his* doing, or Pauline's. They themselves had taken their children in for checkups religiously, and arranged for every possible vaccination!

Then Dr. Amble said, "One good thing."

"What's that?"

"He does relate, you notice. You saw how he clung to your wife when he was upset."

"Well, but . . . he doesn't talk to us much. It's been nearly a month now. He's been awfully slow to get comfortable with us."

"That could be a good sign too. It proves he misses his mother, which means she must have behaved like a mother. Evidently they'd formed an attachment."

It was pathetic, how little it took to fill Michael with pride.


"May I speak to Becoming, please."

"This is Becoming."

"It's Michael Anton, calling about Serenity."

"Ah. Yes."

Michael waited.

"Well, Serenity is no longer with us," Becoming said.

Michael's heart stopped. He said, "What?"

"Last evening when we looked into her room we found she'd left."

"I don't understand."

"She decided to turn her back on what we offer here, it seems."

"But . . . you mean, she walked out? You told me she wasn't capable of making it down the front steps!"

"Oh, she had been progressing, though. She was attending our meetings; she was talking about starting over with her boy. She was moving forward, all of us thought! Now this: a willful refusal to proceed with her rebirth. It happens, sometimes. We're never sure just why."

Becoming's voice was mournful and slightly deeper than usual, like a record spun too slowly. Michael, on the other hand, felt his spirits rising by the second. Lindy had been attending meetings! She'd been talking about her boy!

Of course she had left. She was her normal self again, and she would be wanting her son back. She was coming home to Baltimore to claim him.

He asked Pauline if she remembered how to get in touch with

Destiny. She didn't, but she reminded him that the number must be on one of those old telephone bills he always insisted on keeping. Yes, and now she knew *why* he insisted, he could have pointed out; but he was too busy plowing through the desk, digging up the bill, searching for the number. "You should be the one to call. You've had more dealings with her," he told Pauline. "Ask if Lindy's shown up at the rooming house. Tell her that if she has, she should stay on there until we can wire money for her ticket."

Pagan had gone to a baseball game with George and Sally, as luck would have it. He wasn't around to witness the general upheaval—the desk drawer struck by a hurricane, Michael's hair standing on end where he'd torn his fingers through it, Pauline so flustered she fumbled the dialing and had to begin again. And then it was all for nothing. Destiny told Pauline she hadn't seen hide nor hair of Lindy. Yeah, sure, she would pass on the message if Lindy happened by, and she'd telephone with any news, of course reversing the charges. But to be honest, she didn't hold out much hope for a person who walked away from her own rebirth.

Pauline went into sort of a low spell after she hung up. "Now look! We're back to where we were before," she said. "Our daughter's out loose in the world and we have no idea where!"

It was Michael who was the optimist, for once. "You know how young people are these days. Hitchhiking, catching rides with friends or finding rides on bulletin boards. She's probably halfway here already! I give her till . . . when. Today's Saturday. I bet she's here by Monday. Maybe even sooner, but definitely by Monday."

When Pagan returned from the ball game, solemnly sporting an Orioles cap, he couldn't have guessed that anything out of the ordinary had happened. Pauline was as chipper as ever. Michael was as calm, sustained by his clear, bright vision of Lindy heading steadily toward them. He saw her walking down the middle of a two-lane highway, looking at him directly, smiling. He was picturing her the wrong age, he knew, but he allowed himself that small gift: Lindy as a child, eight or nine years old. Her hair was caught up in two parenthesis-shaped ponytails above her ears. She wore shorts underneath her dress so that she could do cartwheels and handstands anywhere she liked. Her knees were scabby. She was his own funny, feisty, rough-and-tumble Lindy, and she was almost home now.

For one brief period in the Antons' lives, they had owned a dog. An overbred collie, this was, unimaginatively named Lassie—a flibberti-gibbet, yappy and hysterical. Any time one of the children left the house, Lassie would race to the picture window and hop up on her hind legs to nudge aside the curtain with her needle of a nose. Hour after hour she kept a frantic vigil, whimpering and quivering and all but wringing her paws.

That was how Michael felt, those days they were waiting for Lindy. He kept gravitating toward the front of the house, gazing out at the street. Every car, every approaching pedestrian caused something to leap inside him. By Sunday he was stationed at the window almost nonstop, although he tried to hide it from Pauline. (Pauline seemed to have her own expectations. With her, it was the phone, and she made obvious attempts to keep the line free at all times.) George and Sally came for Sunday supper but Michael repeatedly left the table, wandering almost against his will in the direction of the living room. Several times that night he got up and checked again, pretend-ing to head toward the bathroom. And Monday he stayed home from work. He said it was time he gave his manager more responsibility. But then, because his manager had not proved all that competent during the San Francisco trip, Michael kept phoning the store to see how things were going, and Pauline kept saying, "Good grief, Michael, will you please get off the line?" Pagan had been invited to play with Wanda Lipska's grandson, but when Pauline asked Michael to drive him there, Michael said he'd better not; it might turn out that he was needed at the store. Pauline said, "Oh, for—!" and left in a huff, irately jangling her keys. Michael spent the whole time she was gone standing at the picture window. Not one person walked by. No traffic passed but delivery vans, till Pauline's car pulled into the driveway again and Michael dropped the curtain.

Tuesday he didn't work either. He said he had a scratchy throat.

Wednesday he went down to the store at his usual hour.

They didn't speak about it. There was no particular moment when one of them turned to the other and said, "I guess she isn't coming after all." They just grew quieter and more subdued.

And Pagan? For a while, any time Michael made a phone call he would find Pagan magically stationed beside him. But that stopped, by and by. Pagan started going to the swimming pool. He made friends with the little girl two houses down. Pauline enrolled him in day camp. His room became a tumult of train tracks and picture books, Matchbox cars, front-end loaders, the fire engine long since freed from its box, the brown felt kangaroo with her baby, Cracker Jack prizes, crumbled pretzels, plastic dinosaurs, and random arms and eyeballs from a Mr. Potato Head.

Michael had imagined that someday, when things had settled down some, Pagan would tell them a little bit about his life with Lindy. Bits and pieces would emerge, filtered of course through a child's capricious memory but still revealing, still instructive. That never happened, though. Instead, Pagan's past seemed to fall away behind him, and there came a moment when Michael realized that they would never know any more about it than they knew now. It had dissolved, as untraceable as Lindy herself. And Pagan was here to stay.

Driving him to day camp one morning, Michael lost patience when it turned out that for the second time that week, Pagan had left his blanket at home and wanted to go back for it. "Maybe you could do without it, just this once," Michael said, and Pagan said, "But I need it, Grandpa. I have to have it." So Michael slammed on the brakes and swerved into someone's driveway, and just as he was reversing he had a sudden recollection of a book he used to read to his daughters. *Heidi,* it was called. Heidi was a little girl who was sent to live with her grandfather high in the Alps. As near as he could remember, the whole focus had been on Heidi's adjustment to her new surroundings. Lots of goat milk and fresh air, new roses in her cheeks . . . But what occurred to him now was, How about the grandfather? Did anyone ask what the grandfather felt, adjusting to life with a child again?

Now the old man's grace seemed heroic, and Michael was filled with a mixture of admiration and envy.

* * *

On Labor Day they gave their traditional barbecue. It had become just a family event, over the past few years, but even so the guest list was a long one. Karen would be there, having finished with her summer job in Ocean City, and George and Sally, of course, and Pauline's father and her sisters and brothers-in-law, as well as those of their children who still lived in the area. Pauline had Michael set out the extra lawn chairs from the garage. Then she went into one of her preparty frenzies. She started worrying that they wouldn't have enough food, and so she fixed a second batch of coleslaw and she telephoned George and asked him to bring more ground beef when he came, and minutes later she phoned him again and added hamburger buns. "I don't know why we go on doing this," she told Michael. "It's not as if we enjoy it. I'm a frazzle!" And her face did have a strained, lined, wired look to it.

Michael decided he'd get out of harm's way, go pay a visit to Eustace. It was a custom of his, now that Eustace was subsisting on Social Security checks, to drive into the city from time to time and slip the old man a few dollars. So he left, calling, "Back in a while!" All right, maybe he didn't make absolutely certain Pauline heard him. But he'd been remarking for several days that he planned to do this. She could have figured it out.

She didn't, however—or claimed she didn't. When he got home (feeling bloated from the Dr Pepper Eustace liked to serve), she met him at the door demanding, "Where in the world have you been?"

"At Eustace's. I told you. Why?" he asked. He glanced at the clock behind her. Only four-thirty, and the party wasn't starting till five.

But Pauline said, "You did *not* tell me! I've been going out of my mind! Daddy got here half an hour ago and he's sitting on his own with no one to talk to but Pagan, and Karen went for ice and hasn't been heard of since, and you haven't even fired up the grill yet!"

"There's plenty of time for the grill," he said. But he was speaking to her back, because she had already flounced off.

From that point until the end of the evening, he didn't have a chance to exchange two words with her. She was racing around in a thousand directions. But finally the last guest left, and Karen volunteered to put Pagan to bed, and that was when Michael realized that Pauline was still mad at him. When he brought a stack of plates into the kitchen she snapped, "I can do that, thank you very much!" and she grabbed the plates away from him and set them down so hard it was a wonder they didn't break.

"Now, Poll," he said.

"Stop calling me Poll!"

"Pauline, I'm sorry I went out this afternoon but I only went to see Eustace, and you know it would hurt his feelings if I didn't sit a minute; what would he think if—"

"Oh, *Eustace's* feelings; yes, by all means let's consider *Eustace's* feelings—some old man who quote-unquote worked for you a million years ago. Never mind that I've got an entire enormous party on my hands and a three-year-old child underfoot and poor Daddy wondering why nobody's made him feel welcome!"

"Well, how was I to know your dad would show up early?"

"He's family, Michael! He can show up whenever he wants to! But you think just your own family counts, your own cantankerous mother who I cared for till the day she died without a word of thanks and then you wouldn't so much as lift a finger to help us look for *my* mother the time she wandered off and got lost!"

"I helped you look for her lots of times! Lord, those last two years of her life I swear I made a *hobby* out of looking for your mother! But one lone, single, isolated evening, when nobody else was around to close the store—"

"Oh, the store, the store! Always your precious store! What do *you* want?" Pauline asked Karen, who had appeared in the kitchen doorway.

"Nothing," Karen said hastily. "Just saying good night." She ducked out again.

"Night, hon," Michael called after her, but Pauline refused to speak. (The woman had no partitions; if she was angry at one person she let her anger spill over onto the world at large.)

"Even when your own daughter ran away from home," she said, "where were you? At the store! The everlasting store!"

"Well, naturally. It was a weekday. Where would you expect me to be? While you, on the other hand, who had nothing on this earth to do but keep track of our three children—"

"Oh, that is low, Michael. That is low and base and unjust. You're going to try and blame me for Lindy's leaving? How about you? How about a father so cold and remote that his own children can't wait to get away from him and find some affection elsewhere? That his daughter absconds with the first boy she meets and his son gets married before he's through college and his youngest won't even come home for summer vacation?"

Michael often reached a point, in his fights with Pauline, where he was overcome by such helpless rage that he had to leave the room. Pauline would call it withdrawing—further evidence of his coldness. But Pauline had no idea. It was either leave or choke her into permanent silence. Sometimes, he felt his fingers actually tingling with the urge to grasp that corded neck of hers tighter and tighter and tighter.

He spun on his heel and walked out the back door, letting the screen slap shut. On the darkened patio, where chairs still sat about in friendly clusters, he grabbed the farthest chair and slung it around so it was facing away from the house. He threw himself into it and tipped his head back, forcing himself to breathe slowly while he gazed up at the sky.

Behind him, the lights of the house blinked off one by one; he could tell by the way the night sky grew deeper and the stars began to show. He heard a series of doors slamming: kitchen door, bedroom door, and probably a closet door. But he sat on, willing his breaths to stay even.

Such a frantic, impossible woman, so unstable, even in good moods, with her exultant voice and glittery eyes, her dangerous excitement. Why, why, why was she the one he had chosen to marry? When it could have been some sturdy, sweet Polish girl from the neighborhood, or one of those kind young women at the Red Cross canteen in Virginia! Why had he headed instead for somebody out of control?

She had no right to criticize his relationship with the children. He'd been so much closer to them than his father had been to him, and so much more involved in their lives! And as for the store, well, where did she think the money came from for their camps and music lessons and college tuition and trips? Oh, she never had appreciated how well he'd done with the business. First she'd badgered him into abandoning the old location, even though it provided them with a perfectly decent income. (And it *was* an abandonment. He'd known from the start that the buyer planned to turn the place into a liquor store.) Then she'd wanted a full-fledged supermarket, one of those fluorescent-lit monsters with aisles so long that you couldn't see to the end of them; but Michael had had the good sense to realize that what was lacking out here in the suburbs was a version of the old neighborhood grocery, small-scale and personal, with the emphasis on service. Clerks who greeted the customers by name and put their bills on the tab and offered cookies to their babies. Now he had a clientele that wouldn't dream of shopping elsewhere. But did Pauline give him credit for that? No, to this day she continued lobbying for expansion, and when he argued she would remind him that she'd been right about moving the business, after all. She would point out what had happened in the city—the crime and the decay and lately those dreadful race riots. "If not for me, you'd still be there, wouldn't you," she said. "Selling three half-pints of milk every day to three old ladies!"

Sometimes he felt they were more like brother and sister than husband and wife. This constant elbowing and competing, jockeying for position, glorying in I-told-you-so. Did other couples behave that way? They didn't seem to, at least from outside.

He believed that all of them, all those young marrieds of the war years, had started out in equal ignorance. He pictured them marching down a city street, as people had on the day he enlisted. Then two by two they fell away, having grown wise and seasoned and comfortable in their roles, until only he and Pauline remained, as inexperienced as ever—the last couple left in the amateurs' parade.

He closed his eyes and wished for someone to discuss this with. But who? He had lost touch with most of the men in the old neighborhood, who anyhow confined their talk to baseball and the weather. His social life these days was a matter of prearranged gatherings—cocktail parties and sit-down dinners here in Elmview Acres. In fact, he had no friends. Did he even like anyone? Did anyone like him? Could it be true that he was cold and remote?

Wait, though. The screen door twanged open and gently closed. Bare feet padded toward him across the flagstones. Michael felt a melting sense of relief. You could always say that Pauline was his friend. She was closer to him than his own skin; she was the one who had freed him from his stunted, smothering boyhood.

Except that this was somebody smaller, and shorter and lighter-weight. Somebody who made effortful sounds while pulling up a lawn chair; who had to struggle to climb into it. Michael opened his eyes. After a moment, he reached over and laid a hand on Pagan's hand, and the two of them sat gazing up at the night sky.

# 6. Killing the Frog by Degrees

On September 26, 1972, Michael and Pauline celebrated their thirtieth wedding anniversary with a small family dinner. It was a Tuesday—not the best night for a social event, as both George and Karen pointed out. But Pauline had strong feelings about observing the actual date. She liked the thought of announcing, "At this moment thirty years ago, your dad and I were just boarding the train to Washington for our honeymoon." She would have liked it even better if she could have said that this was the moment when the minister had pronounced them man and wife, but since they'd had an afternoon ceremony that wouldn't be possible. Neither one of her children was the type to take off work early. (George did something important with mergers, whatever mergers were. Karen was in her second year of law school.)

There were seven around the dinner table: Pauline and Michael at either end, Karen next to Pagan on the window side, and George and Sally on the buffet side with JoJo in a high chair between them. In Pauline's imagination, a noticeable space gaped where Lindy should have been, but she fancied she was the only one who saw it.

JoJo was the reason they were eating at six p.m. He was only twenty months old. He was a darling, chuckly, dimply boy, the light of Pauline's life, and she had flat-out refused to hear of his being left at home with a sitter. "If we don't include our grandchildren, what's the point of celebrating our marriage?" she asked when Sally apologized for JoJo's spoon-banging during the blessing. Then she reached over and gave her other grandchild a little squeeze. Pagan was also the light of her life, although now that he'd turned seven he was less tolerant of cuddling. He grinned but ducked away from her, intent on the slice of bread he was buttering.

The menu was a total bore. She'd fixed the same old standbys, roast beef and baked potatoes and iceberg-lettuce salad, with a chocolate cake for dessert. This was her concession to Michael. "For you, sweetheart," she said, raising her glass. "No experiments. Nothing gourmet. Not a mushroom or an anchovy or an artichoke to be seen. Everything plain and simple, just the way you like."

Michael stopped chewing long enough to raise his own glass and say, "Well, thank you, hon." The glasses had champagne in them, but that he didn't object to. You couldn't very well serve National Bo when a marriage had endured thirty years.

Michael's hair was iron-gray now and his face had grown lined and leathery, although he was as lean as ever. Pauline's hair was who-knew-what-color, probably pure white underneath the Miss Clairol blond. She'd kept a pretty good watch on the pounds, though, not counting the bit of a tummy that she didn't seem able to do anything about. Yes, all in all she thought they were still a very nice-looking couple. And she was proud of the picture they made as a group: everybody in Sunday best, neatly combed, scrubbed and shiny. Even Karen, who could get sort of straggly when she was absorbed in her studies, had made an effort tonight. She wore pants, as usual, but tailored ones, with a top that matched, and she'd exchanged her unbecoming glasses for the contact lenses that she always claimed made her eyes itch.

It was Karen who presented their gift. First she caught George's eye with a series of meaningful glances that her parents pretended not to notice, and then when George had excused himself and returned with a flat, tissue-wrapped rectangle she said, "Ahem! May I have your attention, please."

"Why! What's this?" Pauline cried, and Michael said, "Aw, hon, you-all didn't have to get us a present."

"Right," Karen said sarcastically, and everyone laughed, because a longtime family joke was how Pauline put so much stock in marking occasions with gifts. Pauline made a shooing gesture with one hand (people tended to exaggerate her character, she felt), and Karen went on. "Mom, Dad, this is from all of us. We wanted to give you something to remind you of these past thirty years." And she took the package from George and set it on Pauline's lap.

Clearly, it was some sort of framed picture. Pauline could tell that from the squared-off edges and the indentation at the center. She supposed they'd enlarged a wedding snapshot, or maybe commissioned a watercolor version of one. So it came as a surprise when she tore away the tissue to find, instead, two black-and-white ovals set side by side in ivory linen. The first was a photo of a very young Michael in a rough plaid jacket, squinting against the sun. The second showed Pauline, also young, laughing and holding on to her hat. Both pictures were familiar to her—Michael's from a shoe box of photos handed down from her mother-in-law, and her own from her sister Donna's wedding album—but they looked so different as ovals, outlined in gilt and matted, that it took her a second to place them. Even then, she didn't understand their relevance to her anniversary. "Isn't that nice!" Michael said when she turned it his way, and he spoke so bluffly that she knew he too was at a loss.

Sally was the one who explained. "It's you two just before you met," she said.

"Before we met?" Pauline asked.

"Donna's wedding was November eighth, 1941. And Michael's picture has somebody's handwriting on the back: 'Thanksgiving 1941 at Uncle Bron's.' So it was just weeks—days, really—before you walked into the grocery store."

"Is that a fact!" Michael said.

Pauline, though, was struck speechless. That those two photos should document, coincidentally, almost the very last moment of their lives as separate people . . . Oh, see what children they were, so innocent! Even the sunlight on Michael's face seemed innocent—watery and gentle—and the lilting curve of the feather on Pauline's hat.

"We didn't have the faintest idea," she said in a wondering tone.

"We didn't suspect a thing! There we were; nothing had happened yet. No Pearl Harbor, no war; we hadn't laid eyes on each other. Our children didn't exist. Our grandchildren weren't imaginable."

"Well! Happy anniversary!" George broke in.

"Remember when you plastered that bandage across my forehead?" Pauline asked Michael. "I thought you were so good-looking. I still think of that time whenever I smell adhesive tape."

"You wore your red coat," he said, "and when we went off to join the parade I lost sight of you for a moment but then I caught this flash of red, and it seemed like all the blood came rushing back into my veins."

"And those crazy quarrels we had," she said. "Once I jumped off a Ferris wheel because you'd gone to Katie Vilna's birthday party without me, remember?"

"While it was still moving!" Michael told the others. "When we were still at least four feet above the ground!"

"The attendant had a conniption," Pauline added, laughing.

"And the time I mailed all your letters back during special training," Michael said.

"And the time I got so mad at you for calling me a butterball when I was eight months pregnant."

"You set off for your parents' house in your nightgown, remember that?"

Then Michael stopped speaking, and Pauline, following his gaze, saw that none of the others seemed to share their amusement. Only Sally wore a smile—a slight, abstracted smile that she directed at JoJo while she fussed with his bib.

"Well. In any case," Michael said. "This was awfully nice of you kids."

"Yes, thank you," Pauline chimed in.

And all of the grown-ups stirred and sat straighter and reached for their champagne glasses.

"At this moment thirty years ago," Pauline said, "you and I were just checking into the President Lincoln Hotel in Washington, D.C."

She stepped out of her dress, gave it a shake, and slipped it onto a hanger. There was the teeniest little dot of pink powder on the collar, but if she covered it with a brooch of some kind she could wear it one more time before sending it to the cleaners.

"A bunch of soldiers and sailors were milling about in the lobby, remember?" she asked Michael. He was emptying his pockets onto the bureau, scrutinizing each note and receipt before he laid it aside, and he didn't answer. She went on, anyhow. "I sat down on a chair and waited for you to register for the two of us. I held on to my purse with my left hand so everyone could see that I was married."

She'd been so nervous that her mouth had felt as dry as flannel. She'd kept trying to recall the advice from the book her mother had given her, *A Young Woman's Guide to Matrimony.* "Relax," the book had told her. Ha! "Trust your husband to instruct you." From where she sat, Michael had looked tentative and awkward, the naked back of his neck as spindly as a schoolboy's.

"It's funny how something can seem so long-ago and yet so recent, both at once," she said. "Why, I can still see the row of nail heads tacked around the end of the chair arm! Brass, they were, and hammered, so that they had this kind of dented feel when I rubbed my fingers across them."

She gave him time to chime in if he wanted, but evidently he didn't. He dumped a handful of coins into the china saucer she had set there for that purpose.

"And then this soldier came over," she said, "a lieutenant colonel, as I recall. He said, 'Miss? Are you alone?' and I said, 'No, I'm waiting for my husband to check us in'—the very first time I'd ever said those words in public, 'my husband.' And all of a sudden there you were, standing in front of me fit to be tied. I never did convince you I hadn't been flirting! We rode up in the elevator with you in a sulk and me chat-chattering on so the bellboy wouldn't suspect."

"Yes," Michael said, "that sounds about right." At long last he turned to look at her. "Fighting on our wedding night, even."

"Oh, I wouldn't say fighting, exactly. It was more like a misunderstanding. And we patched things up in no time. Why, it turned out to be a lovely wedding night! Remember, sweetheart?" she asked, and she was glad now that she had stripped to her slip, the sexy one with the ribbon threading in and out of the bodice.

But he didn't appear to see it. "Jumping off Ferris wheels," he said. "Running away to your folks. Did you hear us tonight, Pauline? Did you hear what we were saying? All of our remember-whens were quarrels. I don't think I'd ever noticed before. Did you see our kids' expressions?"

"Not *all* of them were quarrels, Michael. Goodness!" Pauline said. (Meanwhile, she was rapidly reviewing the kids' expressions. It was disconcerting when Michael popped up with one of these uncharacteristically sharp-eyed observations.) "I was telling how you bandaged my forehead," she said. "You were telling about my red coat—"

"Hauling forth yet again the one and only peaceful moment the two of us ever experienced," he said.

"What?"

He didn't answer. His mouth was a straight line and his eyes had that dark, dense look they got sometimes when his hip ached.

She stepped closer to him and set a hand on his arm. "Oh, Michael," she said. "Why, that's just not true! We've had all kinds of good times! Times we were romantic, times we told each other our fears and worries, times we laughed. The comical things the children used to say when they were little—remember? Remember how Karen used to call club soda 'busy-water'? And the griefs we shared, all the troubles with Lindy, and how you were such a comfort to me when my mother's mind started going . . . So what if we fight a bit? I just think that proves we have a very *spirited* marriage, a marriage with a lot of energy and passion! I think it's been a *fun* kind of marriage!"

But he said, "It has not been fun."

She dropped her hand.

"It's been hell," he said.

She thought even as she was hearing the words that she was mishearing them. He couldn't be saying what she thought he was, could he? And not even in the heat of battle! In a perfectly reasonable voice!

"All this shouting and weeping and carrying on," he said. "Stalking off, slamming doors, kicking furniture, throwing my clothes out the window, locking me out of the house—"

"Why don't you leave, then," Pauline said.

He stopped speaking.

"If you're so miserable, leave! If I make you so unhappy. If your life is such a torment. Go! What are you waiting for?"

He looked at her a moment longer, and then he snatched his car keys from the bureau and turned on his heel and walked out.

So. Some anniversary night. Pauline took off her ribboned slip and rolled it into a tube shape to remind herself to launder it on Delicate in the morning. Her hands were a little shaky, she noticed. She felt weak and empty, as if she had gone too long without eating, and her heart was beating too high in her chest the way it sometimes did when she was afraid.

She took off her bra but not her underpants, and she put on a long-sleeved nightgown. (Any time she was anxious, she slept in her underpants and her most modest gown—a habit left over from girlhood.) She washed her face, brushed her teeth, removed her pearl button earrings and placed them in her jewelry box. She padded down the hall to Pagan's room to make sure his light was off, and then she returned to her own room and climbed into bed.

He would be back. No question of that! As soon as he had cooled off he'd come back, but she would be sound asleep without a care in the world. He'd rattle around, shutting a drawer too noisily, dropping his shoes too heavily to the floor. That was how he operated, not apologizing but just pointedly presenting himself, *Here I am,* waiting for her to make the first move. He could be aloof and uncommunicative for days, and she'd say, "Michael, please don't act like this!" and he'd say, "Act like what? I'm not acting any way." Lying through his teeth. He was not an honest man. He fought in a dishonest manner. He didn't have a tenth of her forthrightness.

Look at how he behaved with the children, for example. "Your mother says this," and "Your mother says that." "Your mother doesn't want you out so late." "Your mother wants you to phone us when you get there. You know how she frets." Always putting her in the role of the bad guy; it was never "*I* want such-and-such." He did that to this very day, with Pagan. As recently as tonight he'd asked, "Didn't Grandma say it was bedtime, Pagan?" And then he got to look so easygoing, so lenient, so let-it-be by comparison.

She switched off the lamp and lay flat, pulling just the top sheet over her. It was a warm, humid night, more like summer than fall, and through the open window she heard the chitter and buzz of insects in the shrubs. A car swished past out front, but it didn't slow or turn into the driveway.

And the way he called her "old lady" during those three months of every year when she was older than he was—thinking he was so witty although he knew, she had certainly told him often enough, that her age was a sensitive topic. "What?" he would ask, all injured bewilderment. "What did I say? I was only being funny. Can't you take a joke?" So she would look like the humorless one; he would look happy-go-lucky.

When the truth was that he was as dour as a judge, and as lacking in feeling.

After they lost track of Lindy in San Francisco that time, Pauline had wanted to hire a private detective to look for her. She'd heard of a man named Everjohn, recommended by a friend of a friend, and she proposed to Michael that they call for an appointment. But Michael had refused. Why bother, was how he had put it. "She knows where we live. She knows we have her son. Suppose this guy managed to find her, what then? Would he rope and tie her and carry her bodily back to Baltimore? She doesn't want to see us, Poll. So, okay. I don't want to see her, either."

Michael in a nutshell. Give up, as easy as that. Wash your hands. Never cared anyhow.

Once he'd told her, out of the blue, that he'd learned a new phrase from a customer: "killing the frog by degrees." "Guess where it comes from," he said.

"I don't even know what it means," Pauline said.

"It means doing something so gradually that nobody happens to

177

notice. Like reducing the size of a cereal box; that's what brought it up. 'The prices stay the same but the boxes get smaller and smaller,' this customer was saying. 'They're killing the frog by degrees.' I said, 'Excuse me?' Guess where it comes from."

"Where?"

"Seems if you put a frog in a kettle of cold water and light a slow flame underneath, the water heats up one degree at a time and the frog doesn't feel it happening. Finally it dies; never felt a thing."

"Why are you telling me this?" Pauline asked.

"Hmm?"

"What made you mention it?"

"Why, I just thought you'd be interested, hon."

"You meant something by it, didn't you."

"What?"

"You told me this for a reason, I know."

"I don't know what you're talking about!"

"You think *we're* being killed by degrees, don't you. Our marriage. And you're trying to claim that I'm the one who's doing it."

"Are you out of your mind?"

No, she was not out of her mind. She supposed it might sound that way to an uninformed observer, but she'd been married to Michael long enough so she knew what he was implying, all right. She could read him like a book. She knew.

Eventually she dropped off to sleep, although she was so keyed up that she hadn't thought she'd be able to. She woke with a start some time later and looked over at the clock: 3:15. It was pitch-dark and silent, the insects quiet, no traffic, and Michael's side of the bed was empty. Maybe he'd had an accident. Yes, he must have! She knew it with such certainty, all at once, that it seemed she had received some kind of telepathic transmission. How else to explain his absence? He would never spend the money for a hotel room. He didn't have any friends he could stay with. No, he'd driven into a ditch somewhere, befuddled with champagne and lack of sleep. And now he was bleeding to death underneath his car, and it was up to her to telephone the police. Except she was too embarrassed to phone. What would she say? "My husband walked out in a snit and I know he must have been in a wreck; I can feel it." "Sure, lady," they'd say. Besides which, she had the illogical sense that she'd used up her quota of calls to the police when Lindy left. "Hey, Sarge, it's that Mrs. Anton. Seems as how she's mislaid another loved one."

Michael had no right to put her in this position. No right at all. She willed herself to sleep again.


In the morning while she was fixing breakfast she had a sudden realization. He must have spent the night with one of the children. Wasn't that spiteful of him! He'd have told them she'd kicked him out of the house; they'd have felt sorry for him. Karen was the more likely possibility, because she had an apartment downtown, very convenient, just off the Jones Falls Expressway. Pauline stopped buttering toast and turned to eye the phone. Call Karen and ask? Or not. She could hear sounds from Pagan's room—the rat-a-tat of last night's baseball scores on his clock radio. If she did call, she should do it before he came into the kitchen. She considered for another moment, and then she picked up the receiver and dialed.

"Hello," Karen said.

"Hi, sweetie! Did I wake you?"

"No, no, I've been up for ages. I'm trying to finish a paper that's due first thing tomorrow."

"Well, I just wanted to thank you for making time for dinner in the middle of the week."

"Oh, that's okay."

"I know how busy you are."

"That's okay."

There was a pause.

"And thanks again for our gift," Pauline said. "What a wonderful idea!"

"That was all Sally's doing."

"Yes, I sort of figured. Sally's such a good organizer. But it was nice of you to chip in on it."

"You're very welcome," Karen said.

"So!" Pauline said. Pagan's radio grew louder, which meant he must have opened his door. "So, did Dad stop by your place last night?" she asked in a hurry.

"Dad? Stop by . . . here?"

"I guess not."

Pagan entered the kitchen, carrying his knapsack by the straps. "Why would he come here?" Karen asked.

"Oh, no reason, really!"

"I thought he was home with you."

"Yes, but we had this little . . . you know; something blown way, way out of proportion . . ."

Pagan dropped his knapsack to the floor with a thud, or more like a boom—what must it weigh?—and settled into his chair and looked over at her expectantly.

"What," Karen was saying, "you had a fight on your *anniversary?*"

"Well, not exactly a—"

But she didn't want to say the word "fight" in front of Pagan. "It was nothing, really," she said. "Heavens, look at the time! I should get Pagan to school."

"Are you saying Dad has gone off someplace?"

"Hmm? Oh. Well, he isn't here right at this moment, but—"

"Can I have Cheerios?" Pagan asked her.

"No, Pagan, I already made toast. Sorry, sweets, I have to go!"

"Wait," Karen said, but Pauline hung up.

"I'm tired of toast," Pagan said. "I had toast yesterday. Can't I have Cheerios?"

"Fine. Here," Pauline told him. She took the Cheerios box from the cupboard and set it down smartly in front of him. Then she reached for the phone again and dialed George.

"But where's a bowl? Where's milk?" Pagan asked, at the same time that Sally said "Hello?"

Drat. Oh, well. "Good morning, Sally!" Pauline said.

"Oh, hi, Pauline."

"Just wanted to thank you for coming last night and for that lovely, lovely picture!"

"I'm so glad you liked it. You don't think the gilt is too froufrou, do you?"

"The gilt. Oh, my, no! No, it's lovely, Sally."

"George said it should have been just a plain white mat. When I brought it home he said, 'Why the gilt edging?' I said, '*Now* you tell me. I asked you before I took it in; I said, "Do you have anything special in mind you want to do with this?" and you said you didn't know anything about such things; you'd leave it in my hands.' But if you'd like me to get it rematted, Pauline—"

"Goodness, no! I love the gilt! I think the gilt's the best thing about it!"

"Oh," Sally said. "Does that mean . . . Do you wish there'd been gilt on the frame as well?"

"Absolutely not," Pauline said firmly. "Both of us like it just the way it is. Michael expressly said so. He isn't here right this minute or I'm sure he'd want to tell you himself. Gosh, I'm not sure *where* he is! You haven't seen him, have you?"

"Seen . . . Michael? Wouldn't he be at work?"

"Well, I'll have him call you when he gets home so he can thank you in person."

"Oh, there's no need for . . . Was he supposed to be coming here? I don't understand."

"Not as far as I know, he wasn't," Pauline said. "Well, thanks again. Bye-bye!"

She hung up but went on standing at the phone a moment, pinching her lower lip between her thumb and index finger.

"Grandma," Pagan said, "I need a bowl for my Cheerios."

"Oh, for God's sake, Pagan, you're old enough by now to get your own bowl!" Pauline said.

But she reached for one anyhow, and slammed it onto the table so hard that Pagan blinked.

Driving back from Pagan's school, she passed by the grocery store. It was right on her way, almost. She just had to dip the eentsiest bit to the south to come upon it: a narrow, one-story brick building set between a pharmacy and a real estate office, with a long black signboard across the top reading ANTON'S FINE FOODS in gold italic letters. Tasteful plantings occupied so much of the gravel parking strip out front that Michael himself always parked in back, among the Dumpsters and trash cans; so she had no way of knowing whether he was there. She pulled into a space near the pharmacy, as far from the grocery as possible, and shut off her engine and sat a moment, debating. Then she made up her mind and got out of the car.

Funny how this new Anton's—so much airier and brighter than the old one—still had the same smells, more intimate somehow than the smells in a supermarket. But the shelves were lined with expensive foods nobody in St. Cassian's could have afforded, and there was a meat counter here and even a florist's department. Over by the produce section Pauline spotted Michael's manager, a pale, fat, damp-haired man who always wore a gold cross on a chain so tight that it seemed embedded in his neck. She walked up to him and said, "Morning, Bart! I guess he's in his office"—using an indulgent, wifely tone of voice.

"Yes, ma'am," Bart said. "Or somewheres nearabouts. I just saw him."

So there hadn't been any accident, any car overturned in the ditch. Her worries had been for nothing. She felt more angry than relieved. "Well, thanks," she told Bart. "I'll go track him down," and she set off toward the rear of the store, bypassing two young women in identical layered hairdos who were arranging a tennis date.

The office door, she saw, was open. Michael leaned against the door frame with his back to her, listening to what's-her-name, the girl who'd taken over the books when Mrs. Bird retired. Letitia, that was it. Letitia was skewed around in her chair asking Michael some question, and Michael was nodding slowly and deeply. There was no reason that he should have grown aware of Pauline's approach—she had a light step, she wore Keds—but he turned, all at once, as if he had somehow sensed her, and the look that came over his face was such a guilty, cornered look that she fancied, for an instant, that she'd interrupted a tryst. Then she understood that this was something worse, that he was sorry she had found him. (Had "tracked him down," to use her own phrase.) She couldn't have said how she knew this, but she knew it for a fact. He wasn't happy to see her. The knowledge slammed into her so cruelly that she took a sharp step backward, bumping into someone's grocery cart.

"Hi," Michael said, and Letitia said, "Oh, hi, Mrs. Anton," and gave her a cheerful wave and swiveled around to her adding machine.

Pauline said, "I was just wondering if you'd be home for supper tonight."

Michael glanced toward Letitia, and then he came forward, closer but still at some distance. Almost too softly to be heard, he said, "I don't think so, Pauline."

The way he added her name at the end was humiliating—so solicitous and concerned, as if he were trying to break bad news gently. She felt stung. She said, "Well, good!"

Some tension eased in his expression. She heard herself say, "Wonderful! Just wonderful! Just stay away forever!" Her voice was somebody else's, some wild, elated madwoman's voice. She spun around, bumping again into a grocery cart—maybe the same one—and rushed down the aisle, past the registers, out of the store to her car.

She told no one. She spent the day discarding things, straightening drawers, cleaning closets. Supper was thrown together from stray tins she had unearthed while reorganizing the kitchen, but only Pagan ate. Pauline herself just watched from her end of the table. "Where's Grandpa?" Pagan asked.

"At a meeting," she told him.

He seemed to accept this, although Michael had never been known to attend a meeting before.

After supper Pagan went downstairs to watch TV and Pauline settled on the living-room couch facing the picture window. Dusk fell as she sat there but she didn't switch on a lamp. She pleated the hem of her sweater between her fingers, over and over, and stared out at the trees growing steadily blacker behind the house across the street. From here the TV sounded like barking—*ruff-ruff-ruff*—cowboys shouting orders to each other above the gunshots. She knew she should go downstairs and check on Pagan, ask if he had any homework, offer to read him a book or play a board game, but she didn't.

When the headlights blazed into the driveway she felt her pulse take a leap. She thought of Michael's description the evening before: "seemed like all the blood came rushing back into my veins." She reached for a magazine and opened it, blindly, so that when he walked in she appeared to be reading in the dark. He flicked on the overhead light and stared at her. She squinted against the brightness.

"I came for my clothes," he told her.

"Oh."

"Also, I'd like to arrange about Pagan."

"Arrange . . . ?"

"I wouldn't just desert him. We should talk about when I can see him."

"Oh!" she said. "Well, go ahead! See him all you want! Keep him for good, if that's how you feel! I'll collect his belongings."

"Okay," Michael said, shrugging. "Fine."

"No, wait! No!" She stood up, clutching the magazine to her chest. "Oh, Michael," she said. "Why do we have to be this way?"

He gave it some thought before he answered. Then he said, "I don't know."

She saw that this was the literal truth. It was true for both of them. She sank back down on the couch, and he hesitated but turned, finally, and went off toward the rear of the house.

Every sound he made was identifiable. She didn't have to be present. The attic stairway sliding through the trap door in the hall ceiling; his uneven tread up and down, twice, with suitcases clumsily knocking against the wooden steps; and then the stairway sliding back. Drawers in the bedrooms opening and closing, hangers in the closet grating along the rod, medicine-cabinet door squeaking in the bathroom. Then he went down to the rec room. She heard his murmur beneath the cowboys' barks, but no response from Pagan. Probably Pagan's voice was too thin to carry. Another murmur; then a silence. Was that for a farewell hug? (Michael was far more demonstrative with his grandchildren than he'd ever been with his children.) Footsteps—heavier and slower—climbing the stairs again and approaching. When he reappeared in the living-room doorway he had a suitcase in his right hand, a smaller suitcase hanging by its strap from his left shoulder, and a garment bag folded over his left arm.

"I'd like to take Pagan on weekends," he said. "Pick him up Saturday mornings and bring him back Sunday evenings, if that's all right with you."

"Take him where?" she asked.

"I've rented an apartment in that new building across from the store."

Ridiculously, she spent several seconds trying to think which building he was talking about. She believed it might be a beige stucco.

"I'm moving in on Friday," he said. "Till then I'm at the Colts Road Hilton, if you need to get in touch with me."

"The Hilton!" she said. "What that must cost!"

"What's it to you what it costs?" he asked.

Which made her finally, finally understand that her husband truly had left her.

And over such a trivial issue, after all their years together! She couldn't even exactly *remember* the issue! Why that particular one? Why not any of the hundreds of others?

Once again Michael hesitated, but then he turned toward the foyer. She heard the front door latch, and a moment later his car lights lit up and backed out of the driveway. She went on staring straight ahead of her. She had a slippery, off-balance feeling, the feeling a person might get if she were sitting on a stopped train and the train next to hers started gliding away and she wasn't sure, for a second, whether it was her train or the other one that was moving.

Thursday passed, and Friday. Still she told no one, not even her sisters. Not even her girlfriends or her children. (Who didn't bother calling, anyhow. Too busy with their own lives, she supposed.) She was reminded of those first few days after Lindy left: best not to say the words. Saying the words made it real.

And her tendency to see Michael in every stranger—she'd experienced that with Lindy also. When you're looking for someone, she'd learned, you try to turn other people into the one you're looking for. You catch sight of a faraway figure and unconsciously you darken his hair or add six inches or subtract twenty pounds, all just wishful thinking. Just pathetic, wishful thinking.

She thought she saw him dropping a letter into the corner mailbox. Waiting to cross Beverly Drive where it intersected with Candlestick Lane. Talking to a woman outside the Almost Unique Beauty Salon. She felt the same combination of feelings that she'd felt when she'd imagined seeing Lindy: joy and anger, in equal parts. She *hated* him! But was flooded with disappointment when she found it was somebody else.

At home, the telephone seemed to swell with pent-up rings. The house seemed muffled in a cottony hush that she associated with houses belonging to lonely old ladies. She tried to stay away as much as possible, filling the day with errands till it was time to fetch Pagan from school. Never had she been so conscientious about those pesky little tasks like replacing the shower curtain, picking up sacks of mulch, hunting a square of tile to match the cracked piece above the stove. She went to the Safeway for supper ingredients—a revelation. (She was used to having Michael bring their groceries home from work with him. She had never realized how expensive food had become.)

Then at last she could go get Pagan. When they walked in the front door together, the house came blessedly alive again. "I'm hungry!" Pagan announced. "I'm thirsty!" And "Look what I made in art class! Can we frame it? Who ate the pretzels?"

Once or twice she tried to talk to him about Michael's absence. "So," she said Friday evening, "you know you're going to see Grandpa tomorrow."

"Mmhmm," he said, and got very busy rooting through the utensil drawer.

"You know Grandpa's taking a little vacation. Living on his own for a bit."

"Have you seen my long curly drinking straw?" he asked her.

"It's in the dishwasher. People do that, you know. Take vacations from each other. It doesn't mean that Grandpa doesn't love you."

"Like Beth Ann's daddy," he said.

"Beth Ann?"

"Beth Ann's daddy got a new mother."

"A new . . . oh. Well, Grandpa would never—"

"*Where* in the dishwasher? I don't see my straw anyplace!"

"Look in the top rack, Pagan," Pauline said. And she gave up.

He was a beautiful child—olive-skinned and black-olive-eyed, under a smooth, round, upside-down cup of black hair—and she loved him deeply. But there had always been something too self-contained about him, something veiled and shut off that she found frustrating. In a way, she would have preferred it if he'd fallen apart, sobbed in her arms, demanded reassurance.

Although of course it was nice that he was coping so well.

Michael telephoned that evening after Pagan had gone to bed. "How are you?" he asked politely.

"Very well, thanks. How are you?" Pauline said.

"I'm all right. I was wondering if I could come for Pagan around eight o'clock tomorrow."

"Eight will be fine," she said.

"Well, good. See you then," he said.

"Bye."

She replaced the receiver.

It occurred to her during the night that she had, in so many words, ordered Michael to leave. She had out-and-out, unequivocally demanded that he go.

Naturally he'd left! What choice did he have? Naturally he'd stayed away! This was all her fault. It was up to her to fix it.

She rose early Saturday morning and put on a blue scoop-necked dress that she'd bought on sale at Hecht's. But in the mirror it looked too new; it looked as if she were trying too hard. She changed into black slacks and a bright-red blouse. She combed her hair, applied her makeup, checked again in the mirror. The red blouse was a good idea.

Not only did it match her lipstick and bring out some pink in her cheeks; it was a reminder of that red coat she had worn on the day they met.

How many times, when she was weary of dealing with Michael, had she forced herself to recall the way he'd looked that first day? The slant of his fine cheekbones, the firming of his lips as he pressed the adhesive tape in place on her forehead. Really their problem was that they knew each other too well now. Going back to her original vision of him made her remember why she'd fallen in love with him.

She headed down the hall toward the kitchen, pausing outside Pagan's room to poke her head in and ask, "You up?"

"I'm up," he mumbled, from beneath a tangle of bedclothes.

"Come on, sweetie. Grandpa will be here in half an hour."

In the kitchen, she bustled around setting up the percolator, popping toast in the toaster, pouring Pagan's orange juice. "Pagan!" she called. "Breakfast!"

"I'm coming."

She went through the dining room to the foyer, where she opened the front door invitingly and plumped the cushions on the cobbler's bench. Passing back through the dining room, she caught sight of their anniversary gift propped on the buffet. She picked it up and returned to the foyer and set it on the table there, angling it toward the door so that anyone entering would see it. In the morning light the two photos seemed more faded. Also, the young Pauline appeared to have an edge to her that the young Michael did not. She seemed older than he, and harder.

"Grandma? Where'd you get to?" Pagan called from the kitchen.

"Just coming, Pagan," she said. But instead she went back to her bedroom. She took her hairbrush from the tray on her bureau and started brushing and tossing her hair until it fluffed around her face in a more youthful fashion.

"It's Saturday, Grandma! Saturday I have cocoa!"

"Oh, you're right. I'll make some."

But she was fumbling with her buttons now, flinging off her blouse and reaching for another—a pink-and-white rosebud print, softer, with ruffles.

By the time Michael arrived, seven and a half minutes later than he had promised, she was back in her red blouse (the rosebuds had been a mistake), stationed at the front door, smiling and opening the screen for him as he started up the walk.

"Hi," she told him.

"Hi."

"Pagan's just getting his things together."

"Okay," he said. He stepped inside. He was wearing a shirt that she hadn't seen on him in some time—a button-down blue oxford that made him look crisp and businesslike.

"Will he need a sleeping bag?" she asked.

"No, there's a guest bed."

"Your apartment comes furnished?"

"Well, in a manner of speaking," he said. "It's sort of rudimentary."

He wasn't meeting her eyes. He was looking everywhere else, jingling his keys, and she had to restrain herself from stepping purposefully into his line of vision.

"How about a cup of coffee while you're waiting?" she said.

"No, thanks. I thought we might go over the checkbook."

"The checkbook," she said.

"It's pretty straightforward, really. I mean, a bill comes; you pay it. Nothing you can't handle, I'm sure. But I've written a couple of checks that need to be recorded—deposit on the apartment, and such." He was reaching into his shirt pocket, bringing forth a slip of paper. "Here, I've noted them down."

She took the slip of paper but went on looking into his face.

"I opened a new account with Friday's paycheck, but that'll take a few days to clear," he said.

"I see."

"Any other subjects we need to discuss?"

She said, "I'm sorry I told you to leave."

After a pause, he said, "That's all right."

"I didn't really mean it. How could you think I meant it? It's just that you hurt my feelings. You talked like we'd never had a happy moment together. You can see why I would react that way."

There was something patient and forbearing about the way he

stood listening to her, not responding, the jingling of his keys finally stilled. It gave her a sense of defeat. She felt tears spring to her eyes, and she said, "We've been married thirty years, Michael. We've been through so much together! You can't just toss that away because of one little thing I said!"

"It wasn't what you said," he told her. "It was how I felt when you said it."

She waited.

"When you said 'Go,' I felt . . . freed," he said. "I thought, Why, yes, I could go, couldn't I? There's an idea! It came to me like the lifting of a burden."

"A burden," she said.

The tears had stopped, but her cheeks were still damp. Not that Michael appeared to notice. He was looking toward a point slightly to her left. Musingly, he said, "I don't know why I reached that conclusion at just this particular moment. In a way, it's sort of pointless now. I'm too old to begin all over again. But it seems like such a waste to go on being wretched together. Better late than never, as my mother used to say. No use throwing good money after bad, or good *years* after bad—"

"Well, I would certainly not want to be a *burden,*" Pauline said, treading hard on the last word.

Now he looked at her.

"Heaven forbid you should feel any sense of *responsibility,* or *duty,* or *obligation.* No, definitely you should go, Michael. I wouldn't dream of holding you back. Go! Go! Go!"

Pagan said, "Grandma?"

He was standing in the dining-room doorway, hugging an overstuffed duffle bag. Michael said, "Well, sir! How's my boy?"

"What's wrong with Grandma?"

"Nothing, son. Ready to hit the road?"

Pagan looked at Pauline. She made herself smile. "Bye, sweetie," she said.

When they'd left, she fumbled behind her for the cobbler's bench and lowered herself to a sitting position. Her knees were trembling visibly and her face felt overheated.

Over the weekend, she told everyone. The telephone was her lifeline, her only source of oxygen. It seemed that if she went two minutes without connecting to some other person, she grew short of breath and panicky. She started folding laundry but suddenly, unaccountably, found herself dialing her oldest sister on the bedroom extension. "I don't know what I'm going to do, Donna. How will I live? How will I get through the days? He's the center of my life!"

Donna said this would blow over. She said, "Pauline, I'm going to forget you ever mentioned this to me, because tomorrow morning the two of you will be right back the same as always."

"You think?" Pauline asked. She brightened, and after she'd hung up she went off to empty the dishwasher, forgetting about the laundry. But then it seemed she was dialing Katie Vilna on the phone in the kitchen, telling her story all over again.

Katie said, "Oh, Poll. Oh, how could he? Oh, what a rat! You two have been married forever!"

"Thirty years," Pauline said, wiping her eyes on her sleeve.

"Thirty years! Imagine! And to such a—well, I shouldn't say it, but he's always been so holier-than-thou. You know? So calm and cool and virtuous. A person had no hope of looking good, next to Michael! I don't know how you put up with it for so long. Why, the longest I stayed married myself was four years, that second time, with Harold, and I was just barely hanging on by my fingernails for the last three and a half."

"Well, but . . . *Harold,*" Pauline said. Harold and Michael were two entirely different species, she could have pointed out.

Wanda wanted to know what they had been fighting about. Pauline said, "Um . . ." Then she said, "What it was about had very little do with it. In fact, I can't honestly say. Isn't it peculiar how an argument will take off from nothing? Once, I remember, we got into this quarrel over whether it could actually be too cold to snow. Michael said that of course it could; if I ever paid proper attention I would realize that on a really cold night you never see snow falling. I said that was an old wives' tale. How else to explain all that snow at the North and South Poles, I asked. He said I didn't know what I was talking about. I said he had no right to sound so condescending. We practically came to blows, by the end. We didn't speak for days!"

"Mom used to say that marriages were like fruit trees," her middle sister told her. "Remember how she would say that? Those trees with different kinds of branches grafted onto the trunks. After a time they meld, they grow together, and it doesn't matter how crazy the mix is—peaches on an apple tree or cherries on a plum tree; still, if you tried to separate them you would cause a fatal wound."

"Why are you telling *me* this, Megan? Why don't you tell *him*? You think this separation is my idea? I had nothing to do with it! He's the one who walked out. He's got a whole new apartment! A fat lot he cares if he's caused a fatal wound!"

After she hung up, though, the grafted-fruit image stayed on in her mind. She did feel as if she'd been wounded. A raw space seemed to have opened in the hollow between her breasts.

And it struck her as appropriate to view her marriage as a tree. She imagined one of those gnarled, wizened, whiskery trees you see on windbeaten cliffs where there's not enough soil or water.

Mimi Drew said, "Excuse me for bringing this up, Pauline, but I can't help noticing that you're sort of . . . temperamental, shall we say. Sometimes people can find that a bit of a challenge. Maybe Michael just needs a little respite."

"Respite! And how about me? With a house to run and a grandchild to raise! Wouldn't I like a respite too?"

"Well, of course you would. I know that. Don't think I don't know that, Pauline."

Pauline slammed the kitchen phone down and returned to her room, planning to fling herself onto her bed, but there was the half-sorted laundry and so she resumed folding it. "What does *she* know?" she asked a pair of Pagan's jeans. "Mrs. Ideal Wife, with her don't-go-to-sleep-mad-at-each-other and her remember-to-pay-your-husband-one-compliment-per-day, which is all very well and good if your husband is pear-shaped, mouth-breathing, pink-eyed Bradley Drew who's dumb enough to believe anything you tell him."

Her daughter-in-law said, "I don't understand. He's living where?

How did he find an apartment so quickly? Do you know how long my brother and his wife have been looking for an affordable rental in that area?"

"No, and I don't care!" Pauline cried. "His real-estate transactions are the least of my worries!"

"Oh. Right. I'm sorry, Pauline; I was being insensitive. I just thought . . . You know, this is bound to be something temporary. It's not as if this is the first time you two have . . . Well, George is out running errands, but shall I come over and sit with you?"

"No, that's all right. Thanks anyway," Pauline said. She didn't want to be seen right now, all snotty-nosed and puffy-eyed, and especially not by her impeccably groomed daughter-in-law.

"I could bring little JoJo! Little JoJo would *love* to cheer up his granny!"

"Maybe later," Pauline said, and she got off the phone in a hurry.

All new parents thought their children were the only children in the universe, she reflected. They thought no others had ever been born; thought the world had been holding its breath all these centuries just for theirs.

Then Sally must have phoned Karen, who phoned Pauline five minutes later. Pauline had put off telling Karen because she figured Karen might take Michael's side in this, not that there really were any sides. Karen started right in with "Sally says you and Dad have had another of your fights."

"Not just *another* one, Karen. We've separated. The marriage is over."

Stating it so flatly made Pauline's tears start flowing again, although she had wanted to seem unperturbed. She made a snuffling noise, and Karen sighed and said, "Okay, Mom, have it your way," and then, with typical heartlessness, changed the subject. Went on to request Pauline's recipe for Crab Imperial. Pauline got the feeling that Karen was trying to impress some young man. "I'm scaling it down to serve two" was how she put it. She might have had the tact to avoid referring to romance in light of the current situation.

"Has your father not mentioned this himself?" Pauline asked. "Is he leaving you kids completely in the dark?"

"He hasn't mentioned it to *me*," Karen said. "He phoned about an hour ago wanting to know if I'd like to go to a movie with him and Pagan, but I assumed he was calling from home. So anyhow, if I don't have those special shells to bake this in, can I use a CorningWare casserole dish?"

Sherry phoned—Pauline's youngest sister, the baby of the family, who was unalterably convinced, therefore, that she was always left out of things. Her first words now were "I heard. I had to hear it from Megan. You told Donna; you told Megan; where was I in this?"

"Your line was busy," Pauline said, taking a chance.

"Oh. Okay. You know what the problem is," Sherry said. "None of us had brothers. We don't have any hope of understanding what men are up to. We never got an inside view of them."

"We had Daddy," Pauline pointed out.

Mentioning their father gave her a twinge of anxiety. She dreaded breaking the news to him. He had always preferred Michael to any of his other sons-in-law.

"But Daddy was off at work all day," Sherry said. "We didn't get a close-up look the way we would have with brothers."

"Maybe you're right," Pauline said. "I don't understand men in the least. I might not even like them. Can *you* tell me why Michael did this? And why now? Why not years and years ago, if he was so dissatisfied? Back when I was young and pretty and could have found someone else!"

"Also we had the handicap of our parents' happy marriage," Sherry said. "They made it look too easy. That wasn't doing us any favors, believe me! They gave us no preparation for how difficult marriage would be."

"Oh, Sherry, is your marriage difficult, too?"

"It's impossible! It's torture!"

"Come to think of it," Pauline said, "I'm amazed that I stuck it out even as long as I did."

"And now you don't have to anymore. You're lucky."

"I'm lucky," Pauline said, and she started laughing through her tears.

So when George phoned and said, "What's this I hear?" she had no trouble making light of it. "I'll be fine. Really," she told him. "I guess I must have sounded upset when I was talking to Sally, but I'm beginning to adjust now. It may be it's all for the best."

"You two are not serious, Mom. This is just one of your spats."

"It is not a spat. Your father has rented an apartment and opened his own bank account and he wants weekend custody of Pagan."

"Well, of all the absurd . . . I believe I'll have a word with him," George said.

"Oh, George, would you? Do you suppose you could do that? I know he thinks I told him to leave—well, I did tell him to leave, but it was only in the heat of the moment."

"One would expect him to realize as much, after thirty years of this," George said, in the heavy, elderly tone that always made her want to giggle.

It wasn't till after they'd said goodbye that she remembered Michael *had* realized. George wouldn't change Michael's mind in the least. And Michael would hate it that she had told everybody their troubles.

Now she thought she'd been wrong to picture their marriage as a tree. What it felt like, instead, was something spilled—something torn and bleeding and spilling out of its borders, like a sloppily fried egg.

On Sunday, she placed not a single phone call. She went to church, where Michael wouldn't ordinarily have accompanied her anyhow. She came home and had a tuna salad for lunch. Then she changed into slacks and worked in the yard a while, spreading mulch around the azaleas. Her next-door neighbor, Marnie Smith, waved as she got into her car and called, "How's it going?"

"Going fine," Pauline called back in a sprightly voice.

Next she made a clean sweep of the house. She filled a cardboard carton with all that Michael had failed to take with him—the clothes that had been in the laundry when he left, dribs and drabs from various closets, his sweatshirt, his snow boots, the slips of paper he had piled on his bureau that night. WHILE YOU WERE OUT . . . , these slips read, and *Admiral Poultry and Eggs,* and *lemons, peanut butter, ham steak* . . . His coins in the saucer she pocketed, feeling smug and gleeful as if she were getting away with something.

It wasn't a very big carton. Men's lives were more easily contained than women's lives, she was learning. Imagine what she'd have had to pack if she'd been the one to move out! She felt a pang of envy as she pictured Michael's apartment, with its "rudimentary" furnishings and a wardrobe that could be carried off in a single trip to the car.

Well. Enough of this.

She reminded herself of his failings. Of how, when she raised some perfectly reasonable objection—when he arrived home from work a full hour later than promised, for instance—he would say something patronizing like "You're just feeling irritable because you're on a diet; this is not about me." Of his tendency to nudge her along when they were dressing to go out but then disappear, off to the bathroom or some such, when finally she was ready. And the way he grew ostentatiously tranquil during fights—etherized, some might say—as if to point out her own "excitability," her "emotionalism," her need to "simmer down," all those terms he was so attached to.

The telephone rang and she raced to pick it up, but it was only Sarah Vine wanting to rearrange the schedule for the Shut-Ins' Shuttle. Pauline said, "Sure, I'm flexible." Later, though, after she'd said goodbye, she started wondering if she would have to forfeit her volunteer work now and find a paying job. What, exactly, was her financial situation? Would Michael still support her? Would he send her . . . oh, Lord, *alimony?* The word had a brittle, sophisticated sound that seemed completely unrelated to her life.

While she was gazing out the picture window she saw her father drive up. His shiny black Buick slid alongside the front curb and then turned into her driveway inch by inch, like a gigantic, unwieldy barge. He parked and got out and stood patting his suit pockets a minute before he fumbled the car door shut and started trudging up her walk. For some years now he'd been moving at this pace (he was over eighty, stooped and shrunken and arthritic), but she couldn't help imagining that she herself was the cause—that he was bowed down by disappointment at what she had let happen to her marriage. He must have heard the news from one of her sisters. He would never just drop in unannounced for no good reason.

But all he said when she opened the door was "Why, hello, hon," as if it were she who'd surprised *him*. He plodded past her, hands loose at his sides, heading toward the living room.

"What brings you here, Daddy?" she asked as she followed him. Might as well get this over with.

He settled himself in an armchair and adjusted the crease in his trousers. Then he looked up at her with his mild, blue, guileless eyes and said, "Oh, just thought I'd pay a call on my next-to-youngest daughter. Isn't that okay?"

"Of course," she said. "Would you like some coffee?"

"No, thanks. Lately I've been trying to cut back. Seems I haven't been sleeping well."

This she took as a reproach. She pretended not to catch his meaning. "Juice, then," she said. "Or a soft drink."

"I don't believe I care for anything just now."

Resigned, she sat down opposite him and waited for him to begin.

"Where's Pagan?" he said.

"He went to a movie with Michael."

"Oh? What are they seeing?"

"You know, I didn't think to ask," she told him.

Darned if she would be the first to broach the subject.

"I bet I didn't sleep two hours last night," her father told her.

"I'm sorry to hear that."

"The night before, maybe three. I can *get* to sleep all right but then I wake up again."

"Well, it's not as if *I'm* sleeping much," she snapped. A more understanding father, she reflected, would have offered support and sympathy.

"What do you do?" he asked her. "Do you get up or do you just lie there?"

"Well . . . I lie there."

"Me too. I lie there and then I start thinking."

"Oh, yes. Thinking," Pauline said with some bitterness.

"Thinking is the worst," he said.

She set her jaw. Here it came.

"I think of every little cross word I ever said to your mother. Every time I got aggravated when she would repeat herself or act confused."

"It is *stupid* to believe that people can make it through a whole marriage without any cross words," Pauline said too loudly.

He looked taken aback.

"What," she said, "you expect I'd be some kind of saint? There are other sides to these things, you know. People don't get mad if they haven't been provoked."

"Yes, but she couldn't help herself. It was the illness."

Pauline hesitated. "The illness," she said.

"You know: she would wander off like she did and I'd be so worried about her. The neighbors would bring her back and I'd say, 'Doris! Where have you been? What on earth possessed you?' and then I'd see her expression. She would be looking so ashamed, like a little child who'd been scolded, and her eyes would fill with tears and she'd say, 'I'm sorry, I'm sorry,' and I would feel just awful. It wasn't *her* fault. Or when I acted extra-patient. She'd ask me the same question fifteen times in a row and finally I would say, in this extra-patient voice, 'As I already told you, dear . . .' But of course that's not really patience; it's 'See how I'm holding my temper.' It's 'See how well I'm behaving.' I knew I was making her feel bad."

"You did the best you could," Pauline told him.

"Last night I was remembering once when she knocked over her milk," he said. "It had been a trying day and then I burned our supper and I had to fix it again from scratch. I got it all on the table, settled her in her chair, sat down myself, reached for my fork . . . and she knocked over her milk glass. Milk everywhere, on our plates and the table and her lap and the floor, and I clamped my mouth shut and went out to the kitchen for a rag and came back, heaving these sighs, and while I was sponging her skirt she reached out and touched my hair and said, 'You are such a honey.' "

He stopped speaking. He looked away, toward the window, and swallowed.

Pauline said, "Oh, Daddy."

"I worry I'll go to hell when I die," he said, almost too low to be heard.

"You would never go to hell!"

She sat forward in her seat, planning to rise and give him a hug, but some slight motion he made warned her off. He was still looking toward the window. He said, "I worry I'll get to heaven and your mother will say, 'You! What are *you* doing here, after you were so hard on me?'"

"That is never going to happen," Pauline said. "Never. I can promise. You know how it's going to go?"

"How?" he asked, but distantly, as if he were not much interested.

She said, "There you are, climbing the stairs to heaven, and you look up and you're surprised to see that the gates are already open and Mom is standing just inside waiting to greet you. She's not old and sick; she's the girl you first knew, and she'll be all excited. She'll be laughing and saying, 'You're here! You got here! Hurry up and come in!' You'll say, 'Don't I have to clear this with someone? Pass some kind of test?' and she'll say, 'Oh, my, no.' She'll say, 'You've already passed the hardest test there is,' and she'll take you by the hand and lead you through the gates. I promise."

Her father was looking at her directly now. He said, "You're a good woman, Pauline."

For that moment, she believed him.

She fixed him a Sunday supper of raisin oatmeal—a Barclay family tradition—and after they had eaten he left, still apparently unaware that anything in her household was amiss. She walked him out to his car and stood waving as he backed almost imperceptibly into the street. Then she returned to the house.

The carton containing Michael's belongings sat on the cobbler's bench in the foyer. Now it seemed inhospitable to have it so close to the door, implying that he should just grab it and go. She moved it into the living room. Then she went out to the kitchen and cleaned up, humming as she worked. She was doing all right, she realized. She watered the plants on the windowsill. She draped the dishcloth over the faucet and turned off the kitchen light.

When the doorbell rang, she was just starting toward the living room. Was there anyone as pigheaded as Michael? He had a perfectly good key in his pocket. He was merely making a point. She took her time crossing the foyer and opening the door.

But only Pagan stood there, hugging his duffle bag. "Guess what!" he said. "Grandpa's got a swimming pool!"

As he stepped inside, Pauline looked beyond him. Michael's car was already gliding away, no more than a colorless hulk in the dusk.

"You climb up these extra stairs to the roof and there is this full-sized pool with a diving board and everything," Pagan was saying. "If the weather's still warm next weekend, I'm going to bring my swimsuit."

She closed the door behind him.

"And there's a TV in my bedroom. Grandpa let me watch one program after I went to bed."

"That's nice," she said faintly.

"Have we got any ice cream?"

"Grandpa didn't give you a gallon all your own at his place?"

"Huh?"

"Sure, we have ice cream," she told him. "Don't make a mess, though, hear?"

He dropped his duffle bag on the floor and set off for the kitchen, but instead of going with him, Pauline went into the living room. She didn't turn on any lamps. She sat on the couch in the dark and pressed both hands to her cheeks and stared straight ahead.

Pictures passed through her mind, tiny but uncannily distinct. She saw Michael tugging on his plaid jacket the afternoon they met. She saw him shaving in the hotel bathroom the first morning of their marriage—that method he had of grabbing the tip of his nose and moving it aside while he was shaving the skin below it, which had made her laugh out loud. She saw him walking into her hospital room with flowers after Lindy was born, more flowers than she had ever seen and surely more than they could afford, a whole mountain of flowers that almost hid his shy, young, thin, eager face.

In her memory all these pictures were brightly sunlit, and they broke her heart. She didn't cry, though. For once, the tears wouldn't come. She saw that Michael might have been right. It really could be too cold to snow.

# 7. The World Won't End

Originally, the plan had been for Pagan to go to sleep-away camp. He was plenty old enough, after all—thirteen and a half, an eighth-grader come September. He enjoyed most sports and could very well have attended, say, the soccer camp in Virginia where the boy next door always went. But no, he suddenly announced that he wanted to learn guitar instead. And since there was no sleep-away guitar camp—or none that anybody in the neighborhood had heard of—it was decided that he should sign up for the summer music program at the Maestro School for the Arts on Falls Road.

This was where Michael came in. The summer program started at ten o'clock every morning, but Pauline had to be in the office at nine. (She worked part-time as a receptionist for a group of cardiologists.) She telephoned Michael and asked if he could help with transportation. "I can pick him up afternoons," she said, "but I'd need you to drive him there in the mornings. I would drop him off at your apartment on my way to work every day."

"Or the store, would be better," Michael told her. "I head over to the store around eight o'clock, generally."

"Okay, the store. Thanks," she said briskly. Then she got off the line.

Conversations with Pauline were like business dealings nowadays, very starchy and efficient. This was preferable to how it used to be, of course (the tears and recriminations, the clatter of slammed-down receiver), but it always left Michael feeling oddly rebuffed. He hung up himself but then stood there a moment, one hand still on the phone.

The summer program started on a Monday, which made things very easy. Pagan simply slept over at Michael's on Sunday night, instead of going home as he usually did at the end of the weekend. In the morning Michael went to work, and at nine-thirty he walked back across the street to the parking lot behind his apartment building. Pagan was already waiting there, lounging against the passenger side of the car and plucking tentative chords on his brand-new, shiny, hopeful-looking guitar. He'd had a sudden growth spurt over the winter. He slouched as if he were trying to return to his former height, a shock of thick black hair screening most of his face, and when he caught sight of Michael he seemed to have to untangle his limbs from each other before he could straighten. "What ho," he said—his new favorite greeting, picked up who-knows-where. His voice was in that in-between stage, grainy and unpredictable. He wore blue jeans and an oversized T-shirt, more holes than fabric. Michael hoped the Maestro School didn't have a dress code.

The car was already too hot for comfort, smelling of sunbaked vinyl; so they rode with both front windows open and the air conditioner blowing full blast. Michael had to shout to be heard. "You know where, exactly, this place is located?"

"Nope."

"Would I turn north on Falls Road, or south?"

Pagan shrugged and plinked out a guitar chord.

"Didn't you go there to check it out? Take a tour or something?"

"Nope."

"Well, how did you hear about it?"

"Some friend of Grandma's, I think."

Michael took a chance and turned north, heading past a cluster of worn stone buildings and then through leafy green woods.

Much sooner than he had expected, they passed a white sign lettered in crayon tones of red and blue and orange. THE MAESTRO SCHOOL FOR THE ARTS, it read. GRADES 9–12. EST. 1974. "Damn,"

Michael said, braking sharply. He took a left into a driveway, reversed, and cruised back toward the turnoff. It was no wonder he'd overlooked the place. All he could see was trees, no buildings whatsoever. But after several hundred feet of winding, rutted dirt driveway they came upon a huge old frame house with a placard reading MAESTRO SCHOOL! WELCOME! swinging from the porch eaves. Several cars and a pickup truck were parked in the packed-earth yard. A girl who seemed left over from the sixties sat in the porch swing piping on a flute. In spite of her studied pose—the curtain of straight blond hair cascading to one side, her filmy skirt flowing dramatically to the tips of her bare feet—Michael was affected by the sweet sound of her flute. When they had climbed the porch steps he refrained from asking her for directions, not wanting to interrupt the music. "We'll just see if we can find somebody in charge," he said to Pagan. He opened the screen door and stepped in, followed by Pagan, who carried his guitar between his thumb and two fingers.

In the front hall, dark and unfurnished, papered with cabbage roses and smelling of turpentine, they paused to take their bearings. A bearded man dressed all in black was leaning against the far wall whispering over a sheaf of papers. "Excuse me," Michael said, and the man looked up. He was wearing a gold ring in one ear—something that could still take Michael aback. "Can you tell us where the music students should report to?" Michael asked.

"Just down the hall. The big room at the end."

"Thanks."

Michael couldn't help glancing into doorways as they passed. He saw easels, a stack of two-by-fours, a little thicket of music stands. A woman in jogging shorts—another parent, he guessed—and a teen-aged girl stood talking with an old lady who wore a vibrantly patterned dress with a South American look to it.

He and Pagan seemed headed toward an assembly room of some sort, if the rows of folding chairs he glimpsed through the double doors were any indication. Just before they reached it, though, they passed a little room in which a piano was playing. The tune was gentle and measured, as delicate as a trickle of water, so that Michael found himself hushing his footsteps in order to catch each note as it fell precisely into place. He stopped, finally. Pagan kept walking. Through the door to his left Michael saw a woman sitting at an upright piano with her back held perfectly straight, not the slightest curve to it, and her hands placed absolutely level on the keys. He couldn't see her face; just her hair, smooth brown hair descending to her white collar where it turned under evenly all around in what he believed was called a pageboy.

"Pageboy." The word startled a memory out of him—a picture of a young woman pressing a handkerchief to Pauline's forehead—and he said, "Anna?"

She stopped playing and turned and then smiled, unsurprised. "Hello, Michael," she said.

"Anna, what are *you* doing here?"

She laughed. She let her hands drop away from the keys. He could see now that she was older, but she was one of those women who look basically the same as they age, adding only a faint line here, a gray hair there without changing in any fundamental way. "I'm the piano teacher," she said.

"Well, what a coincidence!"

"Not so much as all that," she said. "Who do you think told Pauline about our summer program?"

"She never mentioned it," Michael said. "Gosh, I . . . what a shock! I thought you lived in Colorado or someplace."

"Arizona," Anna said. "But I left there after my husband died."

"Oh. I'm sorry."

"And I'm sorry about your divorce," Anna said.

"Oh, that's okay. I mean . . . Well! It's good to see you!"

"You, too. I hope your grandson will like it here."

"I'm sure he will," Michael said. "So. Well. Okay, goodbye!"

She sat there smiling at him, her posture faultless, hands crossed palms-upward in her lap, while he waved and backed out of the room and stumbled down the hall to find Pagan.

Anna Grant. Well, she wouldn't be Grant anymore, of course. He didn't know the name of the man she'd married—had never even met him, and couldn't remember hearing of his death, although surely Pauline must have mentioned it. Pauline's friendship with Anna had dwindled into one of those distant, annual-Christmas-card arrangements, and whenever she said something like, "Oh! This is from Anna! Look at how big her daughter's grown!" Michael would just grunt and go on opening bills.

And yet . . .

And yet, in some part of his mind, Anna had always stood for the way things might have been if he had chosen differently. Not that he could literally have chosen Anna. She had never given him a glance; he scarcely knew her; they had exchanged maybe half a dozen sentences in their lives. But more than once during his marriage, on those occasions when Pauline had been at her most exasperating, Anna was the woman he had envisioned as her alternative. Anna would never smash a coffee cup in a temper! Anna wouldn't rip up his newspaper when she thought he wasn't listening to her! Or burst into tears in public, or spend his money on frippery, or wake him from a sound sleep to ask him if he loved her!

Sometimes he fantasized that at the very end of his life, he would be shown a sort of home movie of all the roads he had not taken and where they would have led. Suppose, for instance, he had listened to Sister Ursula in ninth-grade science class and decided to be a doctor. If somehow he'd found the money, won a college scholarship . . . and then the movie would show that during his second year of medical school he had volunteered for a drug experiment in order to help with expenses, and the experiment had backfired and he had died at twenty-four. Or had not volunteered, and gone on to discover a cure for cancer. Or had joined a medical mission to deepest Africa, where . . . Oh, all these forks, forking again and yet again!

Suppose that on that day in 1941 when the three girls brought Pauline into the store, he had fallen not for Pauline but for Anna. Suppose he had been smart enough, wise enough, to prefer the quieter, calmer, less exciting girl, and they had started an intelligent conversation about the war, the state of the world . . .

In which case, he might not even have enlisted. It was Pauline who had led him to enlist, with her patriotic enthusiasm that he now recalled as unbecoming fervor. Well, no doubt he would have been drafted anyhow, sooner or later. But he and Anna would have had a mature and considered courtship, and they would have married in a dignified ceremony and produced children who were . . . oh, more *related* to him, somehow.

He had laughed at himself for these notions. He had given a little huff of a laugh all alone in a room. But still, from time to time he had indulged in them.


Pagan began to practice a whole new style of speech. "Right on!" he would say, at every conceivable opportunity, and "Personally, no," or "Personally, yes."

"Would you like another ear of corn, Pagan?"

"Personally, no."

Michael gathered that this was the way people talked at the Maestro School. Also, "Some of us do; some of us don't." Or "Some of us are; some of us aren't."

"Will you be spending this Sunday night at my place, Pagan?"

"Some of us will; some of us won't."

"What is *that* supposed to mean?" Michael exploded.

Pagan just raised one eyebrow—another recent development.

And his clothes; oh, Lord. Leather sandals with no socks—for a boy!—and baggy drawstring pants without a front fly, for heaven's sake, and an influx of new T-shirts (though somehow they already looked old) advertising names like the Band and James Taylor. James Taylor was his hero. Pagan would sit on Michael's couch, not on the seat but on the back of it with his bare feet tucked between the cushions, and languidly strum a few chords and sing in a nasal drawl about him and his guitar always in the same mood, or don't let him be lonely tonight, or never been to Mexico but sure would like to go. He had a chrome-hinged black guitar case now (evidently it was considered gauche to carry an instrument naked, even if one's sole form of transportation was a Buick Regal sedan), and this too looked old, in spite of its staggering cost, because he had plastered it with bumper stickers and might even (Michael suspected) have given it a few purposeful kicks and scuffs. From the looks of it, you would think he'd spent decades hitching around the country playing for free drinks in seamy bars.

Anna said he had talent. She said that Mr. Britt, Pagan's teacher, had mentioned how quickly he caught on to things.

"Well, I don't know where he gets it from," Michael told her. "The Antons have never been musical."

They were sitting on the front porch at the school. Michael had noticed her in the porch swing as he drove up into the yard and he'd told Pagan, "Guess I'll go say hello to Mrs. Stuart"—referring to her in this formal style because both last week and the week before he had invented reasons to come inside when he dropped Pagan off, and he didn't want Pagan getting any ideas. "Why don't I meet this Mr. Britt of yours," he'd said to Pagan the first time, and "Let's have a look at your practice room" the second. On both occasions Anna had seemed pleased to see him, had greeted him graciously and appeared to have no trouble finding conversational topics. She'd inquired the first time about his old store, whether it still existed, and asked where he lived now and how he liked it and described her own living arrangements (a house just off Falls Road that she was renting with an option to buy). Their second encounter took place after she had learned that her daughter was coming for a visit, and that provided all kinds of material on the subject of children in general. "Of course, now, Lindy," Michael had said, "our oldest . . ." and he had paused, not certain how much Anna knew.

Anna had said, "It must be hard not to have any idea of her whereabouts."

"Yes," he'd said. "You never do get used to it. It seems you ought to, but you don't."

She had nodded but asked no questions. She wasn't a prying kind of person, he'd noticed.

Now Michael toed the porch swing back and forth as they watched the students arriving—long-haired teenagers wearing ragged shorts or those absurd drawstring pants, and the dancers (a separate species) all angles in their clingy black leggings that must have felt miserable in this heat. Anna herself wore what amounted to her uniform—a white cotton shirt, short-sleeved to show suntanned arms lightly dusted with freckles, and tailored slacks, gray today, and flat black oxfords. "Elizabeth gets here tomorrow," she was saying, "and it didn't occur to me till this morning that I'll have to plan some kind of meatless meals. She's a vegetarian."

"We had one of those for a while," Michael said. "Karen. Our youngest."

"Did Karen eat seafood?"

"Nope. But she ate dairy."

"Elizabeth eats seafood, at least. So it won't be all that difficult. In fact I may just pick up some crabmeat tonight if I have time after work."

"Why don't I bring you some," Michael said.

She hesitated.

"We've got great crabmeat at the store," he said. "Trucked in fresh every day. I could pack a pound in crushed ice and deliver it to your house."

"Well, that's awfully nice of you, but—"

"And then maybe you could invite me in for a drink."

She studied him for a moment—long enough so that he felt the need to backpedal. "I mean, not that you'd be *obliged* to," he said. "I would still bring you the crab even without the drink."

"I'd be delighted to give you a drink," she said, "but you'll have to let me pay for the crab."

"I couldn't possibly."

"Then I couldn't possibly accept it."

They looked at each other.

"How about this," Michael said. "I don't let you pay for the crab, but you would fix me dinner."

Her smile deepened; it seemed to be concealing laughter.

"What," he said.

"If I fix you dinner I'll have to go grocery-shopping first," she said. "So I might as well just pick up a pound of crabmeat while I'm there."

"No, wait!" he said. "Okay, I take it back. How about *two* drinks? No supper, but two drinks. Three?"

Both of them were laughing now. "Three drinks!" she said. "How would you drive home? All right, you bring the crab, I won't offer to pay, and I'll send out for Chinese."

"It's a deal," he said.

Behind them, the screen door opened and Pagan said, "You're still here!"

"Aren't you supposed to be in class?" Michael asked.

"Some of us are; some of us aren't," Pagan said, and he let the screen door fall shut again.

Anna lived on a tiny street a mile or so south of the school. Her house was a plain white clapboard, the narrow, tall, peaked, rectangular shape of the hotels in a Monopoly game, with a patchy front yard and overgrown shrubs. When Michael rang the doorbell she appeared immediately, looking somehow more put together—freshened up in some way—although she wore the same shirt and slacks he'd seen her in that morning. "Crab man!" he said, singing it out like a street arab, and he held up the plastic bag with its knobby, ice-filled bottom.

She took it from him and said, "Why, thank you," and then, peering down inside, "Jumbo lump! You didn't have to do that."

"None but the best for grown daughters," he said.

But what he really felt was, none but the best for Anna.

He followed her through a living room furnished with decent but elderly furniture and into the kind of kitchen he hadn't seen in years—an expanse of rubbed-down blue linoleum, a sink on porcelain legs, a round-cornered refrigerator, and a huge electric range that must have dated from the forties. A person could have roller-skated in that kitchen; it was so large and spare. "Nice," he told Anna, who was putting the crab away.

She must have thought he was joking, because she laughed. He said, "No, I mean it. Look at that counter! No mixer, no blender, no toaster . . ."

"I've moved around so much," she said, "I haven't had a chance to accumulate many belongings." She shut the refrigerator door and turned to face him. "What can I get you to drink?"

"A beer would be good, if you have it."

"Of course," she said, and she opened the fridge again. The beer she took out was imported, fancier than he was used to. He wondered if she kept it for herself or for someone else. Was there a man in her life? This past couple of weeks he had been picturing her alone, complete unto herself, but how likely would that be for a woman as attractive as Anna? She was pouring herself a sherry now, moving in a slow, fluid way that reminded him of the dance students at the Maestro School.

In the living room, they settled at either end of the couch and then she said, "Oh! I didn't ask if you wanted a glass."

"I'm just an old Polack, remember?" he said. "I drink my beer from the bottle."

He never referred to himself as a Polack. It must have been the influence of this house—its comfortable air of not trying too hard, not needing to try, taking its own gentility for granted. His mother's doilies and crucifixes and even Pauline's "modern" furniture seemed so earnest by comparison. He took a sip of the beer, which had a denser taste than his usual brand. "Where is it you've moved around to?" he asked. "Just Baltimore? Or all over."

"Mostly out west," she told him. "When Paul died Elizabeth was only ten, and I knew I'd have to get a job, so I went to Idaho where my in-laws lived. Then I taught at a school in Cleveland until it closed, and then in Albuquerque. And now here I am! I feel lucky. Faculty positions in music aren't easy to find."

Michael cleared his throat. He said, "Was your husband's death very sudden?"

"No, he had leukemia."

This answered Michael's question, all right, but now he realized it wasn't what he'd wanted to know. What he'd meant was, had she loved her husband? Did she still miss him? He cleared his throat again and drew a line through the dew on his beer bottle.

"We met during the war," she told him. "I guess shortly after you and Pauline got married. I remember you two couldn't come to the wedding because Pauline was too pregnant to travel."

"Oh, right," Michael said, although he had no recollection of that.

"Are you and Pauline still close, at all?"

The question was so like the question he'd wished he could ask her that he felt a little flicker of hope. He sat forward and collected his thoughts. "No, we're not," he told her. "Of course, we're in touch. We have to be. We have our children and their various, you know, events; not to mention Pagan. But I look at her sometimes and I think, Imagine! Once this woman and I were married. It seems so odd, as if . . . oh, as if I'd been another person back then. I'd been this distant acquaintance I'd heard of who married a woman named Pauline a long, long time ago."

What he was saying was the truth, as accurate as he could deliver. So why, all at once, did another thought occur to him? He thought of a day last spring when he had dropped by Pauline's office—something about a check or a signature that she'd needed in a hurry. There she'd been, behind her little window in the waiting room, conversing cozily with two other receptionists as she sorted a stack of folders. "If that is not just like you!" she'd been saying, with a chuckle beneath her words, and in the instant before she'd raised her head and caught sight of him, he had had time to wonder how it could be that he'd once felt that he would suffocate if he couldn't get away from this woman. She wasn't evil, after all. She hadn't cheated on him, abused their children, drunk too much or gambled. In fact she was better than he was, in some ways—kinder and more open, the one who had friends. Had their troubles been solely *his* troubles?

As if she had read his mind, Anna said, "I always did admire Pauline."

He considered that word, "admire," reflecting on its possible undertones.

She said, "I didn't actually know her that well, though we went to the same high school. She belonged to a different crowd. But I liked her peppy spirit, and she never snubbed the rest of us the way some in her group did."

"You were with her the day she and I met, though," Michael reminded her.

"Oh, yes, on account of Pearl Harbor. Wasn't that a time? We were all in it together, seems like; all caught up in it. What we didn't know yet! I lost my brother in that war."

"I'm sorry," Michael said. "I don't think I ever heard that."

She gazed down into her sherry glass. Her face was a series of ovals, Michael noticed—an oval itself containing long brown oval eyes and an oval mouth without that central notch in the upper lip that most people had; and then there was the smooth oval of her head with the hair turned under so neatly all around. He had never before considered what a restful shape an oval was.

Anna said, "Pauline, and Wanda Bryk, and . . . who was the other girl that day?"

"Katie Vilna."

"Katie. Yes. She and Wanda stopped to help after Pauline cut her forehead."

"They're still around," Michael told her. "I think Pauline still gets together with them every so often."

"And how about you?" Anna asked.

"Me?"

"Do you keep up with your old neighbors?"

"Oh, not so much. I see something of my friend Leo, and from time to time I check on Mrs. Serge, who used to live next door to us. I'm not really very sociable, though."

"Me neither," Anna said.

"You're not?"

"You're my first guest since I've moved here."

"Is that a fact," he said. He glanced around the room. He thought now he should have paid it some compliment. "You've done a fine job settling in," he said. "I've lived in my place six years and I don't even have any pictures up."

"Do you not want any pictures?"

"Oh, yes. It's just that I don't know what I would hang."

She tilted her head and looked at him, and he felt he could guess what she was thinking. She was thinking that *she* would know what to hang. Pauline, in the same situation, would have stated as much; Pauline was always so sure that she could set other people's lives straight. But Anna kept her own counsel. It was Michael who said, finally, "Maybe you could advise me?"

"Well," she said. "Maybe."

And then, a moment later, "I'm not sure if it would work, though."

She probably had no idea why he smiled at her so warmly.


The next Saturday afternoon, when her daughter's visit was over, Anna came to Michael's apartment and they walked through it together counting up the number of walls in need of pictures. Then they went to a shop in Towson that sold inexpensive framed reproductions. Pagan went too, since this was one of the days he stayed at Michael's. He didn't seem to find it odd that a member of the Maestro music faculty was helping his grandfather buy artwork. Anna said, "What about you, Pagan? What would you like in your bedroom?"

He said, "A James Taylor poster? I just saw a super one at the record store in the mall. You think I could get it, Grandpa?"

"I don't know why not," Michael said.

He wished he were so clear himself about what he wanted. He was afraid of looking ignorant, choosing something lower-class. He kept glancing toward Anna as he considered different pictures, but she just gazed back at him with a receptive, neutral expression that offered him no clue. "Why don't you choose?" he asked her finally. "I don't know what I like. I don't have any opinions."

"There's no need to make up your mind this very afternoon," she said. "We're not in any hurry."

When he opened the door for her as they left the shop, he set a hand lightly on her back where her shirt was tucked into her slacks. And later, as they were pulling into his parking lot, he asked if she would like to come up for a drink. But she said no, thanks, she had errands to run.


Monday afternoon, he returned to the shop alone and looked through the pictures all over again. A ruddy, pink-haired woman who hadn't been there on Saturday was standing behind the counter, and he asked her, "Which is the best of these? To put up over a couch, for instance. This one? This?"

"The Chagall is nice," she said.

He followed her gaze and saw that it *was* nice—whimsical and dreamy, with people floating across the sky in an unsurprised manner. He bought it, along with van Gogh's sunflowers and another van Gogh of a bedroom, and an antique French liqueur ad and a Grant Wood landscape that he chose on his own because he liked the peaceful effect of the lollipop-shaped trees dotting the green hills. As soon as he got home he hung his purchases—more of a job than he'd anticipated—and then, still sweating from his labors, he telephoned Anna and invited her to come see them the following evening. "I know it's a school night," he said. (He knew very well. It was a night when Pagan wouldn't be present.) "But I could make you supper so you wouldn't have to cook after work. An extremely early supper, I promise."

"That would be lovely," she said.

The next day he left the store in mid-afternoon, laden down with groceries. He came home and roasted a chicken, boiled some potatoes, and put together a salad. It was the simplest of menus (the salad dressing was bottled; the dessert was a cake from the bakery counter), but it seemed that he made every possible mistake, and by the time he'd finished his preparations the kitchen was a wreck. Pauline, he knew, could have produced the same meal without even thinking about it. No doubt most women could. He sent a helpless look toward the pile of soiled pans in the sink, and then he went off to shower and shave.

His couch (the landlord's couch) was upholstered in beige vinyl. His coffee table (also the landlord's) had some sort of wood-grained Formica surface. He should have bought furniture, too. He should have bought rugs to hide the beige wall-to-wall carpet, and clocks and vases and thingamajigs to give the place some character.

This was all too much for him. Too much. He sank onto the couch, making sure to adjust the creases in his carefully "casual" khakis, and tipped his head back and gazed despairingly at the ceiling. A single long thread of a cobweb hung almost down to his nose. What a ridiculous idea to have invited Anna here!

But he would have to say that it had been years since he had felt the way he had these past few days—so alive and energized. Anna was his first thought every morning and his last thought every night. Even in his sleep she seemed to drift across the dark background of his mind, radiating a soft, warm glow and a sense of quiet contentment. In fact, had he *ever* felt this way? Even in his youth? Maybe he had forgotten, but it seemed to him that all of this was new. His life was just beginning, and the heavy summer air felt rich with promise.

If it turned out she didn't love him back, he would still treasure the knowledge that he was capable of such feelings.

She arrived exactly on time, wearing a plum-colored skirt instead of slacks, which made him happy because it implied that she viewed their supper as an event. With her she had a bottle of wine and a round, crusty loaf of bread. "Did you bake the bread yourself?" he asked as he took it from her, but she laughed and said, "Goodness, no. It came from a little place on Falls Road." Then she glanced toward the picture above the couch. "So you bought the Chagall!" she said. "It looks perfect there. And I like how the sunflower print picks up the yellow in your curtains."

"Let me show you the others," he said.

He led her through the dining alcove (the French liqueur ad) and into his bedroom (the second van Gogh and the landscape). "Do you think the landscape is corny?" he asked. "I know it's not . . . abstract or anything."

"No, no, it's an excellent choice."

She sounded as if she meant it. And she gave no sign she had noticed that his bed lacked a bedspread, or that his bureau held no knickknacks except a mayonnaise jar full of pennies.

In the living room he offered her sherry, bought especially for the occasion, and he poured one for himself even though he'd never liked the way sherry clung to his tongue. He settled in the armchair at some distance from her; he didn't want to look pushy. Because there wasn't a table anywhere near his chair he kept hold of his glass, rotating it between his palms as he sat hunched forward with his elbows on his knees. Anna, the picture of poise, occupied the very center of the couch, her own glass placed thoughtfully on a folded paper napkin just as if the coffee table were made of actual wood.

"I ran into Pauline this afternoon when she came to pick up Pagan," she told him. "She says he's begging to transfer to the Maestro School full-time as soon as he reaches ninth grade."

"He's been talking to me about that, too," Michael said. "But . . . well, no offense to the Maestro School, but would he get an education there?"

"Oh, they have English and math and all that during the year," Anna said.

"And then, you know, music is not exactly a profession," Michael said. "For a boy, I mean. I mean, guitar music. Well, unless you're some kind of genius or something. I mean, I realize music has worked for *you*, but . . ."

He seemed to be digging himself into a hole. "So, anyhow," he said, "did you happen to tell Pauline you'd be seeing me tonight?"

"No," Anna said, "it didn't come up." Then she flushed and said, "Also, I wasn't sure whether or not she would mind."

For the first time, it occurred to Michael that maybe Anna too was considering the possibility that they might become more than friends. Maybe this was not just his lone, self-deluding fantasy. She was looking at him steadily, her cheeks still pink, her chin raised in an attitude that struck him as almost defiant. It was his turn to be flustered. "Oops!" he said. "Dinner!" And he lunged to his feet as urgently as if he had something in the oven, although he didn't.

His kitchen was a mere strip of appliances in plain view of the living room; so he had no excuse not to continue their conversation. Luckily, though, Anna took over, asking him easy questions from her seat on the couch. Was cooking a hobby of his? Did he cook for himself every night? Did he ever go to restaurants?

"I'm a terrible cook," Michael said. "The only way I managed this meal was to start at four p.m. so that I could get a handle on things.

Or try to get a handle. I do eat in, mostly, but I just have a peanut-butter sandwich or tuna straight from the can. I don't go to restaurants much because I feel like such a fool sitting all alone at a table."

He set the bowl of potatoes on the counter that divided the kitchen from the living room. Then he looked across at Anna and gathered all his courage and said, "I might start eating in restaurants if you would come with me, though."

She still had her chin raised in that forthright way, and she said, "I would like very much to come with you."

And that was how it began.


They went to Martick's, and Marconi, and a place down on St. Paul Street that made good soups. The place on St. Paul became their favorite and they always tried to get the same table there, a little round one near the window; and if one of them ordered the gizzard soup the other had to order it too because it had so much garlic. They were kissing each other good night now—just tentative, cautious, restrained kisses as of yet—so garlic was an issue.

They went to movies and held hands; her hand was muscular and solid, no doubt from piano playing. Her hair smelled like butterscotch. At suspenseful moments during movies she had a habit of not breathing, and Michael always found himself not breathing either, in sympathy.

They went to concerts, but holding hands there seemed inappropriate because Anna was so focused and entranced. Michael would send her sidelong glances to find out when to applaud. A kind of veil would clear from her eyes when a piece was truly finished, and then she leaned forward and clapped generously.

They ate sometimes at his place (ready-to-eat foods from his store, cold cuts and salads picked up at the deli counter) and sometimes at hers (take-out Chinese or pizza). She wasn't much of a cook. She lacked the most basic equipment—a sieve or a set of measuring cups—and showed no interest in acquiring any. This struck Michael as refreshing. He was impressed as well by her self-sufficiency. If they had a date nearer his place than hers, she would suggest meeting him there rather than expecting a ride, or she might even offer to pick him up. She never rang his doorbell empty-handed; she always brought wine or flowers. She never telephoned him at work even though he wanted her to. And there was something noticeably adult in her dealings with her daughter. No scenes or sulks or silent treatments, or none that she mentioned; just a cheerful, courteous, mutually respectful relationship.

She made no fuss about being alone—spending an evening alone or attending some event alone—and she capably arranged for her tire rotation and her washing-machine repair and the removal of raccoons from her attic. To Michael (who was still taking Pauline's Chevy in every three thousand miles for its oil change) this seemed remarkable. To Anna it was hardly worth notice.

Unlike most dating couples, they saw more of each other on weekdays than on weekends. Pagan was there on weekends and Michael felt uncomfortable about combining the two parts of his life. Gradually, though, as June gave way to July and July to August, he became so accustomed to having Anna with him—so dependent, really—that he began inviting her to various activities on Saturdays and Sundays. She went out with them for burgers or ice cream; she swam with them in the rooftop pool, wearing a dignified one-piece black knit swimsuit that somehow managed to be the most alluring piece of clothing Michael had ever laid eyes on. The tops of her breasts were tanned and freckled like her arms, but they paled where they met the cloth and he had the impression of moon-white, cucumber-cool globes. The slight swelling of her thighs where they emerged from the legs of her suit cried out for the touch of his fingers, and it was all that he could do to look away toward Pagan's back flip.

And had Pagan mentioned Anna to Pauline? Well, he must have. Her name would have had to come up, at some point. ("When me and Grandpa went to Anna's house for lunch . . .") But Pauline said nothing about it, and Michael saw her often enough so she had plenty of opportunities. Maybe she knew and didn't care. Maybe she was glad for him, even. For once, perhaps, she was being a grown-up.

Anna said she'd had no more than the briefest contact with Pauline—the chitchat mere acquaintances exchange when they meet in passing. "After I first moved back we talked about getting together," she said. "She phoned me about the Maestro School; Belle Adams from our old church had given her my number. We said we'd have to have lunch, but you know how those things go. And now it's just as well, because I think it might be awkward."

*Might?* She didn't know the half of it. She seemed to assume that everyone was as sensible as she was.

Once when they were driving on I-83, Michael started telling her about an accident he had had at that very spot. His brakes had failed and he had slammed into a laundry van. "The funny thing was, this thought popped up when I realized what was happening," he'd said. "No control at all, the pedal sliding clear to the floor without the slightest effect; and what occurred to me was, Whee! Not that I said it aloud, or even had time to. But, Whee! I thought. I'm crashing! Splat! All hell is about to break loose! And this enormous sense of relief rushed through me."

"Relief!" Anna said. "Do you mean you were wishing to die?"

"No, no . . ."

"Was this when you were depressed in some way?"

"No, not in the least. I just—"

He felt an unexpected prick of impatience, and he made himself take a deep breath. "I just enjoyed an instant of not . . . having to be responsible," he said.

Anna said, "Goodness."

He saw that there was no hope of making her understand.

Although didn't that prove her virtue? She was purely a woman of reason. She was everything he had longed for when he was married to Pauline. It was miraculous that he had been given this second chance.

The Maestro School announced a program for parents on the last Friday evening of the summer session. There would be a string quartet, a piano solo, a dance from *Giselle,* a reading from *Troilus and Cressida . . .* and a girl singing "Wayfaring Stranger" accompanied by Pagan's guitar.

Pagan groused about the choice of songs—couldn't it be something the whole world hadn't done to death?—and he said the singer had a whiny voice. But obviously this was an honor. (The only other guitar student was relegated to a ragtag group playing background music for *Troilus and Cressida*.) He spent the weekend before the concert practicing almost nonstop, sitting in a C shape on Michael's couch with his head bent so low that his face was completely hidden. "I'm going *the-ere* . . ." he sang, breaking on the high note. Michael got the tune stuck in his head, and during the week that followed he seemed to hear it, forlorn and wistful, while he was reading over invoices or fielding a call from a customer.

Every one of the Antons planned to attend—not just Michael and Pauline but George and Sally and their two little ones, and Karen if she didn't have to work late. Knowing this made Michael nervous. It would be the first time his family saw him and Anna as a couple. But he did *want* them to see; he wanted them to know that she was important to him. So when Anna asked if he preferred that she come in a separate car, he said, "Absolutely not. I'll pick you up at seven." And when they arrived at the school, nearly half an hour early, he led her to the very front row of folding chairs.

The assembly room must once have been a parlor. The tiny plywood stage had a tacked-on look, and the few spotlights were clamped precariously to a mahogany picture rail. Around the perimeter, students' paintings were propped on easels—version after version of the woods behind the school, as well as several still lifes of summer squash and cantaloupes.

Anna was telling Michael about the student who would be playing the piano solo—how petrified he was, how he had forbidden his family to attend, how yesterday he had threatened to back out. She was wearing a dressy black dress and heels. It was nice of her, Michael thought, to have made the effort.

Others began filing in—parents, grandparents, small children. A girl in a leotard peeked out of the door at stage left. A woman in a muumuu rushed past with an armload of binders.

Then Pauline said, "Oh, here you are!"

She stopped in front of Michael, with Karen just behind her. She wore a white blouse and a flowered skirt, her hair was freshly tinted and styled, and her bright red lipstick matched her red button earrings. Karen, on the other hand, was her usual frumpy self in faded jeans and a Greenpeace T-shirt. She waited stolidly, her round, bespectacled face resigned, while Pauline prattled on. "All I can say is, I'm glad tonight finally got here. One more chorus of 'Wayfaring Stranger' thrum-thrum-thrumming away and I swore I'd—hello, Anna! I didn't see you! Karen, did you ever meet my friend Anna Grant, I mean Stuart? I've been meaning to call and thank you, Anna. The Maestro School has been—"

She broke off. She turned from Anna back to Michael. Her eyes grew wide and startled.

What had she seen, though? They certainly weren't holding hands or anything like that. They weren't sitting unusually close; their shoulders weren't even touching. But all at once Pauline got a slapped look, and her mouth snapped shut, and she wheeled away—flung herself away, so that her purse flew out on its strap—and plunged toward the rear of the room. Karen said "Mom?" and sent Michael a dumbfounded glance before she followed.

Anna raised her eyebrows at Michael, but just then the muumuu woman caroled, "Welcome, all!" in a joyous, ringing voice from the stage, and the two of them had to face forward. Michael didn't hear what the woman said after that. He was conscious only of Pauline watching him from somewhere in the rows behind. He felt his neck was turning to wood from the strain of sitting motionless, neither leaning toward Anna nor drawing away from her, keeping his eyes front and center.

The program passed in a blur of white-stockinged limbs and toe shoes, squeaky clarinets, young boys in pasted-on beards, and, yes, somewhere among all these, Pagan's black bowl of hair bent over his guitar and his nimble fingers plucking chords without a mishap while a girl sang "Wayfaring Stranger" in a voice that wasn't whiny in the least. But all Michael thought of was restraining himself from swiveling around to search for Pauline in the audience.

Anyhow, he wouldn't have found her.

She'd gone straight home, evidently. Or straight *somewhere*, clear out of the building, because when the muumuu woman returned to the stage, applauding with just her fingertips, and announced that refreshments would be served in the solarium, Pauline was nowhere to be seen. Neither was Karen. The only Antons were George and Sally, seated at the rear in case one of their children caused a disturbance. JoJo clung to Sally's arm, and Samantha was asleep in her lap. "Good job, kiddo!" George said, rising to give Pagan's hair a tousle, and then he asked Michael, "Where's Mom?"

"Wasn't she sitting with you?"

"Haven't seen a sign of her."

"Well, she . . . must have left early, I guess," Michael said. "Karen must have driven her home." He let a suitable interval pass and then he said, "George, Sally, I'd like to introduce Anna Stuart."

"How do, Anna," George said pleasantly.

But it was Sally who truly looked at Anna, and then looked back at Michael before saying, "It's good to meet you."

"I believe George and I met once before," Anna said. "But that was thirty-some years ago; so I'm not surprised he's forgotten."

"Oh, you're a friend of the family?" Sally asked her.

"From *long* ago. I went to high school with Pauline."

Michael could see that Sally was trying to puzzle this out, but she asked no further questions.

Of course they couldn't skip the refreshments. And of course they had to thank Mr. Britt, and smile through a dozen compliments from various parents and then try to figure out *whose* parents so the compliments could be repaid. Michael's face started aching. He wondered if there was any end to this.

But finally they were free to go. He and Anna and Pagan stepped out into the blessedly quiet night and located Michael's car. It was far enough from downtown so that stars shone by the thousands. Michael wished he could bring Anna home with him. But since it was a Friday, he would have to deliver her to her door and then take Pagan on back to the apartment.

Pagan was unusually talkative, no doubt from relief. He asked

Anna, "Could you tell that I was nervous when I started?" and "Did you notice I came in a little late on the second chorus?"

"You did wonderfully," Anna told him. "It was a really fine performance."

Michael drove in silence through the blackness of Falls Road. He'd been an idiot to imagine that Pauline would have known and said nothing.


Now all at once it seemed *everyone* knew; everyone had an opinion. Wanda Lipska asked why he kept falling for Protestants, and Karen said the least he could have done was give Pauline a little warning, and Pagan (all at once aware of the implications, evidently) grew tongue-tied and evasive every time Anna showed up at Michael's apartment. George volunteered that Anna seemed like an okay lady, but Pauline's sister Sherry called her a Jezebel. "It's an accepted fact that friends don't steal friends' husbands," she said. Sally wondered if Michael might like to bring Anna to dinner sometime, though not of course when the children were awake in case they told Pauline; so maybe they ought to just go to a restaurant instead. Leo Kazmerow said he was glad as hell to hear Michael had stopped living like a monk. Then the staff at the store got wind of things—how, Michael couldn't say—and traded conspiratorial smiles whenever he left work early, inquired slyly about his weekend, asked who'd picked out that new shirt for him.

But what was there to know, really? He and Anna had not discussed their feelings for each other. They certainly weren't sleeping together—nowhere near it. Maybe they were just good friends who happened to sit extra close and kissed goodbye when they parted. Was that the way Anna saw it?

In his shaving mirror he practiced: "Anna, our relationship has begun to mean a lot to me." No: "*You* have begun to—" What a stilted phrase, "mean a lot." Was he capable of "I love you"?

Whenever she was due to come over he changed his sheets and tidied the bedroom, although she had not set foot there since viewing his pictures. And was he capable of *that?* The only woman he'd ever had sex with was Pauline, less and less frequently the last few years of their marriage. He didn't know how people instigated these things. . Ask straight out? Just proceed unless stopped? When he and Anna kissed, her mouth was soft and pliant but her lips stayed closed. He let his hand rest on her rib cage, high enough under her arm so that he could feel the stitching along the edge of her brassiere, but she never made that subtle shift of position that would bring his fingers closer to her breast. She gave no hint of wanting anything more from him than what they already had, and he supposed this was significant, in someone ordinarily so direct and confident.

Maybe he should just give up before he made a fool of himself.

Early in October, Mrs. Brunek from the old neighborhood phoned to say that Mrs. Serge had died. "I know you still looked in on her," she said, "so I thought you should be told. She passed peacefully in her sleep, we think. Her daughter-in-law found her when she stopped by with the day's groceries. The viewing's from three to five today and the funeral's tomorrow at ten."

"Well, thank you," Michael said. "I'll certainly be at the funeral."

"Ask Pauline if she'd like to come too," Mrs. Brunek said.

But Pauline, when he called her, said no. She did have a job, she pointed out. She couldn't skip merrily out of the office anytime anyone died. Mrs. Serge was not just anyone; she'd lived next door to them the first seven years of their marriage. Michael suspected that this had more to do with Anna. Pauline had hardly said a civil word to him since the night she'd seen the two of them together. She'd reverted to the bitter, blaming tone of the days just after they separated. His tactic was the same now as then; he pretended not to notice. "Oh, all right," he said. "I'll just convey your condolences, then."

"I am perfectly able to convey my own condolences," Pauline said icily.

"Good enough. So long!"

He hung up. Then, without stopping to consider his motives, he called Anna and invited her instead.

Anna had barely met Mrs. Serge. In fact, he was impressed that the name meant anything to her. "I don't think I've seen her since your wedding," she said, "but she was such a sweet person. I remember she brought a present bigger than she was!"

"An epergne," Michael said.

"A what?"

"A foot-high plaster slave boy holding two plates to put pastries on."

"My," Anna said.

"I guess I just want your company. It's always so depressing going back to the old neighborhood. Everything's falling apart or torn down and there's only a handful of people left that I used to know. But I realize tomorrow's a school day. I just thought maybe, on the off chance—"

"It's the day I don't have morning classes, though," Anna said. "Could I be back by one o'clock?"

"I guarantee it."

"Then I'll come."

After he had hung up, he told himself that she must like him a little more than she would just a friend, or why would she have said yes to this? Then he felt ashamed that he was viewing poor Mrs. Serge's death as an opportunity for a date.

He wore black to the funeral and so did Anna, he was pleased to see. St. Cassian's people put stock in such things. It was a beautiful fall day, crisp and brilliantly sunny, and Michael had allowed enough time to swing by the old store on their way. A mistake, he realized as soon as he turned the corner. That the building had gone from groceries to liquor to secondhand clothing he already knew; he was braced for the sight of bleach-spotted housedresses and brittle, crumpled work boots in the window. But today the window was covered over with brown paper, and a hand-lettered For Sale sign was tacked to the door. He pulled up to the curb and peered more closely. On the second floor—uninhabited for years now, probably used for storage— yellowed paper shades gave the windows a sightless look. "Oh, what a pity," Anna said.

"I'm just glad my mother can't see this," he told her.

"It seems smaller than it used to, doesn't it?" she asked. "I know everybody says that about places they go back to, but this seems tiny. It's hard to believe people found all the groceries there they needed, once upon a time."

"Well, they didn't need as much, in those days," Michael said. "Or as much variety, at least."

As he drove on toward the church, he reflected on his store in the suburbs, with its sense of space and light. Sometimes he looked around at the merchandise—the English water biscuits, Spanish olives, French mustards in their cunning blue-and-white pottery jugs—and he felt as if the place were not really his. He felt deceitful and pretentious. Although of course it had all been his idea. Pauline might have been the one to urge the move, but it was he who'd had the vision of something higher-quality to suit the tenor of their new neighborhood.

He parked behind the elementary school but then sat there with his hands on the wheel. Anna sent him a questioning look, and he told her, "Last Christmas, I drove downtown to give Eustace his usual Christmas envelope. Do you remember Eustace? No, I don't guess you would—colored guy who used to work for me at the old place. He retired when I sold it but we still keep in touch. So I knocked on his door and this young fellow answered—big frizzy hairdo, African-print gown or smock or whatever hanging out over his jeans. I said, 'Is Eustace here?' He said, 'Who wants to know?' I said, 'Only his old employer, come to give him his Christmas envelope.' He said, 'He don't want your envelope!' I said, 'Excuse me?' He said, 'Get away from here with your envelope!' Then I heard Eustace somewhere at the back of the house. He was calling, 'Who's that, Jimmy? Jimmy, who's there?' but this young fellow said to me, 'Who do you think you are, anyhow, coming round here with your envelopes?' and he shut the door in my face. I don't know if it was just him who felt that way or Eustace too. But I surely didn't mean any harm! I'd been bringing that envelope for years; Eustace always just thanked me politely!"

Anna said, "Well. Times change, I guess."

"They certainly do," he told her.

Then he sighed and opened his door.

Times had changed at the church, too. He could see that as soon as they entered. Oh, physically it was the same—dim and glimmery, smelling of wax candles—but only the very oldest mourners were in black. The others had on every color of the rainbow, clothes they'd never have dreamed of wearing to church in his youth—T-shirts, polo shirts, khakis, sneakers. Wanda Lipska walked down the aisle dressed for a yachting trip, it looked like, in a navy blazer and white pants. Leo Kazmerow, seated one pew ahead, wore an electric-blue nylon windbreaker, and when he turned to say hello, Michael saw the emblem of a gasoline additive emblazoned on his chest pocket. "Mikey boy," Leo said. "Look who's here, hon," and he nudged his wife, whom Michael had not at first recognized because she'd put on so much weight. Her back had grown as broad and beefy as a truck driver's, and her hair—a harsh, artificial brown—was the consistency of cotton candy, so puffed up that he could see air through every wisp.

He would have introduced Anna, or reintroduced her, but just then the service started. A priest he'd never seen before stepped up to the altar and the organ changed its tone of voice, after which six weedy young boys wheeled a gleaming casket forward. These must be Mrs. Serge's grandsons. Michael seemed to recall that Joey had had a whole swarm of children.

Anna sat just close enough for him to feel the warmth of her arm and the slight motion of her breathing. At some point, she placed her hand next to his and he took hold of it, gratefully, and folded his fingers around it. His thoughts wandered to an evening the week before when she was leaving his apartment and he had said, "Don't go," and she had said, "Stay?" and he had said, "Stay." And for a moment it had seemed that she might, because she smiled at him so seriously. But then she'd leaned forward to kiss his cheek—not his lips but his cheek—and said good night and left. He wished now he hadn't been so forward. He hoped he hadn't ruined things.

At the end of the service, when Leo's wife turned to resume their conversation, he had to resist the impulse to drop Anna's hand like a hot potato. In this neighborhood he was still a guilty, furtive boy. And when Mrs. Brunek said, "Give my love to Pauline, hear? That poor, poor woman, having to raise her grandson all on her own," he hunched his shoulders stoically and made no effort to defend himself.

It was barely past eleven o'clock; the service had been a short one. "Didn't I promise you'd be back in plenty of time?" he asked Anna as they descended the steps. They weren't going on to the cemetery. "We can have a bite to eat, even. Shall I take you out to lunch?"

"No, thanks, I'll grab something at home," she said. "There's a lot I'd like to get done before I go to school."

This was the kind of thing that kept him off balance. Didn't *he* have a lot to get done? But he would gladly have postponed everything for Anna's sake. Anna, evidently, didn't feel the same way.

He was quiet on the drive to her house. Anna glanced at him from time to time, but she didn't comment.

On the off ramp from I-83, merging onto Northern Parkway, they were crowded to one side by a speeding sports car. Michael had taken note of the car several minutes before. He already knew the driver was a maniac. So he slid over easily, without any sense of emergency. Anna, though, was less prepared. She flinched, and then she laughed at herself. "Sorry," she told Michael.

"That's okay," he said.

They reached Falls Road and he turned left. He was replaying her reaction in his mind—her sharp intake of breath and her involuntary recoil. Always before she'd sat so calmly, the most relaxed and uninvolved passenger. She had never so much as pressed her brake foot to the floor.

He flicked his turn signal on and took another left at Wickridge Street, then a right into Anna's driveway, where he came to a stop.

"Thank you, Michael," she said. "Are we still meeting for dinner tomorrow?" She had a hand poised on the door handle.

"I think you like me," Michael told her.

There was a brief, shocked pause. Even he was shocked.

Then she said, "I think I love you."

They started spending their weeknights together, usually at her place because her place was cozier. Lying on his back in the dark, his left

229

arm needles and pins from the weight of her head on his shoulder, Michael marveled at how natural this felt. They might have been an old married couple. In her sleep she had a way of grasping his free hand and flattening it against her stomach as if she owned it, which tickled him; awake, she was not so bold. She wore cotton pajamas to bed, always white. She woke up cheerful but quiet; she didn't like to talk in the early morning. She was modest to a fault and turned away from him as she dressed.

They told each other their darkest secrets. Anna had fallen out of love with her husband some time before he died; Michael worried he was to blame for what had happened with Lindy. "I think I wasn't a close enough father," he said. "I remember how relieved I was when I found out she was a girl, because then less would be demanded of me."

Anna always listened through a whole story before she commented. He appreciated that. Then she asked questions, sometimes unexpected ones. For instance: "What if Lindy wasn't really Pagan's mother?"

"What?"

"How can you be sure she wasn't just watching him for a friend? You remember how it was in those days, all that communal living, those young people acting like one big extended family."

"Well, in fact we *can* be sure," Michael said. "We tracked down his birth certificate before he started school. Lindy was his mother, but his father wasn't named."

"Someone Spanish," Anna said meditatively. "Considering his hair and those brown, brown eyes."

Another time she asked why he and Pauline hadn't gone to a marriage counselor. Michael said, "What for? What would we have said was wrong?"

"Just that you were unhappy, I guess."

"I think you have to give them a better reason," Michael said. "Like 'She did this' and 'He did that.' It doesn't work if you're simply not the right type for each other."

"But you were the right types when you first met."

"You know, I can't even remember what I was thinking back

then," Michael said. "Maybe I just wanted a girlfriend. I was young and I wanted a girl and Pauline was the one who was there."

Anna studied him. He could say anything to her. She never over-reacted the way Pauline used to do. She didn't take things person-ally; she didn't say, for instance, "But I was *also* there!" although she certainly could have. And she never stored up his confessions to use against him later.

On weekends they spent their nights separately, because of Pagan. Michael agreed that this was the right thing to do, but he couldn't help chafing against it as Saturday and Sunday dragged on. Pagan had reached the stage of life where friends were more important than family—a small crew of boys dating from his elementary-school days, and lately a few girls as well. Often he'd be out till ten or eleven at night, and there Michael sat, alone, and Anna sat alone at her place for no practical purpose. "This is ridiculous," Michael told her on the phone. "I'm just a doorman! My only function is to let the kid in the door when his curfew rolls around."

"That's very noble of you," she said teasingly, and then he had to laugh.

Pagan got along well with Anna face to face. At least, he was per-fectly amiable when she showed up on weekends. In her absence, though, he campaigned against her. Or maybe not so much against her as in favor of Pauline. "I don't understand why you and Grandma don't get back together," he would say. "It's so silly! You're married!"

"Well, actually we're not," Michael said.

"My friends don't know where I am when they want to get in touch with me."

"Oh, is *that* what the problem is," Michael said.

Young people were amazingly self-centered. Even his grown chil-dren, not so young at all anymore, had sulked like two-year-olds when he filed for divorce. "This is not the normal order of things," George had told him. "There are supposed to be two of you."

"There *are* two," Michael had pointed out.

"Two together. Two parents."

"Oh, for God's sake, George, you're a parent yourself by now;

what do you care? Besides, it's not as if there was anything I could do about it. Your mother told me to leave, remember?"

"She'd been telling you to leave for years. That didn't mean you had to go."

Unreasonable, the lot of them. Next to them Anna was like cool, clear water.

Christmas that year was bare and brown, not a snowflake to be seen, but in January a good foot of snow fell during the course of one night. Michael woke unusually late on a Sunday morning to find his bedroom filled with an eerie white glow, and when he rose and looked out the window he saw that the trees had turned into white pipe-cleaners and the cars down in the parking lot were igloos.

He went to Pagan's bedroom door and knocked and stuck his head in. Here the curtains were closed, so that the light was gloomy and the air smelled used and musty. Pagan was just a mound beneath the blankets, breathing snuffily. Michael said, "Hey. Guess what, it snowed."

Pagan stirred and groaned.

"I'm going to have to go shovel Grandma's walk," Michael told him.

No response.

"So you'll need to get your own self up and dressed in time for Anna's. Do you remember we're invited to Anna's for waffles? I'll expect you to be ready by the time I'm back, say at a quarter to ten."

Pagan said, "Mmf."

"Did you hear me?"

"Mmf."

Michael hoped for the best and closed the door.

By the time he'd showered, shaved, dressed, and located his gloves and the boots he hadn't worn since last winter, it was almost nine o'clock. The sidewalk at the rear of the building had been cleared but the parking lot was still buried, and he had to wade to his car laboriously and then kick away the drifts that were piled up against the door before he could get it open. First he started the engine and turned on the heater and defroster. Then he began scooping armloads of snow off the roof and windshield. His scraper would have been too puny; this was deep, billowing snow, but so fluffy that when he started driving it compacted easily beneath his wheels. He had no trouble reaching the street and traveling the short distance to Elmview Acres.

Pauline's front walk was an untouched stretch of white. It was a pity he couldn't start shoveling inward from the curb, because his boots left corrugated prints that would be harder to remove. Taking as few steps as possible, he made his way to the door and pressed the bell. Pauline appeared at once wearing a red ski jacket and a white knit hat with a pompom. "I just phoned you!" she said. "No one answered."

"Shoot, that means Pagan must have gone back to sleep."

"I thought I was going to have to shovel the walk myself!"

Other women did that all the time, but Michael didn't say so. In a way, he sort of enjoyed performing these duties—the husbandly tasks that she still expected of him, married or not. It made him feel responsible and accomplished. He was aware of an added swagger in his stride when he set off toward the carport where she kept the shovel.

The snow was almost weightless, and shoveling it was like shoveling clouds. He dug swiftly from the house to the curb, and then he worked toward the driveway where he cleared a path for Pauline's car. Pauline followed with a broom, sweeping the last thin haze of white that he left on the concrete. "Wasn't this a shock!" she called. "I woke up and looked out the window and I couldn't believe my eyes!" Her voice rang bell-like in the clear air, and her face was bright-pink and cheery. Evidently the snow had made her forget her resentment. Michael forgot it too; he stood smiling at her when he'd finished, watching as she whisk-whisked her way toward him. She was wearing red mittens, and her knit cap concealed her sculpted, middle-aged hairdo. Only a few ruffles of blond poked out around the edges, reminding him of how she had looked as a girl.

"What about your pipes?" he asked her. "Are you remembering to leave the basement faucet trickling?"

"Well, not up till now, but I guess I ought to start."

"At least for tonight you should," he said. "Keep an eye on the thermometer. I'd say anytime it falls into the teens, you ought to leave that tap on."

"Would you like some coffee, Michael? I've just made up a fresh pot. I've decided I'm skipping church today."

"Oh!" He fumbled his jacket cuff away from his watch. "No, thanks. I'd better be going," he told her. He walked back to the carport and set the shovel in the corner. Other tools were clumped there in a tangle—a hoe, a rake, an edger—and he realigned them against the side of the house before he returned to the driveway. "I have to collect Pagan," he said.

"I'll bet he's thrilled with the snow," Pauline said.

"He would be, if he'd wake up."

"He's like George at that age. Remember? George would sleep till it got dark again, if we'd let him."

"Must be something adolescent," Michael said.

He was walking toward the curb now, with Pauline close behind. When he reached his car he turned, and she stopped and looked up at him, hugging herself against the cold. "Thank you, Michael, for coming," she said. "I don't know how I would cope if I had to handle all this myself—the snow, the pipes . . ."

"That's okay."

As he drove off he saw her in his rearview mirror, waving one fat red mitten like a child.

It was ten till ten when he got back to the apartment, but Pagan wasn't even awake, let alone ready to leave for Anna's. Michael said, "Hey! What happened here?" and he yanked the curtains open. Now the stuffy smell depressed him, and the swamp of cast-off clothes littering the floor. "Pagan? Hear me? Up and at 'em! Anna's waiting for us!"

Pagan stirred and groaned and sat up. One cheek was creased from his pillowcase, and his eyes were slits. "Did you know it snowed?" Michael asked.

"Mmf."

"Look out the window!"

Pagan looked but then flopped backward onto his bed.

"Anna's fixing waffles, Pagan. We should have left five minutes ago."

"Do I have to come?"

"Yes, you do," Michael told him firmly. Then he went out to the living room to phone Anna and say they'd be late. Her line was busy, though. He supposed she was talking to her daughter. Sunday was their usual telephone time.

Once Pagan was up and dressed, he showed more interest in the snow. "This is great!" he told Michael as they walked toward the car. "You think they'll close the schools tomorrow?"

"Who knows?" Michael said. "They might."

"Darn, I don't have my sled! Let's drop by Grandma's and get it."

"We're late as it is, Pagan. We'll pick it up after Anna's."

"Do I really have to go to Anna's? I'm missing all the fun! I bet Keith and them are already out in this!"

"*I'll* bet they're sound asleep," Michael said, "if they're anything like you." He unlocked the passenger door and then went around to the driver's side.

Most of the main streets had been plowed by now, and the sun was high enough so that the surfaces were black. "See there?" Pagan moaned. "It's melting!"

"It's no such thing. Every bit of it will still be there long after you've eaten your waffles and thanked your hostess politely for inviting you."

Michael had given Anna a waffle iron for Christmas; that was why she was doing this. He had also given her an electric percolator, a toaster, and a mixer. "So you'll have too many belongings to move around anymore," he'd told her. She had laughed, but he was speaking in earnest.

By the time they parked in her driveway, it was ten twenty-five. She came out onto the porch, wiping her hands on her apron, and Michael called, "Sorry we're late!" as he was stepping from the car.

"Don't apologize. I just worried you'd got stuck in the snow."

"It was Pagan who was stuck. Stuck in bed."

"Sure, blame me," Pagan grumbled. He slammed his door shut and called to Anna, "Like I could wake *myself* up, on a Sunday! Grandpa was out shoveling Grandma's sidewalk and I didn't have a clue; for all I knew it was the middle of the night."

Michael hadn't planned to admit that he'd gone to Pauline's. Not that it was a secret, exactly, but he certainly wouldn't have volunteered the information. He glanced toward Anna, trying to read her reaction, but her face showed nothing.

Anna's own sidewalk was cleared and bone-dry. She must have shoveled it very early. Even her driveway was cleared, and the last traces of snow had been removed from her car. As Michael climbed the porch steps, he said, "If I'd only gotten here sooner I could have shoveled for you, too."

"Oh, well," she said, accepting his kiss on her cheek. "I think I can still manage to shovel my own snow, thank you!"

She sounded matter-of-fact, but he wondered why she'd turned her cheek to him instead of her lips.

Inside the house, a fire was burning in the fireplace and the air smelled of hot maple syrup. "You two sit at the table and I'll start the waffles," she said. "Coffee? Orange juice? Pagan, I've made cocoa." She moved between the kitchen and the dining room, looking uncharacteristically domestic in the white pinafore apron that covered her sweater and slacks. Pagan, meanwhile, was still on the topic of sledding. "Everybody'll be out on Breakneck Hill by now," he said. "By the time I get there they'll have used up all the snow."

"You can't *use up* snow, Pagan," Michael said.

"Sure you can! You just watch! Keith and Rick and them will be making all these sled tracks, and pretty soon there'll be nothing but bare ground."

Michael studied him a moment. It was true that these days, Pagan was at a disadvantage—shuttled between two homes, not entirely a part of either neighborhood. In fact, you couldn't call Michael's area a neighborhood at all. His apartment building was inhabited by elderly widows and young married couples just starting out, and everything around it was commercial.

"I'll tell you what," he said. "As soon as we've finished eating, I'll run you by Grandma's to pick up your sled and then I'll drop you at Breakneck Hill."

"Really? Great! I've *already* finished eating."

"Well, I haven't," Michael said, and he reached deliberately for the syrup pitcher. "So I suggest you fortify yourself with another waffle."

To his surprise, Pagan took his advice. The prospect of joining his friends had put him in a better mood, apparently, because he ate two more waffles and drank a second mug of cocoa, and when Anna asked him what kind of sled he had, he embarked on a lengthy monologue about various types of snow equipment. "Rick, now, he's got this really cool number from Sweden that's a whole different shape—thinner, like—and you should see the speed he makes! But it cost a bundle, I bet." Anna listened, smiling, taking occasional sips of coffee. She was good at talking with young people. She seemed to view them as interesting foreigners; she asked questions about their habits, their music, their leisure activities as if she were writing a guidebook, and even Pagan—now a socially clumsy fourteen-year-old—warmed up and grew expansive once the conversation got going. He gestured widely with both hands as he outlined the shapes of different sleds, often narrowly missing the syrup pitcher or his cocoa mug.

But Michael thought Anna was looking only at Pagan and not at him, and he worried this meant she was mad at him.

Then after breakfast, when he suggested she come with them to Breakneck Hill, she said she couldn't. "It's the day of Ed's concert, remember?" she said.

Michael didn't remember. He suspected her of making it up. He said, "A concert at this hour?"

"At one p.m. He's giving a cello recital. So I guess we should just get together afterward, don't you agree? You'll drop off Pagan at, what, it will be noon by then, I imagine; and since you'll have to pick him up again in just another hour or two, it makes sense that we go our separate ways and then meet later."

"Fine," Michael said. "Right. Might as well do the sensible thing, here."

She drew in a breath to speak, but he turned away briskly and went to fetch his jacket.

At Pauline's house the front walk was dry now—a satisfaction. Pagan bounded up to the door and disappeared inside while Michael waited at the wheel. A few minutes later Pagan reemerged, wearing black nylon gloves and big rubber boots with the clasps unfastened. He set off, jingling, toward the carport, and Pauline opened the storm door and called after him, "Don't forget your scarf!"

"I can't wear a scarf when I'm sledding!"

He vanished into the carport just long enough for Pauline to shrug helplessly at Michael, and then he came out with his sled, a sturdy old Flexible Flyer that used to belong to George. "You'll catch pneumonia!" Pauline called. She was in her stocking feet but stepped onto the front stoop anyhow and stood shading her eyes as she gazed at Pagan.

"A scarf would get caught in the runners and I'd die a gruesome death by strangulation," Pagan said, not breaking his stride.

Pauline turned to look at Michael again. Michael just grinned.

When the sled was safely stowed in the trunk and they were driving toward Breakneck Hill, Michael said, "How long do you expect to be sledding?"

"Long as I can, I guess."

"I have to know when to come and get you, Pagan."

Pagan thought about it. Then he said, "Why don't I just walk back to Grandma's whenever I'm done. Me and the guys might go to Keith's house after, and you'd have to drive me to Grandma's all over again this evening. So why not say you'll just leave me off now for the week."

"What about your things?" Michael asked.

"Everything I need is at Grandma's. It's just clothes and stuff at your place."

"Okay."

Michael stopped at the foot of the hill. It was a long, gentle slope—not really breakneck at all—leading from a wooded ridge to the northern boundary of Elmview Acres. Colorful little figures dotted the expanse of white, climbing up or coasting down on sleds and plastic saucers and sheets of cardboard. It looked like a scene from a Christmas card, and after Pagan had set off with his sled Michael sat a while taking it in.

Now where?

Anna would be getting ready to leave for her concert. He still had time to drive back to her house and offer to go with her, if he wanted. But he didn't. Let her go by herself, if she was miffed with him. Let her be as independent as she liked!

He shifted gears and pulled onto the road and headed for home.

She could be off-putting, on occasion. She could be almost too honest; not that honesty was a flaw. "What did you used to think of me, back when we were young?" he'd asked once, and she had said, "Why, I didn't think anything, really." He had been offended, although he knew that was unreasonable of him. Of course she hadn't thought anything! He was merely a chance acquaintance, the boyfriend of a casual friend. But he almost wished that she had lied; or not lied, exactly, but fooled herself. "I always did sense that there was something special about you." Anna Grant, however, was not a woman who fooled herself.

He turned into his parking lot and parked on the bare rectangle his car had occupied during the night. Most of the other cars were still buried in snow. It was a Sunday, after all; people hadn't needed to get out. He pictured those young married couples sleeping late, eating in, snuggling close on the couch as they read or watched TV. But he himself had more in common with the widow ladies, he thought as he stumbled through the snow, all alone, to his empty, echoing apartment.

When he walked in his front door it seemed that the smell of sleep had spread from Pagan's room throughout the entire place. And Pagan's history homework still lay scattered across the coffee table; so it wasn't true that he had all he needed with him at Pauline's. Now Michael would be expected to gather it up and make a special trip to Pauline's before school. Damned if he would, though. Let Pagan deal with that on his own! It was no affair of Michael's.

He sat a while in the armchair, looking out the living-room window even though all he could see was sky. It occurred to him that he had no hobbies. No interests. Nothing to do. How had he filled the time before he met Anna?

Forget about Anna.

He was used to bringing home a newspaper from his store and therefore had none today, when the store was closed. And the effort of standing up to switch on the TV seemed insurmountable.

At three-thirty, when the phone rang, he was still sitting idle in the armchair. He started and then stared at the phone while it rang again and then again, six rings in all without his lifting a finger. Served her right. But when the phone went silent he thought, Wait! He sat sharply forward. He'd made a terrible mistake. He stood up, already moving toward the phone to dial her number—"Did you call? I was in the bathroom," he'd say—when it started ringing again. He lunged for it. "Hello?"

"Michael?"

"Oh, hello, Anna."

"Where are you?"

"Obviously, I'm at home."

"I mean . . . I was expecting we'd get together after the concert."

"I had something to do."

"Oh."

A little pause.

"Well, should I come to your place?" she asked. "Have you collected Pagan yet?"

"No, I won't need to. He's going to walk to Pauline's when he's done sledding," Michael said.

So that Anna was forced to ask again, "So should I just . . . come to your place?"

"I've got an awful lot to catch up on," he said. "Why don't we skip it."

"Oh. All right."

"The world won't end if we fail to get together every single evening!"

"That's true," she said, after a moment.

"Okay, then. Bye," he said, and he replaced the receiver.

Then he went into his bedroom and settled at his desk and paid his bills. Sealed the envelopes. Pounded stamps onto the corners.

Jerked out all his drawers and cleaned them, throwing away old circulars and paper clips and rubber bands and business cards.

After that he went to the kitchen and cooked himself an actual, time-consuming meal. He boiled rice and he blended several canned soups and stews to form a sort of goulash that he ladled on top. He cut up vegetables for a salad—unfortunately a larger salad than he needed, once he'd combined what he'd chopped, but he ate every bit of it anyhow. He ate standing at the counter, forking the salad straight from the salad bowl and the goulash straight from the saucepan. Then he cleaned the kitchen. Then he went back to the living room and turned on the TV.

Shortly after eleven, while he was watching the late news, his doorbell rang. He rose to peer through the peephole. Anna's face was small and distinct and, he thought, expressionless, but when he opened the door he saw that tears had made shiny trails down her cheeks. He said, "Anna?"

"I don't know why you're behaving this way," she told him. "I don't know what's made you angry." She stepped inside, wearing a quilted red jacket that he hadn't seen before, keeping her arms crossed over her chest. "I thought we were having a perfectly nice Sunday together, and now you don't want to be with me!"

He said, "That's not true, Anna. Of course I want to be with you." Then all at once he was horrified. "My God," he said, "what have I done? I didn't mean to hurt you! Anna, don't cry. Please," he said. He'd never seen her cry before. He wrapped his arms around her and led her into the room. "Please, Anna . . . here, have a seat. Oh, God, where's the Kleenex? Please don't cry!"

He placed her on the couch and settled next to her, trying to take her hands except that she was digging the heels of her palms into her eyes. "Please. Please," he kept saying. He hugged her. "You have to listen to me. I don't know what was wrong with me. I've been just sort of crazy all day; I jumped to all kinds of crazy conclusions. I think maybe I'm just . . . unsure of you. We're in such an unsure relationship. Always juggling our time, spending our nights apart when Pagan's here . . . I think we ought to get married."

Anna gave a little snorting laugh as if she didn't take him seriously, but he said, "No, I mean it." And he did. "Just so this won't happen anymore!" he said. "These strains, these misunderstandings, each of us not certain of the other . . . Please, Anna. Marry me."

She lowered her hands and drew away and looked at him. Her face was wet and her lashes were damp and the whites of her eyes were pink. She drew a shaky breath and said, "Well. Maybe you're right."

"Is that a yes?"

"I guess," she said.

"You'll marry me?"

"I guess."

"Oh, Anna, you won't regret it! I'm going to take such good care of you!"

And he gathered her close again.

He should have been the happiest man in the world at that moment. But even as she relaxed in his arms he felt a kind of leftover, lingering ache. It seemed that somehow this day had done some damage, not to her but to himself, or maybe to the two of them.

# 8. A Cooler Spot on the Pillow

It was ironic that Pauline overslept, because all night long she had wished for morning. At one point, surfacing from an edgy half-dream about a bill she'd neglected to pay, she had been relieved to see that her alarm clock read 6:10—an acceptable time to get up. But the room had seemed strangely dark, and when she checked the clock again she'd realized that it was actually 2:30. She had groaned and thrown off her blanket, turned onto her back, yawned aloud, retrieved the blanket (it was April, a betwixt-and-between time of year), switched to her side . . . and all at once it was nearly nine and the world had started without her. She could hear the Bennett children next door jumping on their trampoline, and the garbage men clanging trash cans in the distance, and, oh, Lord, she'd forgotten to put the garbage in the alley for the Saturday pickup. She hauled herself out of bed and went over to the window, pried two slats of the blind apart and saw the tail of the garbage truck just disappearing around the bend. Carrie Bennett was planting pansies in the plot between their backyards, and the sun was a bright, warm yellow and much too high in the sky.

Then she couldn't get any hot water. What on earth? She stood naked on the bath mat, one hand reaching behind the shower curtain to test the temperature, for one whole minute and then for two. Stone cold. There were days when she felt this house was out to get her. She turned off the water and considered awhile. All she knew about hot water was that it came from a tank in the basement. And it was heated by gas—a scary, invisible substance. What if gas were flooding the basement at this very moment?

Pagan was away at college, and she didn't like to phone Michael because his wife might answer. It would have to be George. She checked the clock once more as she tied her bathrobe sash, and then she sat down on her bed and dialed George's number.

"Hello?" Samantha said.

Oh, goody. Pauline felt a little rush of happiness just at the sound of Sam's voice. She said, "Hi, sweetheart! It's Grandma."

"Hello, Grandma," Samantha said. She was one of those comically middle-aged children—eleven going on forty, with a self-assured, declarative manner. "Guess what, we're getting a puppy," she said.

"A puppy! I thought JoJo was allergic."

"He is, but Mom read in the newspaper that even allergic kids can have poodles, because poodles don't get dandruff."

"I didn't know *any* dogs got dandruff," Pauline said. "Can that be right? And poodles: aren't they sort of high-strung?"

"Not the big kind. Mom's done research. Also poodles are one of the most intelligent breeds and they're especially known for—"

"Pauline?" Sally broke in.

"Oh, hi, Sally. I was just—"

"I hate to interrupt your conversation, but we have an appointment with this dog lady out in Phoenix."

"Yes, Samantha was just telling me, you're getting a poodle! Isn't that exciting!"

"Can we call you back this afternoon?"

"Well, actually I wanted to speak to George about a household emergency."

"George has gone to the hardware store. Tell you what, I'll leave him a note to phone you when he gets in. Okay? Bye, now."

There was a click. Pauline was left holding a dead receiver. She couldn't help but feel hurt, a little, although she knew that Sally was merely in a rush.

She phoned Karen. "Karen?"

"Oh, hello, Mom."

"The most upsetting development: I don't have any hot water."

"You don't?"

"I went to take a shower and the water just ran cold, never even got to lukewarm."

"Well, gosh. Maybe you should call the electric company."

"It's not electric, though. It's gas. At least, I'm pretty sure it is."

"So? The *gas* and electric company; they're the same thing. Look, Mom, I've got to run. I'm late for a meeting at work and I haven't had my breakfast."

"It's Saturday! You don't work on Saturday!"

"Not usually, no, but if we don't get on this case a whole family's going to be evicted by Monday morning, so . . ."

"Oh, fine. Go, then," Pauline said, and she hung up.

Far be it from her to take Karen away from her precious Poor People.

Unshowered, unshampooed, irritable and hungry, Pauline dug through her bureau drawer for lingerie. It was at times like this that she especially missed Lindy. Lindy had always been the most sympathetic of her three children, the most watchful and attuned, whereas Karen was too wrapped up in saving mankind and George was, face it, under the thumb of that Sally. (Illogically, she knew, Pauline blamed George for not being there when she phoned.) The pair of them; what a disappointment they were!

Whenever somebody warned Pauline that an experience would be difficult—complicated or painful or requiring great stores of patience—her answer was "Are you kidding? I've had *children!*"

She stepped into a pair of slacks and pulled a T-shirt over her head. This past couple of years she'd been wearing her hair cut very short and fluffy, but since she hadn't been able to wash it this morning it clung too closely to her scalp and made her look like a monk. She ran a brush through it with brisk, snappy strokes, frowning into the mirror. The underside of her upper arms reminded her of their old Dodge's felt ceiling, which had somehow come unstuck from the roof and used to hang down in loose swags.

It never failed to amaze her that she was sixty-four years old now. Sixty-four sounded to her like some other person's age.

She padded barefoot to the kitchen and turned on the stove, braced for disaster, but the burner lit right away; so the water heater's problem couldn't be the fault of the gas line. What, then? She thought about going down to the basement but decided against it. Instead she started a pot of coffee, poured herself a glass of orange juice, and put two slices of bread in the toaster. Really, she reflected (settling with her orange juice at the sunlit kitchen table, curling her feet around her chair rungs), things were not so bad. It was going to be as warm as summer today, and the trees were sprouting green stars of new leaves, and the chittering of the birds outside the window gave her hope that there might be a nest in her little dogwood this spring. She loved her house. The children had urged her to move to an apartment after the divorce, but she'd lived here so many years—thirty-six come September—she couldn't imagine feeling comfortable anywhere else. Even its dated elements soothed her: the kidney-shaped coffee table in the living room, the out-of-synch "Colonial-style" maple cobbler's bench in the foyer, the rec room's ridiculous built-in brick TV niche too shallow for a color TV. She could have redecorated if she wanted, but why would she? She could remember when every piece of furniture had been her dream possession, pored over in magazines for months ahead, scrimped and saved for. It would have broken her heart to see it all out in the alley waiting for the bulk-trash collector.

She wasn't like some people, who could toss away the past without a backward glance.

Her sister Sherry called. Still the baby of the family at age fifty-six, she was ever ready to throw a tantrum over one thing or another, and today it was the dry cleaner. "I walk in, I tell the man I've brought six sweaters. He asks me where's my ticket. I say, 'What do you mean, where's my ticket? I'm just now bringing these in!' He says, 'You *brought six sweaters,* you told me. What was I supposed to conclude?' All short-tempered and crabby, like I was the one at fault."

Pauline tsk-tsked. She said, "You'll never guess—"

"This is the very same cleaner that gave me the wrong dress that time, a nasty unbecoming magenta, size twenty-two. Twenty-two! I ask you! I almost think it was deliberate."

"I have no hot water," Pauline said.

"Hmm?"

"I got up this morning, went to take my shower, and not a thing came out but cold."

"I had that happen once."

"What did you do?"

"I don't know; Pete took care of it."

Pauline said, "Oh."

"Or probably it was the plumber," Sherry went on blithely, "but Pete was the one who called him."

"Nice for *you*," Pauline said.

"What? Oh, honey, I'm sorry; I wasn't thinking. Oh, it's awful that you have to see to these things by yourself! It's just not fair! You want me to try and wake Pete?"

"No, that's okay. George is supposed to phone me as soon as he's back from the hardware store."

"I don't know how you can bear it," Sherry said. "I would be so mad! I'd be calling Michael up and saying, 'Get over here this instant, you rat!' "

"Now, now," Pauline said. It made her feel sublimely tolerant when Sherry went on the way she did. "Really I've gotten past all that," she said. "Well, I'd be pretty bad off if I hadn't! I've moved on. I'm not going to waste my energy nursing grudges."

"You're amazing," Sherry told her.

Pauline said, "It's not so hard." And she meant it. Over the years, she had lost her rancor toward Michael. Or maybe she'd just expended it all, worn it out with overuse. She could tell herself, nowadays, that she might very well be better off without him; for what kind of man would discard a whole marriage on the basis of one little quarrel? His problem was that he was not a forgiver. Things were so permanent, with Michael. Words once said could not be unsaid; deeds could not be undone. So there he was, stuck forever with that stiff-faced, dull-faced Anna.

Pauline would have to admit that she did still hold a grudge against Anna.

\* \* \*

When the doorbell rang she thought for a moment that George might have come in person, but it was one of those itinerant workmen who stopped by in the spring and the fall. "Want me to clean your gutters? They're a mess," he said, but Pauline said, "No, thanks. Theoretically, I have a roofer who does that."

"Theoretically?" he said. He laughed. He turned to a teenage boy hanging back at the curb and called, "Lady's having her gutters cleaned 'theoretically'; never mind."

So Pauline didn't ask if he knew anything about water heaters, which she'd half planned to do when she saw who it was. "Thanks anyway," she said with as much dignity as possible, and she closed the door in his face.

When had she turned into the general population's one-dimensional, cookie-cutter, cartoonish notion of a middle-aged woman?

And where *was* that roofer, anyhow? He should have been here last December! You couldn't rely on anyone nowadays!

She phoned George again but nobody answered. She phoned Mary Kay Bart, who was a nurse in Pauline's office and whose husband, if Pauline understood correctly, had something to do with kitchen remodeling (which was not unrelated to water heaters, was it?), but nobody answered there either. Everybody was off on jolly, bustling, family-type Saturday-morning pursuits. Well, okay. She hung up and returned to the bedroom for her shoes. No point sitting home moping.

At the Giant on York Road, she bought a few groceries to see her through the week—fruits to take to work for lunch and lo-cal frozen dinners for supper. Then she returned a blouse at Stewart's. She told the saleslady that her husband hadn't liked it. Even when she'd had a husband, he had never argued with her taste in clothes, but she didn't want to give the real reason, which was that the plunging neckline that had looked so enticing in the changing booth had turned all at once pathetic when she got it home. Her cleavage had developed this sort of puckery texture, seemingly overnight.

No wonder she spent less money nowadays! Nothing looked good on her anymore. That made it a whole lot easier to stay within her budget.

One of the cosmetics counters was offering free makeovers. A woman was being swabbed with foundation while several other women watched, and Pauline slowed to watch too but only for a moment. Then she walked out of the store and found her car. She drove home the longer, prettier way; well, partly because it was prettier and partly because she took a wrong turn. The radio was playing oldies that celebrated spring, and she started singing "April Love" in harmony with Pat Boone and forgot to watch where she was going.

As soon as she reached the house she telephoned George again. This time he answered. "Oh! Mom! Hi!"—all surprised and innocent.

"Did Sally tell you about my water heater?" she asked him.

"Water heater? No-o-o. She did leave a note saying to call you and I was going to do that, I was just about to, as soon as I finished—"

"I have absolutely no hot water. It stays cold no matter how long I run it."

"Ah."

She waited a moment. "What should I do?" she asked finally.

"Well. That may require a plumber, Mom."

"A plumber! Oh, God. A plumber on a Saturday; you know what he's going to say. He'll say he can't come till Monday and that means a whole entire weekend without—"

"Of course it could be just the pilot light," George told her.

"Pilot light?"

"What's happening in the basement, do you know? Is there water on the floor? Because if there is, you'll probably need a new unit; but if there isn't, it might be just the pilot light and that's a very simple matter."

"Oh, maybe it's the pilot light," Pauline said.

"Is there water on the floor?"

"I'm not sure."

"You're not sure," George said.

"I'm scared to go see."

"Mom," George said, too patiently.

"All right! All right! But you stay on the line, okay?"

She laid the receiver on the kitchen counter and walked down the corridor to the basement stairs. Three steps from the top, she stopped and held her breath and listened, but she didn't hear anything alarming. The rec-room carpet—a flat, fuzzy green like the surface of a pool table—looked dry from where she stood; so she took heart and descended the rest of the way. She tiptoed across the rec room and peered through the doorway to the left of the bar. There the machinery of the household—the furnace, water heater, washer, and dryer—hulked in the dim light from the single high window. The concrete floor was not even damp. She detected no smell of gas. Maybe things were not so bad after all.

"It must be the pilot light," she told George when she got back to the phone.

"Well, good. All you have to do is relight it, in that case."

"Me?"

"You know how to strike a match, Mom."

"I'm scared it might explode."

George made her wait through several seconds of silence. Then he said, "All right. I'll come do it myself."

"Oh, thank you, sweetie!"

"But first I want to finish up here. I'm trying to get a doghouse assembled before they bring home the puppy."

"How long will that take?" Pauline asked.

"Couple of hours? I don't know."

"The reason I ask is, I've got lunch with the girls in . . ." She glanced at her watch. "Just over an hour."

"Fine. I'll come once you're back."

"No! Wait! How will I shower and dress for my lunch? Can't you come now instead?"

"No, I can't," George told her.

"Oh, George."

"I promised Sally I would do this," he said. "You call me when you get home again and I'll come right over, I promise."

"Well. All right, I guess," she said.

She hung up very slowly and sadly, as if he could see her.

It was Katie Vilna's turn to be hostess, and as usual she had gone all out: cocktails with umbrellas in them, and gigantic floral arrangements everywhere you looked. (Katie had a habit of marrying rich. She lived in Ruxton now and her house was a real showpiece.)

They had long ago abandoned any pretense of cardplaying. First they had drinks in the living room (grand piano, Persian rugs, uncomfortable Victorian furniture studded with glass-headed tacks that dug into your back), and then they went into the dining room. The floral arrangement there was so towering that Katie had to remove it so they could see each other. Katie herself sat at the head of the table, wearing a flowing caftan that might have been a bit too eveningy for a ladies' luncheon. Wanda, who had given up trying, slouched at her right in a baggy denim skirt and a big green cardigan, and across from Wanda sat Marilyn, a shadow of her former self after undergoing chemo for breast cancer. Her hair stuck out all over her head like a baby chick's feathers, and instead of one of her tony pants sets she wore a sweat suit. Pauline had the seat at the foot of the table. She had stayed in her slacks but exchanged her T-shirt for a dressy red polyester top, with a paisley silk scarf fashioned into a sort of headband that she hoped would hide the fact that she hadn't shampooed.

At first the talk was all Marilyn's health; they had to get *that* out of the way. Was she feeling less tired? What tasted good to her? She really ought to eat more. "I can't," she told them. "I try, but even the idea of food makes me want to throw up. Sorry, Katie," because she hadn't touched Katie's famous Crab Salad on Avocado Spokes.

Pauline could see everyone thinking how nice it would be not to feel hungry, and then deciding against voicing the thought. Oh, by now she knew these women so well! It was funny, though, that her closest friends were people from the St. Cassian stage of her life. She used to be tired to death of Poles—their unspellable, unpronounceable names, their oompah music, their heavy food, their folksy costumes on holidays—but now any time she heard the jiggety-jig of an accordion she got all weepy and sentimental.

And Wanda, with her "You should start eating yogurt, Marilyn.

I'm going to give you the name of this really healthy brand that's got special beneficial bacteria . . ." Granted, Wanda could be bossy, and Katie had a trashy streak, and Marilyn was given to boasting too much about her children; but Pauline had lost the ability to pass judgment on these women. She didn't even know if she liked them, in fact, and perhaps she *didn't* like them, but by now it hardly mattered because how would she ever start over with somebody new, at this point?

Katie asked if they had noticed what a wide range of life events the four of them had experienced. "We've got a widow here"—nodding toward Wanda—"two divorcees, one of them remarried and one not, a child who's died, a child who's vanished, a hysterectomy, and now a case of cancer."

"Someday," Marilyn said, "it will be one of *us* who dies."

Only she was brave enough to state it.

And since once again Pauline knew what everyone was thinking (it would be Marilyn herself who died, most likely), she jumped in to change the subject. "Say! Guess what! Tonight I've got a date!"

"Who with?" they all wanted to know.

"Well. There's this man at my church? Dun Osgood? He and his wife moved here a couple of years ago from Minnesota. And his wife died last Christmas—completely out of the blue, a heart attack in her sleep after a nice Christmas meal. So ever since then I've tried to make conversation with him, told him how sorry I was, asked how he was managing; and last Sunday he came up after services and invited me out to dinner."

"So, let's see," Wanda said, counting on her fingers. "January, February, March . . . four months. That's an awfully short mourning period, if you want my honest opinion."

"Well, maybe he's just looking for companionship. That's all right! I don't mind that! We could get on a comfortable footing and then, you know, on down the line . . ."

"You have the most amazing luck finding men, Poll," Katie said. "Here I am, scraping the bottom of the barrel—went six years without a serious feller, last time, till I met Gary—and you've been seeing men by the dozens!"

"Well, hardly dozens," Pauline said. "And a lot of them were disasters, believe me."

"Still. What's your secret? Remember the day she met Michael?" Katie said to Wanda. "She walked in the door and—wham! He never looked at *us* that way."

"Pauline had cut her forehead," Wanda told Marilyn, "and we took her to Michael's mom's grocery store for a Band-Aid."

Marilyn, who had surely heard this story any number of times, peered obligingly at the threadlike white scar Pauline revealed on her temple.

"She was bleeding like a stuck pig! I mean, she didn't look very romantic right then. But Michael went into this, you'd have to say, trance. Insisted on bandaging her himself, walked her out of the store, and stayed with her forever after."

"Not *quite* forever," Pauline said drily.

"We all thought she'd slipped him a potion! We studied her clothes, her hairdo, her laugh—remember, Katie? For a while we painted little perky points on our upper lips; we thought maybe *that* was her secret. Except hers were real and stayed and ours kept rubbing off. And then Richard; remember Richard?"

"Richard was the dentist," Marilyn said.

"No, Norm was the dentist. See what I mean? We can't keep count of them all! Norm was the dentist she saw while she was still just separated, and Richard came afterward. He was the ophthalmologist."

"Optician, actually," Pauline said.

"He was the longest-lasting; he wanted to get married. Or sounded like it, at one point, the way he started talking."

"He was too critical and judgmental," Pauline said.

"Listen to you!" Katie cried. "Do you know how many women your age would jump at the chance to marry a man like Richard?"

"They're welcome to him, is all I can say."

Katie flung out both hands and rolled her eyes at the others in a way that made Pauline feel reckless and dashing.

*　*　*

Driving home, though, she was grim-faced, and when "April in Paris" began drifting from her car radio she switched it off. Things were never the way they seemed from outside. All those men supposedly thronging around her; well, yes, there had been a few. But Norm the dentist wore gold neck chains and his fingernails were buffed—two things Pauline couldn't stand. And the one who came after him (Bruce, who'd had real potential) had stopped calling; she wasn't sure why. She suspected it might have had to do with an argument they'd had one evening when he arrived late for dinner. Some men just wanted people to keep all their feelings bottled up and festering.

As for Richard: he hadn't started out judgmental. At first he had been so admiring; he had complimented traits in her that everyone else took for granted. She had such a green thumb! She was the most creative cook! He loved her laugh and her enthusiasm. Of course she'd realized that such a state of affairs couldn't continue forever. Eventually the newness would wear off. Still: he had asked one day if she would switch from vinegar to lemon juice on her salads so they wouldn't keep clashing with the wines he brought, and although she knew he meant no harm she had felt slightly offended. Vinegar clashed with wine? He'd disapproved of her salads all this time but bitten his tongue? Suddenly she'd felt less desirable, less certain of her powers.

Then his daughter in Ohio invited him for Christmas. He told Pauline he would decline because he wanted to celebrate with her instead. "Although," he said, "it's true my daughter's marriage is in trouble and I know she's probably hoping for support at a difficult time . . ."

So of course Pauline said oh, he should go then; children came first; she understood. And then he let slip that he had already bought his plane ticket. He had been counting all along on her pressing him into going!

Pauline had not been able to hide her sense of injury. "I see," she had said. "Is *that* how it is. Okay! I get the picture!"

And he'd said, "Now, now, you're making too much of this."

Which had had the ring of one of Michael's pet phrases. "Making too much of this." "Overly emotional." "Get ahold of yourself, Pauline."

She dropped Richard cold. She was unavailable when he returned from Ohio; she wouldn't answer the phone and she blandly, breezily brushed him off when he showed up at her door. He thought it was because he'd gone ahead and made the trip, but it wasn't that. It was his, "Now, now . . ."

She refused to let history repeat itself, even if it meant living out the rest of her life alone, dealing with water heaters alone, driving her car alone over roads that mysteriously ended up where she least expected or turned into other roads, wrong roads, completely unfamiliar roads . . . Oh, Lord, it was like swimming through fog! This was such a big planet and she was drifting about on it, entirely unprotected!

She saw a traffic light up ahead and she took a left and then, thank goodness, all at once she knew where she was. A few blocks more and there was Stewart's, dear old dowdy Stewart's. She was so relieved that she turned into the lot and parked and went inside.

At the cosmetics counter they were still doing makeovers. A young girl examined the results in a mirror: black-lashed eyes, glowing cheeks, a mouth like strawberry jam. Pauline slowed to look too and the woman behind the counter said, "How about you? Would you care to try our products?"

Pauline owned drawersful of products—blushes, glosses, powders, and potions, many of which she'd used only once. Even so, she found herself saying, "Oh, well, why not?" She did have a date that evening. It wouldn't hurt to doll up a bit.

And there was something so soothing about the pat-pat of the saleslady's fingertips, dabbing cream onto the tired, hot skin beneath Pauline's eyes. The cream smelled like rose petals. The saleslady's fingers were cool and smooth, and while she worked she hummed to herself in a cozy, unself-conscious way, her sweatered pillow of a bosom inches from Pauline's face. Now and then she offered a compliment. "Don't you have a nice browline!" And "I think I'll just accent these lovely blue eyes with blue shadow." The final outcome was not exactly miraculous—same old Pauline, only shinier—but it did lift her spirits, and the three or four other customers who had paused to watch murmured appreciatively. She ended up buying an entire skin-care regimen, along with a set of "her" customized colors cleverly packaged in what looked like an artist's paintbox. The saleslady threw in a free travel kit with the company logo on the side. Pauline needed two shopping bags to carry everything home.

George said it was the pilot light, just as he had thought. He'd relit it and she ought to have hot water in half an hour. He closed the basement door behind him, looking fat-cheeked with satisfaction, and tucked a matchbook into his shirt pocket with two fingers. "You could have done that," he told her.

"I know, dear heart, I'm very silly," she said. "I shouldn't be so dependent." She waited a beat, in case he cared to contradict her. Then she said, "But *why* was it the pilot light?"

"Why?"

"I mean, what caused it to go out? How can we be sure it won't go out again the minute you leave?"

"Well, if it does, you need a plumber."

"Are you saying that it might?" she asked. She straightened up from the counter she'd been leaning against.

"I'm not saying anything, Mom. The pilot was out; I relit it; everything should be fine. You're the one who's talking about its happening again."

"It's just that if there wasn't any reason the first time, you see, then there's nothing to prevent it a second time. If you follow me."

He sighed. He said, "Why go borrowing trouble, Mom?"

"Well, you're right. You're perfectly right! I'm just a worrywart, is all. This house is solely my responsibility. You can't blame me for being anxious."

"We've said for years you ought to move to an apartment."

"Oh, George, I raised you children here! It's my home! I would die if I had to live in some little dinky apartment!"

"Dad did it, for a while," George said.

"Well, that was your dad's own choice," she said huffily. "Besides, he's a man. Men don't have the same feeling for houses."

George was making sure he had his billfold, the way he always did when he was getting ready to go. She could read him like a book. She said, "Would you like a cup of coffee?"

"No, thanks."

"I can fix it in a jiffy. Or a soft drink? Juice? A beer?"

"The kids will be expecting me," he said. He chuckled. "That puppy's a handful."

"What about now, where your dad's living now?" she asked in a rush. "Anna's house. Is it homey?"

"Hmm?"

"Does it feel like, you know, a family house, warm and comfy and lived in?"

"It feels fine," he said, turning his gaze toward the kitchen window.

"Because I've always thought—correct me if I'm wrong—that Anna's not that domestic. I can't picture how she would decorate a home. Are there knickknacks and photos and afghans? Or is it more, how would you put it, sterile. Does she go for any particular period of furniture?"

"Oh, Mom, I don't know," George said. He was moving toward the dining room now, heading for the foyer. "I don't know one furniture period from another," he said. "It's just a house, is all."

"But you must have some impression of it," she said as she followed close on his heels. "You must get some sort of feeling when you enter it—alienated or out of place or dislocated or . . . what? You can't have absolutely no opinion!"

He turned at the front door and stooped to brush her cheek with his lips. "Along about, say, five-fifteen," he said, "check and see if you've got hot water."

He opened the door and walked out.

Sometimes she could just stomp on George.

\*   \*   \*

She did have hot water, finally. She took a long, soaking shower and then she blow-dried her hair and put on a pale-blue dress and blue pumps. (She wasn't sure where Dun was taking her to eat. She figured a dress would be safest.) Last, she applied her new cosmetics: ivory foundation, a touch of pink blush, rose lipstick, and pale-blue eye shadow almost exactly the color of her dress. The woman who gazed out of her mirror was pink-and-gold, her hair a blond mobcap around her face. Pauline didn't hope anymore to look beautiful. She was trying instead for acceptable, unobjectionable, *likable.* She remembered how when she was a girl, the sight of an older woman who'd gone to the effort of lipstick and finger waves had filled her with grateful relief. There was no necessity, then, for pity.

She was just getting into her blazer when the doorbell rang. It was six o'clock precisely, which she found encouraging. Punctuality signified eagerness. (Or was it only that *lack* of punctuality signified *lack* of eagerness?) When she opened the door Dun Osgood was already smiling, as if he had been practicing—a wide, fixed, determined smile, shaky at the corners. He was a tall man with an apologetic stoop to his shoulders and an appealingly craggy face topped by a fan of straight gray hair. "Well, hi there!" he said. "How're you doing?"

"I'm fine, Dun. How are you?"

"Got an awfully nice evening for this. You sure you're going to be warm enough?"

"I'm sure." She took her purse from the cobbler's bench and stepped out the door and shut it behind her. Dun, she saw, was dressed up to about the same degree she was—a sport coat over an open-collared white shirt and good gray trousers. When they started down the walk he took light hold of her arm just above the elbow, and he opened the car door for her and made certain she'd tucked her hem inside before he closed it.

"Think you're going to like the place we're going to," he said as they pulled away from the curb. "Pincers. Have you been?"

She shook her head.

"I used to eat there every Wednesday night with Mattie. Wednesday night is dessert night. Order one dessert, get another of equal or lesser price for free. Mattie would order the Boston cream pie and I'd have the chocolate nut cake."

"That sounds lovely," Pauline said.

"Although tonight is not a Wednesday, of course."

"That's all right," Pauline said. "I've never been a huge dessert-eater."

"You don't mean to say!" Dun exclaimed, astonished beyond all proportion, in Pauline's opinion. He came to a halt at a four-way stop sign and embarked on a lengthy after-you dance with the other driver before he started up again. "Well, you and Mattie wouldn't have much in common, then," he said. "Mattie had such a sweet tooth! At home she always fixed a dessert even when it was just the two of us for dinner. Pies like you wouldn't believe, flakiest crusts in the world."

Pauline summoned up a mental image of Mattie Osgood, who had, in fact, seemed the pie type—soft but not fat, with a sun-speckled, cozy face. "You must miss her very much," she said.

"Oh, yes. Oh, yes."

His *o*'s were Minnesota *o*'s, rounder-sounding than most, quaint and naive and sincere.

"There are times I forget she's not with me," he said. "I think, I should tell Mattie such and such! or Wait till Mattie hears this! Then it all comes back to me."

"Or that feeling you get when you're walking down the street," Pauline said, "that the person you've lost is walking beside you. This warm, accompanied feeling along one side of your body, and then you recollect, and your whole side goes cold and sort of breezy."

"I've had that!" Dun said. He sent her a quick, darting glance.

They traveled for several minutes in silence, Pauline allowing him his private thoughts. The light was fading now and the country-side was losing its colors. The pink blossoms on the trees were a bleached white, the white houses a pearly gray.

"Tell me, Dun," she said when she felt a suitable time had elapsed. "How did you come by your name? 'Dun' is so unusual."

"Well, that would be from my mother's folks," he said. "Dunnis-ton, they were. But I've always been just Dun myself."

"I think it's very attractive."

"Why, I like *your* name, too," he said.

She settled deeper into her seat, contentedly. They turned east and merged with a stream of other cars. It felt good to be a part of the Saturday-night celebrations. She loved the rituals of dating—the dressing up, the little flutter of anticipation, the process of leading somebody from small talk to real discussion. Dun Osgood's awkwardness just made him more of a challenge. And anyhow, she'd never cared for a man who was too smooth.

She said, "I don't think I've asked you, Dun. Do you have children?"

"No, no." Those *o*'s again, sorrowful-sounding now. "We wanted them," he said, "but you don't always get what you want in this world."

"Isn't *that* the truth!" she said.

"It wasn't so hard on me personally, but I know Mattie was disappointed. She just doted on her nephews. Doted."

"And do her nephews live nearby, so they can give you some company now?"

"Oh, no."

She waited.

"Well, I have a son and two daughters, myself," she offered finally.

"Is that a fact!" He pulled into a parking lot, beside a restaurant with a neon crab above the door. "Daughters are what Mattie would have liked, I know," he said. "She believed that daughters would stick by you more than sons."

"Did she really," Pauline said. She considered debating the point, but she decided to wait for some other topic on which he was better informed.

The restaurant was spookily, unnaturally quiet—not even any canned music—and so dark that the hostess had to lead them to their table with a flashlight. They passed only a few other diners, some of them sitting alone, most nursing cocktails garnished with maraschino cherries or slices of fruit. An old people's restaurant, then. Pauline was familiar with those. This would be its busiest time—five till six-thirty or so. She settled comfortably onto the banquette and accepted an enormous laminated menu. The table was made of some rough, dark wood and laid with paper place mats. A candle shaded by a little tin hat flickered in the middle. She tilted the hat to shed light on what the menu offered. Caesar salad, crab cakes, strip steak, surf 'n' turf . . . She smiled across at Dun. "Isn't this nice!" she told him. She spoke barely above a whisper, but even so her voice was the loudest sound in the room.

"You think you can find something you're able to eat?" Dun asked.

"Why, yes."

"Mattie, you know, she couldn't eat seafood. It seemed like such a waste, moving to the East Coast and then not able to take advantage of that good fresh crab and fish. But she had all these digestive troubles. She did enjoy the strip steak, though. You might want to order that."

"No, I think I'll have the crab cake," Pauline said firmly.

"And to drink?" a waitress asked, standing over them with a pad and pencil.

Pauline hadn't realized she was actually placing an order. She had counted on a little slower tempo. "Well, um . . . a glass of white wine?" she said. She looked at Dun to see if he would suggest they get a bottle, and when he didn't, she told the waitress, "The house brand will be fine."

"Just tomato juice for me," Dun said.

Pauline said, "Oh. Are you not having a cocktail?"

"Puts me right to sleep," Dun said. "But you go ahead; don't mind me. And the strip steak," he told the waitress, "well done, with fries and the salad, French dressing."

"What vegetables for you, hon?" the waitress asked Pauline. She was still a very young girl, gawky and ponytailed, but already she had that maternal, waitressy tone of voice.

Pauline said, "Oh . . ." She peered again at the menu. "Coleslaw? And the string beans?"

She waited till the girl was out of earshot before she said, "I didn't *have* to have wine. I could just as well have had juice."

"Oh, now, I want you to enjoy yourself," Dun told her. "And

what I said earlier about the desserts: I hope you won't hold back from ordering one just because it's not Wednesday. Why, I plan to get one! Half-price or not! Make the most of life while you're able, I always say!"

"Let's just see whether I have the space for it," Pauline told him.

"Oftentimes, you know what we'd do? Mattie and I? We'd splurge and get a third dessert and split it. What Mattie always said was, it wasn't like we were *paying* for three. On Wednesday nights, that is. But we could even do that tonight! It's a special occasion!"

Pauline looked directly into his eyes and said, "It *is* an occasion, isn't it?"

"Yes, sirree," he said.

"It's our first time going out together, just the two of us alone."

His gaze slid toward the waitress, who was approaching with their drinks. He watched intently as Pauline's chunky wineglass was set in front of her. He watched as his little tumbler of tomato juice arrived, a tree of celery jutting out of it at a slant.

"Cheers," Pauline said, lifting her glass.

"Yes, cheers," he said.

They sipped and set their drinks down.

"You know what I like to ask people?" Pauline said. She leaned toward him confidingly, the fingers of one hand curled around her wineglass stem. (She was good at this. She had to be. Other women—long-married and taking too much for granted—could afford to sit back passively and let a conversation drift, but Pauline had had to learn to be entertaining and thought-provoking.) "It's a little sort of personality test," she said, "when I'm trying to get to know somebody. I ask about their house dream."

"Their dream house?"

"No, their . . . See, I believe that almost everyone dreams now and then about the house they're living in. They dream that one day they climb a set of stairs they hadn't noticed before or open a door that wasn't there before and, presto! They find a whole new room! An undiscovered room that they never knew existed! Have you ever dreamed that dream?"

"Well," Dun said, "it does sound kind of familiar, now that you bring it up."

"And here's what I've observed: half of the people think, Isn't this wonderful! Someplace new to explore! And the other half thinks, Just what I need: another maintenance problem. This room has not been tended in years and now I can see daylight through the ceiling."

Dun knotted his forehead.

"Which do *you* say?" Pauline asked him.

"Oh, why . . ."

"Would you look at that room as a gift, or a burden? Because I feel it's very revealing, don't you?"

The waitress set their plates in front of them. "Anything else I can get you?" she asked.

"Not a thing," Dun said. "Unless you, Pauline . . ."

"No, thanks," she said. "Don't worry; there's not a right or wrong answer. It's just a . . . symbol, you know? A symbol of which style of person you are."

"Actually," Dun said, "I'm not sure I've had that dream after all."

Pauline said, "Oh."

"But it's an interesting question."

He cut into his steak and examined it. Helpfully, Pauline tilted the candle shade to send him better light. "Me," she said, "I get this sense of possibility. A brand-new room! A new adventure! But my husband, on the other hand . . . His version of the dream was, he discovered a second story when, as you know, our house is a ranch house, and the floor was puddled with water and snakes were swimming around in it."

"How could that have happened, though?" Dun asked her.

"What? Well, it was only a dream."

"Was your loss a very recent loss?"

"My . . . ?"

"Your husband. When was it he passed?"

"He didn't. We're divorced," Pauline said.

"Oh, I hadn't realized."

"We parted ways thirteen years ago," Pauline said.

"I'm sorry to hear that," Dun told her.

"Don't be sorry! I'm over it!" She took a bite of her crab cake. Her words seemed to hang in the air a moment; she heard a ring of bravado that she hadn't intended. "It was all very friendly and civilized," she said, softening her voice. "No long-drawn-out court battles or anything like that."

"Well, still," Dun said, "I can guess it must have been painful. I don't know what I'd have done if Mattie'd asked me for a divorce! Would you believe she and I never had a serious quarrel? I don't mean we didn't disagree—she'd want the thermostat higher and I'd be sweating; she'd want to go to some shindig and I'd prefer to sit home. But we never what you'd call fought; we never regretted we were married to each other. I consider myself lucky that way. I feel I've been very fortunate."

"Yes," Pauline said, "you *are* lucky. Yes, not many can say that."

She was overcome, suddenly, by a sense of boredom so heavy that she envisioned it as a vast gray fog seeping soundlessly through the room.

So when the crash came—a heart-stopping *wham!* and a clatter and a series of tinkles—she welcomed the diversion. She straightened in her seat and glanced hopefully over Dun's shoulder. In the open, tiled space just in front of the hostess's podium, their waitress slapped her own cheeks and stared down at a mangle of crockery. "Mercy sakes!" Dun said, but Pauline said, "Don't look!"

"Pardon?"

"That's what my daughter tells me—Karen. She once took a hostess job to help with her law-school expenses and to this day, if we're in a restaurant and someone drops something, she tells me, 'Don't look, whatever you do! Pretend you haven't noticed.' That poor waitress; she must be mortified."

"I thought there'd been an explosion," Dun said, returning obediently to his steak. He cut himself another piece while behind him, the waitress tucked her skirt up and knelt to gather half-moons of plates and cups missing their handles. *Chink-chink,* they landed on her tray. The other diners watched with interest, but Pauline gazed tactfully to her left where, she suddenly noticed, a white coffee cup sat all by itself in the center of the aisle. Dun was saying, "You have a daughter who's a lawyer?"

"Yes, she works for this advocacy group that helps people who are on welfare," Pauline told him. The cup stood right side up, a single flash of white in the gloom, and as far as she could see it wasn't even chipped. This made it appear to have been set there for some purpose. Should she point the cup out to the waitress? Or would that be interfering? She forced herself to look again at Dun, who was saying, "I'll bet you're proud of her."

"Proud?"

"Having a lawyer in the family."

"Well, yes, though you'd never *know* she was family, because she's changed her name to Antonczyk."

Dun stopped chewing and asked, "Why would she do that?"

"Isn't it the limit?" she said. All right, she would gather the energy to try one more time. She laughed and shook her head. "That was my husband's last name two or three generations ago. They changed it to Anton, I don't know when, and now here she is, Antonczyk, back to her roots and so forth. We all said, 'Who?' We said, 'What?' But that's Karen—a mind of her own."

"One of Mattie's nephews did the exact same thing," Dun said.

"He did?"

"Only he changed his first name. He changed it from Peter to Rock."

Pauline thought this over.

"He said it meant the same thing and it had a more snazzy sound, but I don't know; the family was pretty upset. Mattie told him that someday he would want to change it back. He mentioned that to me at her funeral. He said, 'Already I'm *starting* to want to. Aunt Mattie was right.' He thought the world of her; all of them did. She never forgot a birthday. She sent them cards for every occasion, Christmas and Easter and Valentine's Day and Thanksgiving and Labor Day, even."

Over Dun's left shoulder, Pauline saw a very old couple entering the restaurant. They paused at the hostess's podium, but the hostess was nowhere in sight. They looked at each other. The man advanced a few steps and glanced back at his wife. She seemed doubtful. The man had a felt hat in his hands and he turned it nervously by the brim as he advanced yet another step and another, while behind him, his wife ventured a step or two herself. The man gathered speed; he seemed focused on a certain table somewhere to Pauline's rear, and he kept his eyes fixed on it as he walked smack into the white cup. *Ching!* It rang against the tiles and took off, spinning like a top, with a circular, metallic sound that brought the hostess rushing up out of nowhere. The couple froze and then pivoted in unison and stumbled toward the door. The expression on the husband's face in the instant before he turned—pure bewilderment; how in heaven's name to explain such a strange faux pas?—struck Pauline's funny bone and she got the giggles. She tried to keep quiet, of course. She tucked her chin down, shielding her mouth with one hand. But she was laughing so helplessly that she made a kind of honking sound, and tears began running down her cheeks. Dun, who had started slightly at the first *ching* but (perhaps recalling her instructions) remained facing forward, seemed not to notice her behavior. Or maybe he was being diplomatic. At any rate, he went on talking. "Even May Day; remember May Day? Most people don't. I can't figure what happened to May Day. Folks used to hang baskets of flowers on people's doorknobs and Mattie still did, the prettiest little baskets she bought in bulk at the crafts supply and trimmed with ribbon. I'll be so broken up when May Day comes this year. I don't know what I'm going to do."

Pauline collected herself, finally. "Yes," she said, "it's going to be hard. I'm so sorry she won't be here." And other things, other consoling, murmuring, commiserating things. But her mind was a mischievous animal cavorting elsewhere as she wiped her eyes and tucked her hankie away and started slogging through her crab cake and her coleslaw and green beans.


In spite of everything, she asked him in when he brought her home. She just hated to walk alone into an empty house. She hated the abruptness of it, the sudden contrast. So she said, "Won't you come in? I've got cocoa"—sensing that cocoa would be his beverage of choice.

"Cocoa!" he said. "From scratch?"

"Naturally from scratch."

It was Nestlé's Quik, but he would never know.

She settled him on the living-room couch and she made him take off his sport coat, and when she brought him his mug of cocoa she sat on the couch also, even though she had no interest in him and would, in fact, have felt repelled if he'd moved any closer. (Not that there was the remotest chance of that.) His cragginess struck her now as dried-upness; his midwestern accent seemed priggish. But she said, "This has been so much fun! I don't know when I've had such a nice evening." And when he handed back his mug and said he couldn't believe he had stayed this late, she said, "It's just like that song, isn't it? Like 'Two Sleepy People.' I used to think of that song when my husband and I were courting. We'd come in from a date and we'd both be falling on our faces with tiredness but you know how it is; there was still so much to talk about, so much we wanted to tell each other . . . and it always made me think of that song about the couple who couldn't bear to say good night. Do you remember that?"

"Oh, yes," Dun said. "I remember it well." But he was reaching for his sport coat as he spoke.


She phoned Pagan at his dorm. It was only nine o'clock—the shank of the evening, for him. Some other boy answered and then shouted for him raucously. "Anton! Pay Anton?" he bellowed. But finally he said, "Sorry. Guess he must be out."

"Well," Pauline said, "tell him that his grandma called, please. No special reason; just wanted to gab." She didn't suppose Pagan would ever get the message, though. He lived in a way she couldn't imagine, boys and girls tumbling all over each other and dreadful music blaring down the halls, although he seemed to be thriving.

She phoned Katie on the pretext of thanking her for lunch. But Katie said, "Oh, you didn't have to—what, sweetheart? It's Pauline," so Pauline knew enough to say a quick goodbye. Katie didn't even ask how her date had gone; that was how eager she was to get back to her husband.

She phoned Wanda. They could talk about Marilyn. How was Marilyn *really* doing? Why was she still feeling sick? Shouldn't she be over that now? But Wanda's telephone rang ten times without an answer. She must be at one of her daughters'. Wanda was very close to her daughters.

Years ago, so long ago that Michael had still been doing the leg lifts prescribed by the physical therapist, he had told Pauline that if he ever got a terminal illness, a part of him would rejoice because at least then he could stop exercising. Pauline had been scandalized. "What a thought!" she'd said, but he had gone on to add, "And cocktail parties, and dinner parties, and visiting back and forth and talking with meaningless people about politics and the weather—I could give it all up. I could shut myself away and give up, and no one would blame me."

"I can't imagine," Pauline had told him. "Me, I'd be doing the opposite. I'd be trying to cram as much as I could into the time I had left. I'd be dancing till dawn! I'd be *greedy* for people!"

Well, there you had the difference between them. It seemed unjust that she should be the one who was living on her own now, while he was happily ensconced in another household.

("You should see the two of them," Karen had once reported, in the amused and rueful tone she often used for Michael. "Sitting at their kitchen table drawing up their household budget, recording their gas expense and their mileage, sorting coupons for free car washes and carpet-cleaning discounts. Like two peas in a pod.")

Pauline walked through the house turning off lights. In the bedroom, she adjusted the blinds and changed into her nightgown. The water in the bathroom sink ran plenty hot, she was glad to find. She ought to apply her new Nighttime Renutritive Cream, but it seemed like too much trouble.

She slid under the covers and reached for the magazine she had been reading the night before. An article on . . . what? On how to organize her time. It had put her to sleep, and no wonder. How to *fill* her time was the problem. She turned the page. She flipped past ads for colognes, for ladies' razors, for tummy-slimming pantyhose. Her eyelids felt like heavy velvet draperies. A man in a tuxedo fastened a string of pearls around a beautiful woman's bare neck. A noted nutritionist wrote about the hidden calories in our diet. Calories hidden in salad dressings, in so-called healthful granolas . . . so-called healthful granolas . . .

She woke with a start, and look! It was morning! No, that was just the lamplight. She sighed and flicked the switch off. Then she slid flat in her bed, but wouldn't you know, now she couldn't get back to sleep. She was like one of those dolls whose eyes close when they're laid down, except she'd got it backwards. Lie down and she sprang instantly awake. In the past she had tried sleeping pills, but they had made her so groggy that she had felt helpless and frightened. Better just to struggle toward sleep on her own. Turn onto her side. Turn onto her back. Search for a cooler spot on the pillow.

It was thinking that made her nights so long. All the bad old thoughts came crowding to the front of her mind. She had lived her life wrong; she'd made a big mess of it. She had married the wrong man just because that was the track she'd been traveling on and she hadn't known how to get off; so she'd gone ahead with it and behaved forever after like someone she wasn't, someone shrewish and difficult. She had let the people she loved slip through her fingers—even Michael, whom she did love, it had turned out, wrong man or not: his patience and his steadiness and his endearingly earnest nature. How could it be possible that Michael really had left her?

And Lindy. Sometimes it seemed to her that Lindy was the one she'd loved most, although of course a mother loves all her children the same. Sometimes when the car radio played one of those old songs ("Are You Going to San Francisco?" was the saddest, so lost and faraway-sounding), she had to blink the tears back in order to see the road. Yet she had failed to keep Lindy from harm. She hadn't protected her, hadn't held fast to her, hadn't even waited up for her when Lindy went out in the evenings. She had felt powerless, was why. She'd had no idea how to deal with it all. Her own girlhood had been so innocent and safe.

Still, other parents had managed. Other parents' children hadn't disappeared.

And she should have helped her father more during her mother's illness. She should have had him to dinner more after her mother died. What could she have imagined to be more pressing than that?

She thought of her mother-in-law, aged and tremulous, whom she'd railed at for her ditheriness and her packrat ways. "Don't *badger* me so; I'll have a stroke," Mother Anton had told her, and Pauline had snapped, "Fine. Let's say you've already had one and you're lying on the floor; just tell me from there which of these magazines I can throw out." This long-ago exchange came back now word for word, and Pauline winced and covered her eyes with one hand.

Now she remembered that it wasn't Michael, after all, who had stayed up late with her talking. Was it? No, it was someone else, some earlier boy whose name she couldn't recall. She couldn't picture his face, even, and she certainly couldn't say what they had been discussing. All she knew for sure was, the two of them had talked and talked, and Pauline had not been alone.

# 9. Longtime Child

One cold, gray morning in February of 1990—cold enough to have frosted overnight—George was scraping his windshield when he heard the sound of an engine starting up nearby. He glanced down his block of stately Colonial houses, each with its two or three vehicles parked out front, but the car spitting puffs of smoke belonged to no one he knew. It was a white Ford Falcon, ancient, dulled, rusted, dented, chattering as it idled in place. George turned away and finished scraping his windshield. Then he tossed the scraper onto his rear seat, settled behind the wheel, and started his own engine, which barely whispered as he slid away from the curb. He drove a Cadillac Eldorado— the last of the good *decent*-sized cars, in his opinion.

Braking for a bus at North Charles, he glanced into his rearview mirror and happened to notice the Falcon just behind him. Its windshield was completely cleared, not scraped-looking but gleaming warmly from edge to edge; so he knew the car must have been running for some time. Maybe it had come from elsewhere to drop off a neighbor's cleaning woman. By now the bus had lumbered on by. George focused forward again and took a right onto Charles Street.

His office was in Towson. He was a vice-president at Jennings, Jensen and had his own parking space, designated by a white wooden sign that read RESERVED GEO. ANTON. After he had locked his car he walked around to the trunk to retrieve his briefcase, and that was when he saw the Falcon backing out of the lot. Apparently it had turned in by mistake, because only members of his firm were allowed to park here. He watched it chug away toward York Road, its rear end unfashionably high off the ground. Then he forgot about it.

Several days passed before he saw the Falcon again. It was parked on Allegheny, a block and a half from his office. He noticed it as he stood saying goodbye to a client he'd had lunch with, and he faltered in mid-sentence when he caught sight of that distinctive rear end and the rust-freckled, crumpled trunk. A CARTER/MONDALE sticker hung in tatters from the bumper. Nobody sat inside, though. He collected himself and turned his attention back to his client.

Late the next Monday afternoon as he was driving home from work he saw the Falcon parked on Greenway, not far from his own street. This time it was occupied. He slowed and peered inside, but the car behind him honked and he was forced to drive on. Anyhow, he had seen enough to reassure him. The driver was a woman, mid-fortyish and nonthreatening and almost certainly a stranger, although he couldn't swear to that in the half-light. Besides, she'd turned her face away when she saw him looking in. But that was only natural. Nobody likes to be spied on.

He parked in front of his house and locked up, took his briefcase from the trunk, and waved to Julia Matthews who was just slipping into her Buick two doors down. As he started up his front walk he heard another car brake and reverse, and something made him turn to look. It was the Falcon, maneuvering itself into the space behind his Eldorado. The space was more than big enough but the driver had to make three passes before she managed to fit in, and even so she ended up about two feet away from the curb. Throughout the whole process, George stood waiting, facing the Falcon squarely and holding his briefcase at his side.

The woman got out and shut her door and started toward him. She was colorless and shabby, one of those people who dress for cold weather by piling on disorganized layers—not a single, appropriate-weight coat but a series of thick sweaters in various competing lengths over a cotton print dress. Wool knee socks and felt clogs gave her a bohemian air. Her dark, straight hair hung to her shoulders (a witchlike style in older women, George had always thought), and her eyes were brown and small and noticeably bright, even at a distance.

She stopped a few feet away from him. She said, "George?"

He had a feeling there was something that he was avoiding knowing.

"George Anton?" she said.

He took a breath and said, "Lindy?"

"It *is* you!" she cried, but she seemed just as disbelieving as he was. She started to step closer but then appeared to change her mind.

He had pictured this moment a million times. Now that it was actually happening, he felt uncomfortably aware of his forty-five-year-old self. Lindy's own aging he had imagined with each passing decade, at least in a vague, theoretical way, but somehow he had never envisioned himself standing before her in his wide beige camel-hair coat, a chunky, faded-blond businessman with a briefcase in his fist.

"I've been following you for days," she told him. "I hope I didn't spook you. I was trying to get my courage up."

"Courage!" he said. "Why would you need courage for *me?*"

"I found your name in the phone book. You were the only one."

She was clutching her purse with both hands—some sort of Native American–looking woven cloth pouch. Yes, she did seem nervous. "I looked for Mom and Dad," she said, "for Karen . . . not a mention. Not even Anton's Grocery. Where has everyone gone? What's happened?"

It was he who stepped closer, finally. He thought of giving her a hug or kissing her cheek, but that seemed too intimate for a woman he no longer knew. Instead he took her arm and said, "Come inside, why don't you."

She could have pursued her questions, but she didn't. Maybe she feared the answers. To cover the awkward silence, George made more of the walk to the house than he needed to, at one point steering her elaborately around a minuscule unevenness where a tree root had lifted a flagstone. Her clogs made a padding sound, like paws. Something she wore jingled. She would be the type to favor heavy, non-precious jewelry whose purchase benefited some disadvantaged tribal craftsmen.

He was relieved to hear the burglar alarm beep when he opened the door. Sally and Samantha must be out. Just for now, he would prefer this to be a two-person conversation. He set his keys on the credenza and crossed the hall to punch in the code. "Come on in," he said, removing his coat. "May I take some of your . . . wraps?"

She didn't answer. She was gazing around the room at the tapestry he and Sally had brought back from Florence, the little arched leaded-glass window, the French doors leading to the rest of the house. A crystal chandelier directly above her lit the top of her head, pointing out tiny flyaway wires of gray hair that gave her a hectic look. Her face had gone slightly soft, developed a sort of extra layer, and all her sharp angles seemed blunted. (As if she'd been wrapped in a sheet of fondant, George fancied.) But her voice still had the unmodulated, don't-care-how-I-sound quality that he remembered from their childhood. "This is quite a place," she said, and the squawking tone she gave "place" was eerily familiar.

He said, "Let's go sit where it's comfortable."

He walked ahead of her, turning on lights, and Lindy followed. In the living room, she plopped herself on the sofa. George sat in the wing chair across from her, a low, glass-topped table between them. He was conscious of keeping his shoulders back, holding his stomach in.

Even so, she said, "You look a lot different."

"Yes, well, I've been meaning to go on a—"

"Are you the last one left?" she asked him. "Tell me. I have to know."

He said, "No, of course not."

"In the phone book—"

"Oh, the phone book," he said. "Karen changed back to Antonczyk; that's why you wouldn't have found her. And Dad: after he and Mom divorced—"

"Divorced!" Lindy cried.

"After they divorced, he remarried and moved to his wife's house and so the telephone listing—"

"But what about Pagan?" Lindy broke in.

"Pagan's fine."

It wasn't till she sank back against the sofa cushions that George realized how tensely she had been sitting. She said, "He grew up okay? He's happy? He's all right?"

"He's fine, I told you. But as I was starting to say—"

"Was it Mom and Dad who raised him? They stayed together long enough?"

"Oh, yes. Or, no . . . I mean, they didn't stay together long enough but they shared the care of him; so it all worked out. But anyhow, Dad's listed under Anna's name, Anna Stuart, and—"

"Anna *Grant* Stuart? Mom's high-school friend?"

"I didn't realize you knew her."

"She came to see us once, when we were still on St. Cassian Street. She brought us a box of chocolate turtles."

"I have no memory of that," George said.

"Was Anna the reason for the divorce?"

"No, no. Good Lord, no; the divorce was, what, six or seven years earlier," George said. He paused to remind himself where he was heading. "So, as far as Anton's Grocery, well, first Dad moved it out to the county and changed its name, and then he sold it to World O'Food, must have been a couple of years ago now . . ."

"Dad hated World O'Food! He said chains would be the ruin of us!"

". . . and that's why you wouldn't have found Anton's Grocery in the phone book," George plowed on. "Now, as for Mom, well . . ."

He swallowed.

"Mom, um, in fact, she . . . died," he said.

He felt a kind of jagged break in the air between them. He wished that he had thought of some less shocking term, maybe some ambiguous term that Lindy would misunderstand for a moment.

"She had a wreck," he said. "Driving the wrong way on an exit ramp. Back in '87, March of '87."

Lindy said, "Mom *died?*"

Her eyes seemed all pupil.

"The police thought first she must have been drinking," George said, "or high on drugs, or unconscious. They couldn't believe that somebody in her right mind could have made such a mistake, till we explained to them that that was just how she drove."

He attempted a light chuckle. Lindy failed to join in.

"But Pagan," she whispered, finally. "Pagan's all right, you say."

"Pagan's fine, Lindy."

The shade of impatience in his tone surprised even him. She sent him a quick, sharp glance, and he ducked his head and mumbled, almost apologetically, "Though it does seem a bit late for you to be concerned."

She went on looking at him.

"In *my* opinion," he added after a moment.

She opened her Native American pouch and started rummaging through it. A warped leather billfold emerged, and a set of keys strung on red yarn, and a newspaper clipping folded to the size of a credit card.

I am sitting in my living room with Lindy, George was thinking. The actual Lindy, in person, after all these years. She's wearing ordinary tan suede clogs with a brown leaf stuck to one sole. She drives a sixty-something Ford Falcon, and one of her sweater buttons is hanging by a thread.

Lindy unfolded the newspaper clipping and examined it. A peculiar, airy, buzzing sensation surrounded George's ears.

"Here," Lindy said. She handed him the clipping.

George found a grainy black-and-white photo of two men—one elderly and mustached, one young. It took him a second to realize that the younger man was Pagan. He could have been almost anyone, with his shock of black hair and generic gray cable-knit sweater. Underneath, a caption read:

> Dr. William Gamble, developmental psychologist, and Pagan Anton, longtime child and family advocate, discuss the merits and drawbacks of the proposed legislation.

"Did you notice the wording?" Lindy asked.

"The wording," George said.

Lindy nodded, smiling encouragingly, inviting him to share her amusement at something.

"Well," he said, "yes, I suppose . . . considering that Pagan is only twenty-five . . ."

"I mean the way they broke the lines up. Or maybe there should have been a hyphen, because it looks as if they're saying Pagan is a longtime child, doesn't it?"

She gave a rough-edged giggle and reached for the clipping. George hadn't quite finished studying it, but he could tell she felt some urgency about getting it back and so he released it.

"I found it lying on a desk," she said. "Isn't the world amazing? All these years I've been thinking about him, trying *not* to think about him, trying to keep him out of my head . . . Well, not at first, of course. Not when I was so wrecked and bad off. Back then I couldn't think about anything. But, you know, after I married and all . . . I married a guy with two children. We met when I was still in the commune. You wouldn't have heard about the commune, but that's where I cleaned up my act. And Henry came to lead this poetry workshop; he was a high-school English teacher in Berkeley at the time, except now we live in Loudoun County—"

"Loudoun County, *Virginia*?" George asked.

Lindy nodded. "We moved there last year," she said. "Oh, I realize how it looks! It looks as if I planned it; plotted to inch closer. But honest, it was coincidence. Just a coincidental job offer, and now that Henry's children are grown . . . But I was going to say, so I married him and he had these two kids, aged six and nine. And first they were just, you know, baggage, but bit by bit I got fond of them. I started, let's say, loving them. And here's what's funny: as soon as that happened, as soon as I felt attached to these kids who were no relation to me, why, all at once I found myself thinking more and more about Pagan. I missed him to death! I thought I would die of it! It's like those kids were a constant reminder. Well, I knew I had no right. By then he was settled; he'd moved on in life. I vowed I would keep away from him. But then . . ."

She turned her head sharply and gazed toward a porcelain lamp on her left. For a moment George assumed that something had caught her eye, till he realized she was blinking back tears. After a long, painful silence she turned back to him and said, "Then I found that clipping."

George said, "I see."

"I was clearing off Henry's desk so I could play a game of solitaire, and there was this stack of articles about educational issues. And I swept them together and started to put them in the drawer, and that's when I saw his name. Pagan Anton."

She spoke the name lingeringly, giving each syllable its full share of attention. George cleared his throat.

"For one split second I thought I'd made it up. I thought I was hallucinating. But when I looked at the photo, I knew it had to be *my* Pagan—that Mexican hair like his father's. I asked Henry, 'Where'd you get this? What newspaper is it from?' He didn't know. The principal had just handed him a file folder, he said. And there weren't any clues in the clipping itself. On the back was an ad for mail-order steaks. I said, 'But he's a child and family advocate! Couldn't there be, I don't know, a heading for that in the Yellow Pages?' Because already, some time back, I'd tried to look him up in the Baltimore phone book. I was like a stalker or something. I was like someone demented. But all I found was you. Not Karen, not Mom or Dad . . ."

Her eyes filled with tears again, but this time she went on facing George. "I see now that I always imagined the whole lot of you right where I left you," she said. "Mom in her miniskirt. Dad wrestling with that old lawnmower. You and Karen kids still."

"Pagan's here in Baltimore," George blurted out. He felt ashamed of his earlier impatience.

Lindy watched him steadily.

"But he lives at the school where he works. That's why he's not in the phone book. He teaches an experimental music program for autistic children. He married his college sweetheart and they have a baby boy."

"I'm a grandmother," Lindy said. And then, "Does he hate me?" For a moment, it seemed she was asking whether her grandson hated her.

"He never mentions you," George said.

That sounded so harsh, though, that he hurried to add, "But I don't know. Who can say? He was so little at the time, I'm not sure he remembers you. Or, rather . . ." Because that, too, sounded harsh. He started over. "When Mom and Dad first got him," he said, "he didn't mention *anything*. He was . . . kind of silent. Kind of deaf and dumb."

Kind of autistic, in fact—a thought that hadn't occurred to George till this very moment. Did that explain Pagan's choice of careers, which George had always viewed as discouraging if not futile?

"But gradually he warmed up," he said. "With Mom, for instance—I remember at first he acted as if he didn't know she existed, but every time she left the room you could see him sort of stiffen, and then he would relax again when she came back."

"So he adjusted, by and by."

"Oh, yes! By and by he settled in and had a perfectly normal childhood."

It seemed, though, that George couldn't leave well enough alone. He felt compelled to go on. He said, "The only thing I'm not sure of is, has he really forgotten you? Or does he remember and just not let on? Because sometimes I get the feeling . . . well, sorry to say this, but . . ."

Why *was* he saying it? But now he was forced to finish what he had begun. "I get the feeling he's sending the message that we're not allowed to bring your name up," he said. "It's like he's silently forbidding us. Though of course I could be imagining things."

He stole a glance at her face. At least she had stopped crying; she was listening to him calmly. "I could very well be mistaken," he told her.

She said, "I don't know which to wish for: that he remembers, or that he's forgotten. We were so close, once. We did everything together! We were all each other had. But once—"

She looked at the lamp again. This time the pause was longer.

"Once I threw him down a flight of stairs," she said.

"Oh, well. Well, now!" George said. He shifted in his seat. "Gosh, I'm sure you—oh, why, these things happen! Gosh. Anyhow. So—"

"And how about you, George?" Lindy asked.

"Me."

"Are you married? Do you have children?"

"Why, yes, Sally should be home any minute, in fact." He wished she would hurry. He and Lindy had had ample time alone, he felt. "We have a son at Princeton, and a daughter still in high school. I'm a vice-president with a firm that facilitates mergers for small businesses."

"Mergers for small businesses," Lindy repeated. George glanced at her suspiciously, but she seemed merely to be turning the phrase over in her mind. "You used to make model airplanes covered with tissue paper," she told him.

He gave a short laugh and said, "Not anymore."

"And Karen? Is she married too?"

"Nope. She's a hotshot lawyer, something to do with the homeless."

He expected Lindy to be impressed, and might even have been trying for it. (Karen wasn't really as hotshot as all that.) But she wore the distracted expression of someone preparing to speak the instant the other person shut up; and almost before George had finished she said, "Please, George, will you call him for me?"

He didn't have to ask whom she meant.

"Please?" she said. "And then if he wants—if he doesn't say no— I could get on the line."

"Well," he said.

"I couldn't bear it if *I* called and he hung up on me."

No convincing excuse came to mind. He couldn't explain even to himself why he was so reluctant. In the end he had to say, "Well, all right, Lindy."

He rose and waited for her to rise too. "The phone's in the den," he told her.

"Oh," she said, but she went on sitting there. Then slowly, like a much heavier woman, she collected her purse and hauled herself up and wrapped her layers of sweaters more closely around her. "I'm scared to pieces," she told him. "Isn't that ridiculous?"

He led her back across the front hall without answering.

In the den, he switched on a lamp and settled her in a leather recliner. Then he sat down at his desk and reached for the phone. It was a newfangled phone with automatic dialing—a mystery to him, but Sally was good at these things and she had programmed it for him. All he had to do was punch a single button. In Lindy's presence, this felt like showing off: See how effortlessly I, at least, can get in touch with your son? And it was misleading as well, because Sally was the one who kept in touch with the family, most often. Still, when Pagan answered, George did his best to sound hearty and familiar. "Pagan. Hi. It's George," he said.

"George? What's up?"

Somehow, the Antons had reached the stage where a phone call meant bad news; you could tell it from the apprehensive note in Pagan's voice. It must have been Pauline's death that had led them all to that expectation. So George drawled his answer out long and slow and easy. "Oh, nothing much. Not a whole lot. Can't say much is doing at *this* end, but . . ."

Oddly enough, he felt his heart start to pound. And Lindy, perched on the edge of the recliner, was gripping her bag so tightly that he could see the waxy white of her knuckles beneath the skin.

". . . but I do have something of a surprise for you," he said. "You'll never guess who I've got sitting across from me."

"My mother," Pagan said flatly.

George said, "You knew?"

Lindy raised her chin and watched him.

"No," Pagan said, "but who else would it be?"

"Right. You're right. So. Would you like to tell her hello?"

"Why not," Pagan said.

George passed the receiver to Lindy and then (against every inclination) rose to leave. He was nearly out of the room before she spoke. "Hello?" she said.

He hung around in the hall long enough to hear her say, "Oh, I'm fine. And you?"

In the living room, he sat back down in his chair and stared into space. The unreal feeling still buzzed around his head. He searched his mind for images of the Lindy he had known—a bony child, all knees and elbows, forever clambering over him or nudging him aside or reaching past him for something. Her shins covered with bruises from roller-skating and stoopball. Her hair matted and tangled, no matter how often their mother tried to comb it.

He remembered how they'd compete with each other, fight over every candy bar and comic book. "Me first!" Lindy would tell him, and he would say, "No fair!" and their mother would call, "Stop that, you two!" He saw Lindy playing jacks on the sidewalk in front of the store, snatching up ninesies and tensies in a heedless, all-out swoop that kept the backs of her fingers perpetually scraped raw. He pictured the bedroom on St. Cassian Street that he and his sisters had shared, which had formerly been their parents' room and long before that, their grandmother's—he and Lindy in the double bed and Karen in the crib. At night Lindy whispered stories to him. "Once there was a man with no eyes who died in this very house, did you know that?" He would clap his hands over his ears but then remove them, horrified and intrigued in equal parts. "And then what?" he would ask.

Maybe the woman in the den was an impostor.

The front door slammed, and Sally called, "George?" He heard her heels tapping across the parquet. When she appeared in the living-room entranceway she seemed to have come from a whole different planet, with her ash-blond hair as sleek as brushed aluminum, her cheeks bright from the cold, the collar of her cashmere coat standing up around her face. "George, is Sam home yet? I forgot to tell her— what is it?"

"What's what?" he said.

"Why are you looking like that?"

"I'm not looking any way."

"What's going on, George?"

"Nothing's going on!" He stood up with elaborate slowness and loosened his tie. "Though one thing I guess I should mention," he said. "Lindy's here."

"Lindy who?" Sally asked.

"Lindy, my sister."

She stared at him. She said, "Here in this house?"

"She's on the phone just now with Pagan."

At that moment, Lindy arrived in the hall behind her. Sally spun around.

"How'd it go?" George asked.

But she appeared not to hear him. She was looking at Sally with a strangely blank expression. Just as George was realizing that he ought to make introductions, Sally rushed over to her and seized both her hands and said, "Lindy! Oh, this is so exciting! This is so unexpected! I'm Sally, by the way—George's wife. I am so, so happy to meet you!"

Lindy used to hate it when people fussed like that. (Their own mother, for instance.) But now she took it in stride, or perhaps didn't even notice. She allowed Sally to lead her to the couch.

"Have you been here long? Where'd you come from? How'd you find us?" Sally asked. She perched next to her, still in her coat, so that she seemed to be the one visiting. "What do you think of your brother? Would you know him? You don't much look like him, do you? I guess you got your dad's coloring."

George said, "Sally, could we just hear how her talk with Pagan went?"

"I'm sorry! Listen to me run on!" Sally cried. Then she sat up straighter and laced her fingers together and waited primly for Lindy to speak.

Lindy said, "Oh. Well."

"Was it very emotional?" Sally asked. "I can't even imagine! All these years, and then, why, you must have had so much to say to each other!"

"Not really," Lindy said.

"Was he just speechless with amazement?"

George said, "For God's sake, Sally, let her talk, will you?"

Sally blinked. Lindy said, "That's all right."

She spoke somehow without moving her lips, her face stiff and numb-looking. "His voice had changed," she said. "That's the kind of thing you don't think to brace for—that he wouldn't have that clear little sweet little voice anymore."

"But what did he say?" Sally asked, and then she shot a quick glance at George.

"He was perfectly polite. He asked how I was; he said it was nice to hear from me; he said yes, he had a family now . . . I said to him,

283

I said, 'Do you think maybe we could meet?' He said, 'Meet.' He said, 'Oh.' He said, 'Oh, I don't know. I don't really see the point, do you?' "

Sally said, "Point!"

"Well, I suppose that's understandable," George said.

Both women looked at him.

He said, "In view, I mean, of the . . . you know, circumstances."

"No, we do *not* know," Sally told him, and then she turned back to Lindy. "I hope you convinced him otherwise."

"No, I just said, 'Fine,' " Lindy said. "I said, 'In case you ever might want to get in touch, though, I'll leave my number with George.' "

"He was just taken unawares," Sally decided. "He's very kind-hearted; believe me, he is. It's just that he wasn't expecting this. He'll call back! I promise he will. That phone's going to ring any minute."

"No, I don't think it will," Lindy said. She gathered her sweaters around her. She said, "I should be getting home now."

"Right now? But we've barely met!" Sally cried.

"I do have a husband waiting."

"You're married? Where do you live? I don't know anything about you!"

"George will tell you," Lindy said. "I just seem to be really, really tired. I have to go."

She rose and started toward the front hall, holding her bag in both hands. She moved as if her feet hurt.

George said, "Wait."

She paused, not bothering to look at him.

"What about Dad and Karen?" he asked. "Aren't you going to see them?"

"Maybe some other time," she said.

A tantalizingly familiar mixture of frustration and bafflement swept through him, and he said, "Suit yourself."

But Sally said, "Lindy. Please. Reconsider. They'll be *desperate* to see you! Couldn't we just phone them and invite them over? Just for a little visit? A few little minutes, maybe?"

"You know," Lindy told her, "I really feel I might be about to die of tiredness. I'm sorry. You seem like a very nice person. But all I want to do is go home and go to bed. George, I left my number on your desk pad if Pagan wants it. But he won't."

The peculiar thing about it—the unjust thing—was that everybody blamed George. Sally said he'd acted so passive, he'd given up so easily, he had seemed almost pleased when Pagan turned Lindy down. "Pleased!" George said. "Excuse me, but who was it who phoned him, may I ask? Who told him she wanted to speak to him?"

"I swear you looked downright satisfied when you heard he wouldn't meet her in person. You said, 'Oh, well, I suppose that's understandable.'" (Here Sally made her voice sound booming and pompous, really nothing like George's.) "Admit it: you were on his side. *You* didn't think he should meet her, either. You're an unforgiving person, George Anton."

"All I meant," he told her, "was that it might have been anticipated that a three-year-old thrown to the wolves by his mother would possibly not have much to say to her all these decades later."

"He's not a three-year-old anymore; he's twenty-five. And of course he has things to say to her, even if they're angry things! You should have called him right back, George, and told him to get himself over here. You shouldn't have left the den in the first place. Lindy probably said everything wrong out of nervousness."

"I was giving her some privacy, Sally."

"Privacy, is *that* what you call it," Sally said. "The fact is, you're exactly like your father. You think standoffishness is a virtue."

And his father? His father, who should have been the most unforgiving of all, behaved as if Lindy had merely been out shopping all these years. "When's she coming back? Did she say?" he asked when George telephoned. "Why didn't you let me know about this? Didn't it occur to you that I would want to see her?" This was a man who'd suffered untold worry and grief, not to mention an entire second round of carpool duty and soccer games and parent-teacher conferences for the sake of somebody else's child, but now all he wanted to know was "Did she at least ask about me? Did she wonder how I was doing?"

"Naturally she asked," George said. (Well, more or less she had.)

"Was she upset about your mom?"

"Oh, yes."

His father gave a ragged sigh. "Poor, poor Pauline," he said. "It kills me that she didn't live to see this."

"I know, Dad."

"She never gave up hope, I could tell. She never stopped believing that one day, sooner or later . . . Why, that time she had a chance to go on a cruise, remember? She could have gone with a group from her church but she said, oh, she would have to be away so long, she just didn't think she ought to. And I was arguing with her, do it! We would manage just fine! You were already in college by then and Karen was, what; well, if you were, say, eighteen then I guess Karen would have been . . ."

Ever since his retirement, George's father had grown more trying. His conversations were so long-winded now, so shapeless and convoluted and pedantic, full of repetitions, qualifiers, self-corrections, pauses to search for just the word he had in mind, dogged attempts to nail down the exact, specific date or street or name even when it made no difference to his story. All due to loneliness, no doubt. The grocery had been his whole social life. Ordinarily, Anna could be counted on to move things along. "Well, June or July, one or the other. At any rate . . ." she would gently suggest. But she couldn't help over the telephone; so it was up to George to break in, finally, and say, "It's true that Mom always seemed to be kind of . . . looking out the window for Lindy."

"She kept every single one of Lindy's belongings in case she ever came back, did you know that? Her clothes and books and papers and cosmetics and LP records."

George certainly did know that. It was he and Karen who'd discovered it all, while they were still in that state of disbelief that follows a sudden death. (Marilyn Bryk, his mother's old friend, had phoned George on a rainy March evening—Marilyn the cancer patient, who should have been the one to die first, by all rights. She'd gotten word before anyone because the police found a birthday card from her in Pauline's purse.) Imagine how it felt to come upon a faded black turtleneck, a pair of black jeans studded hip to cuff with silver rivets, a voluminous, wrinkled black raincoat bristling with buckles and epaulettes—a sad little time capsule of a wardrobe that George's daughter Samantha had instantly claimed for her own. Samantha had a kind of crush on Lindy, or so it seemed to George. She hadn't even been born till years after Lindy left home, but she was always asking questions about her, poring over photographs of her, making her into some mythical, magical being.

When Samantha heard now that she'd missed Lindy's visit, she was beside herself. "Lindy was here? In this house? The person I've most wanted to meet for as long as I've been on this earth? I cannot believe that you let her get away before I could see her!"

"Is it my fault you didn't come home from school till after dark?" George demanded.

"Well, it sure wasn't *my* fault! I was waiting for my tennis coach! Mom forgot to tell me he'd canceled! And anyway, how long did Lindy stay here—three and a half minutes? Why did she leave so fast? What did you say to cause her to go? Did you make her feel not welcome?"

Gina was even more accusatory—Pagan's bossy wife, Gina Meredith, a feminist type who'd kept her last name and refused to shave her legs and breast-fed her baby in public. "Pagan told me his mother's shown up," she said when she telephoned. "Is she still there?"

"No, ah, she's left, Gina."

"Well, I feel strongly about this, George. I feel he should meet with her. I feel we both should. We *all* should, as a family."

"But Pagan himself said—"

"First and foremost, I need to ask if she took drugs in her first trimester."

"You do?"

"These things can have lifelong effects. We need to be informed."

"Well, I'm sorry, Gina, but Pagan told her he saw no point in seeing her."

"You might at least have argued with him," Gina said.

"I didn't think I had the right to argue. Nor do you, in my humble opinion," George told her, gathering steam. "Pagan's the injured party, after all. He should be the one to decide if he wants to see her."

"Well, this is just unacceptable," Gina said.

George said, "Lots of things are unacceptable. That doesn't mean they don't happen."

Although he had a strong suspicion that Gina was still too young to believe that.

Only Karen saw George's side of things. First she demanded all the details. What Lindy had looked like was tops on her list (could she still fit into those jeans, provided she felt the inclination?), followed by why she hadn't stuck around till Karen could get there, and what exactly her conversation with Pagan had consisted of. "At least he didn't hang up on her, did he? Or *did* he? Do you think he asked her anything about who his father was?"

"I don't have the faintest idea," George told her.

"Well, I can't say as I blame him, if you want to know the truth. She dumps him without a word, disappears, leaves him to fend for himself, and now all at once she says, 'Dearie me, didn't I have a child someplace? I wonder what's become of him.' Damn *right* he shouldn't have to meet her."

George didn't talk with Karen very often. Oh, they liked each other well enough, he supposed, but they led such different lives. Also, he sensed that she was not all that fond of Sally, although she had never said anything. Now, though, he felt a surge of warmth for her. He said, "I wish you'd convince Gina of that."

"Gina?"

"She just now telephoned me in a huff. Thinks I should have, I don't know, put Lindy in a hammerlock till Gina could get over here and investigate her gene pool. I believe she was envisioning some big family confrontation."

"Oh, then," Karen said. "If *Gina* wants, I guess it's going to happen."

Gina was another subject George and Karen agreed on. George had almost forgotten that.

As if Lindy's visit had lifted some kind of curtain or partition, George was visited over the next few days by what he would have to call flashbacks. They were more vivid than mere memories, and briefer—just single mental images, really. The wooden cane his father used to walk with, its worn, satiny handle that had filled George with love and sorrow any time he saw it hooked over the kitchen doorknob in the apartment on St. Cassian Street. A geranium plant his mother had rescued from a neighbor's trash can and nursed into an overgrown monster that sent its segmented, scaly tentacles sprawling across the windowsill. Counting out change for customers from his father's tall brass cash register. Getting his toes squeezed by the Fitting Lady when his mother took them shoe-shopping before the start of each new school year.

Then he recalled other shopping trips, dragging after his mother as she tirelessly hunted down bargains—the yawning, aching boredom of it. He remembered the time she stepped into a booth to try on a gray cotton dress and called out a few minutes later, her voice breaking up with laughter, "Children? Want to see what your mother would look like as a mental patient?" At the sight of her, Lindy had doubled over with the giggles, but George had felt too anxious to laugh; their mother was so convincing in her institutional gray.

And then the Christmas their father gave her the nightgown—black, with black lace cups at the bosom that were almost transparent. "Why, Michael!" she had said, and their father had looked sweetly foolish, lowering his eyes and grinning. She'd gone immediately into the bedroom to try it on. They were living in Elmview Acres by then, where the master bedroom lay just across the corridor from the living room, but instead of reappearing, their mother called softly, "Michael? Could you come here a minute?" Their father had set aside a box of socks he'd been fiddling with and risen and left, eyes still lowered, and the bedroom door had latched shut again and there hadn't been another sound for ages. At the time the children were, oh, probably twelve, eleven, and seven or so—old enough to send each other embarrassed sidelong glances, although now the memory made George smile.

Well, so much about their parents had been embarrassing. Or did all children feel that way? But it seemed to George that the Antons' lives were more extreme than other people's. That very same nightgown, for instance, had only hours later given rise to a major battle when their mother thought to ask their father how he had known what size to buy. He'd taken Katie Vilna shopping with him, their father said, since he'd guessed that Pauline and Katie were more or less the same build. And then all hell broke loose. Whether it was their father's colluding with another woman or their mother's belief that Katie was flatter-chested than she was, George couldn't say; but at any rate, their mother had exploded, and their father had called her crazy, and their mother had stuffed the nightgown into the wastepaper basket . . .

People didn't stay on an even keel in the Anton family. They did exaggerated things like throwing out their clothes or running away from home or perishing in spectacular crashes.

Or showing up after twenty-nine years and wondering where everyone was.


Well, they did all get together eventually, just as Karen had predicted. Once Gina fixed her sights on something, watch out. She called Anna, she called Karen, she called George for Lindy's telephone number, and then, by some unknown means, she persuaded Pagan to change his mind. Or maybe persuading Pagan came first. At any rate, it worked out that the family met at Anna's house for lunch on a Sunday in March. Everyone attended but JoJo, who was away at school. Pagan brought Gina and the baby; Lindy brought her husband. A pork roast was served, along with an eggplant lasagna for Gina, who didn't eat meat. Nothing particular happened. Nobody threw a scene or stalked out or burst into tears. Lindy did get a little shiny-eyed over her grandson—a standard-issue six-month-old who evidently reminded her of Pagan at the same age—but otherwise she behaved with restraint, and so did Pagan. In fact, they didn't really have much to do with each other. Lindy seemed to have transferred all her feelings to the baby. She avoided talking with Pagan or even looking at him, if possible, and Pagan was his usual courteous, unforthcoming self. At the end of the afternoon the customary pleasantries were exchanged: must do this again, so good to have seen you, must come to *our* place next time . . . and then everybody went home. It was a perfectly civilized occasion.

So why was it that George had such a wretched time?

Slumped glumly on Anna's piano bench before the meal, arms folded, chin on his chest, he surveyed the goings-on through a scrim of cynicism. Every remark called forth in him a silent, acidic "Yeah, right." When Lindy said, "Just herbal tea for me, please, if you have it. I avoid all unnatural stimulants," he rolled his eyes and exhaled a little too loudly. (She sounded like that simpering girl in *Beauty and the Beast*: "Just a single perfect rose for me, please, Father.") And Michael's response—"Oh, certainly! Coming right up!"—was so pitifully ingratiating, his face so eager and highly colored beneath his thin white hair.

Yes, even people's looks were an irritation. Lindy's husband turned out to be a caricature of the male English teacher, with his clipped salt-and-pepper beard you could mistake for the shape of his jaw and his mild gray gaze and suede elbow patches. Anna's smooth pageboy, still mostly brown, seemed expressly designed to flaunt her self-possession. (George had a theory that hairdos revealed personalities—that people with flat, docile hair, for example, tended toward meekness while those with frizzy hair were uncontrolled and disorganized.) Gina was too lush and plummy, the damp spot over each nipple a disgrace. And how about Samantha, all in washed-out black and strung with ropes and ropes of nuts and beads and astrological symbols? A costume straight from Lindy's old bureau drawers, but if Lindy recognized it she gave no sign. Conventional by comparison in a rough-woven peasant dress and fringed shawl, she was too busy mooning over the baby. Samantha, hovering next to her, might as well not have existed.

Here sat the long-lost Lindy, the central mystery of their lives, the break at the heart of the family, and what were they all doing? Discussing when babies' eyes changed color. Placing orders for sherry and club soda and ginger ale, and debating a phone call to JoJo though would he in fact be awake yet? Should they postpone it till after lunch?

"I keep thinking we're just at this normal party," Karen murmured in George's ear. "There's this normal woman guest here, only she happens to be Lindy." What she said came closest to what George himself was thinking. Wasn't this too easy? Could Lindy really slip back amongst them so seamlessly?

Now Gina was zeroing in. "Lindy, I have to ask. What kind of medical heritage did Pagan's father have?"

Lindy said, "Why, I honestly couldn't . . . heritage?" She looked around at the others. "He was just a drummer from some little town in Texas. We were never really a couple, I mean not so as you would notice."

It didn't seem that Pagan even heard this, or cared if he did hear. He sat comfortably at Gina's side and watched as she, oh, Lord, opened her button-down nursing flap and hauled out a breast for the baby. "A drummer!" Gina told Pagan, sidetracked at least for the moment from her medical concerns. "That's where you get your musical talent!"

Pagan said, "Could be," without much interest.

Sally—too obviously changing the subject—asked why so many holiday wreaths were still up. She said, "How much trouble could it be just to pluck a wreath off a door, I'd like to know?"

"I guess it's one of those things that people tend to stop seeing," Lindy's husband ventured.

"They don't stop seeing their Christmas trees, do they? They don't stop seeing their yard decorations! So why is it that a wreath, a simple, lightweight wreath—"

"Oh, Mom. Let them keep their durn wreaths till June, if they want," Sam said. "Why get all in a swivet about it?"

"Well, I'm just curious, Samantha. I'm certainly not in a 'swivet.' I'm just curious about human nature, is all."

George realized that if he closed his eyes, he could have sworn it was his mother talking.

Speaking of which: over lunch they somehow got to telling "Pauline stories," as George called them in his head. He wasn't sure how this tradition had developed—trading reminiscences of his mother's zanier moments while his father chuckled affably and Anna looked on with a tolerant smile. As a rule George would participate, but today he sat quiet while Karen led off with a description of Mimi Drew's birthday dinner at Haussner's—huge old Haussner's Restaurant with its acres and acres of tables. "It was hosted by a woman Mom had never met," Karen told Lindy, "and when she got there she found she didn't know a soul. But she sat down anyhow and started a conversation, till it dawned on her that not even Mimi was there. She thought, Oops, I'm at the wrong party, and right then she spotted Mimi clear across the room, but she was having such a good time that she decided to stay where she was."

"She was always doing things like that," Sally said as she passed the lasagna to Lindy. (Who didn't eat meat either, it turned out.) "Once when we were downtown she gave a dollar to a homeless person, except he wasn't homeless after all; he was a tenured professor. 'Madam,' he said, 'I'm a tenured professor,' but Pauline waved a hand and said, 'Oh, well, keep it anyhow,' and I said, *'Pauline . . . !'*"

Lindy's husband gave one of his furry, bearded heh-hehs.

And then the driving stories. The time Pauline got lost in her own alley and the time she confused the brake with the accelerator and the time she backed into a pedestrian, knocked him down, stuck her head out the window, called, *"I'm sorry!"* and pulled forward, put her car in reverse, backed up and knocked him down again. It was Sam who told this last tale but it was George who'd lived it, as a mortified fourteen-year-old, and even though it had happened more or less the way she said, somehow it sounded untrue. His mother had not been some fluffy-headed *I Love Lucy* dingbat; she'd been—at different times—scared and scary, angry, bitter, remorseful, unhappy, jealous, hurt, bewildered, at a loss. He said, "That's not how it was!" but Sam caroled, "Oh, well, close enough," and the others went on laughing.

Only Lindy met his eyes, for an instant. Only Lindy seemed to know what he meant. Lindy wasn't laughing.

\* \* \*

Okay, so: must get going, must do this again, must come to *our* place, blah, blah . . .

Was that the sum of it?

George stood at the edge of Anna's front yard and pecked Lindy's cheek and shook her husband's hand. With the others, he stood watching as the Falcon bobbed off down the road, high-tailed and rakish and battered. The others were saying, "Wasn't that nice?" and "Didn't you think that went well?"

Blah, blah, blah.

What George should have asked, he saw now, was Why did you do it, Lindy? Was it worth it? How terrible could our family have been? What was so important that you had to rip our world apart like that? Doesn't it ever bother you? Don't you ever regret it? Did you give us any thought, all those years? Did you wonder about us? Miss us? Did you dream about us at night? Did you ever think you'd been wrong, or selfish, or cruel, or even . . . wicked?

Wasn't I enough to keep you here?

Was I so easily forgotten?

How could you have left me, Lindy?

# 10. The Man Who Was a Dessert

Michael woke from a dream that had the landscape of a fairy tale—soft green hills and valleys, little thread of a road winding toward the horizon. The atmosphere of the dream colored his early morning. Showering, shaving, dressing, eating breakfast with Anna, he imagined wisps of fog clinging to his hair. Anna's gentle voice traveled toward him across a great distance: She might be home late tonight. They ought to start making Christmas plans. She must remember to call Mollie Picciotto over the weekend.

At 8:45 he drove her to work—a routine that had developed after his retirement. It got him up and forced him out of the house, gave a little shape to his day. Then generally he ran a few errands. This morning he planned to buy window caulking. It was a more entertaining errand than some others. Hearing Anna remark last night upon the draft from the dining-room window, he had felt a quickening of enthusiasm. Now he reviewed the possibilities. Rope putty? Strips of felt? Or should he go for the more professional approach and buy an actual caulking gun? "I'm trusting I'll find what I need at Schneider's," he told Anna. "I'd hate to have to drive to Home Depot."

Anna said, "Pardon?" and then she said, "I don't believe you've heard a word of what I've been saying."

Hastily, Michael rewound his mental tape recorder. "Calvin," she had mentioned. That would be her principal. "Problems at school," he hazarded. "Old Cal acting up again."

"From nine to three, we're working nonstop. Even lunch is work, because we're supposed to eat with the students. But then he expects us to sit through these endless after-school meetings! And this one's on a Friday, when all any of us can think of is getting back home and collapsing."

He flicked his turn signal on and took a left at the Maestro School driveway. "Anna," he said, steering through bare, wanly sunlit woods, "There's a simple solution. Quit. You are eighty years old. It's absurd that you're still teaching."

"I don't want to quit," she told him.

"You and I could be traveling," he said. He pulled into the packed-earth parking lot and faced her. "We could be spending more time with the grandchildren. You could see more of your daughter."

Anna wore her can't-budge-me expression. She was still a lovely woman, despite the gray hair and the netting of lines, but when she turned stubborn, something about the angle of her jaw reminded him of a nutcracker. She said, "Teaching is very important to me. I would never give it up willingly."

"Well, listen to what you just told me," he said. "Didn't you say all you could think of was getting back home and collapsing? And I'm saying there is something you can do about it."

"But I don't want to do anything about it."

"Okay," he said. "I give up."

"I'll call if the meeting runs too late for me to walk home," she said as she got out of the car. "Have a good day, dear."

"You too," he said. "Bye."

But as he reversed and pulled out of the lot and started back down the driveway, he was turning their conversation over in his mind. If a person mentioned a problem, wasn't it only natural for the other person to offer some helpful suggestion? Particularly when the other person was your spouse! Married couples supported each other. But not according to Anna. Anna needed no one. To her, Michael was merely a frill. A luxury. A dessert.

Well, maybe he should feel liberated. He was under no obligation; it was not up to him to fix things. What a relief, right?

He turned onto Falls Road and said, out loud, "She can be *my* dessert, too."

This was not as satisfying as it sounded.

He and Anna would be married twenty-two years come next June. Amazing; it still felt so much like a second marriage. Peaceful though it was, it felt like an *extra* marriage, not quite the real thing—in fact, maybe just an extreme, extended reaction to one of his fights with Pauline. Although if he lived another eight years after that, he could say that he had actually been married longer to Anna. And the chances were that he *would* live eight years; it was entirely possible. His doctor had told him he had the heart of a man of sixty. At first, Michael had missed the point. "Sixty!" he'd said. "That's ancient!" He didn't see himself as old. He had a stoop to his back, a tremor to his hands, and his face was some stern old codger's he didn't recognize in the mirror; but internally he was still twenty, riding off to war while a girl in a red coat waved goodbye.

Today was Pearl Harbor Day, and they were making more of a to-do about it than usual because it was not just the sixtieth anniversary but the first one after the World Trade Center attack. Patriotic movies had been showing all week on TV. Veterans were being interviewed—creaky-voiced old fellows with eyes so hooded in wrinkles that you wondered how they could see. Now the car radio was replaying Roosevelt's speech. Day of infamy, he said. Michael turned left onto Northern Parkway and found himself behind a rush-hour river of brake lights. Damn, he should have taken Harvest Road. He came to a stop and wriggled out of his wool jacket and laid it on the seat next to him.

It always surprised him that when he and Anna disagreed, the disagreement remained unconnected to the rest of their lives. Anna never linked it to other disagreements, never dredged up past issues or seemed to harbor any ill will afterward. Two minutes later she'd be going about her business again. And even when they out-and-out quarreled, she didn't appear to imagine that this could mean

the end of the marriage. Oh, once or twice in the early days he himself had brought up the possibility, out of a kind of reflex. "You can
always get a divorce if you feel so strongly about it." But Anna's
clear gaze had registered incomprehension. "Divorce?" she had said,
wonderingly.

In that dream last night, he was walking through a misty valley
trying to find his way home. Somebody was helping him, a beautiful
golden-haired woman with a wand. Why, it was the Good Witch
from *The Wizard of Oz*. Only now did he recognize her. She told him
not to let anyone kiss him behind the left ear, and not to let the sun
get behind his left shoulder, and not to listen to footsteps following
behind him on the road. "In short," she said in her buttery voice,
"don't ever look back, if you want to see your home again." And then
he had awakened.


At Schneider's he decided rope putty was the answer—inexpensive,
convenient, hard to mess up. (He was not so adept as he used to be.)
After he had chosen a box, he took a look around the rest of the store,
which was no bigger than some closets but managed to contain just
about everything a person could need. He studied an array of adhesive-
backed hooks. Hadn't he wanted hooks for some purpose just a couple
of days ago? He read the fine print on a sack of sidewalk de-icer. Trouble was, so many of these products damaged your grass and your
grouting.

The only other customers were a little three-person family—a tall
young father in glasses and a tiny, dark-haired mother about half the
father's height and a very small boy in a buzz cut. They were paying
for a sled, the old-fashioned wooden kind with metal runners that
Schneider's displayed on the sidewalk out front, and the little boy was
beside himself with excitement. Michael couldn't help smiling at
him. "You suppose you'll actually get to use that?" he asked, and the
child stopped his dance of joy just long enough to think the question
over.

Nowadays Michael came in contact with so few small children

that he had almost forgotten how to talk to them. George's son and daughter were certainly old enough to have children of their own, but JoJo at thirty was still living the life of a teenager, touring with a rock band called Dark at the End of the Tunnel, and Samantha was single-mindedly pursuing her medical studies with no apparent thought of marriage. Neither one of them seemed likely to produce any little ones, at least not any time soon. As for Pagan's two, they were way past the toddler stage—twelve and ten, more interesting to talk with now, surely, but no longer all chatter and giggles and unself-conscious glee. Bobby was bristling with braces that made his mouth look bunchy and misshapen. Polly had adopted a very unfortunate hairstyle: two fat, ball-shaped ponytails where a teddy bear's ears would be, the resemblance magnified by scrunchies of brown fake fur.

Polly's real name was Pauline.

Why had nobody thought to name a child after Michael?

Sometimes at family gatherings, when people started telling funny stories about Pauline, Michael felt a pinch of jealousy. Didn't they remember how difficult Pauline used to be? How demanding? How irritating? ("I had to give my homeless person a five today because I didn't have any ones," she said on the very last occasion he had seen her, and just that word "my," its cozy presumption, was enough to make him remember why they had divorced.)

He moved up to the counter and paid for his purchase, handing over exact change to the penny, declining a bag. Outside, he examined an array of snow shovels before proceeding reluctantly to his car. There was something so reassuring about hardware stores. We can help you deal with anything, was the message he drew from them. Drafty windows, icy sidewalks, mildew, moths, weeds . . . We've seen it all! You'll be okay!

If he were closer to Lindy he might get to know those children— her granddaughters, or step-granddaughters, he supposed they would be: three-year-old twins and an infant. But his relationship with Lindy was little more than polite, an improvement over the old days but still nothing much to brag about. They saw each other just once or twice a year, usually at Pagan's place when there was some family gathering. Their conversations tended to skate across the surface a while and then break through to dark water with a crash. Last summer, for instance, Lindy had announced that their family used to remind her of an animal caught in a trap. Out of the blue she had said that! With no provocation! They'd been discussing Bobby and Polly's recent visit to the circus and Michael had asked, merely holding up his end of things, whether Lindy remembered her own circus trips as a child. "Lord, yes," she'd said. "Good Lord above, those eternal family excursions! 'Just us,' Mom would say, 'just the five of us,' like that was something to be desired, and I'll never forget how claustrophobic that made me feel. Just the five of us in this wretched, tangled knot, inward-turned, stunted, like a trapped fox chewing its own leg off."

He was traveling east on Northern Parkway, driving aimlessly, facing pale, wintry sunlight with one finger on the steering wheel. The radio was playing "The White Cliffs of Dover." Why couldn't music today sound like that? He liked the way the singer kept her voice so plain and ordinary, too intent on expressing her sadness to concern herself with effect.

Not till he hit Rock Road did he realize he was heading toward the old store. Silly of him. It was true that a half-gallon of milk was on today's mental to-do list, but there were plenty of groceries nearer to hand than Anton's. Or World O'Food, rather. He hated that name. He hated the whole chain-supermarket concept, and felt miserable any time he set foot in the place, but somehow his car kept finding its way there. Now he relaxed and gave in to it, listening absently to an interview with a man who had served in France. He had lost both his brothers, three cousins, and his best friend in that war, the man said, speaking in a reflective voice, showing no sign of outrage. Imagine the youngsters nowadays accepting such a state of affairs! They would look for someone to sue, Michael thought. (Lindy certainly would.) Somewhere along the way, people in this country had developed the assumption that life should be unvaryingly logical and just. There was no recognition of random bad luck, no allowance for tragedies that couldn't be prevented by folic acid or side air bags or FAA-approved safety seats.

He passed a strip mall that he could have sworn had not existed a month ago. He passed the dry cleaner where he used to take his clothes when he lived in his old apartment, except now it was a video shop. Then here came the grocery, expanded to engulf the businesses that had once stood on either side of it, repainted in World O'Food's signature blue and green with the O a little globe. The gravel parking lot had been paved, admittedly an improvement. His tires rolled over the asphalt with unsettling smoothness. He parked between two SUVs and inched out from behind the wheel, favoring the one hip, and shrugged himself into his jacket. It was disheartening to see so many cars—far more cars than there had been when the place was his.

Inside, even the layout was different. They'd moved the florist department to the front. They'd replaced the registers with scanners and added a blond wood display case at the rear with a neon O'CUISINE in cursive lettering above it. Sushi rolls, pasta salads, chicken couscous, alfalfa-sprout wraps . . . What on earth? At the meat counter, a Middle Eastern–looking young woman in jeans and clunky-soled shoes that added several inches to her height was comparing jars of caviar while the young man with her—vividly blue-eyed, speaking in an Irish accent—asked whether imported could really be all that much better than domestic. A toddler in a full set of ski clothes begged her mother for tofu hot dogs.

Even the dairy case sported changes. Michael noticed a new line of milks and creams bottled nostalgically in glass, but he chose a carton of plain old Cloverland and headed for a checkout counter.

The clerk wore a nose ring and an eyebrow ring. It was hard for Michael to look at her.

Outside, the cold air was a relief. World O'Food had been overheated. After he'd put the milk in his trunk he stood a moment weighing his keys in one hand, postponing getting into the car again.

Then it occurred to him that next on his schedule was his exercise walk. Why not stroll up Rock Road a ways instead of trudging his neighborhood streets the same as on every other day? He dropped his keys into his pocket and set off.

Thirty minutes each morning, the doctor had advised. Michael checked his watch. He'd do fifteen minutes and turn back. He never went overtime, because walking wasn't really something he enjoyed. It was too empty-headed and too slow, especially now that his limp had worsened with old age. The skewed rhythm of his gait always set up the same meaningless refrain in his mind: *I THINK so but I don't KNOW so, I THINK so but I don't KNOW so,* his good leg coming down hard on "think" and "know," the bad leg sliding across the softer words in between.

His war wound, Pauline used to call it. He'd grown so accustomed to the phrase that he could almost imagine he had actually seen combat, although of course he hadn't. Would he ever get over feeling guilty for that? In the old days he used to hold Pauline responsible. (If he hadn't been so upset by her frivolous behavior, by her letters describing canteen dances and handsome jitterbug partners, he never would have started that crazy feud with his bunkmate.) Now, though, he thought it had been his own basic nature that was to blame. He was the kind who stood aloof while others waded in. He had no illusions whatsoever that he would have made a good soldier. In fact, he would most probably have been killed in his first real battle. So it wasn't that he wished he'd gone to the front, but that he wished he'd been the *type* to go. He wished he had inhabited more of his life, used it better, filled it fuller.

. . . *THINK so but I don't KNOW so, I THINK so but I don't* . . . and then a honking pickup truck blotted out the rest. He supposed he made drivers nervous—an old man limping unsteadily on the shoulder of the road. Old man! A shock all over again.

Lately he had noticed in himself a tendency to start a sentence and then let it run on automatically while he thought of other matters, often with bizarre results. Intending to tell Anna "This tastes delicious" at supper last night, he had heard himself say, "This tastes ridiculous." And only a few minutes afterward: "Why don't you sit and rest while I put the dishes in the computer?" He wondered if his mind was going—every old person's nightmare. Or maybe it was just that he had said those identical sentences so many hundreds and thousands of times, his tongue had begun rebelling against the sheer monotony.

Another honk, this one so loud it made him start. He lurched farther off the pavement and looked for someplace safer to walk, and what should he spy across the street but the gateway to Elmview Acres.

Funny how dowdy it looked—the wrought iron pocked with rust, the brick pillars gone porous and greenish. EST. 1947—a date that had once been so modern, but now it sounded quaint. And when he crossed Rock Road and started up Elmview Drive, he was surprised by the height of the trees. Even in December, the development's scalped look was gone. The houses ("ranch" houses, outmoded now) had skirtings of thick greenery where once there had been bald earth and spindly starter shrubs.

He chose the right-hand fork, the one that curved toward Beverly Drive. *I THINK so but I don't* . . . A woman in a plaid coat was walking her dog. A woman in her bathrobe came out on her stoop for her paper.

At least it was the same place, more or less, although most of the people living here hadn't even been born when he and Pauline first moved in. St. Cassian, on the other hand . . . He'd gone back there this past fall, he and Anna, to visit the Kazmerows one Sunday. They were still in their old row house (though their daughter had a mansion in Guilford, and one of their grandsons did something with high finance), but much of St. Cassian was boarded up now, dead or dying. The original Anton's Grocery had a padlock on the door and graffiti sprayed across the front, and when he and Leo walked past after lunch he thought he heard a scrabbling inside—a rat, or a drug addict, or a ghost. Neighboring streets had gone all chic with artists' studios and overpriced antique shops and whimsically named pubs frequented by college kids, according to Leo—defaced in a whole different way. Oh, and did he know, Leo said, that Ernie Moskowicz was in a nursing home now, and the last of the Szapp boys had died of a stroke, and the

Golka twins had died too within a month of each other, one of cancer and the other of pneumonia? And anyhow, they had long before then moved away from the neighborhood.

Walking down St. Cassian Street, Michael had felt like the survivor of some natural disaster. Wanda Lipska had died in '98 (heart attack) and one of her daughters had died, even—the oldest one, who'd been born a few months before George—and Katie Vilna was dead of lung cancer and Johnny Dymski of liver cancer. And going all the way back, there were Michael's parents, dim as old photos, and his brother, Danny, still and forever a boy of nineteen, although if he hadn't fallen ill he might very well be dead of old age by now anyhow. In the end, everyone dropped away, and someday it would be Michael's turn even if he half fancied that he would go on forever.

When they'd telephoned him about Pauline, he'd had trouble taking it in. This will be the first whole day I've lived on the planet without her, he had thought when he woke the next morning. But still it had seemed unreal. He had been able to picture parts of her so clearly: those two piquant points on her upper lip, the quirky sprig of lashes at the inner corner of each eye where most people's lashes don't grow, her eyes themselves so pansy-blue and trustful and expectant. He knew that he and she had been unhappy together, but now he couldn't remember why. What were the issues they'd quarreled about? He hadn't been able to name even one. He'd remembered the cold, hateful fury she could call up in him, the nights on the couch, the sharp silences, the ripped feeling in his chest, but what had it all been *about*?

"You were ice and she was glass," Lindy had told him recently, in one of their conversational crashes. "Two oddly similar substances, come to think of it—and both of them hell on your children."

He'd said, "Lindy, show some charity, here. We did the best we could. We did our darnedest. We were just . . . unskilled; we never quite got the hang of things. It wasn't for lack of trying."

*I THINK so but I don't KNOW so.* He was crossing Beverly Drive to make the turn onto Winding Way now, one palm on his lower back where it was starting to give him that twanging sensation. The oak tree on the corner, once the only full-size tree in Elmview Acres, had been cut down. All that remained was a stump.

And maybe it was the sight of Pauline's street, or maybe that the effort to dredge up one memory had accidentally unearthed another, but all of a sudden he recalled a party they'd thrown in the early seventies, a cocktail party for the neighbors, where Pauline had pulled him aside and whispered, "You'll never guess what Dr. Brook just did. He reached into my potpourri bowl and popped a handful into his mouth."

"He did *what*?" Michael asked, and she nodded, pink with suppressed laughter.

"That bowl on the buffet," she said. "And here's the worst: I saw him do it in plenty of time to stop him, but I didn't. I watched him reach into the bowl while he was talking to the Derbys, and then I left! I just left! I just turned on my heel and walked off!"

And the laughter had burst forth, finally, and she had clapped both hands to her mouth like a child, her eyes glinting wickedly above them.

Or the time they'd gone to New York together, just before Pagan came to live with them. They started down the stairs to the subway platform and she asked him for a token. "I already gave you a token," he told her.

"Yes, but I need another," she said.

"What happened to the first one?"

"Well, I ate it," she said.

"You what?"

"I put it into my mouth for some reason and just accidentally . . . I ate it, all right? I went ahead and ate it. Why make such a big deal about it?"

He smiled now, if he didn't smile then.

He could almost pretend to himself that Pauline had still been alive all this time, pursuing her own routine in her own corner of the world. He could imagine her in the front yard of her house, which lay just around the next bend. She was filling the bird feeder or picking up stray twigs under a sun that was, unaccountably, more like an

August sun, as golden as forsythia and warm and almost liquid. When his footsteps drew closer—their familiar, uneven rhythm—she would stop work to listen, and when he came into view she would straighten, shading her eyes with one hand. "Is it you?" she would ask. "It's you! It's really and truly you!" she would cry, and her face would light up with joy.

He began to walk faster, hurrying toward the bend.